D0034801

∾THE∾
JEWEL

THE JEWEL

AMY EWING

HARPER TEEN

An Imprint of HarperCollinsPublishers

SANTA CLARA PUBLIC LIBRARY
2635 Homestead Road
Santa Clara, CA 95051

HarperTeen is an imprint of HarperCollins Publishers.

The Jewel
Copyright © 2014 by Amy Ewing
All rights reserved. Printed in the United States of America.
No part of this book may be used or reproduced in any manner
whatsoever without written permission except in
the case of brief quotations embodied in critical articles
and reviews. For information address HarperCollins
Children's Books, a division of HarperCollins Publishers,
195 Broadway, New York, NY 10007.
www.epicreads.com

Library of Congress Cataloging-in-Publication Data
Ewing, Amy.
  The Jewel / Amy Ewing.
      pages cm
  Summary: Violet, a poor girl from the outer city, finds forbidden
romance and uncovers brutal secrets when, after three years of
training, she is purchased by a royal family as a surrogate mother for
royal children.
  ISBN 978-0-06-223579-4 (hardback)
  ISBN 978-0-06-236900-0 (int. ed.)
  [1. Fantasy. 2. Courts and courtiers—Fiction. 3. Slavery—Fiction.
4. Surrogate mothers—Fiction. 5. Social classes—Fiction. 6. Love—
Fiction. 7. Magic—Fiction.] I. Title.
PZ7.E9478Jew 2014   2014001881
[Fic]—dc23   CIP
                                                                          AC

Typography by Anna Christian
14 15 16 17 18 LP/RRDH 10 9 8 7 6 5 4 3 2 1

First Edition

For Jess.
For everything.

One

TODAY IS MY LAST DAY AS VIOLET LASTING.

The streets of the Marsh are quiet this early in the morning, just the plodding steps of a donkey and the clinking of glass bottles as a milk cart rolls by. I throw off my sheets and slip on my bathrobe over my nightdress. The robe is a hand-me-down from my mother, dark blue and worn at the elbows. It used to be huge on me, the sleeves hanging past my fingertips, the hem dragging on the floor. I've grown into it over the past few years—it fits me now the way it used to fit her. I love it. It's one of the few items I was allowed to bring with me to Southgate. I was lucky to be able to bring as many as I did. The other three holding facilities are stricter about personal items; Northgate doesn't allow them at all.

I press my face against the wrought-iron bars on my window—they are arched and curl into the shape of roses, as if by making a pretty pattern, they can pretend they're something they're not.

The dirt streets of the Marsh glow dull gold in the early-morning light; I can almost imagine they're made of something regal. The streets are what give the Marsh its name—all the stone and concrete and asphalt went to the wealthier circles of the city, so the Marsh was left with a thick brown mud that smells briny and sulfuric.

Nerves flutter like tiny wings in my chest. I will get to see my family today, for the first time in four years. My mother, and Ochre, and little Hazel. She's probably not so little anymore. I wonder if they even want to see me, if I've become like a stranger to them. Have I changed from who I used to be? I'm not sure if I can remember who I used to be. What if they don't even recognize me?

Anxiety thrums inside me as the sun rises slowly over the Great Wall off in the distance, the one that encircles the entire Lone City. The wall that protects us from the violent ocean outside. That keeps us safe. I love sunrises, even more than sunsets. There's something so exciting about the world coming to life in a thousand colors. It's hopeful. I'm glad I get to see this one, ribbons of pink and lavender shot through with streams of red and gold. I wonder if I'll get to see any sunrises when I start my new life in the Jewel.

Sometimes, I wish I hadn't been born a surrogate.

WHEN PATIENCE COMES FOR ME, I'M CURLED UP ON MY bed, still in my bathrobe, memorizing my room. It isn't much, just a small bed, a closet, and a faded wooden dresser. My cello is propped in one corner. On top of the dresser is a vase of flowers that gets changed every other day, a brush, a comb, some hair ribbons, and an old chain with my father's wedding ring on it. My mother made me take it after the doctors diagnosed me, before the Regimentals came and took me away.

I wonder if she's missed it, after all this time. I wonder if she's missed me, the way I've missed her. A knot tightens in the pit of my stomach.

The room hasn't changed much since I came here four years ago. No pictures. No mirror. Mirrors aren't allowed in the holding facilities. The only addition has been my cello—not even mine, really, since it belongs to Southgate. I wonder who will use it once I'm gone. It's funny, but as dull and impersonal as this room is, I think I'll miss it.

"How are you holding up, dearie?" Patience asks. She's always calling us things like that, "dearie" and "sweetheart" and "lamb." Like she's afraid of using our actual names. Maybe she just doesn't want to get attached. She's been the head caretaker at Southgate for a long time. She's probably seen hundreds of girls pass through this room.

"I'm okay," I lie. There's no use in telling her how I really feel—like my skin is itching from the inside out and there's a weight deep in the darkest, lowest part of me.

Her eyes scan me from head to toe, and she purses her lips. Patience is a plump woman with gray streaks in her wispy brown hair, and her face is so easily readable, I can guess what she's going to say next before she actually says it.

"Are you sure that's what you want to wear?"

I nod, rubbing the soft fabric of the bathrobe between my thumb and forefinger, and scoot off the bed. There are perks to being a surrogate. We get to dress how we want, eat what we want, sleep late on the weekends. We get an education. A good education. We get fresh food and water, we always have electricity, and we never have to work. We never have to know poverty—and the caretakers tell us we'll have more once we start living in the Jewel.

Except freedom. They never seem to mention that.

Patience bustles out of the room and I follow behind her. The halls of Southgate Holding Facility are paneled in teak and rosewood; artwork hangs on the walls, smudges of color that don't depict anything real. All the doors are exactly alike, but I know which one we're going to. Patience only wakes you up if you have a doctor's appointment, if there's an emergency, or if it's your Reckoning Day. There's only one other girl on this floor besides me who's going to the Auction tomorrow. My best friend. Raven.

Her door is open, and she's already dressed, in a pair of high-waisted tan pants and a white V-neck. I can't say if Raven is prettier than me, because I haven't seen my reflection in four years. But I can say that she is one of the most beautiful surrogates in Southgate. We both have black hair, but Raven's is cropped short, stick straight and glossy—mine falls in waves down my back. Her skin is a rich caramel color, with eyes nearly as dark as her hair, shaped like almonds and set in a perfect oval face. She's taller than me, which is saying a lot. My skin is ivory, an odd contrast with my hair color, and my eyes are violet. I don't need a mirror to tell me that. They're what I was named for.

"Big day, huh?" Raven says to me, stepping into the hall to join us. "Is that what you're wearing?"

I ignore her second question. "Tomorrow will be bigger."

"Yeah, but we can't choose our outfits tomorrow. Or the day after that. Or . . . well, ever again." She tucks her hair behind her ears. "I hope whoever buys me lets me wear pants."

"I wouldn't get your hopes up, dearie," Patience says.

I have to agree with her. The Jewel doesn't seem like the type of place where women wear pants, unless maybe they're servants who work in the unseen places. Even if we get sold to a merchant family from the Bank, dresses will probably be the required attire.

The Lone City is divided into five circles, each separated by a wall, and all of them but the Marsh have nicknames based on their industry. The Marsh is the outer circle, the poorest. We don't have industry, we just house most of the laborers who work in the other circles. The fourth circle is the Farm, where all the food is grown. Then the Smoke, where the factories are. The second circle is called the Bank, because it's where all the merchants have their shops. And then there's the inner circle, or the Jewel. The heart of the city. Where the royalty lives. And where, after tomorrow, Raven and I will live as well.

We follow Patience down the wide wooden stairs. Scents from the kitchen waft up the staircase, fresh-baked bread and cinnamon. It reminds me of when my mother would make sticky buns on my birthday, a luxury we could almost never afford. I can have them whenever I want now, but they don't taste the same.

We pass one of the classrooms—the door is open and I pause for a moment to watch. The girls are young, probably only eleven or twelve. New. Like I was once. Back when *augury* was just a word, before anyone explained to me that I was special, that all the girls at Southgate were. That thanks to some genetic quirk, we had the ability to save the royalty.

The girls are seated at desks with small buckets beside them, and a neatly folded handkerchief next to each one. Five red building blocks are spread out in a line in front of every girl. A caretaker sits at a large desk, taking notes— behind her on the chalkboard is written the word *GREEN*. They're being tested on the first Augury, Color. I half smile, half wince, remembering all the times I took this test. I watch the girl closest to me, turning an imaginary block in my hands as she turns a bright red one in hers.

Once to see it as it is. Twice to see it in your mind. Thrice to bend it to your will.

Veins of green spread from where her fingers touch the block, creeping across the red surface like vines. The girl's eyes are screwed in concentration, fighting the pain, and if she can hold on just a few seconds longer, I know she'll have done it. But the pain wins, and she cries out and drops the block, red winning over green, then grabs the bucket, coughing up a mixture of blood and saliva. A thin trickle of blood runs from her nose and she wipes it away with the handkerchief.

I sigh. The first Augury is the easiest of the three, but she's only managed to change two of her blocks. It's going to be a very long day for her.

"Violet," Raven calls, and I hurry to catch up.

The dining room is only half full—most of the girls are already in class. When Raven and I enter, all talking stops, spoons and cups are put down, and every girl in the dining room stands, crosses two fingers on her right hand, and presses them against her heart. It's tradition on Reckoning Day, acknowledging the surrogates who will be leaving for the Auction. I've done it myself every year but this feels strange, having it directed at me. A lump forms in my throat and my eyes itch. I can feel Raven tense beside me. A lot of the girls saluting us are going to the Auction themselves tomorrow.

We take a seat at our usual table, in a corner by the windows. I bite my lip, realizing that, in a very short amount of time, it won't be "our" table anymore. This is my last breakfast at Southgate. Tomorrow, I'll be on a train.

Once we're seated, the rest of the room sits, and conversation starts again but in low whispers.

"I know it's a sign of respect," Raven mutters. "But I don't like being on this side of it."

A young caretaker named Mercy hurries over with a silver pot of coffee.

"Good luck tomorrow," she says in a shy voice. I barely manage a smile. Raven doesn't say anything. Mercy's face goes slightly pink. "What can I bring you for breakfast?"

"Two fried eggs, hash browns, toast with butter and strawberry jam, and bacon, well done but not burnt." Raven rattles off her breakfast list quickly, like she's hoping to trip Mercy up. Which she probably is. Raven likes messing with people, especially when she's nervous.

Mercy just smiles and bobs her head. "And for you, Violet?"

"Fruit salad," I say. Mercy scuttles off into the kitchen. "Are you really going to eat all that?" I ask Raven. "I feel like my stomach shrank overnight."

"You are such a worrier," she says, adding two heaping spoonfuls of sugar to her coffee. "I swear, you'll give yourself an ulcer."

I take a sip of coffee and watch the other girls in the dining room. Especially the ones going to the Auction. Some of them look the way I feel, like they'd be happy to crawl back into bed and hide under the covers, but other girls are chattering with excitement. I never quite understood those girls, the ones who bought into all the caretakers' lines about how important we are, how we are fulfilling a long and noble tradition. I once asked Patience why we couldn't come home after we've given birth, and she said, "You are too precious to the royalty. They wish to take care of you for the rest of your life. Isn't that wonderful? They have such generous hearts."

I said I'd rather have my family than the royalty's generosity. Patience didn't like that very much.

A younger, mousy-looking girl at a nearby table suddenly cries out in pain and surprise as her water glass turns to ice. She drops it and it shatters on the floor. Her nose starts to bleed, and she grabs a napkin and runs out of the dining room as a caretaker hurries over with a dustpan.

"I'm glad that doesn't happen anymore," Raven says. When you start learning the Auguries, they're hard to control, and the pain is always worse when you're not expecting it. The first time I coughed up blood, I thought I was dying. But it stops after a year or so. Now I only have the occasional nosebleed.

"Remember when I turned that whole basket of strawberries blue?" Raven says, almost with a laugh.

I cringe at the memory. It had been funny at first, but she couldn't make it stop—everything she touched turned blue, for a whole day. She became violently ill, and the doctors had to isolate her.

I look at Raven now, calmly adding milk to her coffee, and wonder how I'm supposed to live without her.

"Did you get your lot number?" I ask.

The spoon tinkles against Raven's cup, her hand trembling for the briefest moment. "Yeah."

It's a stupid question—we all got our lot numbers last night. But I want to know what Raven's is. I want to know how much longer I'll be able to see my best friend.

"And?"

"Lot 192. You?"

I exhale. "197."

Raven grins. "Looks like we're hot commodities."

Every Auction features a different number of surrogates, and they're all ranked. The last ten to be auctioned are considered the highest quality and therefore the most desirable. This year has one of the highest number of surrogates being auctioned in recent history—200.

I don't care about my ranking so much. I'd rather be with a pleasant couple than a rich one. But it does mean that Raven and I will be together until the end.

The dining room falls silent as three girls enter. Raven

and I stand with everyone else and salute the girls who will be joining us on the train tomorrow. Two of them make for a table under the chandelier, but one, a petite blonde with big blue eyes, bounces over to us.

"Morning, girls," Lily gushes, plopping down in one of the plush chairs, a gossip magazine clutched in her hands. "Aren't you just so excited? I am so excited! We get to see the Jewel tomorrow. Can you imagine?"

I like Lily, despite her overwhelming enthusiasm and the fact that she falls into that category of excited girls I don't understand. She didn't come from such a good family in the Marsh. Her dad used to beat her, and her mom was an alcoholic. Being diagnosed as a surrogate actually *was* a good thing for her.

"It'll definitely be a change from the usual," Raven says dryly.

"I know!" Lily is completely oblivious to sarcasm.

"Are you going home today?" I ask. I can't imagine Lily would want to see her family again.

"Patience said I didn't have to, but I'd like to see my mother," Lily says. "And she said I can have a Regimental escort, so Daddy can't hurt me." She smiles widely, and I feel a sharp pang of pity.

"Did you get your lot number?" I ask.

"Ugh, yes. I'm 53, can you believe it? Out of 200! I'll probably end up with a merchant family from the Bank." The royalty allow a select number of families from the Bank to attend the Auction each year, but they can only bid on the lower-ranked surrogates. The Bank doesn't need the surrogates the way the royalty do—women in the Bank are capable of bearing their own children. To them, we're just a status symbol. "What did you girls get?"

"192," Raven says.

"197."

"I knew it! I knew you both would get amazing scores. Ooooh, I'm so jealous!"

Mercy bustles over with our breakfasts. "Good morning, Lily. Good luck tomorrow."

"Thanks, Mercy." Lily beams at her. "Oh, can I have blueberry pancakes? And grapefruit juice? And some sliced mango?"

Mercy nods.

"Is that what you're wearing?" Lily asks, frowning with genuine concern.

"Yes," I say, exasperated. "This is what I'm wearing. This is my favorite thing to wear, and since it's the last time I'll ever get to choose my own outfit, I'm choosing this, because I love it and it's mine. I don't care what I look like."

Raven hides her smile in a mouthful of eggs and hash browns. Lily looks a little confused for a second but recovers quickly.

"So did you hear? About the Electress?" She looks at us expectantly, but Raven is more interested in her food and I've never paid much attention to the politics of the Jewel. But some of the girls follow all the gossip.

"No," I say politely, spearing a piece of cantaloupe on the end of my fork.

Lily puts the magazine on the table. The Electress's young face stares out at us from the cover of *The Daily*

Jewel, above the headline ELECTRESS TO ATTEND AUCTION.

"Can you believe it? The Electress, at *our* Auction!" Lily is beside herself. She loves the Electress, like many of the girls at Southgate. Her story is quite an unusual one—she is from the Bank, not true royalty at all, but the Exetor saw her during a trip to one of her father's shops and fell in love and married her. Very romantic. Her family is royalty now, of course, and living in the Jewel. A lot of the girls see her as a sign of hope, as if their fortunes could be changed like hers. I don't see what's so bad about being a shopkeeper's daughter in the first place.

"I never thought she'd come," Lily continues. "I mean, her precious little boy was only born a few months ago. Just imagine—she could choose one of *us* to carry her next baby!"

I want to shred the lace tablecloth with my fingernails. She makes it sound like we should be honored, as if it were our choice. I don't want to carry anyone's baby, not the Electress's or anyone else's. I don't want to be sold tomorrow.

And Lily looks so excited, like it's a real possibility that the Electress would bid on her. She's only Lot 53.

I hate myself as soon as I think it. She is *not* Lot 53, she is Lily Deering. She loves chocolate, and gossip, and pink dresses with lace collars, and she plays the violin. She comes from a horrible family and you'd never know it because she has a nice word to say about everyone she's ever met. She is Lily Deering.

And tomorrow, she'll be bought and paid for, and living in a strange house under a strange woman's rules. A woman who might not understand her, and her endless, boundless enthusiasm. A woman who might not care, or know how to speak to her.

A woman who will force her own child to grow inside Lily, whether Lily wants it or not.

Suddenly, I am so angry I can hardly stand it. Before I realize it, I'm on my feet, hands balled into fists.

"What—" Lily begins, but I don't even hear her. I catch only a glimpse of Raven's surprised expression before I march through the tables, ignoring the furtive, curious looks from the other girls, and then I'm running out of the room and up the stairs, slamming the door to my bedroom.

I grab my father's ring and shove it onto my thumb, the biggest finger I have, but the ring is still too big for it. I curl my fingers into a fist around the chain.

I pace back and forth across the tiny cell of my room—I can't believe I thought I'd miss it here. It's a prison, a place to contain me before I'm shipped off to become a human incubator for a woman I've never met. The walls start to close in and I stumble into my dresser, knocking everything off it onto the floor. The brush and comb make tiny slapping sounds as they bounce off the wood, and the vase shatters, strewing flowers everywhere.

My door opens. Raven looks from me to the mess on the floor and back again. Blood pounds in my temples, and my body is quivering. She picks her way across my room and wraps her arms around me. Tears well up and spill over, trickling down my cheeks and seeping into her blouse.

We're quiet for a long time.

"I'm scared," I whisper. "I'm scared, Raven."

She squeezes me close, then starts picking up the scattered shards. I feel a hot surge of embarrassment at the mess I've made, and bend down to help her.

We put the remains of the vase back on my dresser and Raven wipes her hands on her pants. "Let's get you cleaned up," she says.

I nod and we walk, hand in hand, down the hall to the powder room. The girl who dropped the icy glass is in there, dabbing at her nose with a wet cloth—her nosebleed has stopped, but her skin is covered in a light sheen of sweat. She starts at the sight of us.

"Out," Raven says. The girl drops the cloth and hurries out the door.

Raven takes a clean facecloth and soaks it with water and lavender soap.

"Are you nervous—" I almost say "about the Auction," but change my mind. "About seeing your family again?"

"Why would I be nervous?" she says, wiping my face with the wet cloth. The scent of lavender is comforting.

"Because you haven't seen them in five years," I say gently. Raven's been here longer than I have.

She shrugs, dabbing the cloth under my eyes. I know her well enough to drop the subject. She rinses out the cloth and starts running a comb through my hair. My heart thrums as I think about what will happen after this day.

"I don't want to go," I confess. "I don't want to go to the Auction."

"Of course you don't," she replies. "You're not insane, like Lily."

"That's mean. Don't say that."

Raven rolls her eyes and puts the comb down, arranging my hair over my shoulders.

"What's going to happen to us?" I ask.

Raven takes my chin in her hand and looks straight into my eyes. "You listen to me, Violet Lasting. We are going to be fine. We're smart and strong. We'll be fine."

My lower lip quivers and I nod. Raven relaxes and gives my hair a last pat.

"Perfect," she says. "Now. Let's go see our families."

Two

ELECTRIC STAGECOACHES TAKE US THROUGH THE DUSTY streets.

Thick velvet curtains protect us from the flakes of dried mud that swirl through the air—the ones that used to stick to my skin as a child. I peek through the fabric, unable to help myself. I haven't been outside the holding facility since I was twelve.

The streets are lined with one-story mud-brick houses; some of the roofs are rotted or caving in. Children run half naked in the streets, and potbellied men lounge in alleys or on stoops, drinking strong spirits from bottles hidden in paper bags. We pass an almshouse, its shutters closed, its doors padlocked. On Sunday, there will be a huge line down this street, families waiting for whatever food and clothing and medicine the royalty has donated to help the unfortunate. However much they send, though, it's never enough.

A few streets later, I see a trio of Regimentals pushing an emaciated boy away from a greengrocer's. It's been so long since I've seen any men besides the doctors who examine us. The Regimentals are young, with large hands and noses, and broad shoulders. They stop harassing the boy when my coach rolls past, standing at attention, and I wonder if they see me peeking through the curtains at them. I quickly cover the window.

There are four of us in the coach, but not Raven. Her family lives on the other side of Southgate. The Marsh is like the tire of a bicycle, encircling the outer reaches of Lone City. If the Great Wall should ever crumble, we'd be the first to go, consumed by the terrible ocean that surrounds us on all sides.

Each circle of the city, with the exception of the Jewel, is divided into four quarters—North, South, East, and West—by two spokes that form an X. In the middle of each quarter in the Marsh is a holding facility. Raven's family lives on the eastern side of Southgate, mine to the west. I wonder if Raven and I would ever have met, if we hadn't been diagnosed as surrogates.

No one speaks in the coach, and I'm grateful for that. I rub my wrist, feeling the hard circle of the transmitter they implanted just under my skin. We all got one before we left for our homes. It's only temporary—they'll dissolve in about eight hours. It's Southgate's way of enforcing the rules: Do not talk about what goes on inside the holding facility. Do not talk about the Auguries. Do not talk about the Auction.

The coach drops us off, one by one. I'm last.

My whole body is trembling by the time I reach my house. I listen for some sign that my family is out there, waiting for me, but I only hear the dull thud of my pulse in my ears. It takes all my strength to reach out and turn the brass handle on the carriage door. For a fleeting moment, I don't think I can do it. What if they don't love me anymore? What if they've forgotten me?

Then I hear my mother's voice. "Violet?" she calls timidly.

I open the door.

They stand in a line, wearing what must be their best clothes. I'm shocked to see that Ochre has grown taller than my mother—his chest and arms are muscled, his hair cropped short, and his skin tough and tanned. He must have gotten a job in the Farm.

My mother looks so much older than I remember, but her hair is still the same red-gold color. There are deep wrinkles around her eyes and mouth.

Hazel, though . . . Hazel is almost unrecognizable. She was seven when I left, eleven now. All arms and legs, her sad, tattered pinafore hangs loose on her bony frame. But her face is just like Father's; she has his eyes, exactly. We have the same hair, long, black, and wavy. This makes me smile. Hazel edges a little closer to Ochre.

"Violet?" my mother says again.

"Hello," I say, surprised by my formality. I step out of the carriage and feel the thick marsh-dust between my toes.

Hazel's eyes widen—I don't know what she thought I'd be wearing, but probably not a nightdress and bathrobe. None of my family is wearing shoes. I'm glad I'm not, either. I want to feel the dirt beneath my feet, the grimy dust of my home.

There is a second of awkward silence, then my mother stumbles forward and throws her arms around me. She is so thin, and I notice a slight limp that I'm sure she didn't have before.

"Oh, my baby," she croons. "I'm so happy to see you."

I inhale her scent of bread and salt and sweat. "I missed you," I whisper.

She wipes the tears from her eyes and holds me out at arm's length. "How long do we have?"

"Until eight."

My mother opens her mouth, then closes it with a tiny shake of her head. "Well, then. Let's make the best of it." She turns to my siblings. "Ochre, Hazel, come hug your sister."

Ochre strides forward—when did he get so big? He was only ten when I left. When did he become a man?

"Hey, Vi," he says. Then he bites his lip, like he's worried about addressing a surrogate so informally.

"Ochre, you're huge," I tease. "What has Mother been feeding you?"

"I'm six feet," he says proudly.

"You're a monster."

He grins.

"Hazel," my mother says, "come say hello to your sister."

Then Hazel, my little Hazel, who I used to sing to at night, and sneak cookies to after lights-out, and play

Jewel-in-the-Crown with in our backyard, turns her back on me and runs into the house.

"SHE JUST NEEDS A LITTLE TIME," MOTHER SAYS A FEW minutes later, as she pours me a cup of chrysanthemum tea.

But time is something I don't have.

I take a sip of tea and try as hard as I can not to make a face. I've forgotten the bitter, astringent flavor, my taste buds so used to coffee and fresh-squeezed juice. Guilt slides into my stomach as I swallow.

My mother and I sit at the wooden table on chairs that my father made. The house is smaller than I remember it. Only one room for the kitchen and sitting area. There is a sink, a little paraffin stove, a side table with a cabinet underneath for plates and cutlery. There is only one couch, its stuffing poking out in places, and a rocking chair by the fireplace. My mother used to knit in that chair. I wonder if she still does.

"Hazel doesn't remember me," I say glumly.

"She does," Mother replies. "Just . . . not how you are now. I mean, goodness, Violet, look at you."

I look down. Do I really look that different? My arms are plumper than hers, and my skin has a healthy pink flush to it.

"Your face, sweetheart." My mother laughs gently.

My throat goes tight. "I . . . I haven't seen my face in a while."

She purses her lips. "Would you like to see it now?"

I can't swallow. My hand slips into the pocket of my robe and I squeeze my father's ring. "No," I whisper. I don't know why, but the thought of my reflection terrifies me. I stare at my mother's hands, folded in her lap—they are gnarled with arthritis, blue veins popping out like rivers in a topographic map.

"Where's your ring?" I ask.

Her cheeks turn pink and she shrugs.

"Mother," I press, "what happened to your ring?"

"I sold it."

I can feel my eyes bugging out of their sockets. "What? Why?"

She looks at me, her expression defiant. "We needed the money."

"But . . ." I shake my head, bewildered. "What about the stipend?"

A yearly stipend is given to the families of the surrogates, compensation for the loss of a daughter.

My mother sighs. "The stipend isn't enough, Violet. Why do you think Ochre had to drop out of school? Look at my hands; I can't work as much as I used to. Do you want me to send Hazel to the factories? Or the orchards?"

"Of course not." I can't believe she would even suggest that. Hazel is too young to withstand the brutal labor in the Farm—there's barely an ounce of muscle on her. And she'd never survive the Smoke. I cringe at the thought of her operating some heavy piece of machinery, choking on the dust that saturates the air.

"Then don't judge how I provide for this family. Your father, rest his soul, would understand. It's only a piece of gold." She wipes her hand across her forehead. "It's only a piece of gold," she mumbles again.

I don't know why I'm so upset. She's right, it's just a thing. It's not my father.

I squeeze his ring one last time, then take it out of my pocket and place it on the table. "Here. You can have this back now. I can't keep it anyway."

There is a look in my mother's eyes as she picks up the ring, and I see what it cost her to sell hers.

"Thank you," she whispers.

"Can I keep the bathrobe?" I ask.

She laughs, and her eyes glitter with tears. "Of course. It fits you so well now."

"It'll probably get thrown out. But I'd like to keep it for as long as I can."

She reaches out and squeezes my hand. "It's yours. I'm surprised they let you visit us in your pajamas."

"We can wear whatever we want. Especially today."

Silence falls, pressing down on me like a pillow, smothering all the things I want to say. A fly buzzes in the window over the sink. My mother strokes the back of my hand with her finger, her expression distant, worried.

"They do take good care of you there, don't they?" she asks.

I shrug and look away. I can't really talk to her about Southgate.

"Violet, please," she says. "Please tell me. You can't imagine how hard it's been. On me, on Hazel and Ochre. First your father, and . . . look at you, you're all grown up and . . . and I missed it." A single tear escapes and runs down her cheek. "I missed it, baby. How am I supposed to live with that?"

A lump forms in my throat. "It's not your fault," I say, staring very hard at her hands. "You didn't have a choice."

"No," my mother murmurs. "No, I didn't. But I lost you, all the same. So please, tell me some good has come out of it. Tell me you have a better life."

I wish I could tell her that I do. I wish I could tell her the truth, about the three Auguries and the years of pain and the endless tests and the doctor visits. I wish I could tell her how much I've missed her, how there is more tenderness in her finger stroking my hand than in all the caretakers combined. I wish I could tell her how much I love playing the cello, how good I am at it. I think she'd be proud of me, if she knew. I think she'd like hearing me play.

The lump in my throat is so swollen I'm amazed I can still breathe. My mind flits back to that awful day when the Regimentals came, a memory that is so old, so tangled, like a jigsaw puzzle with missing pieces. Me, crying, screaming, begging her not to let them take me. Hazel's eyes, wide and pleading, her tiny hands clutching my ragged dress. The cold glint of a Regimental's gun. And my mother, pressing her lips against my forehead, her tears saturating my hair as she says, "You have to go with them, Violet. You have to go with them."

Suddenly, the room is too hot. "I—I need some air," I gasp, pushing my chair back and stumbling out the back door.

The backyard is just a patch of dry earth and yellowing grass. But I feel better as a cool breeze tickles my skin, rustling the leaves of the lemon tree in the center of the yard.

The lemon tree that never once produced a lemon. What was that song Father used to sing?

> *Lemon tree, very pretty*
> *And the lemon flower is sweet*

It was some sort of analogy about the dangerous nature of love, but all I remember thinking whenever he sang it was how much I wanted to eat a lemon. It was the first thing I tried when I got to Southgate. In my excitement, I bit right through the rind. The sourness was so shocking.

"You look different."

I whirl around. Hazel is sitting on an upturned bucket against the wall of the house. I didn't even see her.

"That's what Mother says." My voice comes out a little breathless.

She studies me for a moment. Her eyes are sharp and intelligent. It hits me again how much she looks like our father.

"She says you're going to the Auction tomorrow," Hazel says. "That's why they're letting you see us."

I nod. "They call it Reckoning Day. To . . . settle the accounts of your past before starting your future." I don't know why I say it. The phrase I've heard from the mouths of caretakers a hundred times tastes bitter in my mouth.

Hazel stands. "Is that what we are? An account to settle before you go off and live in some palace in the Jewel?"

"No," I say, aghast. "No, of course not."

She balls her hands into fists, exactly the way I do when I'm angry or hurt. "Then why are you here?"

I shake my head, shocked. "Why . . . ? Hazel, I'm here because I love you. Because I missed you. And Mother, and Ochre. I miss you every day."

"Then why didn't you write to me?" Hazel shouts, and her voice cracks, and my heart cracks with it. "You told me you would. 'No matter what,' you said. I waited every day for a letter and you never, ever wrote, not once!"

Her words punch at my chest. I thought she would've forgotten that promise. It'd been so clear that it could never happen once I was inside the facility. "Hazel, I couldn't. We're not allowed."

"I bet you didn't even try," Hazel spits. "You just wanted your fancy things, new clothes and fresh food and hot water. That's what you get in there, I know it, so stop lying."

"Yes, I do get those things. But don't you think I would give them all up in a second if it meant I could live with you again? If I could tuck you in at night, and sing to you? And we could make mud pies when it rains, and then throw them at Ochre when he's not looking?" The images well up, threatening to consume me. The life I could have had. Poor, yes, but happy. "Do you really think I'd abandoned my family for running water and clothes? I didn't have a choice, Hazel," I say. "They didn't give me a choice."

Hazel doesn't say anything, but she looks unsure. I take a step toward her.

"I celebrate your birthday every year," I say. I'm risking setting the transmitter off, but I don't care. "I make them bake a cake, chocolate with vanilla frosting, and they write your name on it in green icing and put a candle in it, and my friend Raven and I sing happy birthday." We do that for Raven's brother, too, and Ochre.

Hazel blinks. "You do?"

A tear trickles down my cheek and lands on the corner of my mouth. "Sometimes, I talk to you after lights-out. I tell you jokes I've heard, or stories about my friends and life in the facility. I miss you every day, Hazel."

Suddenly, she crosses the distance between us and throws her arms around me. I hold her tight, her bony frame so fragile and shaking with sobs. More tears drip down my own cheeks and into her hair.

"I thought you didn't care." Her voice is muffled by my robe. "I thought you left me forever."

"No," I whisper. "I will always love you, Hazel. I promise."

I am so glad I get this tiny slice of time. No matter what happens after, no matter what result the Auction brings, I am grateful that at least I get this one last moment with my sister.

Dinner that night is a small roast duck that is mostly bones, boiled potatoes, and a few wilted string beans.

I feel guilty thinking of all the dinners I've eaten, the endless choice of the freshest foods. And my family treats this humble meal as though it's a feast fit for the Electress.

"Ochre's brought cream from the dairies!" Hazel exclaims, tugging on my sleeve. "We can have ice cream for dessert."

"What a treat," I say with a smile, before passing the potatoes to Ochre. "So, you work in the dairies?"

Ochre nods. "Most of the time," he says, scooping a large amount of potatoes onto his plate—Mother grabs the bowl away from him before he can take them all. "I like working with the animals. The foreman says in a year, I could start learning to plow the fields." His chest puffs out a little as he says it. "As long as I can keep working for the House of the Flame, I'll be happy. They treat their workers fairly, give us good long water breaks and decent hours and everything. Remember Sable Tersing? He works for the House of the Light, and apparently they're awful. The foremen have whips and they're not afraid to use them, and they'll dock your pay if they catch you smoking, or—"

"What is Sable Tersing doing smoking?" Mother demands. Ochre flushes.

"No, I didn't mean *Sable*, just that—"

"Ochre, I swear on your father's grave, if I catch you with a cigarette—"

"Mother." Ochre rolls his eyes. "All I'm saying is, it isn't fair to the workers, not knowing how you'll be treated from one royal house to the next. There should be fixed rules, and we should be allowed to take our case to the Exetor if they aren't enforced."

"Oh yes, because I'm sure the Exetor has nothing better to do than listen to the complaints of a few teenage boys," Mother says. But I can't help smiling.

"You sound like Father," I say to Ochre. He scratches the back of his neck in a self-conscious sort of way and shovels a few potatoes into his mouth.

"He made some good points," Ochre mumbles through the food.

Hazel tugs on my sleeve again, demanding my attention.

"I'm in the top of my class at school," she says proudly.

"Of course you are," I say. "You're my sister, aren't you?"

Mother laughs. "You didn't get into nearly as much trouble as this one. The year has only just started and she's been in two fights already."

"Fights?" I frown at my sister. "Who have you been fighting, Hazel?"

Hazel shoots our mother a look. "No one. Just some stupid boys."

"Yes, and if it happens again, there will be extra chores and no games for a week," Mother says sternly. Hazel pouts at her plate.

Jealousy twists inside me, listening to the daily life of my family. There is so much love around this table it is tangible—a real, pulsing, living thing. I watch as Ochre and Hazel bicker, and Mother laughs and shushes them. I can see how I would have fit here, how I should have completed this family.

I am seized by the desire to make sure my mother knows I'll be all right. Even if I don't believe it myself, even if it's a lie. I don't want to do anything to endanger the happiness in this room.

"You don't have to worry about me," I say. Everyone falls silent and stares—I probably shouldn't have said it so bluntly. "I mean . . ." I look at my mother. "I'll be okay." She puts down her fork. I force a smile on my face and hope it looks genuine. "Tomorrow I'll be living in the Jewel. Isn't that exciting? I'm sure they'll take great care of me there."

Hazel's eyes are wide as saucers. "But, you should know . . . I mean . . . please know how much I love you. All of you." My voice falters and I take a sip of water. My mother's eyes are filled with tears, and she presses a hand against her mouth. "If there was any way I could stay with you, I would. I—I'm so proud to be a part of this family. Please know that."

Their eyes burn into me, and suddenly I can't look at them anymore. The fire is low in the grate, and I stand. "The fire is dying," I say awkwardly. "I'll get more wood."

I rush out the back door, gulping at the cool night air, my hands shaking.

Don't cry, I tell myself. If I cry, they'll see how scared I am. I can't let them see that. They have to think I'll be happy.

I lean against the wall of the house and stare up at the night sky, glittering with stars. At least, wherever I end up, it'll be under the same sky. Hazel and I will always look at the same stars.

I turn to the woodpile, when my gaze falls on the lemon tree, silver in the moonlight, and an idea hits me.

The third Augury, Growth.

I hurry over to it and run my hand against its familiar bark. This will hurt, but I don't care. The pain will be worth it, for once. And I know I can do it—I'm the best third-Augury student at Southgate.

I find a small knot in one of the branches and press my hand against it, repeating the words in my head.

Once to see it as it is. Twice to see it in your mind. Thrice to bend it to your will.

I picture what I want in my mind—a heat builds in the center of my palm at the same time the ache begins at the base of my skull. I can feel the life of the tree, a moving, shimmering thing, and I pull at it, tugging on it like strings on a marionette, drawing it out. A tiny lump forms under my palm, a green leaf peeking out between my fingers. The tree resists a little and I gasp as fire rips down my spine, and it feels like needles are being shoved into my brain—my back arches and my head spins, but I've experienced worse pain in my four years at Southgate, and I'm determined to succeed in this. I force myself to focus, biting my lip hard to keep from crying out, coaxing the threads of life one by one, like strands of gossamer, pulling them out, shaping them, and the lump grows bigger, until it fits comfortably inside my hand.

A lemon.

I release it and my knees buckle—my palms hit the ground, and I stay doubled over, panting. A few drops of blood splash on the dirt, and I wipe my nose with the back of my hand. I lean my forehead against the tree and count backward from ten, the way Patience taught us, and gradually the pain subsides, until all that's left is a dull ache behind my right ear. Shaking, I get to my feet.

The lemon is perfect, its skin a rich yellow, its plump little body dangling from the branch. Hazel will love it.

I can still feel the life of the tree inside me, and I know that I've given a piece of myself to it, too. This tree won't be barren anymore.

I turn away, picking up some wood off the pile, and head back inside to join my family.

Three

THE ENTIRE HOLDING FACILITY STANDS ON THE PLAT-
form to see us off.

Southgate has its own train station, as does Northgate, Eastgate, and Westgate. We are the last stops in the
Marsh—the trains don't go any farther than the holding
facilities. The stations that transport workers to the other
circles of the city are farther on, closer to the wall that separates the Marsh from the Farm. I remember walking my
father there once when I was little, frightened by the big
black steam engine with its piercing whistle and its chimney
belching clouds of white smoke.

It's very early in the morning, just after dawn, and many
of the younger girls are bleary-eyed and stifling yawns. But

the ceremony is mandatory. I remember my first ceremony—
I was cold, and tired, and I didn't know any of the girls
going to the Auction. I just wanted to go back to bed.

It's strange, standing on this side of the platform. We
won't know what we'll be wearing until we get to the preparation rooms at the Auction House, so we're dressed the
same—knee-length brown shift dresses, with SG and our
Lot numbers stenciled on the left side.

I am now officially Lot 197. Violet Lasting is gone.

A representative from the Jewel stands behind a podium
and gives the usual speech. He is a large man, with wire-
rimmed glasses and a brocade waistcoat. On his left hand is
a ring—a ruby that sits like a fat, glittering cherry, encircled
by tiny diamonds. I can't take my eyes off that ring. It could
feed three families in the Marsh for a year.

He has a bland, droning voice, and the wind picks up
most of his words and carries them off. I'm not listening
anyway—it's pretty much the same speech year after year,
about how noble the tradition of surrogacy is, how essen-
tial we are to the continuation of the royalty, how esteemed
we'll be in the eyes of all the residents of the city.

I don't know about the Bank and the Jewel, but I'm
fairly sure the rest of the city couldn't care less about the
surrogates, unless you live in the Marsh and it means losing a daughter. None of the lower circles—the Smoke, the
Farm, and the Marsh—are allowed to have surrogates.
Sometimes parents try to hide their daughters, or pay off
the doctors who test them. The blood test that indicates
surrogacy is mandatory for every girl in the Marsh once she
reaches puberty. They don't know why only girls from the

poorest circle have the strange genetic mutation that causes the Auguries, but the royalty won't let anyone slip through the cracks. If you're caught trying to avoid the test, the sentence is death.

I shiver, remembering the first public execution I ever witnessed. It was seven months ago. A girl had been caught after three years in hiding. They brought her to the square in front of the gates of Southgate—we were kept behind screens, transparent on our side but opaque on the other, so that the gathering crowds couldn't see us. I searched for my mother in that crowd, but she wasn't there. It's nearly an hour's walk from our house to Southgate. Besides, she probably wanted to keep Ochre and Hazel away. She and Father never attended the public executions—"grotesque," Father used to call them. But I remember being curious, wondering what they were like.

Seeing one, though . . . I understood what he meant.

The girl was wild, long black hair tangled around her face, framing eyes of a brilliant, almost shocking, blue. There was something fierce and untamed about her appearance. She couldn't have been more than a few years older than me.

She didn't fight or struggle against the two Regimentals restraining her. She didn't cry, or beg. She looked strangely peaceful. When they put her head on the block, I could swear she smiled. The magistrate asked her if she had any last words.

"This is how it begins," she said. "I am not afraid." Her face saddened, and she added, "Tell Cobalt I love him."

Then they chopped her head off.

I forced myself to watch, to keep my eyes on her mutilated body and not cringe and look away, like Lily and so many of the other girls did. I thought she deserved to have someone be as brave as she was, as if it would somehow validate her life and death. It was probably a stupid idea—I had nightmares for a week—but I'm still glad I did it.

Whenever I think of her, I always wonder who Cobalt was. I wonder if he ever found out that he was the last person she thought of before she died.

I turn my attention back to the man from the Jewel, who finishes his speech and wipes his glasses with a silk handkerchief.

There are only twenty-two surrogates going to the Auction from Southgate this year. Most are coming from Northgate and Westgate. Our train is a plum-colored steam engine with only three carriages—much smaller and friendlier than the train my father took to work.

Our head doctor, Dr. Steele, shakes the fat man's hand, then turns to address us. Everything about Dr. Steele is long and gray—long chin, long nose, long arms, gray hair, gray eyebrows, grayish eyes. Even his skin has a grayish tinge. Lily once told me she heard that Dr. Steele is addicted to opiates, and it washes out all of his natural coloring.

"And now, ladies," Dr. Steele says in a frail, whispery voice, "it is time to depart."

He waves a long-fingered hand, and the doors on the steam engine open with a loud hissing sound. The surrogates begin to file into the carriages. I look back and see Mercy dabbing her eyes, and Patience looking as placid as ever. I see the rose-shaped bars on the windows of the dormitories, set in the pale pink stone of the holding facility. I see the faces of the other surrogates, the girls who will go back inside once this train leaves and never think of us again. My gaze falls on a young girl with bulging brown eyes. She is so thin, and clearly malnourished; she must be new. Our eyes meet, and she crosses the fingers on her right hand and presses them against her heart.

I step into the carriage and the doors close behind me.

THE CARRIAGES ARE AS DEVOID OF PERSONALITY AS OUR bedrooms at Southgate.

Purple curtains cover the windows, and a bench hugs the walls of the rectangular space, lined with plum-colored cushions. There are only seven of us in this particular carriage, and for a moment, we stand awkwardly in the sparse compartment, not quite sure what to do.

Then the train lurches forward and we break apart. Raven, Lily, and I take a spot in one corner. Raven pushes back the curtains.

"Are we allowed to open them?" Lily asks in a hushed voice.

"What are they going to do?" Raven says. "Shoot us?"

Lily bites her lip.

The ride to the Jewel takes two hours. It's dizzying, how quickly the certainty in my life dwindles. I'm certain this train will take us through the Farm, the Smoke, and the Bank, to the Auction House in the Jewel. I'm certain that I'll go to a prep room, then to a waiting room, then to the Auction. And that's it. That's all I have left. The unknown stretches out in front of me like a vast, blank sheet of paper.

I stare out the window, watching the mud-brick houses flash past, dark brown against the pale gray sky.

"It really isn't much to look at, is it?" Raven says.

I kick off my shoes and tuck my legs under me. "No," I murmur. "But it's home."

Raven laughs. "You are so sentimental."

She puts on a good show, but I know her too well. She'll miss it. "How was your Reckoning Day?"

She shrugs, but her mouth tightens. "Oh, fine, you know, my mother was over the moon about how healthy I looked, and how tall I was, and how *excited* I must be to see the Jewel. As if I'm going on a vacation or something. Yours?"

"What about Crow?" I ask. Crow is Raven's twin brother.

She untucks her hair from behind her ear, letting it fall to cover her face. "He barely spoke to me," she mumbles. "I thought . . . I mean, I didn't . . ." She shrugs again. "He doesn't know how to talk to a surrogate, I guess."

I try to remember what I thought about the surrogates, before I knew I was one. I remember thinking that they were something other, that they were special. Special is just about the last thing I feel right now.

At that moment, Lily begins to sing. Her small hand wraps around mine, her eyes bright as she watches the Marsh pass by us. Her voice is sweet and she sings a traditional Marsh-song, one we all know.

"Come all ye fair and tender ladies
Take warning how you court young men . . ."

Two other girls join in. Raven rolls her eyes.

"It doesn't really suit the moment, does it?" she mutters.

"No," I say quietly. "It doesn't." Most of the Marsh-songs are about girls who either die young or get rejected by their lovers—they don't really apply to us. "But it's nice to hear it, all the same."

"Oh, love is handsome, love is charming
Love is beauty while it's new
But love grows old and love grows colder
And fades away like morning dew."

A thick silence follows the song, broken only by the rhythmic pumping of the wheels beneath us. Then Lily laughs, a sort of crying-laugh, and squeezes my hand, and I realize I'll probably never hear another Marsh-song again.

THE TRAIN SLOWS, AND I CAN HEAR THE MASSIVE IRON doors grate and screech as they retreat into the wall that separates the Farm from the Marsh. I'd learned about the Farm, of course—we learn about all the circles in history class—but seeing it is something entirely different.

The first thing that strikes me is the colors. I never knew so many shades of green existed in nature. And not just green, but reds and pale yellows and bright oranges and juicy pinks.

I think of Ochre—he must be in one of the dairies by now. I hope he'll be able to keep working for the House of the Flame. I hate to think of him supporting our family on his own.

The other amazing thing about the Farm is the land-scape. In the Marsh, everything is flat; here, the ground has a sort of rolling feel to it. The train chugs over a bridge, where a river separates two hills. On their slopes, gnarled vines are trained in neat rows, on sticks and pieces of wire. I remember that this is called a vineyard, where grapes are grown for wine. I've had wine a couple of times—the caretakers let us have a glass on our birthdays, and on the Longest Night celebration.

"It's so *big*," Raven says.

She's right. The Farm seems to go on and on, and I almost forget that there is a Marsh, or a Jewel, or an Auction. I can almost pretend there is nothing except this endless expanse of nature.

As soon as we pass through the iron doors that separate the Farm and the Smoke, the light dims, like the sun's been turned down a few notches.

The train runs slowly on an elevated track through a maze of cast-iron behemoths, factories that tower over the streets, their chimneys belching smoke in a variety of colors—dark gray, white, greenish-purple, dull red. The streets are teeming with people, their faces gaunt, their backs bent. I see women and children mixed in with the men. A shrill whistle blows, and the crowd thins as the workers disappear into the factories.

My heart jumps as I realize there's only one more cir-cle left after this one. How much longer until we reach the Jewel? How many more minutes of freedom do I have left?

* * *

"OOOOH." LILY SIGHS AS WE ENTER THE BANK. "IT'S SO pretty."

The sunlight returns to a bright, buttery yellow, and I almost have to shield my eyes as it glints off the facades of the shops that line streets paved with pale stones. Arching windows with silver shutters and ornate signs wrought in gold are commonplace here. Neat rows of trees with thin trunks, their canopies trimmed into perfect green spheres, line the sidewalks, and electric stagecoaches are everywhere. Men in bowler hats and cleanly pressed suits escort women wearing dresses made of colorful silks and satins.

"Looks like Patience was right," I say. "No pants for women here."

Raven grumbles something unintelligible.

"Isn't it lovely?" Lily leans her head against the glass. "Just imagine—the Exetor might have met the Electress in one of these very stores."

Raven is shaking her head slowly. "It's crazy. All this . . . I mean . . . we've seen pictures but . . . they have so much *money*."

"And we haven't even seen the Jewel yet," I murmur.

"All right, girls, settle down," an older caretaker named Charity says as she comes in, followed by Dr. Steele. She carries a silver tray bearing different colored tablets in neat little rows. I glance at Raven.

"What are the pills for?" I whisper, but she only shrugs.

"Curtains closed, please," Charity says. Lily is quick to obey, but I see some of the other girls looking nervously at one another as they pull the curtains shut. The dull purple light in the carriage feels ominous.

"Now, now, don't look so anxious," Dr. Steele says. His voice is flat and not remotely reassuring. "This is just a little medication to relax you all before the big event. Please remain seated."

My heart is pumping in my chest and I reach out for Raven's hand. The doctor moves calmly around the room. The tablets are coded by Lot number, and each girl sticks out her tongue while Dr. Steele drops it into her mouth with a pair of tiny silver tongs. Some of the girls cough, others lick their lips and make sour faces, but other than that, nothing dramatic happens.

He reaches Raven. "192," he says, picking out a light blue tablet. Raven stares up at him with her deep black eyes, and for a second, I think she's going to refuse to take it. Then she opens her mouth and he drops it onto her tongue. She keeps staring at him, and doesn't give the slightest reaction to the tablet at all. It's the only defiance she has.

Dr. Steele doesn't even notice. "197," he says to me. I open my mouth and he drops a purple tablet onto my tongue. It stings, and tastes sour, reminding me of that time I bit into the lemon. In a second, it has dissolved. I run my tongue along my teeth and swallow. The tablet leaves a tingling sensation behind.

The doctor nods his head. "Thank you, ladies."

Charity bustles after him as he leaves the carriage.

"What was that?" Raven asks.

"Whatever it was, it didn't taste very good," I mutter. "I thought you weren't going to take yours for a second."

"Me too," Raven says. "But it would've been pointless,

wouldn't it? I mean, they probably would've just—"

But whatever Raven thought they would have done, I never hear, because unconsciousness engulfs me suddenly, and the world goes black.

Four

WHEN I COME TO, I AM ALONE.

A bright light shines overhead—too bright, it hurts my eyes. I'm lying on something cold and flat. Straps press down on my arms and legs and I realize, with a jolt of panic, that I'm naked.

Instinctively, my body lurches, trying to free myself and cover myself at the same time. A scream builds in my throat, but before I get a chance to release it, a soft voice murmurs, "Don't panic. I'll take those off in a moment. They're for your protection."

"Where am I?" I mean to shout, but my voice comes out in a scratchy whisper.

"You're in one of the preparation rooms. Calm down,

197. I can't take the restraints off until you do." The voice has a strange quality to it—too high to be a man's but too low for a woman's. My chest heaves and I try to relax my muscles, slow my breathing, and not think about how exposed I am.

"There. That's better." The voice moves closer. "I promise, 197, the very last thing I want is to harm you in any way." I feel a pressure around my arm, and something cold presses against the inside of my elbow. The pressure tightens.

"I'm just taking your blood pressure," the voice says calmly. The tight thing around my arm relaxes; then it's gone. I hear the scratching of a pen on paper. "Look up for me, please?"

There's nowhere else to look but up, and suddenly a bright light shines in my left eye, then my right. I blink furiously, but it's like my retinas have been seared—all I can see is a green glow. The pen scratches again.

"Very good, 197. Almost done. I'm going to touch you now. I promise I will not hurt you."

All my muscles clench into tiny fists, and I blink harder, but I still can't see. Then I feel a gentle pressure low on my stomach, first on the left side, then the right.

"There we are," the voice says soothingly. "All done."

The glow fades from my eyes and the face behind the voice comes into focus.

It's the face of a man, but it's oddly childlike, with delicate features, a narrow nose, a thin mouth, cream-colored skin. His head has been shaved except for a circle of chestnut hair on his crown, which is tied up into an elegant topknot, a hairstyle that I remember from my classes on royal culture and lifestyle. It means he's a lady-in-waiting.

Ladies-in-waiting are more than just the highest of servants—they're confidantes and advisors to their mistresses. They are selected and trained from a young age, and some of them are men, castrated so they can be considered "safe" to work so closely with royal women.

Humiliation washes over me at being naked in front of a man, and I squirm against the restraints. He waits patiently, looking only at my face, ignoring my body, and something in his expression makes me wonder if he knows how I'm feeling, what I'm thinking. I stop struggling. He smiles.

"Hello. I'm Lucien. I'm going to take the straps off now, all right?"

My voice seems to have disappeared, but he doesn't wait for an answer. As he reaches over me to undo the restraints, I notice he's wearing a long white dress with a high lace collar and long sleeves. His fingers are manicured and his body is slim but soft, like the muscle hasn't been toned under the skin.

"You have beautiful eyes," he says, undoing the last strap. "Why don't you sit up, and I'll get you a robe?"

He disappears and I scramble into a sitting position, hugging my knees tight to hide my body. My eyes still have a hard time adjusting; I hold up my hand to block out the brilliant light overhead.

"Oh yes, let's do something about the lighting." Lucien's voice drifts from the darkness. The light goes out. At first, it's terrifying—then slowly, light seeps back into the room. Different colored globes, attached to gold fixtures on the walls, begin to glow, and their colors blend together until the room is lit in a comfortable shade of pinkish yellow.

"Here you are." Lucien hands me a dressing gown made of ice-blue silk. I slip it on quickly, the delicate fabric soft against my skin, and try to pretend that it's my mother's bathrobe. He holds out his hand, an offering, not a command; I ignore it and hop off the table onto trembling legs.

"First things first. Let's get rid of this ghastly table." He gives me a conspiratorial smile, but the muscles in my face aren't working—I can only stare at him blankly. He presses a button on the wall and the floor underneath the table drops down, a platform being lowered into nothing, and then another piece of wood slides over the gaping rectangular hole, clicking into place and fitting so perfectly, I would never have guessed it was there. "I don't suppose you see many false floors in the Marsh, do you?"

I blink, and look from him to where the table used to be, and then back again. Suddenly, I feel like I'm twelve years old again, just entering Southgate, when everything seemed so new and bright and fancy.

Lucien sighs. "You don't talk much, do you, 197?"

I clear my throat. "My name—"

He holds up a finger and shakes his head. "Sorry, honey. I can't know your name."

Even though I have no attachment to this man, and I'll probably never see him again, the fact that he isn't allowed to know my name, *my* name, not some number I've been assigned, brings tears to my eyes. My chest tightens.

"Don't cry." Lucien says it gently, but there is an urgency in his tone. "Please."

I take a deep breath, willing the tears back, away from my lashes, from their precarious balance on my lids, back down into the deep well inside me. In a second, they're gone.

Crying will be useless from now on anyway.

"All right," I say, my voice steady. "I'm not crying."

Lucien raises an eyebrow. "No, you're not. Good girl." The way he says it, it doesn't sound condescending. He seems impressed.

"So," I say, hoping I sound braver than I feel, "what happens now?"

"Now," he says, "you look in a mirror."

My heart plummets to my toes so fast it leaves my head spinning. I force myself to breathe normally as all the colors of the room blur together.

Lucien puts a hand on my shoulder. "It's all right. I promise, you'll like what you see."

He leads me over to a lumpy, covered thing in the corner. It's elevated on a little platform, and Lucien indicates that I should step onto it. My legs are still shaking.

"Do you want to close your eyes first?" he asks.

"Does it help?"

"Sometimes."

I nod and squeeze my eyes shut. In the darkness behind my lids, I remember the last time I saw my own reflection. I was twelve. I kept a little mirror on the dresser in the room Hazel and I shared, and I was brushing my hair. Everything about my face was thin and pinched. My nose, my cheekbones, my eyebrows, my lips, the little point of my chin. Everything but my eyes. Huge and violet, they seemed to take up half my face. But the memory is old; it's been taken out and pored over so many times, like a letter, read and reread until it's wrinkled and creased and some of the words are blurred.

There is a gust of air and a swish of fabric. "Whenever you're ready," Lucien says.

I hold my breath and focus on my heart as it punches against my chest. *I can do this. I won't be afraid.*

I open my eyes.

I'm surrounded by three identical women. One looks directly at me, the other two at angles on either side. There is no thinness in her face, except maybe in the tiny point of her chin. Her cheeks are round, her lips full and parted slightly in surprise. Black hair cascades over her shoulders. But her eyes . . . her eyes are exactly as I remember them.

She is a stranger. She is me.

I try to reconcile those two thoughts, and as I move my hand to touch my face, I start laughing. I can't help it. The girl in the mirror moves with me exactly, and for some reason I find this funny.

"That's not the usual reaction," Lucien says, "but it's better than screaming."

That brings me up short. "Some girls scream?"

He purses his lips. "Well, now, we don't have all day. Let's get you ready. Please, sit."

He gestures to a chair beside a table littered with makeup. I take one last look at the stranger in the mirror, then step off the podium and sit down. There are so many tubes and creams and powders, I can't imagine what they're all for or that they could possibly be used on just one person. Three hourglasses sit on a small shelf above the table, in different sizes with different colored sand.

Lucien dips his hands into a basin of sweet-scented water, drying them on a fluffy white towel. Then, very carefully, he turns over the first hourglass, the largest one, full of pale green sand.

"All right," he says. "Let's get started."

WHENEVER I'D IMAGINED THE PREP PROCESS, I ALWAYS thought it might be the only fun part of the Auction. Someone doing your hair and makeup and all that.

It's actually incredibly boring.

I can't see anything Lucien's doing, except when he manicures my hands and polishes my toenails, or covers me from head to toe in a fine silver dust—I have to take my robe off for that, and I put it back on as quickly as I can. But for the most part, I just sit in the chair. I wonder how Raven is faring, and who is prepping her. She must be hating this.

"Where are the other prep rooms?" I ask, as Lucien applies a thin layer of translucent powder over my neck and shoulders.

"They're all on this level, or the one below it," he replies, frowning at some imperfection on my collarbone.

"When does the Auction start?" I hope I sound casual.

"It's already started."

I feel like I've been punched in the stomach. I have no idea how long I was unconscious; I have no idea what time it is. "How long?"

Lucien mixes some powders together on a little palette. "A long while," he says.

My fingers dig into the leather-covered arms of the

chair, and I try to keep my face smooth, but all I can think is, *Lily has been sold by now.*

Lily's gone.

"I'm going to work on your face," Lucien says. "Try to keep as still as possible. And close your eyes."

It's like he's giving me a little gift, shutting out the world for a while and staying in darkness. I think about my mother, and Hazel, and Ochre. I see our house in my head and picture Mother knitting by the fire. Ochre is at work. Hazel is in school. I wonder if she's found my lemon yet.

I think about Raven, and the first time we met. She was thirteen and had been at Southgate for a year already, but she kept failing her Augury tests (on purpose, she later told me). I was learning the first Augury, Color, and she was in my class. I tried and tried but I couldn't turn my building block from blue to yellow—they start you off with one block, and you can't advance to another level until you've changed it. I didn't understand what they wanted from me. I didn't know how I was supposed to do it. Raven helped me. She taught me how to relax my mind and then focus it, how to see it before it happened, and she held the bucket for me when I coughed up blood. She gave me her handkerchief to stanch my nosebleeds, and showed me how to pinch the bridge of my nose to help them stop, and she promised me it wouldn't always be this bad. My head was pounding and my body ached, but by the end of the day, that block was yellow.

I have no idea what Lucien's doing to my face, and I hope I still look like myself after this. Layer after layer after layer is applied to my cheeks, my lips, my eyelids, my eyebrows, even my ears. He spends a lot of time on my eyes, and uses soft powders and cold creams and something thick and hard, like a pencil.

"Done," he says at long last. "You have incredible patience, 197."

"What's next?"

"Hair."

I watch the hourglass, the tiny trickle of green sand that has been slowly filling the lower bulb. Lucien's fingers are gentle and deft, and he uses hot irons and steam curlers to manipulate my hair. I hope I don't lose it when I see myself again. Maybe I won't have to look in the mirror. Maybe I'll just go straight to the Auction.

My stomach tightens at the thought.

"May I ask you a question, 197?" Lucien says quietly. I wish he'd stop calling me that.

"Sure."

The silence that follows is so long, I wonder if he's forgotten what he wanted to ask. Then, in a voice barely above a whisper, he says, "Do you want this life?"

My muscles freeze. I feel like this question is not allowed, not permitted to be asked, or even thought about in the Jewel. Who cares what the surrogates want? But Lucien asks me. It makes me wonder if maybe he'd like to know my name, too.

"No," I whisper back.

He finishes my hair in silence.

THE SECOND HOURGLASS IS SMALLER AND FILLED WITH pale purple sand.

I stand in front of one of the three closets while Lucien

pulls dresses off the racks and I squeeze myself into them. He picks ones that are a hair too tight, telling me it's to "emphasize my curves." Some of the dresses are outrageous things, like costumes, with wings sprouting out of them, or finlike attachments. Thankfully, Lucien gives up on those pretty quickly.

"Definitely not your style," he says. I don't know what my style is, but I'm glad he agrees that it's not *that*.

I try on a series of dresses made of heavy brocade, relieved when Lucien dismisses those as well—they make me feel like I weigh a thousand pounds. There are dresses with full skirts, short skirts, long sleeves, no sleeves, made of silk, damask, taffeta, lace, in every color and pattern imaginable. Lucien's brow furrows as I try on more and more, the pile of discarded fabrics growing higher and higher. A light sheen of sweat beads on his forehead, and he glances at the hourglass—the purple sand has nearly filled the bottom bulb. We're running out of time.

Suddenly, a smile breaks across his face and he gives me a look that makes me immediately suspicious.

"You know what?" he says, tossing aside a long dress made of red velvet. "*You* choose."

I blink. "What?"

"You choose. Just poke around in the closets and pick what you like best."

For a second, I'm too stunned to move. Isn't this sort of important, what I wear for the Auction? Won't it influence who buys me? Isn't this his *job*?

But then I wonder if he's giving me another little gift, like closing my eyes for the makeup. I remember what Raven said yesterday, about how it was the last day we'd ever get to choose our own outfit. Lucien's giving me one more choice.

"Okay," I say. I ignore the first closet, where most of the costume-y stuff is, and head straight for the second. I run my hands along the racks, seeing which materials feel best. The farther back I go, the simpler the dresses become.

The moment I touch it, I know.

It's made of muslin, in a purple so pale it reminds me of the sunrise yesterday, of the sky just before it exploded with color. It has an empire waist and falls in a clean line to the floor. It has no ornamentation. It doesn't even look expensive.

I love it.

Lucien laughs when he sees my choice. "Try it on," he says, and when I do, he laughs again and claps. "I don't think that dress has ever been used by a surrogate in the history of the Auction," he says. "But, honey, it fits you like a glove."

Five

"WHAT'S NEXT?" I ASK.

"You look in the mirror again," he replies.

I swallow. "Do I have to?"

Lucien takes my hand in both of his—his skin is soft, like a child's. "Yes. It's required. You've seen yourself as you were, and now you have to accept who you are, and embrace your new life and your future." It's like he's reading from a script, but something in his eyes contradicts the words. Like he's really telling me he's sorry.

"All right." I manage to breathe steadily as I approach the mirrors. I keep my head down, step onto the podium, count to three, and look up.

The stranger in the mirror has been transformed.

I blink rapidly, trying to reconcile her with the image I had of myself in my head. The image of a pretty girl, slightly plump, full face, big eyes. The woman I am looking at now is beautiful. Stunning. Her cheeks seem thinner, molded to accent her high cheekbones, and her eyebrows arch delicately over luminous eyes, lined in rich purple with accents of lilac and gold. Her lips are glossed in pale pink, and her hair tumbles over her shoulders in thick curls, one side pinned up with a jeweled clip, encrusted with amethysts that form the shape of a butterfly. There is a shimmer to her skin, almost like she's glowing. The color of the dress works perfectly and its simplicity only makes her features stand out more.

"What do you think?" Lucien asks.

I am speechless.

He takes a step closer, so our reflections touch. "I wanted you to still look like you."

"Thank you," I whisper.

Lucien picks up the last hourglass—it's tiny, and the sand inside it is dark red.

"This one is for you," he says. "You have this time to do whatever you want. Look in the mirror. Sing. Meditate. Just don't mess up your hair and makeup."

"What are you going to do?"

He gives me a sort of sad, pitying look. "I'm going to leave, 197. A Regimental will take you to the Waiting Room when your time is up."

My heart sticks in my throat. "You're leaving?"

Lucien nods. "My apologies about the mess," he says, his eyes lingering on the scattered clothes and smudges of makeup on the vanity. "The servants can't come in to clean until you're gone." He gives me a small smile. "It has been a pleasure to prep you, 197."

He turns the hourglass and walks to the door.

"Lucien, wait."

He stops. I'm nervous and want to chew on my bottom lip, but I'm worried about what he said about not messing with my makeup. I don't know what I want to do, in these last minutes before I'm sold. But I do know that I don't want to be alone.

"You said . . . I can do anything I want?"

He nods.

"Okay. Then I want to talk to you. I want you to stay."

For a second, it's like he doesn't understand me. Then a slow smile spreads across his face.

"Well," he says, smoothing his topknot. "This is a first."

He sits on one of the claw-footed sofas, daintily crosses his legs, and pats the spot next to him. I smile for the first time since I woke up in this room.

"Ah," he says, "that's what was missing. Now you're perfect."

I sit down. There is a silence in which I can almost hear the trickle of sand through the hourglass.

"What would you like to talk about?" Lucien asks.

"I don't know," I say honestly. "I just . . . didn't want you to leave me."

Lucien's expression softens. "When you think of something, let me know." He brushes the silky fabric of his gown with his fingertips. I notice again how smooth his skin is.

"How old are you?" I ask.

He bursts into laughter. "Oh, honey, you can't start with that. You'll never survive here."

I blush deeply, feeling the heat burn in my cheeks. "Sorry," I mumble. I've lived so long in a place where age was always known, and limited to only a certain number of years.

Lucien pats my hand. "Don't worry about it. You're already doing so much better than most of the other girls I've prepped."

"How long have you been doing this?"

"Nine years. But I don't prep every Auction. I've been doing it so long now, I get to choose who I work on." He bats his eyelashes.

"You chose me?"

"I did."

"Why?" I can't imagine what could have compelled him to choose me. How could he know anything about me?

He hesitates for a moment. "Your eyes," he says.

I'm stunned. "You saw me?"

"We're given photographs of all the surrogates in the Auction. Along with your measurements, of course. How else would I have three closets full of dresses in exactly your size?"

I try to imagine Lucien flipping through stacks of photographs of girls denoted only by lot number and dress size. It makes me feel so small.

I glance at the hourglass—already, half my time is up.

"Are you afraid?" he asks.

"I don't know." The words come out on their own, and I realize they're true. I don't know if I'm afraid. I'm not sure if fear is the right word. I feel strangely detached, like this isn't real, like it's happening to someone else.

"For what it's worth," Lucien says, "I think you'll be fine."

I don't really know what to say to that. The sand trickling through the hourglass is loud in my ears.

"What's out there?" I ask.

But before Lucien can answer, the sand runs out. A lock clicks.

Time's up.

"Lot 197." The Regimental's voice is very deep. He fills the entire doorway, his red military jacket tight over broad shoulders, his eyes dark and impassive. "Come with me."

My mouth has gone completely dry and it's an enormous effort to stand. Lucien stands as well, and for a second his body blocks the Regimental from view and he squeezes my hand. Then he glides away, his expression carefully neutral.

It takes me nine steps to reach the Regimental, and each one seems like an eternity. He turns smartly and walks out the door; I force myself to follow him.

The hallway is carpeted in a dark pink rug so plush that neither my satin slippers nor his boots make any sound. The walls are painted mauve, and the same globes that were in my prep room glow on the walls. Sometimes we pass other doors, and identical hallways appear, branching off the one we're on, but they are all empty. Silent. An uneasiness crawls up my spine.

The Regimental stops so abruptly, I nearly walk into him. The door we're in front of looks just like the others—simple, wooden, with a copper doorknob. He steps back and stands at attention. I wish he would talk to me. I wish he would tell me what I'm supposed to do.

I step forward and slowly open the door.

SOUND BUZZES AROUND ME LIKE A THOUSAND MARSH flies.

There is the briefest pause when I enter, then the buzzing starts up again.

The room is so full of color, it takes my brain a few seconds to process that these are girls—surrogates, not dolls. One pretty blonde stands out, taller than the others thanks to her hair, piled in curls that stretch about a foot above her head. Her pink lace dress flows in endlessly expanding folds to the floor, like an iced layer cake. She's talking to a haughty-looking, black-haired girl, with skin the color of dark chocolate—her features are feline, like a lioness. She wears one of the costumelike dresses. It's strapless, the top crafted out of golden plating that dissolves into a rainbow of tassels that shimmer with the smallest movement. Her hair is sectioned into multiple braids, each one threaded with silver and gold. The whole effect is quite fierce. She sees me staring at her and her eyes narrow, looking me up and down.

I turn away, and my gaze lands on a small figure, alone in the far corner of the room. Then someone grabs my arm and I jump.

"Finally." Raven's voice is so familiar that I feel my bones soften with relief. "I was wondering when you'd get here."

I stare at her, trying to fit this new Raven into the image

I have of my best friend. She is wearing a long robe, styled like a kimono but made of softer fabric, more alluring. It's patterned in red and gold, the empire waist emphasizing how long her legs are. Her eyes are thickly lined in black, elongating their almond shape. The center of her lips have been painted bright red, so it looks like she's constantly making a kissing face, and her hair has been slicked back, arching over the crown of her head like a fan, from one ear to the other. Teardrop earrings, rubies encased in gold, hang from her ears.

I open my mouth, then close it. I don't know what to say.

"I know, I look like an idiot," Raven says.

I want to laugh and cry at the same time. She's still my Raven. "You look incredible," I say. "Those earrings must be worth a fortune."

"It's not like I get to keep them. At least you still look like you. How did you convince your prep artist to do that?"

"I didn't. He chose to make me like this."

Raven's black-lined eyes nearly bug out of her head. "*He?* You had a *man?*"

I've forgotten that this news would be shocking. Lucien no longer feels like a man to me. He's just . . . Lucien. "He's a lady-in-waiting," I explain.

Raven looks incredulous. The expressions on her new face are unsettling. "What was he like?"

"He was . . ." I try to think of the right word. "Kind. He was nice to me. What about you?"

"Ugh, I had this *ancient* woman who probably

singlehandedly keeps the makeup factories in business. She was awful." Raven shudders. "Anyway. It's over now."

"How long have you been here?"

"I don't know. Maybe five minutes? There weren't as many girls here then."

"So this is the last of us," I say, glancing around the room.

"Yeah. Lots 190 to 200. The jewels of the Auction." Raven shakes her head. "We look sort of freakish, to be honest. Well, except you."

Suddenly, a door on the opposite side of the room opens. An older Regimental with salt-and-pepper hair steps through it.

"Lot 190," he calls. "Lot 190."

A waifish girl, in a silver dress that glitters with scales, weaves her way to the door. Her head seems oddly large compared with the thinness of her arms and shoulders. The Regimental gives her a small bow, then turns. She follows him out the door, the scales of her dress tinkling.

I reach for Raven's hand as she reaches for mine.

"This is it," she says.

"We'll see each other again," I say. "We have to."

The door opens again. A different Regimental this time.

"Lot 191. Lot 191."

A large girl in a black velvet dress and wearing an ornate headdress follows him out. I clutch Raven's hand so hard it hurts.

The door opens.

"I'll never forget you," Raven says. "I will never forget you, Violet."

"Lot 192. Lot 192."

Raven holds her head high and walks proudly through the dwindling crowd of girls and out the door.

And then she's gone.

I feel my insides collapsing and the room seems to swirl around me. I have to remind myself to breathe.

Raven's gone.

My whole body shakes. I never even said good-bye to her. Why didn't I say good-bye?

"Was she your friend?"

I start and look down at the girl I saw earlier, the one who was alone in the corner. She can't be older than thirteen. Her hair is a brilliant red, her body thin and wiry, and she wears, to my intense surprise, a ragged pinafore. She has almost no makeup on, just a hint of blush on her cheeks and gloss on her lips. She looks incredibly tiny. And plain. But her big brown eyes are full of compassion.

"Yes," I say. "She was."

The girl nods. "My best friend came here with me, too. But she was Lot 131. I haven't seen her since the train."

"Which holding facility are you from?"

"Northgate. They came with me," she says, indicating the iced cake and the lioness. "But they aren't my friends."

"I'm Violet," I say.

Her eyes widen. "Are we allowed to tell each other our names?"

"Oh. Probably not." I sigh.

The girl bites her lip. "I'm Dahlia," she says. Then she smiles shyly. "I think you're the prettiest of all of us. Especially your eyes. You must've had a really good prep artist."

"I did. What about you?" It doesn't look like she got prepped at all.

"She wanted me to look pathetic. That's what she said. To intrigue the buyers." Dahlia chews nervously on her thumbnail.

The door Raven left through opens. Lot 193 is taken. A few seconds later, Lot 194 follows.

There are only six of us left. The room feels cavernous. A chandelier hangs from the ceiling, dripping with pink crystals and bathing the room in a rosy glow. There is no furniture. Just the dark pink carpet and mauve-painted walls. It's like being inside a giant mouth.

"Are you scared?" Dahlia asks.

Now that it comes to it, the hazy feelings I couldn't identify in the prep room have sharpened to a point. Fear. It stabs at my lungs, claws at my stomach, burrows into the base of my skull. I feel it like something other, something outside of me. My palms itch, and sweat beads in my armpits.

"Yes," I say.

"Me too." Dahlia gnaws at the nail on her index finger. All her nails have been chewed right down to the quick.

"What's your lot number?" I ask.

Her body freezes. "What's yours?"

"197."

She scratches her nose and looks down. "200," she mumbles.

Before I can really comprehend this tiny, tattered girl as the most desirable surrogate in the entire Auction, the door opens again.

It's as if time speeds up. I watch surrogates 195 and 196 leave, one right after the other, too quickly, surely they shouldn't be leaving quite so quickly, wasn't there more time in between the other girls? And then the door is opening again and the Regimental with the dark eyes who brought me to this room is there and he calls my lot number but my feet are cemented to the floor.

Dahlia nudges me. "You have to go, Violet."

The lioness smirks and whispers something to the iced cake, who giggles.

I blink. "It was nice to meet you, Dahlia," I say. Then I force my feet to move, one in front of the other, and the Regimental comes closer until he's looming over me. Our eyes meet, and my fingertips tremble, fear and anticipation merging into a hard knot at the base of my skull. Without a word, he bows and turns, and I follow him into the dark.

Six

THE DOOR CLOSES BEHIND ME AUTOMATICALLY, AND FOR one terrifying moment, all there is is darkness.

Then I hear a low hum, and a narrow hallway is illuminated on either side by a path of small square floor lamps. Their yellowish-green light shoots straight up, showing me the way without revealing where I'm going. The Regimental is a black outline in front of me, his pace slow and even. A weight presses harder against my chest with each step I take, the invisible walls closing in around me. I hear Lucien's voice in my head, telling me I'll be fine, and Raven's, too, saying she'll never forget me. I hold on to them, like talismans, trying to keep the fear at bay.

The hallway curves to the left. Then the floor lamps end

abruptly and the Regimental stops. Silence.

"Where are we?" I ask. My voice is hushed and tiny. For ten long seconds, the Regimental says nothing; then, stirred by some unseen command, he turns to me.

"I thank you, Lot 197, for your service to the royalty. Your place is marked. You must go on alone." He bows low, and steps back so he is behind me.

A rounded, golden door engraved with the various crests of the royal families begins to glow. I have no idea what lies behind it, and suddenly panic seizes me so completely that I think I might pass out. But Raven went through this door. And so did Lily.

My fingertips tremble as they graze the ornamented metal. As if the door was waiting for my touch, it swings open, and suddenly I find myself blinded by a brilliant light.

"AND NEXT UP, LADIES, WE HAVE LOT 197. LOT 197, please take your mark."

The voice is polite, almost pleasant, but I'm having a hard time focusing on what it's saying.

I'm in an amphitheater, rings of seats spiraling upward, but the seats aren't normal seats, they're chaise lounges, and sofas, and one even looks like a throne. And in each one sits a woman, her eyes focused on me, her clothing extravagant beyond anything I saw in my prep closets. Rippling, colorful satins; delicate silks; lace; feathers; crinoline; cloth-of-gold—glittering fabrics sewn with jewels, they are nothing like the ones the dolls in the Waiting Room were wearing. These women are masterpieces, living sculptures of elegance and nobility.

"Lot 197, please take your mark," the voice says again. I see him now, a man in a tuxedo standing to my left behind a wooden podium. He is very tall, his dark hair slicked back. Our eyes meet and he inclines his head.

There is a silver X in the middle of the circular stage. My knees shake as I approach it, this walk by far the longest of all the long walks I've taken today. I hear a rustling of whispers, like a light breeze running through the amphitheater. The man waits until I've reached the X. Then he removes a white candle from inside the podium and places it in a brass holder. His eyes scan the room once before he strikes a match and lights the candle. The flame glows bright blue.

"Lot 197, ladies. Age sixteen, height five feet seven inches, weight one hundred and thirty pounds. Unusual eye color, as you can see. Four years of training, with scores of 9.6 on the first Augury, 9.4 on the second, and a tremendously impressive 10.0 on the third. Prodigious skill with stringed instruments, particularly the cello."

It is frighteningly bizarre to hear myself described this way; a set of statistics, a musical instrument, and nothing more.

"The bidding will start at five hundred thousand diamantes. Do I hear five hundred thousand?"

A woman in a blue silk dress, a massive diamond necklace roped around her neck, raises a silver feather.

"Five hundred thousand from the Lady of the Downs, do I hear five hundred and fifty thousand?"

A dark-skinned woman raises a tiny set of bronze scales with one hand, sipping champagne from a crystal flute with the other.

"Five hundred and fifty thousand, do I hear six hundred?"

The bidding continues. My value climbs to seven hundred, then eight, then *nine hundred thousand* diamantes. My brain has a hard time wrapping its head around such a sum. I can't seem to breathe normally—my lungs feel compressed, like they're being squeezed in a vise. The women don't speak, they just raise an object that signifies their House; I don't recognize them all, and the auctioneer doesn't always address them by title. Suddenly, I wish I'd paid more attention in royal culture and lifestyle class.

"Nine hundred and fifty thousand, do I hear one million?"

A young woman, seated in the chair that looks like a throne, raises a tiny scepter with a diamond the size of a chicken's egg perched on its tip. I feel a collective intake of breath from the other women, and notice the auctioneer's eyes flicker for an instant toward the candle. It has burned halfway down.

"One million diamantes to Her Royal Grace, the Electress. Do I hear one million five?"

The Electress. I am shocked by how young she looks, even younger than in the photographs I've seen of her, almost like a child playing dress-up. Her gown has puffed sleeves and a wide brocade skirt, her lips painted a very bright red. I try to determine if there is anything particularly Bank-like about her, but she looks pretty much the same as all the other women in this room.

I notice a woman in the row above staring at her—the woman's almond-shaped eyes remind me of Raven's.

"One million five to the Countess of the Rose," the auctioneer says, and I am pulled back to the present. An older woman on a chaise lounge is holding up a golden rose. A few seats away, a heavy woman glares at her—no, *heavy* isn't the right word. *Fleshy* would be more accurate. The woman's bulk is squeezed into a black satin dress, leaving her doughy arms bare. Her face is pudgy and her eyes are . . . cruel. I can't think of another word to describe them.

"Do I hear two million?" the auctioneer asks.

The diamond scepter is raised immediately. Then the rose. Then the scepter. My heart slams against my ribs, the rush of my blood roaring in my ears. Could I really be sold to the Electress? It seems foolish that I'd never considered it—I guess I'd always figured the Electress would go for Lot 200. Why go for fourth best when you can have first?

The candle is burning lower now, milky wax dripping down the bronze holder, the blue flame burning brighter as it nears its end. The bidding increases, and my value soars to five million diamantes, an unimaginable sum. It's clear that I will either be the surrogate for the Electress or the Countess of the Rose—all the other women have stopped bidding. I fight the urge to gnaw on my lower lip.

Then it happens.

"Do I hear six million diamantes? Six million?"

The woman with Raven's eyes holds up a tiny blue mirror.

The candle goes out.

"Sold!" the auctioneer cries, and all my muscles turn to

jelly. "Sold for six million diamantes. To the Duchess of the Lake."

SOLD.

The word revolves around my brain without really making sense.

I am sold.

For a flicker of an instant, I meet the dark eyes of the woman who has bought me: the Duchess of the Lake. Then, suddenly, I am sinking through the floor.

The X is on a platform being lowered down below the stage, away from the Auction. This time, I welcome the darkness. It feels safe. I look up and see another platform closing over the circular space where a few moments ago I stood, like a total eclipse. And just before it closes completely, I hear the auctioneer's voice.

"And next up, ladies, we have Lot 198." I wonder which girl is crossing the stage—the lioness or the iced cake. "Lot 198, please take your mark."

The Auction goes on.

"Lot 197?"

I start, aware that I've stopped moving. And it's not completely dark, just dim. I'm in an empty room with concrete walls, circular like the amphitheater above it, and riddled with doors.

"Lot 197?" A woman in a simple gray dress frowns at me. She is holding a clipboard, and her eyes scan it briefly.

I don't think I can speak yet, so I just nod.

The woman nods curtly in response. "Duchess of the Lake. This way."

She opens one of the doors and I follow her down a narrow hallway. There are no glowglobes here—the only light comes from a few flickering torches set in high brackets. Their flames cast strange shadows along the walls, a stark and unsettling contrast to the warm light of the glowglobes in my prep room.

The hallway ends in a plain wooden door and the woman opens it—I follow her into a small, domed room made of octagonal stones that give me the feeling of being inside a beehive. A fire burns low in the grate, casting a dim light on a simple table and chair. There's a lumpy black cloth on the table. Otherwise, the room is empty.

"Sit," the woman says. As soon as I sink into the chair, my muscles begin to shake, and I have to put my head in my hands and take deep breaths through my mouth.

I am sold. I am property. I will never see my family or Southgate or the Marsh ever again.

"There, there," the woman says mechanically. "It's all right."

It is definitely not all right. I don't know if I've felt less all right in my entire life. I press the heels of my hands against my eyes, not caring if I smudge Lucien's makeup. I want to go home.

A pair of cold hands wrap around my wrists.

"Listen to me." The woman's voice is different, almost gentle, and I look up. She is kneeling in front of me, her face close to mine. "Whether I agree with this or not, it doesn't matter, you understand? I don't make the rules around here. But the royalty says that no surrogate is allowed to see her way into or out of the Auction House." I feel queasy as she stands and unwraps the black cloth, revealing first a blue vial, then a syringe. "I'm telling you right now, this won't hurt you. We can do this the easy way or the hard way, it's up to you—I know they don't give you a choice on your way in. The easy way is, you let me put you to sleep. The hard way is, I press a button and four Regimentals come through that door and hold you down, and then I put you to sleep anyway. Do you understand?"

I swallow the bile that rises in my throat and nod.

"So, what will it be?"

I suppose I should be happy that I have a choice at all. "If it's all right with you, I think I'll do the easy way."

The hint of a smile plays at the edge of the woman's lips. She fills the syringe with blue liquid from the vial, then turns my arm over to find a vein in my elbow. I wince as the needle pierces my skin—needles were a part of life at Southgate, but I never got used to them. "You're a smart girl. Maybe smart enough to survive this place."

Her words are ominous, but the blue liquid floods my veins, making my legs heavy and my eyelids droop, and before I can ask her what she means, darkness swallows me up and I sleep.

Seven

"She's waking up. Go fetch Her Ladyship."

I hear footsteps, then a door opens and closes, but it sounds far away. I shift my head and it sinks deeper into something very soft. I'm extremely comfortable, and warm. When I open my eyes, at first all I can see is a hazy yellow glow.

"How are you feeling?" a voice asks. It sounds like it's coming from the end of a tunnel. I blink and rub my eyes, and the world sharpens—hope blossoms inside me when I see a long white dress with a high lace collar and a topknot. But it isn't Lucien. This lady-in-waiting is a woman, older, her eyes bright and scrutinizing, her topknot a rich auburn color. It's strange to see a woman with a partially shaved head. A thin leather belt is fastened around her waist, a full key ring hanging from it.

"Where am I?" I ask, sitting up, my voice still thick with sleep.

"In your new bedroom, of course."

At first, I think she must be joking. The room is enormous. Glowglobes cast a warm light on the walls, papered in pale green, and the furniture scattered about the room is upholstered in shades of green and gold. There are dressers, an armoire, a vanity, plush armchairs with footstools, a sofa, a small breakfast table, and a large fireplace. Dark green curtains cover the windows, gold tasseled ropes hanging at their sides—they block out the light completely, so I can't tell whether it's day or night outside.

It is more beautiful than any room I could have ever imagined. And this woman said it's mine. I can't help the giggle that escapes my lips.

The lady-in-waiting smiles, and her eyes crinkle at the corners. "Welcome to the palace of the Lake."

"This is all for me?" I always imagined my living situation would be similar to the austere conditions of my bedroom at Southgate.

"Not just this, of course. Your private chambers include a powder room, tea parlor, drawing room, and dressing room."

"You mean there's *more*?"

She gives me a condescending look. "Child, you were bought by the Duchess of the Lake. Not some merchant family."

I try to remember what I know about the Duchess of

the Lake. She's from one of the four founding Houses, but I always get the two Duchesses and two Countesses confused. Hundreds and hundreds of years ago, before there was a Jewel or a Marsh or a Farm, this island was divided into two cities—the Duchesses ruled one, and the Countesses the other, and the cities were always fighting against each other. Then an arrangement was made, and the daughter of a Duchess married the son of a Countess and became the first Exetor and Electress, the two cities became one, and the Lone City was formed—divided into five circles with the Jewel at its heart.

I think Lily mentioned the Duchess of the Lake recently, tied to some sort of scandal that I wasn't interested in hearing about. I'm beginning to wish I'd spent less time rolling my eyes at Lily's gossip and more time listening to it. I was so determined to resent the royalty that I never considered there might be benefits to living with them. But as I look around my room, for the first time I think maybe my life in the Jewel won't be so bad.

"Come on, up you get," the lady-in-waiting says. "Her Ladyship will be here shortly."

A handful of butterflies flutter in my stomach.

My bed is so big, I literally have to crawl across it. I have a sudden, childish desire to jump up and down on the mattress, but the woman's presence holds me back. The emerald bedspread is velvety under my hands and knees, and I brush aside the gauzy canopy that floats down from each of the four posters. I realize, as my bare feet sink into the plush carpet, that my clothes have been changed. I'm wearing a white silk nightdress, not unlike the one I wore at Southgate, embroidered with green and gold thread. The lady-in-waiting holds up a jade dressing gown, and I slip into it. Now I match this room.

My room.

A thrill runs up my spine.

"Thank you," I say. "What's your name?"

"Cora," she answers.

"I'm—"

"You are the surrogate of the House of the Lake," Cora says, cutting me off. "That is all."

It seems like Lucien isn't the only one who can't know my name. I'm tempted to just blurt it out anyway.

"Are you hungry?" Cora asks, and I'm immediately distracted, because now that she's mentioned it, I realize I'm famished. She leads me to the small breakfast table, where a plate of green grapes, a triangle of soft cheese, several slices of bread, and a crystal glass of water are spread out, waiting for me. I shove grape after tart grape into my mouth, smearing the bread with liberal amounts of cheese and washing it all down with cold water.

"How long have I been asleep?" I ask between swallows. Cora has retrieved a hairbrush from the vanity and starts brushing out my curls. "Oh, I can do that."

I reach for the brush, but she pushes my hand away. "Eat. The Duchess will be here soon. You'll need your strength."

Suddenly, I'm not hungry anymore. I take a sip of water and push the plate away.

"And to answer your question," Cora says, "you've been asleep since you left the Auction last night. It is now six o'clock in the evening."

I don't know what time I left the Auction, but it sounds like I've been asleep for an entire day.

"Are you finished with the food?" she asks.

"Yes," I say, then add, "thank you."

Cora leads me to an open space in the center of the room, the keys that hang from her belt clinking together as she moves. There are three different doors, one on my left, two on my right, all leading, I guess, to the rest of my "chambers."

"When the Duchess arrives, be sure to keep your eyes down, unless otherwise instructed. Always address her as 'my lady.' That is very important, understand?" I nod. "Her moods can be unpredictable, so I'd suggest that, for now at least, you say as little as possible."

I hear the clacking sound of heels on polished wood and my breath catches in my throat. Cora hurriedly puts the brush back on the vanity and stands behind me.

The clacking stops. One of the doors on my right opens. A man's voice announces, "Her Royal Ladyship, the Duchess of the Lake."

Flanked by six Regimentals, the Duchess enters the room. I gape at her dress, folds of pale silver and pearls, before I remember I'm supposed to keep my eyes down. I stare at my toes, each nail polished to a shine by Lucien.

Though her heels make no sound on the carpet, I can sense the Duchess moving closer to me, until the embroidered hem of her dress comes into view. She stops. My skin prickles, and I fight the urge to look up. A hand reaches out and a finger, thin but strong, hooks under my chin. The Duchess raises my face to meet hers.

Raven's eyes. Again, that's the first thing I notice, their almond shape. Her skin, too, has the same caramel-honey tint as Raven's, though maybe a shade lighter. But as she studies me, I see her eyes are nothing like Raven's—there is no warmth, no laughter in them. They are hard and cold, and the reminder of my best friend fades in the face of this unfamiliar woman.

She's shorter than me by a few inches, and her black hair is swept up and studded with diamonds. She says nothing. Her eyes drift down, taking me in. She moves slowly, circling me, and I try to keep my face relaxed. My muscles are bunched into coils; it's a huge effort to remain rooted in one spot.

When she is in front of me again, she holds my gaze for a long moment.

And then she slaps me hard across the face with the back of her hand.

Pain shoots through my cheekbone as sparks explode in front of my eyes. I cry out and press my hand against my skin, which burns where she hit it. Tears blur my vision. I've never in my whole life been hit before.

For a second, I imagine hitting her back. My free hand even tightens into a fist. But the wall of Regimentals loom behind her and I only glare, clenching my teeth so hard it hurts my jaw.

The Duchess smiles, a bizarrely warm smile, given that she just slapped me. "I don't ever wish to do that again," she purrs, in a voice like velvet. "So I hope you'll remember how it feels."

She folds herself delicately into one of the chairs. Her

body is so graceful. I've never seen anyone move with such elegance. The Regimentals arrange themselves around her, like a red fan. I notice each of them has a tiny blue circle, crossed with two tridents, pinned to the left side of his uniform.

"Yes," the Duchess murmurs, almost to herself. "I think you are exactly what I've been looking for. What do you think, Cora?"

"Time will tell, my lady," Cora replies.

"Yes . . ." The Duchess runs a manicured finger down her cheek. "I've been waiting for you," she says, her dark eyes fixed on mine. "For nineteen years. Your timing couldn't have been more perfect."

I have no idea what she's talking about, and I'm glad I'm not expected to say anything.

"I'm told you play the cello," she says.

When I don't respond, her face turns stony, and I quickly stammer out, "Y-yes." A slight intake of breath from Cora reminds me to add, "My lady." The words turn sour on my tongue. My cheek throbs.

The warm smile comes back, and she stands in one fluid movement. "I will see you at dinner in one hour. My own lady-in-waiting will ensure you are prepared correctly. Won't you, Cora?"

"Yes, my lady," Cora replies.

The folds of her skirt rustle as the Duchess moves across the carpet. She pauses at the door. "You really do have the most extraordinary eyes," she says. There's something in her expression I can't understand—hope, maybe? Then she's gone, the Regimentals trailing after her.

I feel my muscles begin to crumble, and tears prick my eyes again. The left side of my face is throbbing. I sway on my feet a little, until Cora's strong hands grip my arm and elbow.

"You're all right," she says.

She leads me to one of the sofas and sits beside me. "Let me see," she says, tilting my face toward her. "Oh, that's nothing that can't be fixed with a little bit of ice ointment."

I stare at the massive chandelier overhead, crystals and emeralds glittering in the soft light. Suddenly, this beautiful room makes me feel cold.

A door opens and I hear Cora's voice. "Wait in the dressing room."

I don't know who she's talking to and I don't have the energy to look. More doors open and close. When Cora comes back, there's a pale blue jar in her hands. She unscrews it and dabs some ointment onto my sore cheek. Relief is instantaneous; my skin is cooled, the pain in my eye socket numbed.

"Thanks," I mumble.

"You did very well," Cora says.

"Why did she hit me?" I ask. My voice breaks and a tear spills down my cheek.

Cora places a hand gently on the uninjured side of my face, wiping the tear away with her thumb. "This isn't the Marsh, child. I didn't make the rules. But there *are* rules. You're her property now." Cora's lips press together. "She's not a bad mistress, really. There are worse, I promise you. But you're strong. I can see that. You'll be all right." Her eyes glaze a little and her brow furrows. "You'll be all right. . . ." Then she smiles brightly and stands, holding out a hand.

"What do you say we get you ready for dinner?"

I grasp her hand and she helps me up, but a seed of fear has taken root in the pit of my stomach. I didn't like the look on her face when she said I'd be all right.

MY POWDER ROOM IS ABOUT HALF THE SIZE OF MY BED-room, but still enormous.

The sink and toilet are made of dark blue stone, with a big claw-footed copper bathtub taking up nearly an entire wall. Fluffy blue towels hang from copper rods and the plush bathmat beneath my feet is striped in navy and peri-winkle. There is no tap on the bathtub, but to my shock and joy, Cora pulls a lever and water shoots from a wide spout on the ceiling, like a waterfall of rain.

I reach out my hand, mesmerized by the hot water run-ning through my fingers. Cora smiles.

"You've never taken a shower before, have you?"

I shake my head. "Only baths."

"You're in for a treat. Go on, then, and don't dally. We've only got an hour." She eases herself into an uphol-stered blue armchair in a corner by the sink.

"Are you . . ." I pull my jade dressing gown tighter. "Are you staying here?"

"Don't look so embarrassed, child. It's nothing I haven't seen before." When I don't move, she sighs and covers her eyes with her hand. "Pull the curtain around you once you're in."

I strip off my nightclothes and step into the tub. Steam sticks to my skin and wilts the last of Lucien's curls. I pull the curtain, striped to match the bathmat, closed around me. Then I step under the waterfall.

I am in ecstasy.

Water pours over my head, dripping into my mouth and running down my shoulders, its heat relaxing the muscles in my back and legs. I let out an involuntary sigh.

I hear Cora's laughter through the curtain. "It's nice, isn't it?"

I pull my fingers through my hair again and again, luxuriating in the feel of the hot water as it runs over my scalp. There is a copper shelf filled with soaps and lotions and shampoos, and I can't help myself, I try as many of them as I can, and the scents of lavender and freesia and rosewater and mint and watermelon fill the room.

"All right, that's enough," Cora says, though I could stay in this shower for the rest of the evening. The Duchess hitting me across the face feels like a distant memory.

"How do I turn it off?" I ask.

"Just push the lever back down."

The water ceases as quickly as it started, and I shiver. A towel pokes through the curtain. I dry myself, then wrap the towel around me and pull the curtain back. Cora has a smaller towel in her hands and she wraps up my wet hair. I follow her into my dressing room. Its walls are hung with silks of peach and cream; there is a three-sided mirror like the one in my prep room, and a vanity with makeup as well.

Standing in front of the vanity is a girl, about my age, in a dress like Cora's, with a high lace collar, but no shaved head or topknot—her hair is copper colored and tied up in a bun on the crown of her head. Instead of a key ring, a flat black rectangle hangs from a fine gold chain on her leather belt. She is holding a dress, similar in style to the one I wore at the Auction but made of finer thread that glitters in the warm light.

"This is Annabelle," Cora says, and the girl curtsies. "She will be your lady-in-waiting."

"Oh." I didn't realize I'd have a lady-in-waiting. "Hello."

Annabelle's cheeks turn pink, but she doesn't say anything.

Cora sits me down at the vanity and Annabelle hangs the dress up by the three-sided mirror. Then the two of them get to work, combing out the snarls in my wet hair, using powders and creams and glosses to highlight my features, and filing my nails into even more perfect ovals. Annabelle never says a word, and Cora only speaks to give her some instruction or other.

And all the while, I stare at the girl in the mirror, looking somehow smaller and younger than I have seen her.

Eight

"Time to go," Cora says.

Annabelle dabs a little bit of scented oil on each of my wrists and adjusts my hair so that it tumbles over my shoulders.

"Thank you," I say. She smiles shyly.

Cora escorts me to the dining hall. We walk down a small flight of stairs to a door that opens out into a hallway decorated with paintings of flowers. We turn down another hall lined with massive gold-framed portraits—their eyes seem to follow me as I go—and then down a plain, carpeted staircase lit with glowglobes. I catch a glimpse of a room filled with marble statues before I'm distracted by a massive foyer with a glass ceiling, a fountain sparkling in its center. We leave the foyer behind, turning down a different hallway, and I'm just about to ask Cora exactly how much farther we have to go when she stops at a door with a silver handle.

She turns and gives me a final, appraising look, smooths out a nonexistent wrinkle in my dress, then ushers me into a small study with lots of bookshelves and a fire crackling in the grate. The Duchess sits in an armchair in front of the fireplace, sipping amber liquid from a crystal glass. She has changed into a pale blue dress of shimmering material, like water woven into silk. As I enter, she looks up and smiles.

"Good evening."

"Good evening, my lady."

She stands and saunters toward me. I instinctively tense. Her smile widens.

"No, I won't hit you again." She reaches out and traces a finger down the side of my face. Her hands are cool and dry. I see that look again, that sort of hopefulness in her expression. "I've learned from previous experience that it is better to start with the stick, rather than the carrot. I certainly don't need another Garnet, do I, Cora?"

"No, my lady," Cora says.

"I was a slave to fashion then," the Duchess says with a sigh. "I won't be making that mistake again."

A different door opens, and an old man in pinstripe trousers and a black jacket with tails bows his way in. I can hear the low murmur of voices coming from the room behind him.

"All of your guests are here, my lady," he says in a wheezy voice. "The Electress has finally arrived."

"Thank you, James," the Duchess says. "I shall be with them shortly."

The old man bows again and closes the door.

"This dinner is tradition," the Duchess says, turning back to me. "All around the Jewel and the Bank tonight, dinners are being held, just like this one. For a few close friends"—her mouth twists when she says the word—"and their newly purchased surrogates. So we may all see who bought whom." She pauses to sweep away from me and set her glass down on a small table. When she turns back, her eyes are like black fire. "You are not allowed to speak. You may not eat more of any dish than I do. You may not communicate with the other surrogates in any way. Is this clear?"

I swallow. "Yes, my lady."

The strangely warm smile returns. "Good. Prove you can be trusted, and you will be rewarded. Break any of these rules and I will be very disappointed. And I don't think you wish to suffer my disappointment."

A chill runs over my skin, making the hair on my arms stand on end.

"Now," the Duchess continues brightly, "let us greet our guests."

Cora opens the door that the old man, James, went through, and I follow the Duchess into the dining room.

It is cavernous, lit with candles perched on every available surface, lining the polished oak table and dripping from the chandelier. Their light reflects off the walls, papered in maroon, and the furniture, dark wood polished to a high sheen. Ornate flower arrangements are interspersed among the candles, giving off a light, pleasant fragrance. But all these things I notice only in my peripheral vision. It is Raven's face that has my full attention.

Raven!

It takes every ounce of self-control I have not to run across the thick carpet and throw my arms around her. She wears a kimono-like robe, similar to the one she wore the last time I saw her, and her makeup and hair are much more subdued—she looks beautiful. My stomach flip-flops when I see who she's standing next to. It's the fleshy woman from the Auction, the one with the cruel eyes. Her ample figure is stuffed into a dark gray dress, her chestnut hair fashioned up into a strange sort of square-shaped bun. She's in deep conversation with a much smaller woman, and as the two turn to greet us, I see it's the Electress. She still looks impossibly young, her dress a vibrant, almost shocking, shade of pink.

And standing behind the Electress, so small I almost didn't see her, is Dahlia.

She looks so different than she did in the Waiting Room. A soft, golden gown is draped around her wiry frame, and her hair is piled up in brilliant red curls. It feels wrong, too old for her, like a child wearing her mother's clothes. The tattered pinafore felt more fitting, somehow.

"Good evening, ladies," the Duchess calls to the room at large. There are five women and five surrogates in total, including me and the Duchess. I also recognize the lioness and the iced cake.

It's a hard thing, looking at these girls. We have all clearly been given the same instructions—no communication with one another—and we are all trying to follow them while not entirely succeeding. I can't quite conceal my smile as I look into Raven's eyes, and she can't totally hide her frustration at not being able to talk to me. Dahlia looks at me with hope and excitement. The lioness's eyes flicker between us suspiciously.

"Your Royal Grace," the Duchess says to the Electress, "I am honored you chose to attend my small dinner. I know you had many invitations."

With this, the Duchess sinks into a low curtsy. The other royal women follow suit, sinking low to the ground, their skirts bubbling out around them. A few seconds too late, we follow as well. Only the lioness and the iced cake really get it right. I was never very good at all the etiquette stuff, and my balance is a little off, but I'm the picture of grace compared to Raven. Watching her try to curtsy in that kimono, combined with the expression on her face, is enough to make me double up with laughter. I bite down hard on my lip, keeping the giggles inside.

"It is my pleasure," the Electress replies. Her voice is just as childlike as her face. "I couldn't pass up a dinner with the ladies of the four founding Houses. Shall we sit?"

A flash of annoyance crosses the Duchess's face before she smooths it into a welcoming expression. "Of course," she says, gesturing to the chairs set around the table. They are in pairs, one large with curved wooden arms, the other plain and straight-backed. Footmen, standing like silent statues against the walls, spring to life, hurrying forward to pull out our chairs. I sit and stare at all the silverware lined up beside my plate—I've definitely learned what each fork and spoon is for, but at the moment I can't remember which goes with what. I glance at Raven, who looks just as puzzled as I do.

I study the women instead . . . the four founding Houses. These women are descendants of the original families who founded the Lone City. Obviously, one is the Duchess of the Lake. And one House was a flower, I remember that, too.

"I must admit, Pearl, I'm surprised we're here at all," Raven's mistress says to the Duchess. "How long has it been since you last bought a surrogate?"

The Duchess's answering smile is venomous. "Why, Ebony, don't pretend as if you honestly don't know the answer to that."

"Not since your son was born, isn't that right, Pearl?" the Electress pipes up. "Nineteen years is a long time to wait. What admirable patience you have!"

"Thank you, Your Grace," the Duchess replies.

The first course is served, a salad of wilted greens, radish, pear, and asparagus, with a creamy dressing. It is so delicious I want to gobble it all down, but the Duchess only takes two bites before pushing her plate away. The tang of the dressing and the sweetness of the pear linger in my mouth after my plate is cleared.

"Tell me, Alexandrite," the Electress says to the iced cake's mistress, as the next course of roast duck with frisee and figs is laid in front of us, "how did you enjoy the Auction? I know it was your first time."

"Oh, it was marvelous," the woman gushes. Her skin is the color of dark brewed coffee and she is young, nearly as young as the Electress. Her dress is made of glittering bronze silk—and then I remember her, holding up the set of bronze scales. "The Duke of the Scales was so pleased that I was able to return home with such an impressive surrogate. He is certain our daughter will be perfect."

The Duchess of the Lake, the Duchess of the Scales . . . that leaves the two Countesses. I look back and forth between Raven's mistress and the mistress of the lioness— she is old, by far the oldest woman here, with wrinkled skin and hair so gray it's nearly white. She wears a brilliant red dress with long, elbow-length gloves. And then I recall her, too, bidding for me against the Electress. The Countess of the Rose.

"It seems as though everyone who can is having a daughter this year!" the Electress exclaims.

"No doubt the recent birth of your son has had great influence over the ladies of the Jewel," the Duchess says wryly.

The Electress laughs. "Oh yes, I suppose that is true. And the Exetor wishes to get little Larimar betrothed as soon as possible."

"He *must*, Your Grace," the Duchess says with the barest hint of condescension. "Once he announces your son as heir to the throne—as we all expect him to do at the Exetor's Ball—the child must be betrothed within a year. It's the law."

"I'm well aware of the laws of this city," the Electress replies sharply.

"And yet, you bought a surrogate," the Countess of the Rose points out. "Why have a daughter so soon?"

"Well," the Electress says. "It is my husband's wish to see his line continue through our son, but I have always hoped for my daughter to rule when I am gone. I feel a woman would possess more sensitivity to the needs of her people. And I'd like to give some young man from the Bank the same opportunity I was given by our beloved Exetor. It only seems fair, to give back in some way to the circle I was raised in. Wouldn't you agree, Pearl?"

This comment doesn't seem to go down well with any of the royal women at the table. The Duchess of the Lake is gripping her fork so tightly that her caramel skin has turned white across her knuckles. "Whatever Your Grace thinks is best." She turns to Raven's mistress. "And what about you, Ebony? Will the House of the Stone be welcoming a daughter along with everyone else? Or will we be seeing you again at next year's Auction?"

The Countess of the Stone. That's it. Lake, Rose, Scales, Stone. Lily would be proud. I bet Raven isn't even paying attention. The Countess of the Stone pops a fig in her mouth and chews it slowly.

"Oh yes, I believe I will start with a daughter," she says. "Boys can be so terribly difficult, don't you think?"

The Duchess's cheeks flame pink and her eyes narrow.

The Electress giggles. "Yes, how is Garnet, by the way?" she asks. "Staying out of trouble, I hope?"

"He is in his room at the moment, Your Grace. Studying."

Suddenly, the doors to the dining room burst open, and a young man staggers in. I haven't seen any boys my age since I was twelve, except Ochre and he doesn't really count. This boy is . . . well, he's beautiful. His blond hair is slicked back, except for a few locks that have escaped and fallen over his forehead. He is tall, with broad shoulders, and his white collared shirt is partially unbuttoned, revealing a glimpse of his chest. My cheeks burn, but I can't stop staring at him. In one hand, he grasps an empty crystal tumbler.

"Mother!" he cries, raising the glass like he's toasting the Duchess of the Lake. *This* is the Duchess's son? He looks nothing like her. His slightly unfocused gaze takes in the rest of the room. "I beg your pardon, ladies. Didn't realize there was a dinner party tonight." His bright blue eyes land on me, and something seems to click. "Oh, right. The Auction."

The Electress and the Duchess of the Scales are practically in tears, laughing into their napkins. A satisfied smile spreads across the Countess of the Stone's pudgy face. The Countess of the Rose looks politely embarrassed.

"Garnet, my darling," the Duchess says, a steely edge to her voice. "*What* are you doing?"

"Oh, don't mind me," he replies with a wave of his hand. "Just needed a refill."

He swaggers to a side table and uncorks a dark glass bottle, filling his tumbler. The Duchess is on her feet in an instant.

"Will you excuse me for a moment?" she says, gliding to Garnet's side and grabbing his arm. I hear him mumble "Ow" as she walks him out of the dining room.

"And that, ladies, is why I feel this city should be left in the hands of a woman!" the Electress exclaims. The Duchess of the Scales and the Countess of the Stone explode with laughter.

For a second, I meet Raven's eyes. She raises an eyebrow, as if to say, "What is wrong with these people?" I press my lips together, fighting a smile, and give her a tiny nod.

"But that decision is not up to you," the Countess of the Rose interjects. She is the only one not amused by Garnet's bizarre entrance. "It is the Exetor's choice, since the line passed through him." She takes a small bite of frisee. "Of course, you are only a recent addition to the Royal Palace. Perhaps the subtleties of royal succession have not fully been explained."

The Electress stiffens. "Clearly it has been too long since there has been any pleasure in *your* bedchambers, Ametrine, but there is no more powerful weapon of persuasion than a woman's body. I am quite capable of changing my husband's mind."

I blush at the turn the conversation just took. Footmen come in to clear our plates, and I take advantage of the Duchess's absence, shoveling a few extra pieces of duck into my mouth.

"I meant no offense, Your Grace," the Countess of the Rose says. "But remember that surrogacy is a very strange thing. You never know precisely what you are going to get. The Augury scores only tell you so much. Perhaps you will end up *preferring* for your son to succeed to the throne."

"Doubtful," the Electress replies. She beckons to one of the footmen. "Fetch Lucien. Now."

My ears prick and I sit up straighter.

The servants begin serving the next course—smoked salmon with capers and candied lemon—and the Duchess returns.

"My apologies, Your Grace," she says with a low curtsy.

"Oh, no need to apologize. It was rather exciting," the Electress says. "In comparison, dinners at the Royal Palace are positively dull."

The Countess of the Stone's wide mouth curves into an unpleasant smirk. I take a sip of wine and wait for the Duchess to sit down. I'm starving, and I hope she likes the salmon more than the other dishes, so I can actually eat a substantial amount of something.

Then I see a white dress and a topknot and my heart somersaults. Lucien glides into the room, holding a walnut and a silver bowl.

"Thank you, Lucien," the Electress says. "Wait here."

"Of course, my lady." Lucien places the walnut and the bowl on the table and moves back to stand against the wall. Dahlia's eyes are wide with fear, almost pleading, as she looks back and forth between the bowl and the Electress. I hold my breath, wondering what the Electress is going to make her do. Across the table, I see that Raven's expression mirrors mine. The iced cake and the lioness watch intently.

"She was showing me the most magnificent trick earlier," the Electress says. She turns to Dahlia. "Go on."

Dahlia's lower lip trembles as she picks up the walnut in her small hand. Nothing happens. The Electress's eyes harden.

"Go on," she repeats in a sharper tone.

Dahlia's fingers close around the walnut, and when she opens them, it has a slightly transparent look, like it's been turned to brown glass—she's using the second Augury, Shape. Her eyebrows knit together as she concentrates, and suddenly the walnut ripples, shifting and stretching like it's made of water.

I expect her to turn it into a simple shape, like a star or

a flower, but instead she molds it into a miniature statue of the Electress. It's an incredibly difficult feat; Dahlia must be in an extreme amount of pain.

As if in response to my thought, Dahlia cries out and drops the statue—she grabs the silver bowl, coughing up a mixture of phlegm and blood.

The Electress holds up the statue, stunning in its detail, a perfect replica of herself. The royal women clap.

I feel sick. How could the Electress make her do that in front of all these people? These women are actually *applauding* the suffering and humiliation of a young girl.

"Isn't it marvelous?" the Electress says gaily. Lucien glides forward and takes the silver bowl from Dahlia. I see him slip her a handkerchief, so that when she looks up again, her mouth and nose are clean and free of blood.

"That will be all, Lucien," the Electress says dismissively.

"Yes, my lady." Lucien turns to leave and his eyes rest on me for half a second; the shadow of a smile passes across his face. I smile, too.

"An impressive exhibition," the Duchess of the Lake says, cutting into her salmon. "Though you may want to keep your best linens away from her."

"Oh, that doesn't happen every time," the Electress says.

I blanch. How many times has the Electress made Dahlia perform an Augury? It's barely been a day.

The Duchess swallows a bite of salmon and dabs at her mouth with her napkin. "You may want to warm her up a bit before forcing her to sprint."

"I will keep that in mind," the Electress says, patting

the top of Dahlia's head. The action is degrading to watch;
two red spots appear on Dahlia's cheeks.

"Does she have any special skills?" the Duchess asks.
"They don't always, you know. But I do prefer a surrogate
with a bit of talent." She takes a sip of wine. "Mine plays
the cello."

My fingers tighten around my fork, and my shoulders
tense. Everyone is looking at me, except for Raven, who is
glaring at the Duchess.

"That is something I would very much like to hear," the
Electress says. I glance at the doors, petrified, waiting for
some footman to appear with a cello.

But the Duchess only smiles. "I am certain, Your Grace,
that someday you will."

The conversation continues about the surrogates'
unique abilities—the iced cake is a dancer; the Countess of
the Stone brags about Raven's skill with mathematics—then
shifts to our Augury scores. They talk about us like they are
discussing a pet or a prized racehorse. Like we can't hear
them. Like we're not even there.

At long last, the dinner is over and the women are kissing one another's cheeks (or, not quite kissing; they all seem
reluctant to touch one another), and the ladies-in-waiting
are coming in with their cloaks. The Countess of the Stone
also has a male lady-in-waiting—he looks just as unpleasant
as his mistress, with a large, beaked nose and a mouth that
turns down.

Raven is staring at me, her face set, determined, as if to
say "I *will* see you again." I try to smile at her with my eyes.

The Electress is the last to leave. Dahlia glances at me,

terrified, and I do my best to give her an encouraging look, pressing my lips together, the corners of my mouth barely turning up. I hope she knows what I mean. I hope she'll be all right in the Royal Palace.

The Duchess traces a circle slowly around the rim of her wineglass with one finger, watching her guests leave like a cat with its prey. Then she sighs.

"That will be all for tonight," she says, and though she doesn't look at me, she has to be talking to me. There's no one else in the room. Then she drifts through the door to her study, leaving me confused and alone.

Nine

CORA COMES TO GET ME A MOMENT LATER.

I follow her silently back through the halls and up the stairs, the palace taking on a dreamlike quality in the dimmed light of the lamps, like I'm lost in a gilded maze. She opens the door to my chambers, where Annabelle is waiting for me.

"She goes straight to bed," Cora says. Annabelle nods.

"Where are you going?" I ask Cora.

"To attend to the Duchess," Cora says, as though it should be obvious.

"Oh. Well, good night." The caretakers always said good night to us at Southgate, and Cora feels very much like a caretaker.

Her eyes crinkle as she smiles. "Good night."

I follow Annabelle through another door into my bedroom, my head swimming with scenes from the dinner. There seemed to be two teams at play: the Electress, the Countess of the Stone, and the Duchess of the Scales versus the Duchess of the Lake and the Countess of the Rose. Being royal seems exhausting—why invite people to a dinner party if you don't even like them?

I'm so caught up in my own thoughts, I don't notice that Annabelle has removed my jewelry and is unzipping my dress. A silken nightgown is laid out on my bed.

"Oh!" I say. "I can get ready myself."

Annabelle shakes her head.

"Are you not allowed to speak to me?" I ask, my heart sinking.

Annabelle picks up the flat rectangle hanging from her waist and removes something small and white from a pocket on her belt.

It's a piece of chalk.

The rectangle is a slate, I realize, as she scribbles on it and holds it up for me to see.

Can't speak

"What, not at all?" I ask stupidly.

She shakes her head.

"Did something happen to you?"

As soon as the words are out, I realize they're rude. Annabelle holds up her slate.

Born this way

"You've never been able to talk? Ever?"

I remember a girl in the Marsh who couldn't speak, but

she couldn't hear, either. Obviously, Annabelle can hear just fine.

Annabelle shakes her head and taps the slate once with her finger—the writing is erased.

"Wow," I say. "That's a pretty neat device."

She nods halfheartedly, and finishes unzipping my dress. I step out of it and she slips the nightgown over my head.

We go to the powder room, where Annabelle washes the makeup off my face, then it's back to the bedroom. She sits me in front of the vanity and starts brushing out my hair. I study her reflection in the mirror. Her skin is paler than mine, and dusted with freckles. There's a frailty about her, in her thin wrists and shoulders, and a tenderness in the way she runs the brush through my hair.

"Do you ever wish you could?" I ask, and she looks up, surprised. "Speak, I mean."

Annabelle bites her lip and for a second I think I've been rude again. Then she puts down the brush and picks up her slate.

Every day

I try to imagine what that would be like, not being able to express myself with my voice—with a jolt, I realize it sort of happened to me tonight. And I didn't like it at all.

Annabelle finishes with my hair and moves to the bed, pulling back the covers for me. It feels like I've been sleeping for most of the last two days, but I'm still tired. I crawl under the velvety comforter, my head sinking into the feather pillows. Annabelle points to a long strip of patterned fabric hanging down the wall over the nightstand. She motions pulling on it, then points to herself.

"If I ring that, you'll come?"

She nods.

"Where do you sleep?"

She points down, then scribbles on her slate.

Good night

I am suddenly gripped with fear of being left alone in this unfamiliar, extravagant room.

"Annabelle?" I say. "Will you . . . could you sit with me for a little while?"

She hesitates, and I remember Cora's instructions that I was to go right to sleep. But then she nods, and perches herself on the bed beside me. I smile.

"Thanks."

Must be v. strange

I realize that *v* stands for *very*. Of course. It would be a pain writing everything out longhand. I'd use abbreviations, too.

"How long have you lived here?" I ask.

Whole life

I run my fingers along the embroidered edge of the pillowcase. "It's certainly beautiful."

Annabelle nods without much enthusiasm.

"At dinner tonight," I say hesitantly, unsure if I should be talking about the dinner at all, "the royal women . . . they didn't seem . . . I mean, they weren't very nice to one another. Is it always like that?"

Annabelle grimaces, and I take that for a yes.

"The Electress is very young, isn't she? Even younger than she looks in her photographs."

Annabelle nods.

"The Duchess didn't seem to like her much."

Annabelle fidgets, and her cheeks turn pink. I hastily change the subject.

"I saw the Duchess's son." A blush creeps up the back of my neck at the memory of the handsome boy and his disheveled appearance. "He doesn't seem anything like his mother."

Annabelle smiles a very private sort of smile, like my words have amused her in a way I don't understand.

"What's his name?"

Garnet

"Right. Garnet." I remember the Duchess's words in the study, saying how she didn't need another Garnet.

"Have you done this before?" I ask. "Looked after a surrogate?"

Annabelle shakes her head no.

"I'll try not to make your life too difficult."

She smiles and squeezes my hand. It's very warm and comfortable under the covers, and a yawn escapes my throat.

Sleep

"All right," I agree.

She gets up and starts extinguishing the lamps. I roll onto my back and stare at the pale green canopy overhead. My mind flickers to my family. I imagine them in that tiny house, my mother preparing dinner, Hazel at the table doing her schoolwork, Ochre out back chopping firewood. I picture them sitting around the table, eating a meager meal, laughing and talking freely. I wonder if they thought about me at all. A lump swells in my throat.

"Good night, Hazel," I whisper. "Good night, Ochre. Good night, Mother."

I think I hear the scratching of Annabelle's chalk on her slate, but I'm already sinking into oblivion.

THAT NIGHT, I HAVE A DREAM. I'M BACK AT SOUTHGATE, in the music room, trying to play a duet with Lily.

But I can't seem to hold my cello correctly. It keeps slipping to one side and my bow screeches against the strings. Lily lowers her violin and gives me a condescending look.

"You should have listened to me, Violet," she says. I look down and see that my stomach is huge, swollen with the Duchess's baby.

I scream.

I WAKE IN THE MORNING IN A COLD SWEAT, THROWING off my covers and pressing my hands against my stomach.

I'm not pregnant. I'm not pregnant. I repeat the words in my head over and over, a hopeless mantra.

I walk to the bathroom and stare at myself in the mirror over the sink. My eyes are wild, my hair tangled with sleep, my skin paler than usual. I look awful. Is this what I look like every morning? Ugh.

I soak a facecloth with cold water and run it over my forehead and the back of my neck. My stomach growls. I tie my hair back with a ribbon and head into the bedroom, pulling on the fabric that rings for Annabelle. I wonder how breakfast works—do I go to the kitchens? Do I eat in the dining room, with the Duchess?

I swallow hard and my hand moves to my stomach again, the image of my pregnant self looming in my mind.

When will it happen?

I squeeze my eyes shut and try to think about something else, but there's nothing else to think about. It all seemed so distant, so far away in a future I couldn't imagine when I was at Southgate, but now that I'm actually *here*, the thought of being pregnant, of having someone else's child growing inside me, is terrifying.

The door opens and Annabelle comes in, bringing the delicious scent of coffee with her. She places a covered tray on the breakfast table.

The smell of food makes me feel better—I am still hungry after my disappointing lack of dinner last night. My mother used to say that a good meal could ease a troubled heart. Annabelle beckons for me to sit and lifts the cover off the tray.

There are soft-boiled eggs sitting in little silver cups, yogurt with fresh fruit, buttered toast, crisp strips of bacon, and a cold glass of orange juice. Annabelle lays a napkin in my lap and pours coffee into a pink china cup while I attack the food.

She raises an eyebrow.

Hungry?

"Starved," I say through a mouthful of toast and egg. "The Duchess barely let me eat anything last night."

Sleep well?

The strip of bacon freezes on its way to my mouth. I shrug and put it down, taking a sip of coffee instead. "It's a very nice bed."

When I'm finished with breakfast, Annabelle runs me a shower, then laces me into a beautiful gown the color of a ripe peach. I sit at the vanity in my bedroom while she curls my hair and pins it up.

"Am I going somewhere?" I ask.

She shrugs.

"Do you know . . . I mean, do you have any idea . . ." I don't know how to phrase the question. How do you ask someone when to expect to be impregnated? "Do I have a schedule or something?"

Wait for D to call

"Oh." I fiddle with one of the opal-and-topaz earrings dangling from my ears. "All right."

When she's finished, I stand up and study myself in the mirror. With my hair pinned up and dressed in such fine fabric, I look older than the girl who stood in the prep room and gazed at her reflection like it was someone else's.

Pretty

I open my mouth, then close it, unsure of what to say. I do look pretty. I'm just not sure I look like *me*.

The morning is spent exploring my chambers. I have three closets full of dresses in every color and fabric and pattern, from simple daywear to elegant ball gowns. Annabelle opens the curtains in my bedroom, and I get my first glimpse of the outside of the palace. A wide gravel driveway encircles an enormous lake, glittering and smooth, like a crystal mirror, a brilliant and unnatural blue. In the distance, I can see a pair of golden gates.

After a while, we move to the room next to my bedroom. The tea parlor is very pleasant and sunny, all the furniture upholstered in yellows and oranges, with bouquets of marigolds and daisies interspersed on the tabletops. Tall bookshelves line one wall, and the collection contains a mix of familiar and unfamiliar titles. *A Complete History of the Founding Houses* overshadows a battered copy of *The Wishing Well*, a collection of children's stories.

"Oh, I love this book!" I exclaim, sliding *The Wishing Well* off the shelf. I'm surprised to find it in the Jewel—it's a welcome reminder of home. "My father used to read these stories to me. Have you ever read them?"

Annabelle shakes her head no.

The story of the Wishing Well was our favorite, mine and Hazel's. I flip to it now and smile, remembering how we'd wait by the door for Father to come home from the factories, smelling of smoke and grease, and we'd beg him to read to us while Mother fixed his dinner. He had the most wonderful reading voice. The story is about two sisters who find a magic well; they free the water spirit who lives inside it, and in return, she grants them each a wish. Hazel and I would curl up on either side of him and let the words wash over us, and gasp and cry in all the right places. I must have been about ten, then; Hazel was six. A year later, Father was dead.

As I'm flipping to another story, lunch is served. A young maid in a black dress and white apron brings in a tray full of food. If I thought the meals at Southgate were good, they're nothing compared to the Jewel's.

After lunch, I begin to get bored. I read through most of *The Wishing Well*, but my attention drifts. Annabelle sits in one of the armchairs, embroidering a handkerchief.

"Can I see the rest of the palace?" I ask.

Not till D calls

"When will that be?"

Annabelle shrugs.

I sigh and flop back on the couch, but the stays in my dress poke me and I sit up again. Annabelle puts down her embroidery and picks up her slate again.

Halma?

"You play Halma?" I ask eagerly.

Annabelle's smile widens.

"I THOUGHT THIS WAS A MARSH-GAME," I GRUMBLE LATER that afternoon, as I stare intently at the six-pointed star on the board. "How come you're so good at it?"

Annabelle has already beaten me twice, and she appears to be heading for a third win. Nearly all her marbles are in my corner—mine are scattered in the center of the board, making it only too easy for her to use them as stepping stones.

V. old, orig. from F

"The Farm? Really?" I hop over two of her marbles to finally land one of mine in her corner. "I didn't know that."

Annabelle uses my newly placed marble to hop halfway across the board.

Not pop. in J, only serv. play

"Yeah, I can see that," I mutter darkly. I'm not used to losing at Halma—Raven was such a terrible player. She had no patience for it. We'd play with Lily and she'd always get crushed.

It takes Annabelle only three more moves to end the

game. "Rematch," I say immediately.

The door to the parlor opens. A Regimental stands at attention as the Duchess of the Lake sweeps into the room. Annabelle jumps out of her chair, and I scramble to my feet. The Duchess wears a red dress, layers of chiffon falling to the floor, cinched around her waist with braided ropes of silk. A fan dangles from a chain around her wrist. Her face is a carefully controlled mask, but there is a frantic energy about her, like strong emotions are boiling just under the surface.

She looks me up and down appraisingly. "Nicely done," she says, with only the barest glance in Annabelle's direction to indicate that she's speaking to my lady-in-waiting. I wonder if my appearance was some sort of test for Annabelle.

"Good afternoon, my lady," I say with an awkward curtsy.

"Yes," the Duchess replies, "it is a good afternoon, isn't it?" She walks toward me, a tiny smile on her lips, and it takes all my strength not to cringe or lean away. "You were very well behaved last night. I am impressed."

"Thank you, my lady." I wish she'd take a step back. I don't like her being this close to me.

She laughs. "Don't look so frightened. I told you, prove you can be trusted and you shall be rewarded." She waves her fan at the Regimental. "Bring it in."

The Regimental makes a signal, and two footmen enter carrying an enormous wooden crate and place it on the floor. Using crowbars, they pry off the lid and prop it against the box.

"That will be all," the Duchess says, and the footmen bow and leave.

There is a loaded silence during which I look from the Duchess, to the box, to Annabelle, and back to the box again.

"Well?" the Duchess says. "Go on."

I'd really rather open whatever it is alone, but that's clearly not an option. I take a few hesitant steps forward and kneel beside the open crate, pulling out handfuls of packing hay. There is a gleam of varnish, and suddenly my uncertainty turns to excitement. I move faster now, tearing the packing hay out of the way to get to the cello. My fingers brush the strings and a muted jumble of notes echo in my ears.

I uncover it tenderly—it's the most beautiful thing I've ever seen, and I've seen a lot of beautiful things in the past two days. The varnish gives the maple wood a deep red glow; the f-holes are curved more ornately than I'm used to, and I trace my fingers along the purfling, marveling at the inlaid border. I run my fingers over the strings again, plucking each one individually, my throat tightening at their familiar tones.

"Do you like it?" the Duchess asks.

"Is this for me?" I whisper.

"Of course it's for you. Do you like it?" the Duchess asks again impatiently.

I swallow. "Yes, my lady. I like it very much."

"Good. Play something."

I take the cello by the neck and lift it out of the box, sending stray bits of hay fluttering to the floor. A bow and

a block of rosin are nestled in the packing, and I grab them
and head to one of the hard-backed chairs. The weight of the
cello is comforting, and I squeeze its body gently between
my knees, the neck resting against my shoulder. I run the
block of rosin back and forth over the bow and a flood of
memories is released with its sharp, resinous scent—the day
I chose to learn the cello, the first time I ever held a bow,
playing alone in my room late at night, playing duets with
Lily in the music room . . .

"Do you have a preference for composer, my lady?" I
ask.

The Duchess raises an eyebrow. "No. Play whatever you
wish."

I take a deep breath and position my fingers against the
strings, noting idly that I'm going to need to cut my fingernails. Then I draw the bow across the C string.

It's perfectly in tune. The note envelops me, filling the
room, rich and warm and vibrant. I close my eyes.

I play the prelude of a suite in G Major, one of the first
pieces I ever learned. The notes flow easily, falling over
one another like water running across smooth stones, my
fingers moving deftly, sure of their positioning. The room
around me fades and I feel a wonderful sense of release—
my whole being feels altered when I play. I am the music
and the strings and my body is as resonant as the cello's.
We are one instrument, in a place where no one can touch
me, where there is no Jewel and there are no surrogates,
a place where there is only music. The tempo and pitch
increase as I reach the end of the movement, the notes
climbing higher and higher until I pull the bow long across

the final chord, a perfect fifth that hangs in the air, shimmering and flawless.

I open my eyes.

The Duchess's face is transfixed, her expression triumphant. If anything, this scares me more than the mask.

"That was . . . exquisite," she says.

"Thank you, my lady."

She fans herself a few times, then snaps the fan closed.

"She goes to bed early tonight," the Duchess says to Annabelle as she sweeps out of the room, the Regimental at her heels. "Tomorrow we're going out."

Ten

"OUT WHERE?" I ASK ANNABELLE FOR THE HUNDREDTH
time as she finishes brushing my hair that night. "Into the
Jewel?"

She puts the brush down.

Or Bank

"Are you coming?"

She shrugs. I can tell by her face that she honestly doesn't
know.

"Is it . . . am I going to see a doctor?" I ask nervously.

Annabelle shakes her head.

Dr. comes here

"Oh." I chew on my thumbnail, feeling a little better.

Annabelle pushes my hand away from my mouth and

starts rubbing moisturizing cream on my arms.

"I never paid much attention to the Jewel when I was at Southgate. It was my friend Lily who would read the gossip magazines and imagine our life here. I wonder where she is now. She was such a sweet girl. I hope someone nice bought her."

I run my fingers along the polished surface of my vanity and over the velvet top of one of the jewelry boxes.

"She'd love it here." It's nice to talk about Lily—it reminds me that she existed, that she still does, that we were friends, and it meant something. "She loves extravagant things and getting dressed up and all that. She'd have a heart attack over this room. But she was Lot 53. She might be in the Bank now."

Bank is nice

I laugh. "You don't know Lily. Her definition of 'nice' isn't the same as everyone else's." My thoughts drift to the dinner last night. "I saw my best friend, you know. Raven. At dinner yesterday. She was bought by the Countess of the Stone. Do you know anything about her?"

Annabelle shrugs, but her front teeth worry at her bottom lip and her eyebrows knit together. "Raven's tough," I say, more to make myself feel better than to defend her to Annabelle. "Tougher than anyone I've ever met. She'll be okay."

Annabelle nods in an absentminded way and unscrews a jar of cream for my face.

A thought occurs to me and I grab her wrist. "You don't know my name," I say. No one knows my name, but it's disturbing that I never even thought to try to tell her.

Annabelle's eyes widen and she shakes her head frantically.

"Oh, please," I press. "Please?"

She looks away, her expression pained.

"Okay," I say. "Sorry. Never mind."

Her shoulders relax, but I grab the slate and chalk, and before she can take them or look away I scribble:

Violet

Then I tap the slate clean.

THE NEXT MORNING, ANNABELLE DRESSES ME ALL IN black.

There's something different about her mood—she seems on edge, rarely using her chalk and shaking or nodding her head curtly if I ask a question. The gown she chooses for me is similar in cut to my Auction dress, floor length with an empire waist. She ties a choker of black velvet around my neck.

"What's this for?" I ask, rubbing the soft material with my fingertips—it feels nice. Annabelle doesn't respond, she just pins up the front section of my hair, leaving the rest of it down.

Cora bustles in, holding a black lace veil in one hand.

"Is she ready?" She scrutinizes me from head to toe. "Very good," she says to Annabelle, before securing the veil in my hair.

"What's that for?" I ask.

"Don't ask questions. Come with me."

"Isn't Annabelle coming, too?"

"No," Cora says sharply.

Annabelle gives me a small smile as I follow Cora out of my chambers. Anxiety flutters inside me as we walk down the flower hallway, then the hall of portraits, taking a large sweeping staircase down to the glass foyer I glimpsed before the dinner. Sunlight streams through the roof, making the water in the fountain twinkle. The Duchess is waiting for me, her guard of Regimentals surrounding her, a wall of red. She wears a long black skirt, with a black silk blouse under an expertly tailored black blazer. Perched on her head is a black pillbox hat, its netting just barely covering her eyes, which scan me critically.

"That dress is so . . . plain," she says.

"My apologies, my lady," Cora says, curtsying. "She can be changed."

The Duchess waves her hands dismissively. "No, there's no time." She saunters over to me in her black heels, her eyes level with mine. There is something silver in her hands. "Now, I don't necessarily like this, nor do I think you need it," she says, holding up the silver thing. "But there are some people who will use any excuse to slander me. If you behave yourself, I won't use it again unless I absolutely have to. Do you understand?"

I don't understand at all, but her words frighten me. Then she unfolds the silver thing and my stomach drops.

It's a leash.

"You're going to be a good girl, aren't you?" she purrs. My brain is screaming at me that this is wrong, this is horrible, but my muscles have all locked down, freezing me in place, while my heart slams against my ribs like it's trying to escape. All I can do is stare.

The Regimentals move forward, as if they're antici-
pating that I'm going to bolt, but the Duchess holds up a
hand.

"No," she murmurs, keeping her dark eyes on my face.
"Stay back. She understands."

Against everything I am, against every impulse I have,
I allow the Duchess to fasten the silver collar around the
velvet choker on my neck. Part of me is still in shock. Part
of me doesn't want to get hit again, or have it forced on me
by Regimentals. But a part of me does understand, as the
Duchess fastens a bracelet around her wrist, attached to the
long silver chain that now connects us. I understand that
she has an agenda, and that I am part of it, and with this
gesture, she is saying that I'm hers now.

I understand, but I don't care. I hate her for it.

"The veil, Cora," the Duchess says, and Cora lifts the
black lace and lowers it over my face. It covers my eyes, my
nose, my mouth, and falls to my shoulders.

I am chained, bound, hidden. For the first time, I feel
like a prisoner.

"Come," the Duchess says, walking forward. The leash
goes taut and tugs at my neck, and I see the reason for the
velvet choker—it prevents the collar from chafing my skin.

I have no choice but to follow. Humiliation burns in my
cheeks and I clench my hands tightly, my fingernails digging
into my palms. The pain sharpens my focus, a place to concentrate my anger.

A set of glass doors are opened for us by a pair of footmen, and bright sunlight filters through my veil. The sun is
warm, though a cool breeze plays across my skin, raising

goose bumps on my arms and the back of my neck. For a moment, I forget my anger and my embarrassment, and the injustice of this whole situation, because I am standing at the edge of an enormous circular courtyard, surrounded by a palace that looks to be crafted out of sheets of diamond. Its multifaceted surface throws off rainbows in the light and its many turrets are topped with blue flags, fluttering in the breeze. The crystal blue lake stretches out in front of me, and I can see the gates in the distance.

Something moves in one of the windows on the ground floor. I see a figure, a girl, standing with her arms folded across her chest, glaring at me. Or maybe she's glaring at the Duchess. It's hard to tell.

Another tug on my leash lets me know that the Duchess is still walking, toward a vehicle I have only ever seen in pictures. A motorcar. Sleek and white, with a long nose and a wave of metal sweeping over its front tires, it makes the electric stagecoaches look clunky and outdated. A footman opens the door and the Duchess slides into the backseat; I follow unsteadily, nearly bumping my head on the low doorframe. The seats are upholstered in a soft, tan leather, warmed by the sun. The footman shuts the door behind me. A chauffeur, already in the driver's seat, tips his hat to the Duchess and starts the engine. Gravel crunches under the tires as we trundle down the long driveway. It's a very comfortable way to travel, and might actually be enjoyable if I wasn't chained to another person.

I look back at the palace. The girl in the window is gone.

The Duchess ignores me, one finger tapping impatiently on the armrest. She takes a compact out of her black silk clutch and applies a layer of red lipstick. She studies her reflection in the tiny mirror and sighs.

"Getting old is a terrible thing," she says. I stay quiet. I wouldn't know what to say to that anyway—the Duchess hardly looks old.

The golden gates are topped with the crest of the House of the Lake—a lacquered blue circle crossed with two silver tridents. I've seen it around my chambers, over the fireplaces and on top of some of the clocks, as well as on the Regimentals' uniforms. The motorcar pulls out onto a road paved with asphalt, its surface so smooth we seem to be gliding rather than driving. I remember the rutted dirt roads of the Marsh on that last ride to see my family—the mudbrick houses, the smell of dirt and sulfur in the air, the layer of dust that seemed to cover everything. This ride could not be more different.

The Jewel seems to be made up of nothing but palaces, all practically on top of one another but separated by high, thick walls topped with vicious-looking spikes—the palaces themselves are visible only through the large gates that allow entrance to their property. As we leave the Duchess's diamond palace behind, I glimpse a multileveled structure of marble and onyx, with stairs built on the outside at every level, giving it a very geometric look. I'm reminded of the building blocks Ochre and I used to play with when we were little.

Other motorcars join us on the road, and everyone seems to be going in the same direction. We continue to pass palace after palace, many made of different colored crystal—pink, turquoise, emerald, topaz, garnet. Some have tall towers, some are domed, some built in strange shapes I'd never have expected. One palace, like a stack of triangles, reminds me of an evergreen tree, especially since it's made out of jade and gold. Spreading out in front of it is an enormous rose garden, mostly dormant now in the approaching winter, but a few late-blooming buds still cling to the vines, snatches of pale pink and red. The crest on the gates is a green diamond crossed by two roses. A black motorcar sits in the driveway.

"Late, as usual," the Duchess mutters.

Then the walls fall away, and I forget that I don't want to talk to the Duchess, forget the leash and the veil, because I know the incredible structure we're passing and I never thought I'd see it in real life.

"That's the Royal Concert Hall!" I exclaim. An immense facade of rose-colored stone, it is topped with a pale green dome and two golden statues of beautiful women with long, slender trumpets extending from their outstretched hands. I stare, wide-eyed and openmouthed, thinking of all the famous musicians who have played in that Hall—Cornett Strand and Gaida Balaban and my very favorite, Stradivarius Tanglewood. I can't imagine the thrill of being able to play on that stage.

I keep my eyes on the Royal Concert Hall for as long as I can, until it fades in the distance and disappears from sight.

The road begins to climb and we enter a forest, the parade of motorcars winding through trees whose leaves are just beginning to change, splashes of red and orange and yellow visible through the lush greenery. Our driver handles the curves well, but I still grab on to the door handle to keep from sliding across the seat into the Duchess. She stares broodingly out the window.

"I loved this forest when I was a child," she says. "But my father would never let me play in it. It was too dangerous, he said." She shakes her head. "Men and their guns and their ridiculous desire to shoot things for sport." It's hard to imagine the Duchess as a child, much less her playing at all, in a forest or otherwise. "I liked to pretend I could speak to the trees, like the younger sister in *The Wishing Well*. Do you know that story?"

That brings me up short. The Duchess has read *The Wishing Well*?

"Speak," she snaps when I don't answer.

"Yes," I say. "I know it." Then I add unwillingly, "My lady."

"I thought so. It is quite . . . provincial. My governess used to read it to me—she was a very simple woman. My father was furious when he found out. I was supposed to be reading the classics, not fairy stories. He threw my governess into the dungeons. I never saw her again." The Duchess says this so matter-of-factly it sends a chill up my spine. "I imagine your mother read it to you? There aren't any governesses in the Marsh, I should think."

"My father read it to me, my lady."

"Oh?" she says, one eyebrow arching in surprise. "And which circle does he work in, your father?"

"He's dead," I say coldly. And I don't add "my lady."

The Duchess smiles. "Oh, I do like you. You have such an interesting balance of obedience and contempt."

I clench my jaw and stare out the window. I hate that she's given me no way to defy her—my boldness is just as pleasing to her as my compliance.

The forest ends abruptly, and once again I find myself shocked out of my bad mood. The motorcar crawls through a massive topiary—enormous hedge-creatures, ten feet high, line the road, some with trunks outstretched, or claws raised, or snouts to the ground.

"Almost there," the Duchess says brightly.

We slow down as the road becomes packed with motor-cars, climbing even higher and emerging onto a large square with a fountain in its center. In the middle of the fountain is a statue of four boys, back to back, blowing on trumpets; from each trumpet a spout of water arches and falls into the fountain. On the far side of the square is a palace so extravagant, it could only be for the Electress and the Exetor. It's crafted out of a burnished gold material, almost like liquid fire, with pillars and columns and domes and turrets that stretch higher than any of the other palaces I've seen. A series of low, broad steps paved with smooth gray stones lead up to a set of massive double doors.

Royal women, dressed in black, mill around, many of them accompanied by a surrogate, leashed and veiled and all in black, like me. It's a very somber sight—I wonder what's going on.

The driver pulls over and gets out quickly, opening the door for the Duchess. I slide across the seat as the chain tautens, and struggle to stay close to her—I hate the feel of the collar pulling on my neck.

The royal women melt away at the approach of the

Duchess, curtsying to her and murmuring "Your Lady-ship." I search the faces of the veiled surrogates, looking for Raven. She'll have to be here. If this is an event at the palace, wouldn't all four founding Houses be invited?

"Good morning, Iolite," the Duchess says to a red-haired woman with a black stole around her neck. A silver bracelet gleams on her wrist, its chain disappearing under the veil of her surrogate.

"Pearl!" the woman exclaims. She and the Duchess exchange air kisses. "How *are* you?"

The Duchess gives some polite response, but the world is suddenly muted as I take in the surrogate attached to the chain.

She is hugely pregnant.

I can't quite make out her face through the veil, and her eyes are downcast. But she can't be much older than I am.

Reality hits me like a block of cement.

I'm staring at my future.

Sound comes back in a rush.

". . . so sad I wasn't able to make it to the Auction," the woman with the stole is saying.

"Well, of course you didn't need to," the Duchess says.

"Oh, I know, but the lists looked so exciting this year," the woman moans. The lists. I feel nauseous. "Which one did you get?"

"197," the Duchess says smugly.

"She was popular, wasn't she?"

"There was significant interest, yes." The Duchess's gaze flickers to the pregnant surrogate. "Why, yours must be almost due."

"In about a month," the woman says, rubbing her hand over her surrogate's swollen belly and making my skin crawl. The girl keeps her eyes down, showing no reaction to her mistress's touch.

"It seems like just the other day that you bought her," the Duchess says.

"Oh, I know," the woman agrees. "Time simply flies, doesn't it?"

"Have you chosen a name for your son yet?"

"The Lord of the Glass and I have decided to wait until after he's born. But we do have a few in mind," she says with a wink.

This woman must be the Lady of the Glass—one thing I *do* remember from royal studies is that, after the four founding Houses, everyone else is either a Lord or a Lady. Her eyes widen and she waves at someone behind me. "Ametrine!"

What strange names these royal women have, I think, as the Countess of the Rose joins us, leaning heavily on a black walking stick, a mink coat hanging from her shoulders. The lioness is hidden under her veil, but I can feel the tension rolling off her—I bet she's hating the leash more than I am.

"So sad, isn't it?" the Countess says, but her face belies her words—she doesn't look sad at all.

"Yes," the Lady of the Glass replies in a hushed voice, but with the hint of a smile. "And so . . . surprising."

"Indeed," the Duchess says wryly.

I have no idea what they're talking about, but something about their tone makes me uncomfortable.

There is a blaring of trumpets and the massive front doors of the palace groan open. An older man, his black hair graying at his temples, emerges, surrounded by Regimentals. At once, silence falls and the crowd bows low. This time I don't need prompting to know to bow, because this is a face that even I recognize. I've seen it hundreds of times on the covers of Lily's magazines, on the official royal seal, in the newspapers that the caretakers read . . .

The Exetor.

He is tall, and his face, though lined, is handsome. He wears an inversion of the Regimental uniform, a black military jacket with red buttons and the crest of the Royal Family pinned on his left breast—a crowned flame crossed with two spears.

"Her Royal Grace thanks you for your support during this sad time," he says. His voice is a rich tenor. "But she will not allow any surrogate within these walls. If you wish to pay your respects, you must leave them here. Protected, of course, by my own personal guard."

Gasps of shock and murmurs of outrage ripple through the crowd at this announcement. The Lady of the Glass frowns, glancing at her surrogate's belly, but the Countess of the Rose looks positively terrified.

"*Leave* them here?" she hisses to the Duchess. "By *themselves*?"

The Duchess's eyes are fixed on the Exetor. "Very clever," she murmurs. Then she yanks on my leash, pulling me close to her. "You will behave yourself," she says in a voice like shards of ice. "Or you will be punished. Do you understand?"

I grit my teeth and nod. The Duchess holds my gaze for a moment through the veil, then she undoes the bracelet around her wrist, fastening it to mine. Other women follow her lead, many with hesitation.

As a steady stream of black-clothed figures passes through the double doors, bowing and curtsying to the Exetor as they go, another stream of red encircles the surrogates. The Exetor's guard carry rifles, their faces cold. Maybe it's just my imagination, but they seem bigger than the Regimentals at the Duchess's palace. The closest surrogates shrink from them as they tighten the ring around us. As we bunch together, I accidentally bump into the pregnant surrogate, stepping on her foot.

"Oh, I'm so sorry," I hurriedly apologize. The girl says nothing, but her hand moves to caress her stomach. "Is it . . . are you okay?"

"He's kicking," she murmurs, and I don't know if she's talking to me or to herself until she looks up. Her eyes are big and brown, like a doe's, and even more pronounced because of the thinness of her face—her skin is stretched tightly over her cheekbones and chin. A ghostly smile pulls at her lips.

"Is that . . . a good thing?" I have absolutely no idea what it must be like to be pregnant. I have a vague memory of my mother when she was pregnant with Hazel, but mostly I remember wondering about how this new little person would affect *my* life, not what my mother was experiencing. And she'd always seemed happy, glowing, not skeletal like this girl.

"He knows I'm scared." The girl cradles her stomach tenderly. "He knows I don't like being outside."

"How can he tell you're scared?" I ask slowly.

"You'll see," the girl says. "It will happen to you."

Suddenly, someone grabs my arm.

"Fawn?" Another surrogate is staring at me wildly through her veil.

"N-no," I stammer. "I'm Violet." It feels good to say my name aloud.

"Have you seen a girl with dark brown hair and freckles? Did you come from Westgate?"

"No," I say. "I'm sorry. I came from Southgate. Is Fawn your friend?"

"She's my sister," the girl says, tears filling her eyes. "I . . . I can't find her." She turns to the lioness, clutching her wrist. "Have you seen a girl with dark brown hair and freckles?"

The lioness yanks her arm out of the girl's grasp. "Don't touch me," she says coldly.

The girl sniffs and turns to another surrogate, pleading for information. The lioness catches me frowning at her and glares.

"What?"

"I don't understand you," I say. "She was just looking for help."

The lioness laughs. "I don't understand *you*," she says. "All of you. You act like sniveling weaklings, afraid of your mistresses. *We* make their children. *We* have the power."

"Maybe," I retort. "But you didn't choose this life any more than I did."

"Violet!"

The sound of my name cuts off anything else I might want to say.

"Raven?" I gasp.

"Violet!"

"Raven!" I cry louder, pushing my way through the crowd toward the sound of her voice. Raven's boldness inspires other girls, and more names are shouted.

"Fawn!" the girl searching for her sister yells.

"Scarlet!"

"Ginger!"

The crowd of surrogates begins to writhe, like a many-headed monster, rippling and stretching, shoving and elbowing and tripping over one another; I shout Raven's name as loud as I can, and then there she is—I throw myself into her, wrapping my arms around her familiar form.

"Are you all right?" she asks.

"I'm all right, are you—"

Suddenly, gunshots rip through the air, the Regimentals firing their rifles to subdue the crowd. We all skitter together, like a herd of deer, quiet and tense. I clutch Raven's hand.

"How is the palace of the Lake?" Raven asks. "Does the Duchess treat you well?"

"I . . . I don't know. She hit me. But then she gave me a cello. And the food is great." Raven laughs, and I smile. "What about the Countess of the Stone?"

She snorts. "No. I don't think the Countess and I are going to get along very well."

"Why? What do you mean?"

"Don't worry about me, Violet." Raven's lips curve into a wicked grin. "I'm going to make her rue the day she bought me."

"Raven, don't," I plead. I love my best friend's courage, but this isn't like pulling some prank at Southgate. "She could hurt you."

"Yeah. I know." Raven's gaze turns oddly distant. "Have you seen a doctor yet?"

"No."

"You will. And then you'll see." A muscle twitches in Raven's jaw. Then she sighs. "Or maybe not. Maybe the Duchess is different. But the Countess is . . . there's something *wrong* with her, Violet."

"Raven, you're scaring me," I say.

Raven squeezes my hand. "I'll be fine. Don't worry about me."

I'm about to protest when another volley of gunshots explodes into the air—the royal women begin to trickle out of the palace.

"I don't want to leave you," I whisper to Raven.

"Me neither." She smiles bravely. "But we'll see each other again. Founding Houses, right?"

"Right," I say, trying to sound more confident than I feel. Women begin collecting their surrogates, reattaching the bracelets to their wrists and leading the leashed girls to motorcars.

"She can't see me talking to you," Raven says, stiffening. The Countess of the Stone, her enormous figure easily recognizable, is making her way down the stairs. Then my hand is empty, as Raven melts into the sea of black veils.

"So," the Duchess says, suddenly appearing at my side. She unfastens the bracelet and puts it back on her own wrist. "Were you well-behaved?"

"Yes, my lady," I mutter, keeping my eyes down.

"Good. We're going home."

THE FOREST IS A BLUR OUTSIDE THE MOTORCAR WINDOW.

My mind races to try to make sense of what Raven said. What is happening to her in the House of the Stone? What did the doctor do?

"Did you see someone you know?"

The Duchess's voice scatters my thoughts.

"Outside the Palace," she continues. "Did you see someone you know? You seem unsettled."

I try to keep my face smooth.

"No, my lady," I say.

"You really are an appalling liar." She pulls the hatpin out of her hair, removing the pillbox hat and placing it on her knees. "You can lift that veil now. Our mourning period is over."

Gratefully, I pull the lace back off my face. "Who were we mourning, my lady?"

The Duchess traces the corner of her mouth with a long finger. "The Electress's surrogate died yesterday morning."

The world crumples, all the breath knocked out of me like I've been punched in the stomach. Dahlia. She's talking about Dahlia.

"You saw her, remember? At dinner. Such a tiny thing. Let us hope Her Royal Grace is more careful in the future. Title does not protect you from everything."

I can't speak. I can't think. Dahlia was so young . . . she was so small . . .

"How?" I breathe, my lips barely able to form the word.

The Duchess smiles to herself. "I've always found it . . . humbling, how one tiny drop of plant extract can completely destroy a human being. We are so fragile, aren't we? One little sip of wine and then . . . nothing. Life is so easily snuffed out."

My head pounds as I grasp what she's saying. "Why?"

The Duchess raises an eyebrow. "The Electress seems to have forgotten that *I* have been around much longer than she has. *I* am descended from one of the four founding Houses, not some shopkeeper in the Bank. She thought she could change the rules. She is a disgrace to the throne, and an embarrassment to her title, and yesterday she learned that *no one* is untouchable." She glances at my dumbstruck face and her mouth curls into a smirk. "Welcome to the Jewel."

Eleven

When we arrive back at the palace, Annabelle is waiting to take me to my chambers.

The Duchess removes the leash, and I cringe away from her hands, so close to my neck, from the scent of her perfume, from the looming figures of her guard. Everything feels oddly distorted. Unreal. I follow Annabelle up the curving staircase in a daze.

Dahlia is dead. The Duchess *killed* Dahlia.

I am owned by a murderer.

With a shock, I realize it could have been me. The Electress bid on me. It could have been my body being mourned by the black-clad royalty.

I can't make sense of the Duchess's motivations.

Dahlia's only failing was being bought by the Electress. Wasn't it?

By the time we reach my drawing room, anger has usurped the numb disbelief. I push past Annabelle and into my bedroom, tearing the veil out of my hair and throwing it on the ground, ignoring the sharp pain as a few hairs come away with it. Without pausing, I storm through my powder room and into my dressing chamber, fighting to unzip the black dress. Annabelle moves to help me.

"No," I say, pushing her away with more force than I'd intended. "I don't want your help. I don't want any of this!"

The zipper rips, and the sound is so enticing, I rip it further. It feels good, to destroy something of *hers*, in her own house.

And I have three closets, full of her clothes.

I charge to one and throw the door open, grabbing a beaded dress and tearing it along its seam, sending a thousand multicolored beads cascading to the floor. I toss it aside and grab another, ripping at its lace sleeves, scratching at its silken skirts—I want to slash through the entire closet, mangling all the stupid frilly, lacy, silky, ruffled dresses, tearing them to ribbons, shredding them apart until there's nothing left.

Tears are pouring down my cheeks, my breath coming out in aching gasps, and I realize I sound utterly pathetic, helpless, like a child. I sink onto the pile of velvet and beaded lace and crinoline and cloth-of-gold and satin and I wish, more than anything, for my mother. I want her to wrap her arms around me, to envelop me in the reassuring scent of her skin, and tell me that everything will be okay.

The velvet choker is still tied around my neck, and I scratch at it, my fingers clumsy, but I want to get it off. I feel a sting as one of my nails pierces the skin on my neck, but I don't care.

A small hand wraps around mine, holding it still. There is a slight tug and the velvet falls off.

Annabelle strokes my hair, gently cradling my head so that it rests in her lap. I look up at her pale, freckled face.

"She's dead," I say, my voice a cracked whisper. A fat tear leaks from the corner of my eye and trickles down the side of my face into my hair.

Annabelle nods, and in that nod, I know she knows. That's why her mood was so tense this morning.

"Her name was Dahlia." It's suddenly important to me that Annabelle know that Dahlia was a person, not just some nameless surrogate casualty. "She was from Northgate. She waited with me in the room before the Auction. She was . . . she was kind, she . . ."

But my voice trails off, more tears spilling down my cheeks, and Annabelle rocks me tenderly back and forth, on the pile of dresses.

I REFUSE TO LEAVE MY BEDROOM THE NEXT DAY.

I won't get dressed just because the Duchess wants me to. I won't be a pretty little doll that she can prop up and bring around with her to show off, knowing that someone could kill me for it.

The thought splinters inside me like ice cracking, cold and sharp. Someone could kill me. I think about the dinner, the way the women were divided, and with a shudder, I realize the Duchess is outnumbered. The Electress, the

Countess of the Stone, or the Duchess of the Scales could all be plotting my death at this very moment.

Something has to be done. I can't just sit here and wait to be murdered.

Annabelle tries to get me to eat, or to play Halma, or use my cello, but every time I send her away. I don't want to enjoy anything this palace has to offer me. Dahlia is dead. Something is happening to Raven, something bad, but I don't know what and I don't know how to stop it. I think about the pregnant surrogate, her wide eyes, her thin face, the way she cradled her swollen belly with such tenderness. I don't want that. I don't want to be her.

I'd rather be breaking my back in the Farm or choking on soot and ash in the Smoke. I'd happily work as a scullery maid in the Bank, scouring dishes until my hands turned red and raw. But all the paths my life could have taken vanished with one blood test.

I remember the wild girl, whose execution I witnessed. Maybe she had the right idea. Maybe she knew it, and that's why she wasn't frightened at the end. "This is how it begins," she said. I wonder if she saw death as just another way to freedom.

I think until my brain hurts and my eyes are sore, but I can't think myself out of this room, or this palace, or this ruthless, glittering circle. When I finally fall asleep, I dream of Southgate, and Raven, and a time when the royalty were nothing more than pictures in a glossy magazine.

THE FOLLOWING MORNING, I AM WOKEN ABRUPTLY BY the covers on my bed being thrown back.

"Annabelle!" I complain as the cold air stings my bare legs. But it isn't Annabelle who is standing over me.

It's the Duchess.

"Get up," she orders. Annabelle hovers in the doorway, her expression both panicked and pleading. I consider mutiny, but defying the Duchess isn't like defying Annabelle.

Quickly and silently, I climb out of bed and stand in front of her. Even though she is shorter than me, power emanates from her small frame.

"Sit," she says, pointing to an armchair. "We are going to have a talk, you and I."

Her eyes flicker to Annabelle, who curtsies and closes the door, leaving the two of us alone.

I perch on the edge of the armchair. The Duchess sits on the sofa, studying me.

"There are two schools of thought concerning surrogates," she says. "One is that your personalities are a hindrance, detrimental to the development of the fetus. The other is that they are an asset, a useful tool in creating the optimal child. Fortunately for you, I am of the second school. Therefore, I will require your cooperation during our time together. I am not an idiot—I do not expect your love, and I am certainly not your mother. But we are in a partnership, you and I. The Jewel can be a wonderful and terrible place. I expect you'd prefer the former to the latter."

I stare at her blankly, unsure of exactly what she's asking of me.

"You saw what happened when you behaved yourself at my dinner—you received a cello. Continue to behave, and

I will ensure that your life here is as pleasant as possible. You'd like that, wouldn't you? A pleasant life?"

She smiles at me in a way that sets my teeth on edge.

"What do you want?" I ask.

The Duchess purses her lips. "You seem like a fairly intelligent girl. The conversation at dinner the other night mustn't have escaped your notice entirely."

My mind whirs back to the dinner, but mostly I remember the general snideness, Raven's face, and the horrible moment when Dahlia was forced to perform. The Duchess looks disappointed.

"The Electress has recently celebrated the birth of her first child, a son. He will be the future Exetor, and my daughter will be betrothed to him. It is your job to ensure this arrangement. My daughter must be beautiful, but looks aren't everything, as my son proves to me every day. She must be smart and strong. She must have ambition, determination, and courage. I want her to be irresistible. But of course"—she waves her hand—"all of these qualities will come later. To make her truly stand out as an infant, you must make her grow. Faster than the others."

I shake my head, as if somehow I can rattle her words together in my brain in a way that makes sense. "I don't . . . understand."

The Duchess sits up, exasperated. "Do you know how many perfect scores there have been on the third Augury, in the history of the Auction?"

"No."

"Seven—one every fifty years or so. I have researched the Auction extensively. In fact, the last perfect score recorded was from the surrogate my own mother purchased, the one who bore me." She looks proud, as if she had something to do with her surrogate's Augury score. "Of course, my mother did not have the slightest idea how to foster the potential that my surrogate had. I do. I have been waiting a very long time for you."

"So you expect me to make a baby faster than everyone else, and also make her beautiful and courageous and all those other things? How do you even know I'll have a daughter?"

The Duchess frowns. "Perhaps you are not as intelligent as I thought. The royalty are only allowed two children, one girl and one boy. I already have a son."

"But the Electress . . . at the dinner, she said she was going to make her daughter succeed the throne, not her son."

"Well," the Duchess says, "in order for that to happen, she'd need to *have* a daughter, wouldn't she?"

It feels like an ice cube has slipped into my stomach. So that's why she killed Dahlia. To prevent the Electress from having a girl.

"So what, do you plan to kill every surrogate the Electress ever buys?" I ask.

The silence that follows is dark and threatening.

"Is this how you wish to begin our partnership?" the Duchess asks. I press my lips together. "Good. And don't be so dramatic. Death won't be necessary. It wasn't technically necessary this time, since the Exetor will never consent to having a woman succeed the throne. But I did feel that Her Royal Grace's head could do with a little deflating."

This woman makes me sick. She killed an innocent child simply out of spite. "But the Electress said she could convince the Exetor to change his mind," I insist.

The Duchess raises an eyebrow. "Did she? And how did she plan to do that?"

I hesitate, remembering that that moment occurred when the Duchess was out of the room.

The Duchess's eyes harden. "Speak."

I grit my teeth and jut out my chin.

She moves so quickly I have no time to react. One moment, we're sitting across from each other, the next she is towering over me, fingers around my throat. Her grip is like an iron claw, tightening until I can barely breathe. I scratch at her hand, trying to free myself, but she only squeezes harder. Her strength is incredible.

"You listen to me," she says, her voice soft and dangerous. "I have allowed you to mourn for your friend. I have allowed you to destroy an entire year's worth of gowns. I have allowed you to be self-indulgent and I have allowed you to sulk. Do not think there is a single emotion you feel or action you make that I am not aware of and that I could not change or cease if necessary. But I will *not* allow you to disrespect me. Do you understand?"

I try to speak, but only a strangled hissing sound comes out. Her fingernails dig into my skin and stars explode in front of my eyes, my attempts to claw at her hand becoming weaker. A tingling sensation spreads through my fingertips, and my head feels very light and everything goes fuzzy. . . .

Then the world sharpens with painful clarity as the Duchess releases me. I collapse over one arm of the chair, gasping for breath, my throat raw. Air fills my lungs, and I gulp at it greedily, choking in my eagerness to breathe. It takes a few seconds before I can get my body back under control, to stop the shaking in my arms and legs. When I look up, the Duchess is staring at me, her face impassive.

"Do you understand?" she repeats.

I nod weakly. "Y-yes, my lady," I wheeze.

"Good. Now. What did the Electress say?"

"She said . . . she said she could use her body to convince him." I blush at the words.

The Duchess's eyes widen a fraction and she barks out a laugh. "Really? Well, I wish her the best of luck with that." Some strange expression crosses her face, making her features oddly fragile. Then it's gone and she laughs again. "Get your robe. We're going to see the doctor."

The room tilts at an odd angle. "Now?"

"Yes. Now."

The Duchess doesn't seem to notice that I'm falling apart. As I slip my robe on, it's like my stomach has disappeared and my heart has moved to settle in its place. My body feels hollow and my pulse thrums loudly in my ears.

I hadn't expected it to happen so soon. I'm not ready for this.

We make our way down the hall of flowers and through an open gallery filled with colorful paintings. We turn right, then left, down a short hallway paneled in oak. A gilded door sits at the end of it, carved into floral patterns like a grate, and as we reach it, I see that it's an elevator. There was one in Southgate, though not nearly as ornate. The Duchess opens the grate and we step inside. There is a thick blue rug on the floor, and a copper lever that the Duchess pulls—the doors close and the elevator sinks down into darkness.

I press myself against the wall and wish I could disappear. They told us at Southgate that the implantation process would be painless, but that's not particularly reassuring at the moment.

I don't want anything of the Duchess's inside me.

Light covers my feet, then crawls up my calves and over my knees as the elevator slows and comes to a stop.

The doors open to reveal a sterile-looking medical room. It is similar to the one at Southgate, only smaller, clearly just for one person. A tray of gleaming silver instruments sits beside a white hospital bed, and clusters of bright lights perch atop steel supports, like many-eyed silver insects.

I can't move. It feels like something hard is stuck in my throat, making it difficult to swallow.

"Dr. Blythe," the Duchess says, grabbing my arm and yanking me out of the elevator. I see him, hunched over a desk on the left side of the room.

"Good afternoon, my lady," he says. "You are precisely on time."

Like most of the doctors I've been to, Dr. Blythe is older, with deep wrinkles around his eyes and mouth. His skin is a rich brown, with a handful of chocolate-colored freckles spread across his cheeks and the bridge of his nose, a strangely youthful characteristic in such an old face. His black hair, peppered with streaks of gray, is slicked back, though there is a crinkled quality to it. His eyes are a light brownish-green, and there is warmth in them, something I'm not at all used to in doctors. He looks at me like I'm a person, not a sample in a test tube.

"Ah," he says. "Hello."

He is smiling at me. I don't know what to make of that. My head is spinning and I think I might pass out.

His smile fades. "Surely, Your Ladyship, you have informed your surrogate that this is purely a preliminary exam? She looks a bit . . . pale."

Preliminary exam. The words dance around in my head, relief making my legs numb.

"I did not think it necessary," the Duchess says.

The doctor shakes his head. "My lady, we have discussed this. You have agreed to follow my instructions and I must insist that you do."

Immediately, I like this man. Anyone allowed to give the Duchess instructions is okay by me.

"Very well," she says tightly. "I will expect your report this evening."

The doctor bows. "Of course, my lady."

She gets back in the elevator, and it slowly disappears from view—the doctor waits until it's gone before speaking again.

"I'm Dr. Blythe, as you have probably surmised," he says, holding out his hand. "I'll be your primary physician."

I take his hand—it is soft and warm.

"What's your name?" he asks. I hesitate. "It's all right, you can tell me."

"Violet."

"What a beautiful name," he says. "Who chose it?"

"My father," I reply. "After my eyes."

Dr. Blythe smiles. "Yes, they are a most unusual color.

I've never seen anything quite like them."

"Thank you."

"Which holding facility were you in?"

"Southgate."

"Is Dr. Steele still the head physician there?"

I nod.

"What a strange man he is. Excellent doctor, but . . ."
Dr. Blythe shakes his head. "Let's get started, shall we, Violet? As I said, this is only a preliminary exam, but I will
have to ask you to remove your nightdress. You may keep
your undergarments on, and there is a robe for you to wear
if you'd like."

He turns his back while I undress—the robe is not like
the disposable ones I wore at Southgate, but made of white
terrycloth, though there is no belt to keep it closed. I wrap
my arms tightly around my torso, glancing nervously at the
tray of silver instruments.

"Please, sit," Dr. Blythe says, indicating the hospital bed.

I relax a little as he conducts the exam, similar to the
hundreds of others I had at Southgate. He goes through
routine checks of my ears, nose, eyes, throat, takes my
temperature and my blood pressure, makes notations on a
clipboard, checks my reflexes. He asks the usual, unpleasant
questions about my monthly cycle.

"Don't you have this stuff from the doctors at Southgate?" I ask.

Dr. Blythe smiles. "I like to be thorough," he says.
He marks something down on his clipboard, then begins
to attach tiny electrodes to my temples, the insides of my
wrists, then moves to open my robe. "May I?"

I look up at him, startled. "You're the first one to ask," I say.

He smiles and gently places two electrodes on either side of my stomach, just below the line of my underwear, then one on my chest, over my heart. He carefully lifts each of my legs, placing electrodes on the backs of my knees, and then two on the arches of my feet. And finally, he attaches one to the nape of my neck and one at the base of my spine.

"I assume you've only had the head and uterine monitors before?" Dr. Blythe says. I nod. "Well, we like to be a little more accurate, now that you're entering the more . . . practical phase of your surrogacy."

"Am I going to use the Auguries?" I ask. Whenever the doctors used the monitors at Southgate, it always involved an Augury test.

"Yes, but don't worry. Just once for each one." He walks to the wall and presses a red button—a flat white screen descends from the ceiling next to the hospital bed. Pulling up a stool, he sits and taps the corner of the screen—it begins to glow, different colored squares of light checkering its smooth surface. Then he angles the screen so I can't see it.

"Violet," he says, "you are a very special young woman." I fight the impulse to roll my eyes as the doctor touches something on the screen and a yellow glow illuminates his face. "Surrogates have confounded the medical community for centuries, since the very beginning of the Auction. I assume you know your history?"

"The royalty was dying out," I say, repeating what I was told so many times at Southgate. "Their babies were born sick or deformed, and died. Some of them couldn't have babies at all. Surrogates allow the royalty to survive. The Auguries help repair the chromosomal damage to royal embryos."

"Precisely," says Dr. Blythe. "Bloodline is very important to the royalty, but when there are only so many fish in the sea . . ." He taps at the screen. "It was Dr. Osmium Corre, perhaps the most renowned physician in the history of the Lone City, who discovered the first surrogates." This time, I can't help rolling my eyes. All the doctors at Southgate loved talking about Dr. Corre. Raven used to joke that they probably had shrines built to him in their houses. "He identified a strange genetic mutation, found only in young women from the poorest of the five circles—the Marsh— which allowed the royalty to continue having their own children without the risk of birth defects or premature death. But there is more to the Auguries than the miracle of healthy babies. Each Augury is attached to a certain developmental aspect. For instance"—he reaches out to the tray and picks up a large blue marble from among the silver instruments—"the first Augury, Color, affects certain physical aspects of the child."

He gives me the marble—it is heavier than I expected, and very smooth. "Make this red, please."

Once to see it as it is. Twice to see it in your mind. Thrice to bend it to your will.

I draw up the image in my mind, and cracks of red appear on the smooth blue surface. In less than a second, the marble is red. A dull ache pulses behind my left ear, and I rub it absentmindedly.

"Very good," Dr. Blythe says, touching a few more things on the screen. "The first Augury can influence skin color, hair color, eye color . . . it is the easiest of the Auguries. Quite superficial."

I'd never considered that the Auguries would affect anything else except the health of the child. They never told us that at Southgate. But the Duchess's instructions, her expectations of me, are beginning to make sense.

"Now," Dr. Blythe continues, "can you make a star for me?"

The image of a star appears in my head. I close my hand around the marble. My fingers tingle as I feel myself affecting it—the marble becomes malleable, like putty, and when I open my hand, it has turned transparent, scarlet glass. As I draw the lines of the star over and over in my mind, the marble ripples and assumes the shape I want. My headache gets worse.

"Excellent." More notations are made on the screen. "The second Augury, Shape, affects, as you might have guessed, the physical shapes of the child—the length of the legs, the shape of the face or eyes or nose. It also affects organ size, and so is very important to the health of the child. Many women value Shape above the other two Auguries for this reason."

Dr. Blythe takes the star from my hand and puts it back on the tray. My spine stiffens, the pain in my head sharp and staccato, like the beat of a drum. I know what's coming next.

He hands me a flower, just a small bud, petals folded tightly in on themselves—I run my fingers along the stem.

"Make it grow?" I say before he can suggest it. He smiles and nods. I take a deep breath.

The life in this flower is not nearly as strong as in the lemon tree because the flower has been cut. It will die soon. I pull at the wisps of life easily, the familiar sensation of needles boring into my eyes only a mild irritation as the bud explodes into a rose, its petals unfolding in rich waves of dark pink. My nose doesn't even bleed.

I drop the rose on the tray. For a second, I can still feel its life, shimmering in my veins. Then it's gone.

Dr. Blythe's eyebrows are raised. "How are you feeling?" he asks.

I ignore the pain in my head and shrug. "All right."

"That was faster than I had expected. Very impressive."

"I was the best third-Augury student at Southgate." I can't keep the pride out of my voice.

"You were the best third-Augury score at the Auction," he says.

I pick at a loose thread on the robe. "The Duchess said there haven't been many perfect scores in Growth."

Dr. Blythe nods. "She is correct. Though the ranking itself is cumulative. Lot 200 was an outstanding talent at all three, especially given her age. It is a tragedy that she was never able to bear a child."

My eyes itch, thinking of Dahlia.

"Did you know her well?" he asks. "I was told you reacted rather forcefully to her death."

"Does that happen often?" I ask quietly. "That surrogates are . . . killed?"

Dr. Blythe's mouth tightens. "You do not need to worry

about that. The Duchess will take extremely good care of you." He taps the screen a few more times, then clears his throat.

"The third Augury, Growth, is very tricky," he continues. "If successful, it can affect intelligence, creativity, ambition . . . the personality of the child can be influenced."

"How is it tricky?" I ask. It's a little overwhelming, to think that I can custom-make a child.

"It does not always work. We are not sure why sometimes the child comes out with the qualities the mother suggested and desired, and other times with an entirely different result, sometimes an unpleasant one. Often, royal women do not even bother with Growth, because it is so temperamental. But if successful, it can be truly extraordinary. However, usually at the expense of the other two Auguries. It is a risk."

"And this is why the Duchess bought me?" I say. "Because I'm so good at Growth?"

"Has she spoken to you already?"

I nod. "She gave me a whole list of qualities she wants her baby to have. But I don't know how to do any of it."

"Not just that, Violet," Dr. Blythe says. "She wants her daughter to be born *first*. She believes that, with your abilities, her child can be born much faster than the usual nine months. And that it will be . . . more advanced than your typical infant. You can speed up the developmental process as well as the physical."

I feel light-headed. "How quickly do you expect me to have this baby?"

Dr. Blythe's lips press together. "Our goal is three months. One month per trimester."

Three months. Hysteria bubbles up inside me. "What?" I say. "That's crazy."

The doctor just smiles. "We'll see."

"Why didn't they tell us this at Southgate? The Auguries, I mean, what they can really do."

Dr. Blythe types a few more notes, then begins to remove the electrodes. "Violet, they do not tell you anything at Southgate. They do not even allow you to look at yourselves in a mirror. The less you know, the less identity you have, the easier you are to control."

"Then why tell me now?"

"Because your cooperation is vital to the process. And because there is nothing you can do about it now. You are isolated in the Duchess's palace. You will have no further contact with your family or your friends. You will never leave the Jewel." Dr. Blythe presses the red button and the screen disappears into the ceiling. "When you have delivered the Duchess's daughter, you will be sterilized and sent to a facility very much like Southgate, where you will live out the rest of your life with the other surrogates who have fulfilled their purpose."

Back to a holding facility? So I'll always be living under someone else's rules, even after my job here is over.

"The Duchess said the royalty can only have one boy and one girl," I say. "Do I control that, too?"

"No," Dr. Blythe replies. "That is in the hands of the doctors."

"Why can they only have two children?"

"To maintain the purity of blood and, I suppose you could say, the exclusiveness of their club. One child retains the family title while the other is married off to form an alliance with a desirable House. Alliances are always changing here." He sighs and shakes his head. "The Duchess is very disappointed with her son. She has extremely high hopes for her daughter."

The doctor turns away as I slip back into my nightdress. His words swirl around in my head. A baby made in three months. But how can the Duchess believe that I would ever willingly want to *help* her?

Twelve

THE FOLLOWING MORNING, I'M IN THE TEA PARLOR, SIP-
ping coffee and trying not to think about the doctor's
appointment, when the Duchess arrives.

"Come with me," she says.

It's happening. That's all I can think. *She's taking me
back to Dr. Blythe.* I can't seem to make myself stand.

"Where are we going, my lady?" I ask in a half whisper.
Annabelle shoots me a sharp look that I don't understand.
The Duchess frowns, as if she doesn't think I should be
allowed to ask questions at all.

"I have something I wish to show you. Get up."

My bones feel spongy as I follow her out of my chambers, back through the open gallery, and I know where we're

going and my heart starts to panic. But then the Duchess turns down a different hall, by the main staircase, and my relief is so acute it's painful.

Across from the staircase is a set of double doors with golden handles shaped like wings. The Duchess turns to me.

"Dr. Blythe is very optimistic—he feels you will be able to perform the tasks I require. This makes me exceedingly pleased. So." She opens the doors with a flourish, and I smell something warm, like wood and fabric and dust, with a hint of pine. Then I see what's behind the doors, and my mouth falls open.

It's a concert hall. Row upon row of seats, upholstered in red velvet, lead up to a massive proscenium stage framed by thick red curtains with golden tassels. Awe pulls me forward, my feet sinking into the burgundy carpet as I run my fingers over the soft armrests on the seats. The vaulted ceiling is gilded in gold and copper, and glowglobes bathe the room in a rich, warm light. A mezzanine wraps around the upper floor, even more seats stretching higher and higher. I couldn't have imagined a more incredible place to play music, except maybe the Royal Concert Hall.

As if on cue, two footmen appear onstage—one is carrying a chair and a music stand, the other, my cello.

"You may play here whenever you wish, as often as you like," the Duchess says. "I hope it will make you . . . happy." She doesn't sound particularly sincere, but I don't care. My fingers are already itching for my bow. The acoustics in this room must be amazing.

"Can I play now?" I ask, hurriedly adding, "My lady?"

"Of course," the Duchess says. She leaves and Annabelle

takes her place—she must have followed us here. I walk down the carpeted aisle and up onto the stage.

I've never been on a stage before. Looking out over the vast expanse of empty seats, I feel a shiver of excitement. There is so much expectation in them. The only pictures in Lily's magazines that ever interested me were the ones of the concerts. I take my seat and close my eyes, pressing the cello between my knees. I imagine I'm in the Royal Concert Hall and the seats are filled with people in beautiful clothing, all waiting with anticipation to hear me play. I listen to the rustle of their programs, and the whispered conversations that stop as soon as I raise my bow. They are so eager for my performance that with one simple gesture, I can silence a room. I play a courante in C Major, and when I finish, their applause is deafening. I select another piece from the many suites I have memorized, then another, and another. I play for hours. Here, I can pretend that this is my occupation, not baby-maker but *musician*, a professional, as well respected as Stradivarius Tanglewood.

It's late afternoon when I finally stop, exhilarated. Annabelle claps, a tiny flutter of sound in the vast, empty hall.

Done?

"For today, I think," I reply.

Sounds beautiful

"Thanks," I say with a grin. "I hope you didn't get bored."

Annabelle smiles and shakes her head. She presses a button on the wall by a smaller set of doors, and a minute later, two footmen appear to take my cello and the chair back to my room.

"What should we do now?" I ask, climbing down the stairs to the stage and joining Annabelle in the audience. I'm riding a jittery sort of high.

Tour?

"Of the palace?"

Annabelle nods.

"I'd love one."

THE CONCERT HALL IS NOT THE ONLY IMPRESSIVE ROOM in the palace of the Lake.

The upper floor is filled mostly with studies and reading rooms. There is a room full of urns that Annabelle tells me contain the ashes of previous Dukes and Duchesses of the Lake, which I find really creepy, but she assures me that every palace has such a room. There are more art galleries, and guest quarters, but Annabelle only shows half of the upper floor, avoiding the eastern wing.

"What's over there?" I ask.

Men's quarters

"Oh. That's where the Duke sleeps?"

Annabelle nods.

And Garnet

"Right," I say, picturing the Duchess's handsome son. And then, because I can't help myself, I ask, "Is he here now?"

At school, back this eve

"Oh." I fiddle with a button on my dress. "He's very good-looking, isn't he?"

Annabelle blushes.

<u>*Very*</u>

She underlines the word twice and I giggle.

The ground floor is even more of a maze than the upper floor. Annabelle shows me the ballroom, with its parquet flooring and wide, arching windows—a mural is painted on the ceiling, a brilliant blue sky dotted with fleecy white clouds and various colored birds. There is a main drawing room that looks out onto the lake, and a wide, airy gallery filled with nothing but white marble sculptures. We pass by a closed door that emits an unpleasant, pungent smell.

"What's in there?" I ask.

Annabelle makes a face.

Duke's smoking room

"Where is the Duke anyway?" I ask. "I mean, what does he do, exactly?"

Annabelle smirks.

Whatever D tells him to

I laugh.

The last room she shows me is the library, and I'm immediately in love. It is enormous, with high ceilings and stained-glass windows, and it smells wonderfully of old paper, and binding glue, and leather. Long wooden ladders slide along the shelves, and golden spiral staircases lead up to the balcony.

There is an open reading area in its center, with leather armchairs and overstuffed couches scattered around an enormous circular table. The table is studded with little jeweled trinkets that at first I think are brooches—but as I get closer, I see that they're crests. I recognize the circle-and-trident of the House of the Lake.

"What's this?" I ask.

Royal Houses of Jewel

"All of them?" There must be hundreds of crests, arranged within circles of thin silver lines. In the center is the crowned flame of the Royal Palace. The four closest to it must be the four founding Houses. But the others . . .

"See, this is why I never paid attention in royal culture and lifestyle," I say. "There're just too many Houses to keep track of."

Annabelle suppresses a smile. She points to the center crest.

Exetor

"I got that one," I say. "And those four are the founding Houses, right?"

She nods and indicates the next circle, maybe forty or so crests.

1st tier Houses

Then the secondary circle, with about a hundred.

2nd tier

And finally, the outer circle, with the largest number of crests.

3rd tier

"Yes, but . . ." I point at a crest in the second tier, a glittering red oval crossed with two white lines. "This one looks just like"—I point to a third-tier crest, a white oval crossed with two red lines—"*that* one."

Annabelle raises one eyebrow and shakes her head, indicating the second tier, the red oval.

House of the Flame

She points to the third tier, white oval.

House of the Light

"Fine, then," I say. "If you know so much . . . what's that one?"

I point out a silver circle in the first tier, crossed with two golden feathers.

House of Downs

"Okay, that was easy. What about that one?" Third tier, a pale green rectangle crossed with two curved, luminescent lines.

House of Veil

I shake my head. "I give up. You win."

Annabelle smiles ruefully.

She takes me through the stacks, showing me where the art and history books are, and the romance novels, and children's stories. There is an entire row dedicated to music, and I search through it eagerly, discovering old favorites and exciting new pieces that I can't wait to try.

"Am I allowed to borrow these?" I ask.

Of course

I pull out a thick sheaf of paper and sink to the floor, spreading pages and pages of notes across the carpet, deciding which ones I'll take with me.

"Who are you?"

A thin, reedy voice startles me, and I look up to see the girl I saw in the window, the day of Dahlia's funeral. Her beady eyes take in the scattered sheets of paper.

"I'm—" I'm about to say "Violet," but Annabelle holds up her slate. I imagine the word *surrogate* printed on it.

"Oh." She studies me critically, the way the Duchess sometimes does. "You better clean up that mess."

"Who are you?" I ask sharply.

The girl smirks. Her chin and nose form sharp points, and her eyes are set a little too close together. "I don't have to tell you anything. You're just a surrogate."

My cheeks flush, and I go back to sifting through the music, ignoring her command. I can see the hem of the girl's skirt out of the corner of my eye—she stands and watches me for a moment. I spread more papers out. The Duchess can order me around, but not this girl.

The skirt disappears and I look up.

"Who was that?" I whisper to Annabelle.

D's niece

"Is she visiting?"

Lives here

"She's not very nice, is she?"

Annabelle shakes her head.

Servs hate her

Then she puts her finger to her lips and winks at me. I grin.

After a few more minutes of watching me flip through sheet music, Annabelle seems to get that I might be here for a while. She points to herself and writes:

Art books

"All right," I say. "I'll meet you over there."

When I finally have a stack of music an inch thick—and there's still more to look at, more to discover—I put the rest of it away and head off to find Annabelle. I must take a wrong turn, though, because I come out by one of the staircases to the balcony. I turn back, down a long row of leather-bound volumes, and find myself in front of a plain door, slightly ajar. Light leaks through it, sending a long sliver of pale gold across the carpet. I hear the rustling of pages from inside. Curiosity propels me forward, and I push open the door.

The room is small, its shelves filled with books that have ancient, crumbling spines, and piles of faded, yellowing parchment. There is a lone wooden table, and leaning over it is a very familiar figure.

"Lucien!" I squeal.

He looks up, his face blank with shock. "Oh my goodness," he says. "What a very pleasant surprise. But come. You can't be in here."

He takes me by the arm and leads me out of the room. I catch a glimpse of the parchment he was studying—it's all blue lines and measurements, like a blueprint of some sort. Then we're back in the main library and he's closing the door behind us.

"What are you doing here?" I ask.

"I was delivering a message to the lady of the house."

"From the Electress?"

He inclines his head. "The Duchess has the most extensive library in the Jewel. She was kind enough to allow me to peruse it before returning to the Royal Palace." His gentle eyes turn serious. "How are you faring so far?"

I open my mouth and find I don't know what to say. Lucien seems to understand. "Let's sit down for a moment," he suggests.

I follow him to a corner of the library with a small table and two plush chairs. He pulls one out for me, the keys hanging from his belt jangling together.

"You know, I'm perfectly capable of pulling out a chair myself."

He shrugs. "Habit."

I sit and he moves to the opposite chair, taking something off his key ring that I realize isn't a key. It looks like a small silver tuning fork. Lucien puts his finger to his lips, then taps the fork lightly against the table and releases it. It floats an inch or two off the tabletop, hovering in midair, vibrating and emitting a faint hum.

"What is that?" I ask. The tuning fork revolves slowly on the spot.

"It will prevent us from being overheard," Lucien explains. "When you've lived in the Jewel as long as I have, you learn to be careful."

"How long have you lived here?" I assumed Lucien was born in the Jewel.

"Since I was ten."

"Really? Which circle are you from?"

Lucien's smooth face tightens. "Why don't we talk about something a little more relevant? How are you doing?"

"I don't know," I admit. "All right, I guess. Better than some." My throat swells as I think of Dahlia. "Did you get to know her at all?"

Lucien doesn't need to ask who I mean.

"A little," he says sadly. "She seemed very sweet."

"Yes," I say. "She was."

"Was she at your holding facility?"

I shake my head. "I only met her in the Waiting Room."

We are quiet for a moment.

"It was the Duchess," I say, my voice barely a whisper. "She—she killed her."

Lucien nods. "Yes. I know."

I sit up, startled. "You do?"

"It was not difficult to guess." He grimaces.

"Does the Electress know?" My heart starts pumping fast, fear flooding my veins. "Will there be . . . retaliation?"

He pats my hand. "No. The poison used was untraceable. The Electress cannot prove anything, and to attack one of the founding Houses would lose her favor. With her lineage, she can't afford to lose any of the alliances she's made. It isn't worth the risk." His mouth twists. "Besides, she can just buy another surrogate next year."

"What *is* this place?" I say. "How does no one know this goes on?" I would have remembered hearing if a surrogate had been assassinated while I was at Southgate. The news would have spread like wildfire.

Lucien gives me a pitying look. "Nobody cares about the death of a surrogate." He falls silent for a second, his expression distant, his fingers tracing patterns in the grains of wood in the table.

"I saw the doctor yesterday," I say.

Lucien looks up. "And how did that go?"

"The Duchess wants her daughter to be the next Electress."

He sighs. "Yes, I'm sure she does. As does every other daughterless woman in the Jewel who bought a surrogate this year."

"But the Duchess thinks I can do something the other surrogates can't. She expects me to deliver the baby faster— to, I don't know, somehow speed up the whole process. Is that even possible? Have you heard of that happening before?"

Lucien's body has frozen, his expression unfathomable. It's like he's trying hard not to reveal what he's thinking.

"Lucien?" I ask hesitantly. "Are you all right?"

His eyes meet mine, and I notice his are a rich, deep blue. "I would very much like to help you," he says, and there is an urgency in his tone that makes the hairs on the back of my neck prickle. "And it seems I don't have the time I thought I would have."

"Time for what?"

"To set things in motion. To be sure I can trust you."

"You can trust me," I say, sitting up straighter as if that will somehow prove my point.

Lucien smiles. "Yes, I believe I can." He leans forward. "I can get you out of here," he whispers.

The words hang in the air between us. "Out of the palace?" I whisper back.

"Out of the Jewel," he replies.

Footsteps in the row of shelves make us both jump. In one swift movement, the tuning fork is back on Lucien's key ring—two seconds later, Annabelle appears at the end of the stacks, holding a large art book. She takes one look at Lucien and quickly sinks into a curtsy. Lucien stands.

"Ah, I see you've been elevated," he says with a bow. "You are the new surrogate lady-in-waiting?"

Annabelle blushes and nods.

"Your mother must be proud."

Annabelle nods again. My heart is pounding and I try to keep my face casual as Lucien turns to me.

"It was nice to see you, 197." His eyes burn with a silent promise as he says, "We'll meet again soon, I'm sure of it."

I wince at his use of my old lot number, but I don't get the chance to say anything, because Lucien is already disappearing back into the small room. The door closes behind him, and I hear a lock click.

Annabelle gives me a questioning look.

"He was my prep artist," I explain. "For the Auction." I feel disoriented by our conversation, and its abrupt end. Part of me wants to wait in this chair until Lucien emerges again and demand more information. But I'm pretty certain I'm not supposed to be talking to Lucien at all. If he says we'll meet again soon, I'm just going to have to trust that we will. I'll have to be patient. "I—I've got everything I need. I'd like to go back to my room now."

The walk back to my chambers is a blur.

Out of the Jewel.

Lucien has just offered me my freedom.

~ Thirteen ~

I WAKE UP EARLY ON SUNDAY MORNING.

I've been living in the Duchess's palace for a week.

Freedom. The word, teasing and elusive, has been revolving over and over in my mind since I saw Lucien in the library, like a word I made up that has no meaning, until I remember it does. I desperately want to believe Lucien, that there's a way to get me out of here, but the thought of being disappointed tempers my enthusiasm. If I discover he was lying, or he made a mistake, or I imagined the whole thing . . .

My mind wanders to my family. Sundays are a day of rest. Ochre won't have to work, Hazel won't have school. I wonder what they're doing today. I hope, whatever it is, they're having fun. That they're happy. What would they think, if they could see me now, surrounded by all this luxury? They'd probably imagine I'm happy, too.

Maybe Lucien can get me back to them. I could see my mother again, and watch Hazel grow up. I could make my own decisions. I could choose what kind of life I want to lead.

I need to talk to Lucien again. I need him to promise me that this is real.

I sit up and ring for Annabelle.

"So," I say as she sets the breakfast tray on the table, "what does the Duchess want with me today?"

I try to sound casual, like I don't really care. I'm not sure I quite pull it off.

Nothing

"Nothing?"

Annabelle smiles.

Party last night D not feeling well

"Oh." I take a sip of coffee. "Do I see the doctor?"

Annabelle shakes her head.

"What should we do?"

She thinks for a moment.

Garden?

"There's a garden?"

Annabelle grins.

GARDEN ISN'T REALLY THE RIGHT WORD.

The immense backyard of the palace is a riot of color as the leaves on the trees are changing, orange and red-gold. Fall flowers line the gravel paths interspersed with statues and birdbaths and fountains. It gets wilder as we walk farther from the palace walls, the trees becoming denser, the paths sometimes overgrown. There is a giant maze in the center of the garden, constructed out of hedges at least seven feet tall, and Annabelle and I get lost in it, playing a made-up combination of hide-and-seek and tag, laughing and chasing each other until we are out of breath. In the heart of the maze is an enormous greenhouse, where the Duchess's gardener grows all the flowers for the arrangements in the palace. It's warm and humid inside, and the air smells like moist earth mixed with a hundred different floral fragrances. I run my fingers along the fragile petals of an orchid, shades of lavender and magenta and cream blending into one another.

It seems like for every time the Jewel makes me angry or uneasy or sad, I discover something beautiful in it.

I SEE THE DOCTOR EVERY DAY OVER THE FOLLOWING week. Lucien does not return to the palace of the Lake.

Annabelle escorts me to the medical room instead of the Duchess, which is far more preferable. Every appointment begins the same way.

"Is it happening today?" I ask. Dr. Blythe smiles and shakes his head.

"No, Violet," he replies. "Not today."

The appointments are similar to the first, with the Auguries and the monitors, though one of them also includes an invasive exam.

I always hated those exams at Southgate—I close my eyes, cringing at the cold feel of the speculum, and try to pretend I'm playing music, running notes and phrasing over and over in my mind.

As the week progresses, however, the Augury tests become more difficult. Unsurprisingly, Dr. Blythe begins to focus more and more on Growth. Cut flowers are simple—their life is so weak and easy to manipulate. Smaller plants, like ferns or weeds, don't provide much of a challenge either. Saplings are slightly more difficult. It's really the repetition that becomes a struggle, and Dr. Blythe begins timing me, how long it takes to complete the task, how many times I can perform Growth before my nose begins to bleed, how long I can continue after until it becomes unbearable.

"Thank you, Violet," he says at the end of every session. "That was very impressive."

I never know what to say to that.

But the Duchess is true to her word, and my life—aside from those hours spent in the medical room—is actually quite pleasant. I'm allowed to move about the palace freely, though Annabelle is at my side at all times. My meals are always superb, and I get the feeling that the kitchen knows my likes and dislikes. I search the library every day for Lucien, but it's empty except for the occasional maid or footman, and sometimes the Duchess's niece—Annabelle and I always avoid her. We saw Garnet once, too, but he didn't stay very long. Annabelle was blushing so badly she made me hide with her in the romance section until he was gone.

I tell myself to be patient. I tell myself Lucien wouldn't have said something like that if he didn't mean it.

Sometimes, I sit in my favorite armchair in my tea parlor, a big, overstuffed one by the window, and watch the traffic coming in and out of the Duchess's palace. Annabelle fills me in on who's who. The Countess of the Rose visits often—Annabelle tells me that the Rose and the Lake are strong allies. Apparently, the Lake used to be allied with the Stone, but they had a falling-out about thirty years ago and have hated each other ever since. That goes along with what I witnessed at that first dinner.

"Do you know what it was about?" I ask.

Annabelle shrugs and shakes her head.

Happened after D's father died

"Oh. How old was the Duchess then?"

16

Something that might be pity stirs in my chest. It occurs to me that the Duchess and I have something in common, both our fathers dying when we were young.

The red-haired Lady of the Glass is another frequent guest, though I never see her pregnant surrogate again.

The dream of escape is so enticing and so impossible, sometimes I wonder if it's just that—a dream. I hold on to it for as long as I can, but as each day passes without Lucien, it slips a little further away.

ONE AFTERNOON, ANNABELLE HOLDS OUT A PALE BLUE coat for me.

"What's that for?" I ask. "I thought it was time for my doctor's appointment."

Annabelle nods and shakes the coat a little, insisting I put it on. We don't go down the usual path to the elevator, but instead take one of the smaller staircases to the first floor. Passing the ballroom, Annabelle leads me out a back door into the garden. We walk along the neatly trimmed paths and past the hedge maze, to where the trees begin to grow dense and wild. Some of their leaves have already begun to fall, and their branches stretch and groan in the early November breeze.

The path ends at a massive oak tree. Its trunk is so thick, I could hide behind it easily without being seen. Its untamed canopy is just beginning to turn, the outer leaves tinged burnt orange and dull yellow.

"Good afternoon." Dr. Blythe steps out from behind the tree. He wears a tan suit, one hand leaning on a silver-topped cane, the other holding a small black bag. It's strange to see him outside the medical room, and even stranger without his white doctor's coat.

"Why are we in the garden?" I ask. Dr. Blythe nods to Annabelle, who curtsies and hurries back down the path.

"Well, Violet," the doctor replies, "today we are going to begin a sort of special project. Your abilities are indeed the most impressive that I have ever seen, and we have barely begun to test them. So I would like to present you with a challenge. It's good to have goals, wouldn't you agree?"

I frown, unsure of what he's getting at. "What do you want me to do?"

Dr. Blythe's warm eyes move from me to the oak tree. "Make it grow," he says simply.

For a fleeting second, I think he must be joking. I take in the tree, its myriad branches, its tough, wrinkled bark, thick, gnarled roots sunk deep into the earth. It must be very old.

I've never attempted anything like this, ever. "How?" I ask.

Dr. Blythe shrugs. "How did you make the flowers grow, and the ferns?"

"Yes, but . . ." I approach the tree warily. It's not only old, it's so *big*. I reach out and touch the rough bark. Something about this tree makes me feel like a child. It is nothing like the fragile, barren lemon tree in a dusty backyard. This oak has a presence.

I suck in a breath through my nose and hold it for a second. Then I find a crook where one of the smaller branches breaks off from the trunk and wrap my hand around it. The tree smells like dry earth and dying leaves.

Once to see it as it is. Twice to see it in your mind. Thrice to bend it to your will.

Nothing.

I haven't felt nothing since my very first Augury lesson at Southgate.

I close my eyes and focus my mind.

Come on, Violet, I tell myself. *You can do this.*

Once to see it as it is. Twice to see it in your mind. Thrice to bend it to your will.

My fingertips begin to tingle. The oak tree that suddenly fills my mind is not necessarily bigger, but full of color, its leaves more vibrant than they are now. It's in the middle of a field, a wide, empty space with nothing but the wind dancing through its branches. I don't know where this image is coming from, but suddenly, the tree *reacts*.

I gasp and hold on tight to the branch because I don't want to break this connection. I have never felt so much energy before, so much ancient, thrumming power. My body courses with it, an alternate pulse to mine. The life in this tree is so potent, so very much *there*. These are no delicate wisps of gossamer to be pulled at and manipulated, these are thick cables of heat, rooted deep in the earth. I am overwhelmed by this pure, beautiful force of nature.

Very gently, I probe out with my mind, seeing if I can isolate just the one branch. In the instant the tree senses me, pain crackles down my spine and the taste of blood fills my mouth. I cry out and fall to the ground, my hand stinging where it touched the bark.

The ground tilts beneath me, and I can hear Dr. Blythe's voice, but his words are muffled. Blood pours from my nose into my mouth, and for a terrifying second, I can't breathe. I cough it out, violent shudders tearing through my body, and stay hunched over, waiting for the dizziness to subside. I feel at once fragile, exhausted, and buzzing with unfamiliar life, and it takes me a few seconds to understand.

The oak tree is stronger than me.

The world steadies itself, and Dr. Blythe's voice becomes clear.

"Violet? Are you all right?" He hands me a handkerchief and I hold it to my nose, sitting up carefully, so as not to touch the tree.

"I'm fine," I say, but my voice shakes. My spine feels disjointed, like someone cracked every bone in it, and my head pounds but not in the usual way. It's not an ache so much as an . . . awareness. Like my brain has swelled up and my skull can't make room for it.

My nosebleed has stopped. Dr. Blythe cleans up my

face, but the pretty coat Annabelle chose for me is spattered with blood.

"What happened?" Dr. Blythe asks.

I look at the oak and try to picture the warm flow of life inside it. "Nothing," I say. "Nothing happened. I couldn't . . . I couldn't make it grow."

Dr. Blythe sighs. "I suppose I shouldn't have expected you to. Very well."

He helps me to my feet as irritation flares inside me. This is the first time he hasn't told me I was impressive. I don't *want* the compliment, but in this instance, I think I deserve it.

"Dr. Blythe." Cora comes hurrying along the path, Annabelle trotting at her heels.

"Good afternoon, Cora," Dr. Blythe says pleasantly.

"The Duchess needs to see her at once," Cora says.

"Of course. We are finished for the day."

Cora purses her lips at the sight of my bloodstained coat. "Take that off," she says. I hand her my coat, which she passes to Annabelle. She frowns as she takes in my clothes.

"Is something wrong?" I ask. I like what I'm wearing—a simple navy dress with thin straps and a loose-fitting, gray cashmere sweater.

Cora sighs. "It'll have to do, there's no time to change you. Come along." She turns to Annabelle. "I want the stains out of that coat."

Annabelle nods.

Cora leads me to the main drawing room, which is decorated in shades of blue and silver. The Duchess is seated on a couch, her niece sitting beside her. The girl looks sullen, and her dirty-blond hair is pinned up into a plain little bun. Her eyes narrow when she sees me.

"Ah," the Duchess says. "Here she is."

It's then that I notice the two other women in the room. One is obviously royal; her gown is a rich, creamy satin, diamonds hang from her ears, and her face is heavily made up. The other is a surrogate. There is a silver collar around her neck—a fine chain connects her to the bracelet around the royal woman's wrist.

My stomach twists at the sight of the leash.

"This surrogate is going to make my daughter exceptional. She will stand out as no child ever has before," the Duchess says. "An indisputable match for the young future Exetor. And you should have absolute confidence that an alliance with my House will benefit the House of the Flame, both in reputation and wealth."

This woman must be the Lady of the Flame. She owns the dairy that Ochre works at. The image of my brother comes back to me in a rush, that last dinner when he praised her House and how it treats its workers.

My eyes flicker back to the leash.

The Lady of the Flame looks me up and down skeptically. "I don't know, Pearl. You cannot be certain."

"I am."

"And what of the Houses of the Stone, and the Scales? They are also having daughters this year. So is almost every House that bought a surrogate and is lacking a daughter. My goodness, I myself am having a daughter this year, though I have no illusions about a match with the Exetor's son. But there are many who do. How can you be so sure the Exetor and Electress will choose yours?" Without pause, the Lady of the Flame turns her attention to the Duchess's niece. "Besides, *she* is not truly royal. I don't wish to put my son at any disadvantage. Our dear Exetor may survive the stigma, but my House is—"

"The blood of the House of the Lake runs in her veins," the Duchess says sharply. She doesn't look at her niece when she speaks. "She will come with the appropriate price."

"And what of my reputation?" the Lady asks. "It is spotless at the moment. And everyone knows the House of the Lake is not what it used to be."

The Duchess presses her lips into a thin line. "What exactly do you mean by that?"

The Lady of the Flame is quickly backpedaling. "Only that it is no secret that the Royal Palace favors the Houses of the Stone and the Scales. Perhaps the House of the Lake has lost some of its clout. It may be more difficult than you think to arrange a match with the future Exetor."

I take a step back at the chill emanating from the Duchess's small frame. The Lady of the Flame nervously sips her tea. The Duchess plucks a small glazed biscuit from a tray on the table next to her and turns it over in her fingers.

"I assure you, Sapphire, the House of the Lake is as powerful as ever. If some proof of my influence is needed, I will be happy to oblige." She dips the biscuit in her tea and takes a small bite.

"No, that won't be necessary," the Lady says quickly. "I didn't mean . . . I only meant . . . there is the issue of Garnet. . . ."

"You have an issue with my son?"

"Come now, Pearl, you can't pretend to ignore his behavior. It seems every other month there is some new scandal in the papers. He is simply too . . . too . . ." I watch her struggle to find a word that won't offend. "Unpredictable."

The Duchess's lips curve into a wry smile. "Well. What is life without a bit of excitement."

"But it is widely known that you are having difficulty in finding him a wife. Wouldn't it be better to wait until *he* is married before attempting to find a match for your niece?"

"Why, Sapphire," the Duchess says, and I can hear the acid in her voice, "I am touched that you care so deeply for the welfare of my family. But how I run my House is *my* business, not yours. And it is *your* son's future, not mine, that we are here to discuss."

She stands in one fluid motion and moves to my side. "Since you did not allow me to answer your question before, let me answer it now. You asked how I can be so sure that this surrogate will make my daughter stand out." She takes my arm and pulls me to a side table, where a small potted plant sits amid a collection of crystal miniatures. The plant has long stems with pale green leaves and tiny heart-shaped flowers. The Duchess looks at me expectantly. "Go on," she says. "Make it grow."

I clench my hands into fists. It's repulsive, performing for these women like a trained animal. Especially after I nearly suffocated on my own blood in the garden a few minutes ago. I feel brittle, the life of the oak tree still a fading crackle in my veins, my skin hot and tender. But the Duchess's eyes hold the warning of what awaits me if I do not obey her.

My fingers grip the stems of the plant, breaking some of them, crushing the small flowers.

Once to see it as it is. Twice to see it in your mind. Thrice to bend it to your will.

The life of the oak stirs inside me, and the plant explodes.

Thick stems crawl up the shelves on the wall, knocking china plates and glass figurines to the floor. The Lady of the Flame jumps up and backs away, pulling her surrogate with her, and the Duchess's niece is pressed against the window, her eyes wide.

The plant keeps growing.

It climbs higher and spreads out, destroying more shelves. A mirror smashes into pieces, a painting is ripped off the wall, part of its frame crushed, books are knocked to the ground. For the first time, I don't want the Augury to stop. I want to tear this whole palace down. My anger has infused the plant with a new, stronger life, and I feel like my head is on fire, each strand of hair alight with energy.

To the Duchess's credit, she doesn't move. Finally, the fire burns out and the plant stops growing. I take my hand away and swallow back the bile that is rising in my throat. The pain in my neck and back cools to a dull ache.

The Duchess turns to the Lady of the Flame.

"Satisfied?" she asks.

There is a knock on the door.

"Excuse me for a moment," the Duchess says, wrapping her fingers around my arm. My eyes land on the Lady's surrogate for an instant—the girl looks frightened of me. How strange. I give her a small smile and she stiffens and looks down as the Duchess leads me out the door.

"My, my, my," she says as we join Cora in the hallway. "That was . . . well, impressive, to say the very least. Perhaps I should give Dr. Blythe a raise. I thought Sapphire was going to faint. 'Not what it used to be,' indeed . . . idiot woman." She sighs and rubs her forehead with the back of her hand. "I am exhausted by this business, Cora," she says. "It feels as if my life is nothing but arranging marriages at the moment. I can't decide which one is proving more difficult, my niece or my son." She turns to me. "Be grateful you will never have children of your own."

I wince. She says this so carelessly, as if I've made the choice not to have children, as opposed to having it taken from me.

"How is it going, my lady?" Cora asks.

"As well as can be expected, which is to say horrible," the Duchess replies. "Has he arrived yet?"

"Yes, my lady."

"I do hope he's worth the price—they were never this expensive when I was a girl."

"I am certain you will find him satisfactory, my lady."

The Duchess sighs again.

"I may as well get this over with. Come and fetch me again in three minutes' time with some important message. We're not quite done, but I don't think I can last much longer than that."

"Yes, my lady."

"And have the kitchen send up something special for her," the Duchess says with a wave in my direction. "She's earned it."

"Of course, my lady."

The Duchess disappears back into the drawing room, and Cora turns to me.

"You will return to your chambers at once," she says curtly.

"All right."

She nods and hurries off down the hall.

I stand there for a few moments. For the first time since I've arrived at the Duchess's palace, I am alone.

~ Fourteen ~

My pulse is racing as I hurry down the hallway that ends at the ballroom.

I want to explore a little more of this palace on my own, decide for myself where to go and what to see. Several maids are cleaning the windows that look out onto the garden, and I flit past the doors, pausing in between them to make sure I'm not seen.

I pass a sunroom, keeping the sculpture gallery between me and the main foyer. An unpleasant smell tells me I've reached the Duke's smoking room. Hearing the low murmur of voices and the heavy tread of boots, I duck into a small study, peeking through a crack in the door to watch a pair of Regimentals pass by, heading toward the library.

I wait, listening to make sure they're gone, and my gaze falls on a tiny portrait of the Duchess in an oval frame, propped up on a rolltop desk.

An image comes of its own volition and I reach out a finger, gently touching a spot on the Duchess's cheek.

Once to see it as it is. Twice to see it in your mind. Thrice to bend it to your will.

Cracks of hideous green spread across her skin, replacing the light caramel color. I've never done Color so specifically before. Whether I like the doctor's appointments or not, they're certainly improving my Augury skills. I grin—now the Duchess looks as ugly as she acts.

I know it's risky, but I decide to leave it as a little token of me among all this opulence.

I slip back out into the hall, passing the library and turning left, then right. I sneak past the main dining room and find myself in a hallway I've never seen before. Made entirely of glass, it's a promenade that connects the main palace to the east wing.

At first, the east wing seems like the rest of this place. But as I move deeper into it, it becomes almost plain. The halls are painted, not papered, and the colors are dull, muted beiges and mauves. The pictures that hang on the walls are blurred landscapes in simple frames.

I keep walking east, alert. The silence is making me jittery—my own footsteps sound too loud.

"—still don't think it's fair."

An unexpected girl's voice makes me jump.

"I know, Mary, but there isn't anything you can do about it," a different girl answers.

I can't tell where the voices are coming from. I look for a place to hide, trying a door to my left, but it's locked. So is the one on the right.

"The mute is two years younger than me. *I* should have been chosen as the surrogate's lady-in-waiting."

The mute. She's talking about Annabelle.

I hurry back down the hall, trying every door, but they're all stubbornly locked.

"Maybe it won't work out with this surrogate," the second girl says. "The Electress's one is dead. And a few others, too, already. The Duchess won't use the same lady-in-waiting twice."

They're getting closer. I try to retrace my steps, but the honest truth is, I have no idea where I am or where I came from.

"I heard this one is special. The Duchess positively *fawns* over her. I was wondering if she was ever going to buy one. Can you imagine going to the Auction and coming back empty-handed for *nineteen* years?"

This brings me up short. They're talking about me, clearly, but the words are all wrong. The last thing the Duchess does is fawn over me.

"Have you seen her?" the second girl asks. I can hear their footsteps now. I reach the end of the hall and turn down another, but it's a dead end. I'm trapped. There are only two doors to try.

"Once, when I was cleaning the library. She has the strangest color eyes," the girl named Mary says.

I try the first door—locked.

"That's what I heard. Was she nice?"

My palms are slick with sweat as I reach the second door—I can't be caught. What excuse or reason could I possibly give for being here, alone and unchaperoned?

Please, I beg, *oh, please, please* . . .

The knob turns. For a second, I am too stunned to move. Then I throw myself into the room, closing the door quickly and quietly behind me.

I can hear the rustle of skirts, the clacking of heels. I press myself against the door, waiting for them to pass . . .

"How should I know? It's not as if she talked to me. *I'm* not her lady-in-waiting." Mary's voice is practically right outside.

"At least Carnelian will be married off soon. Then we won't have to deal with *her* anymore."

"That wedding can't come fast enough." Mary snorts. The sounds of their footsteps fade, and when she speaks again, her voice is distant. "Did you hear about . . ."

They're gone.

I exhale in a giant whoosh, leaning my forehead against the door and pressing a hand to my heart, willing it to slow.

"Oh, Violet," I whisper aloud. "Stupid, stupid, stupid. Never again."

Then I burst into hysterical laughter, relief making me silly. I turn and find that I'm in some sort of small parlor; there's another door opposite me and a claw-footed sofa behind a low coffee table. Late-afternoon sunlight streams through the lone, arched window and on the wall beside me, there's a large oil painting of a man in a green hunting jacket with a handsome dog at his side.

I'm still giggling when the door across from me opens.

My heart jumps to my throat so quickly I choke on it. There's no time to find a place to hide. A figure steps into the room and suddenly it doesn't matter that I can't hide, I couldn't move even if I wanted to, and a wave of dizziness washes over me.

Standing in the doorway is a boy. Not a boy, a young man—he looks to be about the same age as the Duchess's son. Tall and slender, with tousled brown hair and a strong jaw. His mouth curves a bit at the corners, like he's holding back a smile. One hand rests in the pocket of his pants and his shirt is open at the collar.

But it's his eyes that have me pinned in place. They are a soft gray-green, and they look at me in a way I haven't been looked at since I started my life in the Jewel—like I am a girl, a person, not a surrogate. And yet, it's something more than that; they look at me in a way that makes me feel hollow and strangely buzzy.

"Hello," he says. His voice is soft, musical, lovelier than any instrument—my cello would sound harsh compared to it.

He looks at me expectantly. I have no idea what to say.

"I didn't hear you come in," he says finally. "My apologies if I've kept you waiting."

I can only stare. His mouth curves into a full smile and I feel my lungs contract, making it very difficult to breathe. "It's all right to be nervous. I know you haven't been here very long. The Jewel can be a little overwhelming."

I barely manage a nod, which is better than nothing. How does this boy know who I am?

He shuts the door behind him. The room feels very small with just the two of us in it.

"Would you like to sit down?" he asks pleasantly. I don't think I can move; my lips feel like they've been glued together. I want to say something, but my brain isn't working right. All I can do is watch him, the easy grace of his movements, the curve of his mouth, those exquisite gray-green eyes. He laughs and my heart swells up like a balloon, filling my mouth and throat. "I know you haven't had a companion before, but you can speak to me. It's all right. I'm here for you."

Hope unfolds inside me, spreading through my chest and legs. He's here for *me*?

"Why?" I croak, and my cheeks flush with embarrassment at the sound of my voice.

He seems glad to have finally gotten a response out of me, though. "Didn't your mother ever explain to you about companions?"

I shake my head.

"But surely one of your friends must have had one?"

I think for a moment. "Do all companions . . . look like you?"

He laughs again, louder this time. "Not exactly, but yes."

"Then no," I reply. "Definitely not."

His face turns thoughtful. "Why don't we sit down?"

"Um, okay." I bang my shin against the corner of the coffee table as I move to sit on the sofa.

"Are you all right?" the boy asks.

"I'm fine," I gasp, trying to ignore the pain in my leg.

Am I always this clumsy? It feels like my limbs have discon-
nected from the rest of my body and don't quite know what
to do with themselves.

"Well," the boy says. "Why don't you tell me a little
about yourself?"

No one has asked me that question in so long. "What do
you want to know?"

He leans back and drapes one arm over the top of the
couch. I am hyperaware of his body, the shape of his hands
and arms, the light skin stretched over taut muscle. I wish
my cheeks would stop burning. I wish we could open the
window.

"Anything. Everything. What do you enjoy doing
most?"

"I . . . playing music."

"Really?" His eyes light up. "What instrument do you
play?"

"The cello."

"That's one of my favorites." He smiles. "You know,
I saw Stradivarius Tanglewood play at the Royal Concert
Hall last year."

Suddenly, I forget to be nervous. "You did? Live? In person?"

"You're a fan, I take it."

"A *fan*? Stradivarius Tanglewood is the most talented
cellist in the last century! He's . . . I mean, how could anyone not . . ." I can't frame the sentence correctly. *Fan* seems
like such a trivial word. I nearly wore out the gramophone
listening to Tanglewood's records at Southgate. He was an
inspiration.

"I'm surprised you didn't go," the boy says. "It was an amazing concert."

"I bet it was. Did he play the minuet in D Minor?"

The boy looks delighted. "He did. Though my favorite is the prelude in G Major. I know it's fairly simple but—"

"It's one of my favorites, too!" I didn't mean to shout— the boy looks a little alarmed. "It's, um, the first piece I ever learned to play," I add in a calmer tone.

"Perhaps he'll perform again in the next few months. I'd love to take you. Though, I must admit, I prefer Reed Purling."

My jaw drops. "Reed Purling? Are you joking? Purling is inferior to Tanglewood in every way possible! Technique, style, his phrasing is always terribly clunky, he has the emotional range of a doorknob . . ." I used to have quite a few arguments about this at Southgate with my music teacher. "It's like comparing a finely cut diamond to a piece of quartz."

The boy laughs. "I've never met a Bank girl with such love and knowledge of music." His hand crosses the small space between us and, very gently, he traces his fingertips down the side of my face. "I cannot wait to get to know you."

A riot starts in my chest, my heart pumping so loud it's embarrassing, but all I can focus on is the feel of his fingers against my skin and the way it sends a strange sort of shivery heat through my veins.

Somewhere, in the back of my mind, his words filter through into my consciousness. "What do you mean, 'a Bank girl'?"

He pulls his hand away, his gray eyes wary. "What do you mean, what do I mean? You're from the Bank."

Despair punches through my chest, clouding my vision like a fog, leaking all the color out of the room. Of course. I should have known. He thinks I'm someone else. I'm not even supposed to be here.

He studies my expression. "You're not from the Bank?"

I shake my head, my throat swollen. "The Marsh," I manage to whisper.

He jumps up like I've electrocuted him. "No," he says, shaking his head slowly. "No." He pinches the bridge of his nose between his thumb and forefinger. "Please tell me you're not the surrogate."

The word hits me like a slap in the face, and when he looks at me again, his eyes are different and I know he's seeing me the way everyone else does, the way that identifies me as what I am, not who. He doesn't see *me* anymore.

The truth is plain on my face. I can feel it there, betraying me, shouting at him that I'm forbidden, that I'm dangerous. That I'm not allowed.

"What are you doing here?" he hisses, glancing around like someone might be watching.

"I . . . I . . ."

He grabs my arm. "You need to go. Now."

Suddenly, there is a knock on the door I came through. We both freeze, identical expressions of panic on our faces. "Just a moment," he says, his voice remarkably calm, given the situation. He puts a finger to his lips and pulls me over to a closet, pushing me inside and closing the door. It's dark and smells like mothballs. I crouch low and press one eye against the keyhole.

He runs a hand through his hair, fixes his shirt, and opens the door. "Hello," he says, sounding just as light and casual as when he first spoke to me.

"Good afternoon." The voice is thin and reedy, and I recognize it immediately—the Duchess's niece.

No. He can't be here for *her.*

"My aunt is being insufferable at the moment," she continues. "I'm sorry I'm late."

"Not at all," the boy says warmly. "Please, come in."

I see a glimpse of purple fabric, but the boy's figure blocks my view of the girl as he closes the door. "Would you like something to drink?" he asks.

"No."

He moves out of my keyhole-shaped line of sight. There is a long silence.

"Aren't you going to speak to me?" the girl asks petulantly.

"Certainly. Of course. My apologies. Why don't you tell me about yourself?"

I hate that he asks her the same question he asked me.

"Aren't you supposed to say nice things to me? All my friends who had companions said they told them how pretty they were all the time."

If I hadn't been so desperately hoping for it, I might not have noticed the slight hesitation before he says, "You're very pretty."

There is a rustling of skirts and then the girl moves into view, and I can't help feeling a hint of smug satisfaction at the fact that she is definitely *not* pretty.

"Come here," she demands, and I grind my teeth together. I don't like the way she's speaking to him. The boy moves back into view. "I've never had a companion before."

"I'm aware of that. Your aunt wishes the best for your future, and so she enlisted my services."

The girl snorts. "My aunt doesn't care a diamante about me. She wants me married and off her hands as soon as possible."

The boy shrugs. "That could be true, I don't know. Her Ladyship does not confide in me."

The girl toys with a ruffle on her dress. "So . . . you're going to teach me how to be pleasing to a man?"

What? No. Absolutely not. He can't be here for *that*. Can he?

The boy's mouth curves seductively. "I am here to teach you how to make a man become pleasing to you."

I can't blame the girl for her expression, her beady little eyes widening, her mouth slightly open. "When do we start?" she asks.

He laughs. "Soon. This is just an introduction."

"Oh." She frowns as I exhale with relief. Then she holds out her hand. "I'm Carnelian, Carnelian Silver. But you probably already knew that."

Carnelian. What a stupid name.

The boy takes her hand and presses his lips lightly against it. "It is very nice to meet you, Carnelian. I'm Ash Lockwood."

Ash. His name is Ash. . . . I mouth it silently to the dark closet and smile.

"We're allowed to kiss, aren't we? My friend Chalice

had a companion and she said they were allowed to touch and kiss and everything." Carnelian watches Ash greedily, eager for him to confirm her hopes.

Did I imagine it, or did Ash's eyes flicker to my closet? "We have plenty of time to discuss the rules of my service," he says. "But I imagine it's nearly time for you to dress for dinner."

"Will you be at dinner tonight as well?" Carnelian asks.

"Yes. So I will need to change, too."

Carnelian looks him up and down. "I think you look perfect just as you are," she says, almost shyly. "Maybe living here won't be so bad anymore."

She walks to the door and waits for Ash to open it for her.

"It was very nice to meet you, Carnelian Silver," he says.

She smiles back in what I'm sure she thinks is a winning way. "It was nice to meet you, too, Ash Lockwood. I'll see you soon."

He closes the door behind her and leans his head against it, eyes closed. For an agonizing second, I wonder if he's forgotten about me. But then he strides across the room and throws open the closet door.

"Do you have any idea how difficult that was, with you in here?" he hisses.

"It wasn't my fault." I scramble to my feet but my legs have cramped and I lose my balance. Ash catches my elbow to steady me and my pulse quickens.

"Get out of here," he says. "Quickly. Don't tell anyone you've seen me or spoken to me or . . . or . . . anything. Do you understand?" For the first time, I see a crack in his facade. He seems genuinely terrified.

"Who would I tell?" I say quietly. "Nobody talks to me. Nobody listens."

I see a flash of something that might be pity in his eyes. "Get out of here," he says again.

I stumble to the door, stopping with my hand on the knob. "I don't . . . I don't know the way back."

Ash sighs. "Neither do I," he says with a shrug. "I'm sorry. I can't help you."

I stare at him for a long moment, wondering if I'll ever see him again.

"What?" he asks.

"I've never met anyone like you before," I say. Then I blush furiously—that didn't come out the way I'd intended.

But something about my words makes him laugh, a cold laugh without humor, and he sinks down onto the sofa and puts his head between his hands. "Please," he says wearily. "Just go."

My cheeks still burning with embarrassment, I slip through the door before I say something else I might regret.

Fifteen

I FOLLOW THE HALLWAYS IN A DAZE, THROUGH THE GLASS corridor, left, right, right, left . . .

Everything looks the same but different somehow. I find myself outside the ballroom with no clear recollection of how I got there. My thoughts are lost in a pair of gray-green eyes.

I take one of the smaller staircases to the second floor and run into Annabelle. Her face is panicked, her anxiety wordless.

"I went for a walk around the palace," I say, trying to sound innocent. "Is that not allowed?"

Alone?

"Yes."

NO

"Oh. I'm sorry." I hope my face looks apologetic. Annabelle presses a hand against her chest, and I notice that there's sweat beading on her forehead. "Annabelle, I'm sorry," I say, more sincerely this time.

Never w/o permission

Her writing is sloppy and slanted.

"Or I'll be punished, right?"

Annabelle shakes her head and points at herself. My stomach drops.

"*You'll* be punished?"

Annabelle nods.

"Okay. Okay, I'm sorry. I won't do it again, I promise." How selfish of me, not to have considered what might happen to her if I was caught.

The Duchess is waiting for us when we get back to my chambers.

"Where have you been?" she snaps.

"We were in the garden," I lie, adding, "in the maze." Just in case she checked and didn't see us.

She ignores my explanation.

"I am having a family dinner tonight," she says. "You will attend." She looks at Annabelle. "Have her dressed and in the dining room at seven thirty."

Annabelle curtsies.

"Does this mean I'll finally meet the Duke?" I ask as Annabelle laces me into a pale silver dress with tiny sapphires sewn into a floral pattern on the skirt.

She nods.

"What's he like?"

Annabelle shrugs and makes a face that I take to mean she doesn't find him particularly interesting. She sits me at the vanity and starts curling my hair and pinning it up.

Ash's face appears in my mind for the hundredth time in the last hour. The way he looked at me and spoke to me like a person, even for just a few minutes . . . it was like exhaling after holding my breath for too long.

I stare at my reflection—pink cheeks, tiny smile, bright eyes . . . the girl in the mirror looks truly happy, for the first time.

I've never thought much about kissing, but the idea of Ash's lips against mine—

I giggle. Annabelle gives me a curious glance and I force the smile off my face.

I know I'm being stupid. I'll never be able to kiss him. I'll probably never see him again.

"Oh!" I cry, suddenly remembering. Ash will be at dinner tonight.

Annabelle stares at me with a mix of confusion and concern.

"Oh, um . . . that pin stuck me. Sorry. I'm okay."

Annabelle bites her lip and continues pinning my hair with unnecessary caution.

It feels like my lungs shrink to half their normal size while my heart beats at twice its usual pace. By the time Annabelle dabs some scent on my wrists and pronounces me finished, I'm practically hyperventilating.

"It's perfect," I say. My voice sounds a little strangled. The dress glows against my skin like moonlight, and

Annabelle has adorned my hair with sapphire-and-pearl pins. My lips are glossed in pink, my eyes lined in pale purple, making their color stand out even more. I wonder if Ash will think I look pretty.

Stop it, Violet, I tell myself. *It doesn't matter what he thinks.*

By the time we reach the main foyer, I'm wishing I wasn't invited to this dinner. My nerves are as taut as my cello strings. When we stop outside the dining room doors, Annabelle gives me a once-over, fussing a little with my skirts.

OK?

I nod, my throat too swollen to attempt speech. Annabelle jerks her head at the door and smiles.

Great food

I laugh nervously. She nods to the footman standing at attention by the door. He opens it and announces, "The surrogate of the House of the Lake."

My stomach turns to water as I enter the dining room.

It looks the same as I remember.

Polished oak furniture, maroon walls, a candle-filled chandelier—the only difference is the company. To my left is the Duchess with two men in tuxedos. The Duchess wears a gown of deep blue silk and holds a flute of champagne delicately in her gloved hand. To my right, I see the red-haired Lady of the Glass, Carnelian, and—my heart somersaults—Ash.

It's only been a couple of hours since I met him, but he's somehow even more handsome than I remember. My whole body feels like it's blushing.

Everyone looks up when I enter, except for Ash, who is suddenly very occupied with pouring Carnelian a drink.

I had sort of forgotten Carnelian would be here, too. I note, begrudgingly, that someone has dressed her in a very pretty beaded tunic, and her hair is styled more fashionably than I've ever seen it.

"Come here," the Duchess commands me.

"So, this is the surrogate?" the taller of the two men asks. He is very thin, with coppery skin and a large nose. His eyes are dark, like the Duchess's, but round, and they study me under thick black eyebrows. He takes a sip of amber liquid from a crystal glass. "I was wondering when I'd finally get to see her."

"Oh, darling, you've been so busy," the Duchess says. "What do you think?"

The man shrugs. "You know best, my dear. She's certainly prettier than the one who had Garnet."

This must be the Duke. I don't like the way he says this, or the way he looks at me under those thick brows—it makes my skin prickle.

"My wife tells me you have big plans for her," the other man says. He is portly, the buttons on his waistcoat straining against his large stomach, and his cheeks are red.

"Yes," the Duchess says. "I have been waiting quite some time to find a surrogate like this one. My daughter will be exceptional."

"*Our* daughter," the taller man corrects her.

The Duchess smiles icily. "Quite right. Our daughter."

The door opens, and I hear the footman announce,

"Garnet, son of the House of the Lake."

Garnet swaggers in, looking more put together than when I saw him before. At least, he's not drunk this time. His blond hair is slicked back, his clothing immaculate; his tuxedo jacket fits snugly over his broad shoulders.

I look back and forth between him and Ash. They are both very attractive, but there is something decidedly natural about Ash's looks. Garnet's features are flawless—full lips, straight nose, pale skin. He could have walked out of the pages of one of Lily's gossip magazines. He looks nothing like either of his parents; I assume whatever surrogate bore him was very good at Shape and Color.

"Mother, Father," Garnet says, nodding at the Duke and Duchess and taking a proffered glass of champagne from a nearby footman. "Am I late?"

A muscle in the Duchess's jaw twitches, but just then a bell rings.

"Shall we sit?" the Duke says brightly.

I take a seat on the Duchess's right, the Duke on her left, then Garnet. The Lady of the Glass sits beside me with her husband, then Carnelian, then Ash. The result is that Ash and I are almost directly across from each other.

He doesn't look at me. His eyes seem to skip over me, as if I'm not even there. Like I'm invisible.

The pain of this is a sharp, physical thing, almost like the aftermath of an Augury, except it's not my head that feels like needles are being shoved into it. I try to focus on arranging my napkin in my lap.

I shouldn't be feeling like this. It's stupid. I don't even know him. What does it matter if he looks at me or not?

A servant places a salad of spinach, beets, and goat cheese in front of me, but for the first time since Dahlia's death, I have no desire to eat. My mouth feels like sandpaper.

"Pearl," the Lady of the Glass says as another servant fills her wineglass, "your niece was telling me the most charming stories about living in the Bank. Did you know she actually *helped* with her father's printing press? Imagine!"

The words sound sincere, but the tone is off—I get the impression that the Lady and the Duchess are sharing some sort of private joke at Carnelian's expense.

Red blotches of embarrassment appear on Carnelian's cheeks. "Only one time," she says to her aunt. "When his apprentice was ill."

"Well," the Duchess says, "I'm sure it was very character-building."

The Lady of the Glass hides her laugh in a sip of wine.

"I see you finally got a companion for her," Garnet says to the Duchess through a forkful of beets. He wipes his mouth with a napkin and extends his hand to Ash. "I'm Garnet, by the way."

Ash shakes his hand politely. "Ash Lockwood."

"He's a looker, isn't he, cousin?" Garnet says to Carnelian, waggling his eyebrows at her. "How much is he costing you, Mother?"

The Duchess's nostrils flare, but Ash cuts in smoothly.

"Carnelian was showing me the library before dinner," he says. "You have the most extensive collection I've seen, my lady. It's very impressive."

"Thank you, Mr. Lockwood," the Duchess says.

"Yes, my wife does have the most remarkable preoccupation with the past," the Duke says. "I must admit, I don't understand it at all."

"I wouldn't expect you to, darling," the Duchess murmurs. "The only books you read are the ledgers."

"Someone must look after the finances," the Duke replies with a significant glance at the Lord of the Glass. "Isn't that right, Beryl?"

"Oh, quite, quite," the Lord says with a wink.

"The House of the Lake is one of the four founding Houses," the Duchess says sharply. "My ancestors helped build the Great Wall, without which this island would have long ago been destroyed by the sea. I am a direct descendant of the first Electress, who founded the Lone City and created the five circles, including our beloved Jewel. It is not simply my honor but my *duty* to preserve the literature of their time. Of course, I suppose I understand why it might not be of interest to those whose bloodlines do not extend back that far."

The Lady of the Glass shifts uncomfortably, and her husband busies himself with his salad. The Duke's hand tightens around his fork.

"Oh, come on, Mother, don't belittle Father for climbing up the social ladder," Garnet says, taking a huge gulp of wine and waving a footman over to refill his glass. "You would have done the same if you were born to the House of the Glass."

"Thank you, son," the Duke says tersely.

Carnelian pipes up. "Mama always said it isn't who you

are but what you do that is important."

"Your mother said a great many things," the Duchess snaps. "And none of them need be repeated at my table."

An icy silence settles over the room. I shovel a couple of beets into my mouth just for something to do. I think the last dinner was preferable to this one. At least Raven was there. And Lucien.

"Did you hear," the Lady of the Glass says, leaning forward, almost across me, to the Duchess, "about the Lady of the Locks?"

The Duchess perks up. "What about her?"

"You know she just bought her first surrogate this year?" The Duchess nods. "Apparently, she takes her around *everywhere*!" the Lady exclaims. "On shopping excursions, to luncheons, she even brought her around my house for tea. I can't imagine what she's thinking."

"How embarrassing," the Duchess says. "Do you think she's trying to show off?"

The women burst into malicious laughter. The Duke, the Lord of the Glass, and Garnet are engaged in a debate over a new tax the Exetor plans to levy on the Farm, and Carnelian is prattling away about her plans for the weekend to Ash. I feel incredibly lonely.

"What lot did she end up with?" the Duchess asks.

"102," the Lady of the Glass replies.

"102? And she parades her around like she was in the top ten?"

"I know. Someone should speak to her."

"It's not as if safety is an issue, I suppose—I can't imagine anyone who matters bothering with the surrogate of a third-tier House. It's just a lack of class."

"Perhaps she's trying a new strategy to gain the Electress's attention," the Lady of the Glass suggests, and the two women begin laughing again.

"She's having a daughter, too, I suppose?"

"Of course. But I can't believe the Exetor would ever consider an alliance with the House of the Locks."

"Speaking of," the Duchess says, "did you get your dress for the Exetor's Ball?"

"I did. I was so afraid the Electress might make him cancel it after the whole business with her surrogate. What a disappointment that would be!"

I grit my teeth at the casual mention of Dahlia's death. I wonder if the Lady of the Glass knows that she's speaking to the woman who was responsible for it. I doubt she'd even care.

The footmen clear our plates and serve the next course, lamb with mint jelly and roasted potatoes. The food is delicious, but I can't enjoy it. I'd rather be eating in my rooms with Annabelle than listening to these women talk about surrogates as if they are pets or a new pair of shoes.

My eyes keep wandering to Ash, and I really wish they wouldn't. It's like they're on a mission to notice as much about him as possible. The way he sometimes smiles like he's keeping a secret. How his eyes almost seem to change color, shifting from gray to green. He is patient as he listens to Carnelian, never looking bored or interrupting. His fingers curl around his wineglass and all I can think of is how they felt against my skin. What is wrong with me? He's just a boy. Just an incredibly good-looking boy who knows music and talked to me like a person for a few minutes and made me feel all buzzy and . . .

I take a drink of wine.

"Of course, the Electress isn't the only one who's suffered a loss." The Duchess's words bring me back to the present. "Did you hear about the Lady of the Bell?"

"Yes," the Lady of the Glass murmurs. "I heard they found her surrogate in the bath, drowned. She's completely out of the running for a match with the Royal Palace now. She'll have to wait another year before she can even buy a new surrogate."

The Duchess shrugs. "It serves her right, not protecting her home as she should. One must be extra careful in times like these." She takes a bite of lamb. "Anyway, that's why I never have my surrogate take baths. You can't drown in a shower, can you?"

"Oh, has surrogate hunting season started?" Garnet calls from across the table. His cheeks are flushed, and his eyes are bright when they meet mine. "Better watch your back, new girl. This year is bound to be vicious, what with the precious little Exetor's hand at stake."

The blood drains from my face, and because I'm too aware of him, I see Ash's shoulders tense. The Duchess stands up and slams her palm down hard on the table, making everyone jump.

"You will leave this table at once," she says in a voice so cold I feel the temperature in the room drop a few degrees.

Garnet drains the last of his wine. "With pleasure," he says, standing up and giving the Duchess an overly elaborate bow. Then he turns on his heel and marches out the door.

There is a chilly silence. The Duchess remains standing. The muscles in her jaw clench and unclench, like she's trying to work out what to say.

"Everyone knows how patient I have been over the years," she announces to no one in particular. "I have taken many measures to ensure the safety of my surrogate. *Nothing* will happen to her. I will not allow it."

I feel like she's talking to me without actually talking to me. As if it would be embarrassing to try to comfort me in front of other people.

Dessert arrives and I try to enjoy the cheesecake with fresh raspberries, but I keep wondering how many other surrogates have been killed since the Auction. My thoughts flicker between Raven and Lily.

"Tell me, Mr. Lockwood," the Duchess says. "How long have you been a companion?"

I stare at my fork and listen very hard.

"Three years, my lady," Ash replies. "Since I was fifteen."

"In which circle were you born?"

"The Smoke, my lady."

My head whips up. The Smoke? I assumed he was from the Bank or the Jewel. But from one of the lower circles . . . we sort of have something in common. The thought sends a warm feeling through my chest before I remember I'm not supposed to care.

"Which Quarter does your family live in?" the Duke asks.

"The East, my lord."

"Why, we own several factories in the East Quarter. What did you say your surname was?"

"Lockwood, my lord. But my father makes cabinets at Joinder's Woodworks."

"That's a House of the Stone subsidiary, isn't it?"

"Yes, my lord."

"Darling," the Duchess says, "we must see if we can find this young man's father a more suitable employ at one of our own factories."

"Your Ladyship is very kind," Ash says, but there is a tightness around his eyes.

"I was saying to the Lady of the Glass earlier, it is remarkable that natural conception still has the capacity to produce such . . . excellent results. Your mother and father must be a very handsome couple." The Duchess is staring at Ash with a rather hungry look in her eye as she takes a long sip of wine.

The Lady of the Glass quickly changes the subject. "Carnelian, darling, tell me, what lot number was the surrogate your mother used for you?"

The question seems to make Carnelian uncomfortable. "She didn't care about the rankings. She always said she just wanted me to be healthy."

"Well," the Lady of the Glass says, "I'm sure she got the best she could afford."

"Beryl, all this surrogate talk should be left to the ladies, don't you agree?" the Duke says to the Lord of the Glass. "What do you say to a brandy in the smoking room?"

Just then, the door bursts open and James, the butler, bows his way in.

"Forgive me, Your Ladyship, but an urgent message has arrived from the House of the Glass." He turns and bows to the Lady. "Your surrogate is in labor."

"Oh!" the Lady of the Glass exclaims. "But she's not due for two more weeks."

There is commotion all around as servants pull back chairs and rush to get coats and the Duke and Duchess offer congratulations.

"It will be fine," the Duchess assures the Lady of the Glass. "Garnet was two and a half weeks early and he turned out . . . well, he was healthy, at any rate. You must take my car back, it's faster."

"Oh, thank you, thank you!" the Lady of the Glass gushes, kissing the Duchess's cheek. Her husband and the Duke shake hands, then the couple hurries out the door.

"My dear," the Duke says, "I believe I will retire."

And without even looking at his wife, he strides out of the room.

The Duchess sinks into her chair. "That will be all for tonight," she says with a wave of her hand. "Get out."

I'm only too happy to oblige.

Ash, Carnelian, and I file into the hallway. A maid in a black dress and white apron is waiting for Carnelian, but Annabelle is nowhere in sight.

"Your lady-in-waiting will be back shortly," the maid says, and I recognize her voice from the east wing—the girl named Mary. "She is attending to Garnet in the library."

"Oh," I say. "Thank you."

"How was your dinner, miss?" she asks Carnelian.

"Horrible," Carnelian grumbles. "Can Mr. Lockwood escort me back to my room?"

"That would not be appropriate," Ash says, taking her

hand and kissing it. "But I will see you tomorrow."

Carnelian smiles and allows her maid to lead her away.

The hallway is empty except for the two of us.

Ash realizes this at the same time I do, and he takes a step back, like he doesn't want to be too close to me. I don't know what to say, but I want to say *something*. He starts to walk away, then turns back.

"It's always like that for you, isn't it?" he says. "It's always been like that for the surrogates. I've just never noticed before."

I open my mouth, but before I get a chance to ask him what he means, Ash whirls around and disappears down the hall.

Sixteen

"Does it really need to be quite so tight?"

I was informed a few days after the family dinner that I was to attend the Exetor's Ball with the Duchess and her family. I didn't think going to a ball would entail not being able to breathe for an entire evening.

Annabelle rolls her eyes and finishes tying the strings of my corset. I trace the hard boning with my fingers—I've never worn one before, and I definitely won't miss the experience.

Annabelle turns me away from the mirror and helps me into about a thousand petticoats, then holds up a pile of glittering fabric. Carefully, so as not to muss my hair, she negotiates my way into the dress. She steps back to admire her work, and claps her hands together.

"Can I look now?" I grumble. Preparing me for the Exetor's Ball has taken several hours, and I'm ready to be done with it. Annabelle laughs silently and turns me to face the three-sided mirror.

"Oh!" I gasp. "Oh, Annabelle . . ."

The dress is lavender slashed with gold, the full skirt falling gracefully to the floor, the bodice tight over the corset, which, I grudgingly admit, accentuates my figure. Perhaps a little too much—it's like my body has been squeezed upward, so that I'm showing a bit more skin than I'm used to between the capped sleeves. My hair has been curled and pinned so that it tumbles over one shoulder, and I'm wearing more makeup than usual, especially around my eyes.

Annabelle's face appears over my shoulder, beaming.

"Oh, don't look so smug," I say, but I can't help smiling, too. "The Duchess will be very impressed."

Annabelle leads me to the main foyer, where the fountain twinkles happily in the evening light. Ash and Carnelian are already there, and I can't stop my heart from jumping at the sight of him.

"I didn't realize *you* were coming," Carnelian says. Her pink dress is fancier than mine, with lace sleeves and a much fuller skirt.

"I didn't realize *you* were coming," I shoot back.

Ash doesn't look at me, but his lips twitch.

The Duke and Duchess arrive, Cora trailing behind them.

"We're late," the Duchess says, without any sort of greeting. "Where is Garnet?"

She looks sternly at each of us, as if we might be hiding him in our pockets or something. Then she lets out an exasperated sigh. "I don't even know why I bothered asking. Come."

Her midnight-blue gown gleams under a velvet cloak, and one gloved hand is twined around the Duke's arm as she steers him out the door. Annabelle ties my own cloak around my shoulders as Ash does the same for Carnelian.

"Where is Garnet?" I whisper. Annabelle grins and shrugs.

Two motorcars are waiting in the driveway. The air is chilly, the sky a deep, inky blue, and I pull the cloak tighter around me. The Duke and Duchess move to the first car, and Cora directs me, Ash, and Carnelian to the second one.

The ride to the Royal Palace seems to take forever. Carnelian and I sit next to each other, Ash on the opposite seat facing us. I stare very hard out the window and try to tune Carnelian out as she asks about this palace or that, or giggles at things that Ash says. But he is always there, in the corner of my vision, a black-and-white outline that I can't erase or ignore.

The palaces are even more incredible at night than they were during the day—soft colored lights make them glow like jeweled candies. The Royal Concert Hall is luminous, all pale pink and gold. Ash mentions the Stradivarius Tanglewood concert to Carnelian, who makes me cringe by asking, "Who?"

When we reach the forest, and there is no light other than the motorcar's headlamps, I look up at the sky. Hundreds of thousands of stars are nestled in the darkness.

I remember that night when I looked up at this sky and took comfort in the thought that Hazel and I would always be under it together. I wonder if she's looking at it now. I hope she is.

It occurs to me then that I'll be seeing Lucien again tonight. What an idiot I am, not to have thought of it sooner. All these stupid thoughts about Ash have completely taken over my brain. I shake my head a little, as if that will actually clear it. I need to be focused. I *will* find a way to talk to Lucien. Alone.

We pass through the topiary, the hedge-creatures dotted with hundreds of tiny white lights, and emerge out onto the square with the fountain in its center.

The Royal Palace glows like liquid fire, its domes and turrets and spires searing the darkness, casting a red-gold light across the square. The driver stops at the broad steps, where footmen wait to open our doors and offer their assistance. Ash, Carnelian, and I follow the Duke and Duchess up the stairs to the open front doors. Another servant takes our cloaks, and a footman leads us down a gold-carpeted hallway hung with enormous oil paintings. I hear the faint strains of music coming from somewhere close by.

I can't wait to see Raven, too. It's been nearly a month since the last time I saw her, at Dahlia's funeral. It feels like ages ago. She must be here with the Countess of the Stone.

We reach a set of ornate double doors, which the footman opens with a flourish. Another servant, an old man with a large staff, stands just inside. He bangs the staff on the floor three times and announces loudly, "The Duke and Duchess of the Lake."

The ballroom is packed with men in tuxedos and women in brightly colored dresses, their skirts swirling as they cross and recross, spin out and turn in, dancing to the waltz being played by a small orchestra on an elevated platform on the far side of the room, in front of a wall of windows. At the other end, the Exetor and Electress sit side by side in matching thrones. They are such a strange pair—she looks like a little doll beside him, beaming and laughing, while he sits stone-faced, a wineglass clutched in one hand.

The Duchess leads the way through the groups of men and women clustered around the dance floor, many of whom bow or curtsy to her. The Duke takes two flutes of champagne from a passing waiter and hands one to his wife. I see the coffee-skinned Duchess of the Scales eyeing my Duchess. The iced cake stands beside her, docile and silent. I search for Lucien and Raven. The Countess of the Stone is huge, I should be able to spot *her* easily. . . .

The ballroom is lit by an enormous chandelier with glowglobes hovering in the air around it, like planets revolving around a jeweled sun. The walls are papered in gold and copper and bronze, and the floor is a jigsaw of polished wood. Another waiter passes with a tray of champagne, and Ash takes two glasses, one for him and one for Carnelian.

"It's incredible," Carnelian says, gazing up at the ceiling. "Have you been here before?"

"A few times, yes," Ash says. There is a hint of something in his voice, sadness maybe, or regret, and I wonder what memories this hall brings back to him.

"I've always wanted to go to a ball," Carnelian gushes, oblivious. "But my aunt has never allowed me before."

"That is why I'm here," Ash says. "You needed an escort."

"Garnet escorted me to a party once, for the Longest Night," Carnelian says. "In the Bank. It wasn't anything near as nice as this."

I continue to look for Lucien or Raven, also keeping an eye out for any trays of canapés that might pass by—I bet the food here is outstanding. The Duke has disappeared, and the Duchess is in deep conversation with the Countess of the Rose.

The music shifts.

"Would you care to dance?" Ash asks Carnelian.

She turns bright red. "I-I'd love to," she stammers.

Ash leads her out onto the dance floor. I feel an irrational surge of anger as I watch him wrap his arm around Carnelian's waist, their faces inches apart.

The Duchess isn't paying any attention to me, so I grab a glass of champagne and take a large swallow. Bubbles fizz in my nose.

Another couple is announced at the door. I can't hear their names, but the woman leads a surrogate on a leash. Before entering the ballroom, though, she takes it off and hands it to the footman. I turn away—I've had enough of those leashes to last a lifetime.

There are other young couples dancing, and many of the boys are very handsome; I wonder if they're companions, too, or just surrogate-enhanced royalty. I study the crowd. The royalty hold themselves with a casual arrogance, their eyes darting around the room as though looking for a better conversation, or someone to gossip about.

The surrogates are easy to spot—we all stand mildly to the side of our mistresses, looking uncertain and out of place. The lioness is close by, her braided hair fashioned into an elegant crown. Her eyes narrow at the glass in my hand and I quickly down the rest of my drink and set the flute on a passing tray. I notice the iced cake staring dreamily at the dancers on the ballroom floor. But I still can't find Raven or Lucien.

The Duchess's conversation suddenly catches my attention.

"Soon enough," she's saying to the Countess. "Dr. Blythe has been very pleased with the test results so far."

The Countess laughs. "Yes, Sapphire is telling anyone who will listen about her last visit. I heard your surrogate destroyed quite a collection of glassware."

The Duchess shrugs. "Trifles, really, nothing that can't be replaced. And certainly worth it. I hope the tale reaches the appropriate ears."

"I overheard the Duchess of the Scales saying to the Lady of—"

"Alexandrite is of no concern to me," the Duchess says dismissively. "She is not truly of a founding House, and she only married the Duke two years ago. No, it is Ebony I am worried about."

Ebony—that's Raven's mistress. I move a little closer to the Duchess, listening hard.

"Yes, she's being very secretive," the Countess agrees. "Not a good sign."

"It will be fine as long as my daughter is born first," the Duchess says. "That is the most important factor. It cannot be overlooked. She will be unique even as she takes her first breath. The Exetor will not be able to ignore that."

"And what of the Electress?" the Countess asks.

"In the end, it is not her decision to make," the Duchess replies. "It is his. And no matter how she lies, and parades herself around, and pretends she is equal to us, she is not, and never will be." The Duchess turns, her gaze sharp and chilling as it falls on the Exetor in his throne. "Remember this, Ametrine. No one knows him like I do."

The Countess of the Rose shifts uncomfortably. I feel awkward, too, like the Duchess is having a private moment and I'm intruding.

"Tell me," the Countess says, changing the subject. "How are the marriage arrangements going?"

The Duchess groans. "Which one? The House of the Downs should be giving me an answer this week. At least Garnet comes with a title. Carnelian . . ." I follow their gazes to the dance floor, where Carnelian is looking hopelessly uncoordinated in Ash's arms. "I mean, there is simply no upside to her, is there?"

"The companion you procured for her is *quite* agreeable," the Countess says. "One of the best I've seen in years."

The Duchess smirks. "Oh yes, quite." She has that hungry look in her eye again as she watches Ash; it makes me uneasy. For lack of anything better to do, I steal another glass of champagne and gulp half of it down. My head feels pleasantly light. A tray of crackers with cream cheese and smoked salmon comes my way and I pop one in my mouth while the Duchess's attentions are focused on the dance floor. I keep the champagne flute hidden in the folds of my dress.

The dance finishes, and Ash leads Carnelian back over to us.

"Oh, what fun!" Carnelian gushes. "Mr. Lockwood says we will work on my dancing skills this week."

"A wise idea," the Duchess says dryly.

"You two make a very charming couple," the Countess says, barely concealing her sarcasm.

I can't help rolling my eyes. For a second, I swear I see a flicker of amusement cross Ash's face, but then he turns to address the Duchess.

"I wonder if you might give me the honor of a dance, my lady?"

The Duchess accepts and Ash leads her out onto the floor.

Perfect. It's bad enough seeing him with Carnelian, but watching him dance with the Duchess is creepy. I drain my glass just as the lioness raises one to her lips—she's stolen a flute of champagne, too. I raise an eyebrow. She shrugs and takes an enormous swallow.

Suddenly, someone crashes into me, followed by a burst of raucous laughter. I drop the glass and nearly topple into Carnelian. Some of the pins come loose in my hair; several curls tumble down my back.

"Oh!" I cry, the champagne making me even more unsteady.

"Garnet," the Countess of the Rose snaps.

Garnet's bow tie is askew, his cheeks flushed. It looks like he's gone through quite a bit of champagne himself already. He's with four other boys his age and, by the looks of it, all equally as intoxicated. They attempt to appear sober before the Countess, but don't quite pull it off.

Garnet, on the other hand, doesn't even try. "My sincerest apologies, Your Ladyship," he says with an elaborate bow. "I didn't see you there."

"Really, is it so difficult to behave yourself?" the Countess asks. "Don't you think your mother has enough on her mind?"

"You mean my impending nuptials? Or lack thereof?" Garnet laughs and turns so he's in profile. "Who would have thought that this"—he indicates his face—"would be so difficult to sell?"

Carnelian grins. "You are a pig," she says.

"And you, cousin, are a public relations disaster, but who's counting?" Garnet grabs a glass of champagne. "I will bet you ten thousand diamantes that she finds a match for me before she finds one for you."

Carnelian's face falls. "I don't have ten thousand diamantes."

"True." He turns to his friends. "Let's get out of here before Her Royal Ladyship gets off the dance floor. There's a garden out back."

"Garnet," one of his friends says with a quick nod in my direction. "Aren't you going to apologize?"

"For what?" Garnet asks. His unfocused gaze falls on me. "Oh, that's just my mother's surrogate. Come on."

They push their way through the crowds, their laughter carrying over the music. I touch the back of my head where the pins came loose.

"Is everything all right here?" a familiar voice asks. I whirl around to find Lucien, smiling pleasantly. I open my mouth, but he moves his head just a fraction, and I quickly snap it shut.

"Garnet has just been his usual charming self," the Countess replies. "He seems to have upset this surrogate."

"Oh dear," Lucien says, examining my hair. "How embarrassing. Not to worry, I'll fix her up as good as new before the dance is finished. You," he says sharply, and I jump. "This way."

I follow him through the crowds, keeping my head down and trying to look as meek and unassuming as possible. Lucien leads me out of the ballroom and down a hallway, keys jangling as he unlocks the door to a small powder room. One whole wall is mirrored, and there is a sink and a stone counter littered with makeup and hairpins and perfumes.

"Lucien!" I cry as he shuts the door. "Where have you—"

Lucien puts a finger to his lips and I purse mine together. He takes the tuning fork off his key ring and taps it on the counter; it rises in the air, humming faintly. Then he smiles at me.

"You look stunning."

I can't help smiling back, just a little. "Thanks. I've been checking the library for you. Where have you *been*?"

"It is unwise to meet in the same place twice in the Jewel," Lucien says.

"Were you serious about getting me out of here?" I press.

"Yes. But there's no time for answers now." Lucien studies my hair, lifting the stray curls. "I had a whole plan worked out to get you alone, but the Duchess's son and his ghastly manners offered me a better opportunity."

His eyes meet mine in the mirror and he holds up another tuning fork, like the one that's revolving in the air right now. Very carefully, he secures the fork in my hair and pins up my curls to cover it. "Hide it when you return to the palace. You will need it tomorrow at midnight," he says softly in my ear. "Now, let's return you to your mistress."

He puts the other tuning fork back on his key ring and I follow him silently to the ball, dazed by the turn of events and dizzy at the thought of a secret hidden in my hair.

Seventeen

The Duchess is still on the dance floor with Ash when we return to the ballroom.

"Go back to the Countess and wait for your mistress," Lucien instructs me in a sharp, commanding tone, now that we're in public. I nod, and watch him wind his way through the crowd toward the Electress. When he reaches the royal podium, the Electress beckons him toward the throne. He leans down and she whispers something in his ear. I wonder what she's saying to him.

"Violet?"

I jump at the sound of my name, spoken in a hoarse, whispered voice. Raven stands half hidden behind a pillar, in a beautiful scarlet gown with golden bracelets glittering on her wrists.

"Raven!" I gasp, moving quickly and cautiously to her side.

"Shhh," she hisses. "She can't know I've left her."

She jerks her head over her shoulder. I see the enormous back of the Countess of the Stone, talking with a woman I recognize as the Lady of the Flame. "I've been looking everywhere for you," Raven says.

Once I get over the shock of seeing her, I notice how thin she is. Gaunt, even, her cheekbones more pronounced, and there are dark circles under her eyes.

"Are you all right?" I whisper.

Raven smiles, her lips stretched tight across her face.

"You look beautiful," she says. "Just the way I remember you." Her gaze becomes unfocused. "Do you know, sometimes I wonder if I imagined my life at Southgate. Do you ever feel that way?"

"No," I say. "What are you talking about?"

But Raven doesn't seem to hear me. "There was another girl. She was our friend. She was pretty and silly and she had blond hair. What was her name?"

A lump forms in my throat. "Lily," I say. "Her name was Lily."

Raven sighs. "Yes. Lily. I think I was mean to her sometimes."

She rubs one of her arms absentmindedly, and I see that the golden bracelets are actually handcuffs, attached to each other by a fine, linked chain.

"What are those?" I say, aghast.

Raven's smile is frightening. "She doesn't like me very much. I told her I wouldn't give her what she wants. She thinks she can take my memories away, but I won't let her. I won't forget you. I promise, all right? I won't forget you."

"Raven, you're scaring me," I say.

"You won't forget me either, will you, Violet?" Raven says, backing away.

"No," I say, tears springing to my eyes. "Never."

Raven hurries to her mistress's side just as the Countess of the Stone turns to take a canapé from a passing tray.

A hand wraps around my arm and I jump.

"I thought you'd have found your way back to your mistress by now." Lucien appears at my elbow, a warning in his eyes. "Please allow me to assist you."

I follow him, my mind reeling with the images of Raven's gaunt face, the golden cuffs around her wrists, her insistence that I don't forget her.

"Here she is, my lady," Lucien says, and I blink—we're back with the Countess of the Rose and Carnelian. "Good as new."

The dance ends and the couples begin to leave the floor. The Duchess and Ash will be here any moment. But I can't seem to pull my face together.

"Here," Lucien says, grabbing a glass from a passing waiter. "Have a refreshment. There's no need to look so embarrassed. Everything will be all right."

There is an edge to his voice, and I hear the double meaning in his words and wonder if he knows about Raven, but then he bows and disappears into the crowd.

"You certainly know your way around the dance floor,

Mr. Lockwood," the Duchess says, laughing as they join us again.

"As do you, my lady," Ash replies.

Carnelian pouts a little. The Duchess's gaze sweeps the crowd. "I suppose I should find my husband. Ametrine, let us talk again before we leave."

"Of course," the Countess says.

The Duchess glances in my direction, and I'm grateful for the champagne—it gives me something to do with my hands, and an excuse to hide my face. And it explains the flush in my cheeks and the brightness of my eyes. She snatches the flute out of my hands.

"You do not drink without my permission," she says sharply, handing the glass to a waiter. Suddenly, there is a loud banging, and the music dies down. The Electress and Exetor stand and the crowd falls silent, the men bowing and the women sinking to the ground. My skirt billows around me as I curtsy, my corset poking uncomfortably against my hips.

"We thank you for attending our annual ball," the Exetor says, his voice carrying over the packed room. "You are dear to our hearts and crucial to the continued survival of our great city. We raise our glasses to you in thanks."

The Exetor and Electress raise their flutes—the Electress's smile looks a little forced. The crowd straightens up and follows suit.

"This year is sure to be a very exciting one for our family," he continues. "May I present to you all . . . my son and heir, the future Exetor."

A nurse in a white cap appears in between the Exetor and Electress, holding a baby in her arms. He is dressed in cloth-of-gold with rubies and pearls sewn into the fabric. His tiny face is scrunched up, and as the royalty begin to clap and cheer, he starts to wail, one long, sustained note. The Exetor gives the nurse a sharp look, and the baby is whisked out of the ballroom, his cries fading into the applause.

"Now, let us have some entertainment!" the Electress says. "There are so many new surrogates here this evening. Shall we see whose is the most talented?"

It's amazing, the royalty's ability to ask a question without it really being a question at all. Maybe this is why the Duchess gave me the cello—not as a gift or a reward, but in preparation for some sort of surrogate competition. I glance at her, worried she'll volunteer me, but her eyes are fixed on the Exetor.

"Mine is a dancer, Your Grace," the Duchess of the Scales calls out. "The best I have ever seen." The iced cake, beside her, turns pale.

The Electress laughs gaily and claps her hands. "Wonderful! Clear the floor."

I feel pity for the girl as she is escorted to a section of the dance floor just in front of the royal podium. The crowd surges forward to get a better view. The iced cake's blond ringlets tremble, her eyes darting to her mistress, who nods sharply. I don't want to think about what might happen to her at home if she doesn't perform well.

The girl stops at the edge of the dance floor and removes her shoes. Then, to a chorus of gasps and cries of shock, she unties her skirt and lets it fall to the ground, standing in only her petticoat and bodice.

"Oh my!" the Electress exclaims.

The Duchess of the Scales seems pleased by the attention. "It's the only way she can dance, Your Grace," she says. "Otherwise, the skirt is too long."

The Electress giggles. "I see. Does she require any particular music?"

"No, Your Grace," the Duchess replies with a superior smile. "She can dance to anything."

The Electress calls to the orchestra. "Play a nocturne."

A lone violin starts, a string of melancholy notes quickly joined by a second violin, viola, and cello. I can't help noticing that the viola is just slightly out of tune, the A string a hair sharp.

The iced cake closes her eyes, lifts her arms above her head, and begins to dance.

She is beautiful. I've never seen anyone move with such graceful fluidity—it's like her bones are made of rubber, able to bend and stretch and create shapes that surely no normal body is capable of. I feel like she's telling me a story with every spin and jump. In a strange way, it reminds me of how I feel playing cello.

The song ends, and the iced cake curves into a delicate final position. The Electress begins to clap. Quickly, the crowd joins in and I can't help clapping myself—watching the iced cake was like being in a dream that wasn't quite my own, and I enjoyed it immensely.

The iced cake sinks into a curtsy, then quickly collects her shoes and skirt and joins her mistress.

"That was stunning," the Electress says, and the clapping stops abruptly. "Wasn't it, my darling?"

"Stunning," the Exetor agrees.

"I can't imagine anything more pleasing." The Electress smiles at the Duchess of the Scales, who flushes with pleasure and curtsies. "Alexandrite, I think you may have acquired the most talented surrogate in the entire Auction."

"I would have to disagree with that, Your Grace."

A large intake of breath comes from the crowd, and a cold shiver of fear creeps up the back of my neck. The Duchess of the Lake is still staring at the Exetor, her black eyes glittering in the light of the chandelier. I see the hint of a smile form on his lips.

If the Electress notices this subtle exchange, she doesn't show it. On the contrary, she looks delighted. "Really? You think your surrogate can outshine Alexandrite's?"

The Duchess is practically radiating smugness. "I am certain she can."

"Oh, I do love a good competition. She must perform at once, don't you agree, my darling?"

The Exetor taps a finger against his wineglass. "What is her skill, Pearl?" he asks.

Something flickers in the Duchess's eyes. "She plays the cello, Your Grace."

The Exetor nods. "Take her to the stage," he commands to his footmen. An iron claw grips my arm.

"Do not disappoint me," the Duchess snaps, and then, almost as an afterthought, adds, "please."

I'm marched toward the orchestra, sensing the crowd's eagerness at the challenge, their twisted desire to watch me fail. The stage comes closer, and I trip on my skirts as I'm pulled up the stairs—I hear a smattering of laughter and my cheeks burn.

A man with a gray mustache passes his cello to me with reluctance. I take it, wrapping my fingers around its polished wooden neck, and hold out my other hand for his bow.

I take a deep breath and turn to face my audience. The Exetor and Electress have left their podium—they stand at the foot of the steps, no more than ten feet away. The Duchess is just behind the Exetor's right shoulder, the Duke at her side. Carnelian and Ash stand together close by. And behind them, a mass of faces, all turned toward me, all eyes in the room watching my every movement. The bow trembles in my hand. I've never played in front of this many people before. My imaginary audiences in the Duchess's concert hall were always friendly and encouraging. Gingerly, I sit on the edge of the chair, adjusting my skirts so that the cello rests comfortably between my knees. Its shape relaxes me a little, and I lean its neck on my shoulder.

"Do you have a preference for composer, Your Grace?" the Duchess asks, though whether she's talking to the Exetor or the Electress, I can't tell.

The Electress answers. "I should very much like to hear whatever she enjoys playing the most."

There is some murmuring from the crowd, and I see a few women smirk, but I don't know how that's meant to be offensive, and at the moment, I don't really care. I have to play my best. I take another deep breath and think.

Whatever I enjoy playing the most . . .

In a flash, the entire scene before me changes, because I know exactly what I want to play and I'm not afraid anymore.

The prelude in G Major. The first piece I ever learned. I'm sure the Duchess would rather I play a more modern, complicated piece, something to impress or intimidate. But the prelude reminds me of Raven, and Lily, and all the girls who came with me on that train. It reminds me of the dining hall at Southgate and my tiny bedroom and a cake with Hazel's name on it, of a time when laughter meant something, and of friendship and trust.

I draw my bow across the strings and begin. The notes fall effortlessly over one another, a waterfall of sound, and I leave this ball and float away to a simple music room that smells like wood polish, and the only faces watching me are those of girls who wish nothing more than to hear me play. And not because I'm gifted, not because it makes me different or special in any way, but because I love it. The memories burn inside me like a candle flame, and the bow flies across the strings, the notes climbing higher and higher and I feel free, really free, because no one can touch me in this place, no one can hurt me, and as I draw the bow across the final fifth, a chord that reverberates throughout the cavernous room, I realize that I am smiling and a tear trickles down my cheek.

The room is silent.

I look up and meet a pair of gray-green eyes, no longer soft but blazing. Ash doesn't look away, and neither do I. His gaze is fierce, and open, and it makes me feel alive. He isn't looking at a surrogate—he's looking at *me*.

Then the Exetor begins to clap. The applause is picked up, and soon the noise is deafening, but I feel oddly removed from the situation; the clapping is muffled in my ears, because a glint of gold has caught my eye, and I see the only face that could pull me away from Ash's.

Raven.

She stands out so clearly among the sea of faces, her gold-chained hands pressed against her chest, and she looks happy, truly happy. Our eyes meet, and I cross two fingers on my right hand, and press them against my heart, the symbol of respect from the surrogates of Southgate and a sign that, no matter what, I will never forget her.

Eighteen

THE BALL GETS WILDER AS THE NIGHT GOES ON.

Champagne flows, the dancing becomes more energetic, and the laughter and chatter reach deafening levels.

The Duchess receives many congratulations on my performance, which is ridiculous since *she* didn't do anything. Every time I see Raven, she is firmly attached to the Countess of the Stone's side, head down, chained hands clasped in front of her.

The heat from all the dancing bodies, combined with the champagne, begins to make me dizzy. The Duchess is on the dance floor with the Duke. I've lost track of Carnelian and Ash, and Lucien is involved in conversation with several footmen. Garnet and his friends are laughing and eyeing a group of girls. I need some air, see a door by the wall of windows, and slip through it.

The cool air makes my skin prickle, and I inhale deeply— or as deeply as I can in this stupid corset. I run a hand across my forehead. It is so nice to be alone for a moment.

I'm in a little garden with a fountain at its center. Two shadowy figures are on a bench on the far side, twined around each other. A tall hedge juts out on my right, and I quickly slip around it, out of sight of the couple and away from the noise and laughter of the ball.

The moonlight sparkles off a small pond, with a gazebo behind it. It is so quiet here, so peaceful. I crouch by the water, careful not to get my skirt wet, and tap the glassy surface with my fingertip. The moon's reflection dances as ripples spread out in a circle, growing wider, almost lazy, until the water is smooth again.

"Hello," a voice says.

I nearly fall into the pond. Scrambling to my feet, I see him, Ash, sitting in the gazebo, half illuminated in pale silver, half in darkness—he's taken off his tuxedo jacket, and the sleeves of his shirt are rolled up.

"Hi," I breathe.

For a few seconds, we just stare at each other.

"What are you doing back here?" he asks.

"I . . . I don't know. I was hot. It's loud in there."

"Yes. It is." He looks down. "You shouldn't be here."

"No," I say. "Probably not."

But he doesn't tell me to leave. And he doesn't move.

"That was incredible," he says, his eyes meeting mine again. "I've never heard music played like that before."

"Oh," I say. Too late I add, "Thank you."

"They don't understand," he says, glancing in the direction of the ballroom. "They think your music is *owed* to them. As if their money gives them a right to it."

"Doesn't it?" I say wryly.

He stares at me, his expression hard to read. "No," he says.

"Well, I'm no Stradivarius Tanglewood," I say, trying to lighten the mood. "Or Reed Purling, either, I guess."

Ash looks away, his face turning thoughtful. "I've never done that before, you know. Disagreed with a client. It's not permitted."

"Then why did you disagree with me?"

"I'm not sure. I just . . ." He sighs. "I felt like telling the truth, I suppose."

"You make it sound like such a terrible thing."

"In my profession, it is."

"My profession seems to entail not talking at all," I say. "So you can tell me the truth whenever you want. I can't tell anyone anyway."

"A good point." Ash grins. "The truth is . . . I hate avocados."

I laugh. "What?"

"Avocados. I hate them. They're slimy and they taste like soap."

"Avocados do not taste like soap." I laugh again. "I hate this corset," I say, poking it hard with my finger. "Why aren't the men all forced to wear stupid contraptions like these?"

"I don't think the Duke would pull it off as well as you," Ash replies.

I blush. "I don't pull it off half as well as most of the women in there."

"Don't compare yourself to them," he says sharply. I freeze, startled. He blinks. "I'm sorry. I am so sorry, I—"

"It's fine," I say. "I wasn't." I stare back at the palace. "I'm nothing like them," I murmur.

"No," Ash agrees. "You're not." His words sting like an insult until he adds, "And I mean that as the highest form of compliment."

"How many times have you been here?" I ask.

"To the Royal Palace? This will be the twelfth occasion in which I have had the honor of an invitation."

I can't help smiling. "You don't have to sound so polite. I'm just a surrogate, remember?"

Ash smiles back. "Habit, I guess." He pauses. "That did sound pretty ridiculous, didn't it. Sometimes I don't think I even hear myself anymore. I'm not sure anyone really listens to me anyway."

"I do," I say quietly.

Silence falls. And still, he doesn't move.

"What were you thinking about?" he asks. "When you were playing. It was like you were somewhere else."

"I was imagining that I was back at Southgate—that was my holding facility—and I was playing for the girls there. They liked to listen to me practice."

He stands up. I feel like our moment is ending, and I don't want it to. Suddenly, words start pouring out of my mouth.

"If you ever want to listen, you know, to music, well . . . sometimes I play in the concert hall. Not, I mean . . . just for amusement, not an actual concert or anything but . . ." My voice trails off.

Ash runs a hand through his hair, his expression frustrated. He leaves the gazebo and walks toward me until he is standing so close that the heat from his body radiates against my bare skin. My fingers itch to touch him, to trace the lines of his face and run my hands over his chest. I want him to touch me, too, to press his lips against mine and bury his hands in my hair. The desire is overwhelming and irrational, and I love it.

"Why were you in my room?" he demands. "What were you doing there?"

"I—I got lost," I say.

"You got lost," he repeats, but the way he says it, it's like he means something else. His eyes burn into mine, then he shakes his head, and without another word, turns and leaves me breathless and alone.

I WAKE UP THE NEXT MORNING WITH A POUNDING HEADache.

"Oh," I moan, pressing a hand gingerly to my forehead. My mouth is dry, and tastes terrible. I shouldn't have drunk so much champagne.

Before I ring for Annabelle, I rifle through one of the drawers of my vanity and take out a small, enameled jewelry box, where I hid the tuning fork last night while Annabelle was hanging up my gown. It has a secret, second compartment, and I dump out the earrings and bracelets and pendants and pop the bottom out. The tuning fork is nestled against the velvet lining—I reach out and stroke it with one finger. I don't know what is going to happen tonight at midnight, but I'm eager to find out.

I put the bottom back in, replace the jewelry, and bury the box in my drawer. Then I ring for Annabelle.

I feel better once I've eaten breakfast. Annabelle and I spend a quiet day in my rooms. She beats me at Halma a few times, and I pretend to read for a while, but my mind keeps bouncing back and forth between the memory of Ash at the gazebo and the promise of the tuning fork at midnight.

Suddenly, the door to my tea parlor is thrown open so forcefully that it smacks against the wall. Annabelle and I jump as the Duchess walks in, flanked by her guards.

"Get out," she orders Annabelle, who wastes no time leaving the room.

The Duchess glares at me.

"I have treated you well, haven't I?" she asks.

"Y-yes, my lady," I stammer.

"And your life has been pleasant, as I promised, hasn't it?"

I nod, trying to figure out what I've done wrong. Does she know about Lucien? Did she see me talking to Ash?

"So please explain to me why one of the maids found *this*." She tosses an oval object onto the coffee table.

It's the portrait I changed with Color. The painted Duchess's skin is still a sickly green. Everything inside me shrinks and tightens, and when I look up, I can feel the guilt on my face.

"I . . . I . . ." I have no defense.

"You what?" the Duchess purrs. "Did you think this was funny?"

I shake my head.

"Have you defaced any other pieces of my property?"

She's so calm. Sweat beads in my armpits.

"No, my lady," I whisper.

The Duchess raises an eyebrow. "Let's find out if you are telling the truth."

I've been so focused on her, I haven't been paying attention to the Regimentals. Two of them yank me out of my chair and force me to my knees, while another one pushes my head onto the coffee table next to the painting and holds it there. There is pressure on my ankles, like someone's stepping on them. I've been incapacitated in less than thirty seconds. It is entirely disorienting.

I can only see what's directly in front of me, and the Duchess disappears from view for a moment. I struggle against the men holding me, but it just sends a sharp pain shooting down my shoulder, and the pressure on my head and ankles increases.

The Duchess returns, holding my cello and a silver-headed hammer. I feel like I'm pitching forward into nothingness, like the floor has disappeared beneath me. I am weightless with shock.

"Have you defaced any other pieces of my property?" the Duchess asks again. I try to shake my head, but the hand holding me is too strong.

"No," I say. I can't take my eyes off that hammer. "No, my lady. I swear I didn't."

The Duchess considers this for a long moment. "All right," she says. "I believe you."

Then she smashes the belly of my cello with the hammer. A gaping hole splinters open in the beautiful, varnished surface, and the strings make a sad, discordant whimper.

"No!" I cry, but she raises the hammer again, bringing it down over and over, cracking the bridge, ripping into the body, yanking the strings loose so they hang free and wild, pieces of wire stripped of their beauty. The Duchess beats my cello until it is unrecognizable. Then she drops the remains casually on the floor.

My vision is blurred with tears, so I don't see what gesture she makes, but suddenly my left arm is wrenched out over the coffee table and pinned at the wrist, my fingers splayed across the wooden surface. The Duchess kneels down so that her face is almost level with mine.

"I want you to remember what I said about disrespecting me," she says. She presses the cold face of the hammer against my knuckles. I can't help the tiny sob that escapes my throat. I want to be brave, but I don't know how. The fear is so potent, so *real*.

The Duchess raises the hammer and I brace myself for the pain.

The hammer stops less than an inch away from my fingers.

"If it happens again," she says. "I will break your hand. Are we clear?"

My body is quivering from head to toe, my breathing ragged. "Yes," I whisper. "Yes, my lady."

The Duchess smiles, drops the hammer next to the remnants of my cello, and walks out.

THAT NIGHT, WHEN VELVETY DARKNESS BLANKETS MY room, I sit in bed, turning the tuning fork over and over in my hands.

I can't see the clock over the fireplace, so I have no idea what time it is. Not that it matters. I'm not sure I could fall asleep anyway. For the thousandth time, I rub the knuckles on my left hand. I can still see the raised hammer, still feel the paralyzing fear. I have to remind myself that it didn't happen. I have to keep telling myself that I'm all right.

The tuning fork starts to vibrate. I'm so surprised, I drop it—it falls onto my comforter with a tiny thud, then rises into the air, revolving slowly and emitting a faint hum. I gape at it, unsure of what to do, when I hear a voice.

"Hello?"

"Lucien?" I whisper. "Where are you?" He sounds distant, like he's speaking to me from the end of a long tunnel.

"In the Royal Palace," he says. "Where else would I be?"

"But . . . but . . . how?"

"I call them my arcana. I invented them. They will allow us to speak in secret without being overheard or monitored."

I examine the tuning fork closely. "So . . . we're speaking through this thing?"

"Yes. I have the master. Yours responds to mine. They form a connection." He pauses, then says, "But we have more important things to discuss."

The hair on the back of my neck prickles.

"Can I assume that you are willing, if not eager, to escape the Jewel?"

"Yes."

"Consider this: If caught, you would surely be executed. You may be putting your family in danger. Can you accept that?"

I rub my knuckles again. Am I willing to risk my family's safety for my own? I don't know. But I can't say no to Lucien, not now. "Yes," I say in a hushed voice. "When?"

"I am currently developing a serum that will put you into a coma so deep, it will give you the appearance of death. No one will question it—surrogates often die of medical complications. Or get assassinated by a rival House, as you well know. The Duchess has plenty of enemies who would love to see you dead."

I feel dizzy. "Is it safe?"

"Let me be clear: Nothing about this plan is safe. But if you agree to it, you must also agree to do whatever I say. Any instruction I give, you must follow, regardless of whether you like it or not. Do you understand?"

"Yes," I say.

"Good. The Winter Ball for the Longest Night is being held at the Royal Palace." The Longest Night is the oldest holiday in the Lone City. It takes place in mid-December, still several weeks away. "I will give you the serum then. The following night you will take it. Once you are pronounced dead, you'll be transported to the morgue, where I'll recover your body and hide it on a train scheduled to bring supplies to the Farm. When we arrive in the Farm, I will take you to a safe place."

"Where?" I ask. I can't imagine any place in the city being truly safe from the royalty.

"I cannot tell you that—it's too dangerous for you to know. Now, listen to me very carefully. While you are in the Duchess's palace, you will obey every rule she gives. Not only that, you will be a model surrogate. You will be obedient and submissive. I don't want to hear about any more portraits changing color or shelves being smashed, is that clear?"

I open my mouth to protest, but Lucien keeps talking.

"She *must* believe you are on her side. You have to make her trust you. It is our best chance of getting you out as quickly and safely as possible."

"Fine," I say grudgingly.

"I know it's hard, honey, but I *promise* you—I won't let you down."

"Violet," I say.

"I'm sorry?"

"My name," I say. "It's Violet."

"Violet," Lucien repeats, and I hear a smile in his voice.

I twist the comforter in my hands. "Why are you helping me?"

There is a long silence.

"Something had to be done," he says. "No one deserves this life. No one deserves to have their choices taken away."

I think about Raven, handcuffed at the Exetor's Ball, promising not to forget me.

"Lucien," I say, "I'll do whatever you ask with no complaints, but can you do something for me?"

There is a pause before he replies. "What do you want?"

"At the ball last night, I saw my best friend. Another surrogate. And I was wondering if . . . if you could find out anything about her. Where she is or how she's doing or . . . anything. It would mean so much to me."

I hold my breath, waiting for a response. It takes a long time to come.

"What House is she in?"

I exhale. "The House of the Stone."

"The House of the Stone?" Then, to my surprise, Lucien begins to laugh.

"What?" I ask, hurt.

"I'm sorry," Lucien says, his laughter dying at once. "It's just . . . the Countess of the Stone's estate lies on the western border of the House of the Lake."

It takes a second for his words to sink in. "Wait . . . are you saying . . ."

"I'm saying," Lucien says kindly, "that your friend is living next door."

∼ Nineteen ∼

RAVEN IS NEXT DOOR.

That, even more than Lucien's escape plan, is in the forefront of my mind when I wake in the morning.

All this time, she's been so close.

"I'd like to go to the garden," I say when I've finished breakfast. Annabelle nods and chooses one of my warmer dresses and a coat with a fur collar. We head outside into the November chill.

The air is crisp and smells deliciously of late fall. A few dried brown leaves still cling to the branches of the trees that line the paths, but most of them have fallen. They crunch under my feet as I walk toward the west wall, in the opposite direction of the great oak tree.

Annabelle sits on one of the benches and opens a book. I wander into the wilder part of the garden, just off the path, so I'm partially hidden but still nearby.

My breath makes a white mist in the air as I stare up at the barrier that separates me and Raven. If only there was a way I could talk to her. If we had a pair of arcana, or some kind of sign, a smoke signal, anything to show her that I'm close. If I could, I'd climb up the ivy-covered walls and shout her name.

Then it hits me. The ivy.

I wrap my hand around a slender length of it, feeling the hard knot where a leaf must have died and fallen off.

Once to see it as it is. Twice to see it in your mind. Thrice to bend it to your will.

I feel the life of the vine, and pull at it—a tiny shoot sprouts in my hand. It pokes through my fingers, and begins to climb up the wall. The threads of life in this vine are pliable, easy to manipulate, willing to grow as I ask them to. I barely notice the sharp sting of pain as invisible needles begin to bore into the base of my skull. It is so easy to remain focused.

The image in my mind is clear, and my hand grows hot against the cold air as I push the vine farther and farther up the wall. My back begins to ache, but I won't let go until I've finished.

The vine reaches the top of the wall and I force it farther still, weaving it between a pair of evil-looking spikes, concentrating hard, the image in my head so close to the surface. I make all the tiny strands of life come together, twisting and writhing and forming a flower, whose petals unfold in a rich circle of color.

I've created a violet.

A drop of blood falls from my nose and splashes on the ground, leaving a dark stain. The violet sways in the breeze, innocuous yet full of meaning. I hope Raven sees it. I hope she understands it's from me.

I wander around the wilder part of the garden before slowly making my way back to Annabelle. She closes her book and stands up when she sees me, nodding toward the palace.

"Time to go?" I ask.

Time for Dr.

"HELLO, VIOLET," DR. BLYTHE SAYS WHEN I ARRIVE IN the medical room. "How was your weekend?"

Be obedient and submissive, I remind myself.

"Fine, thank you. How was yours?"

He laughs. "Oh, typical really, nothing exciting. Now, I assume you remember our goal from last week?"

I nod. "You want me to make that tree grow."

"Yes."

"I'm not sure that's ever going to happen." The life of the oak—it's too strong.

Dr. Blythe shrugs. "We'll see." He sticks the electrodes all over my body and brings the screen down from the ceiling.

But this time, instead of handing me an object for the first Augury, he takes a syringe from the tray of instruments and attaches a large needle to it. My mouth goes dry.

"What's that for?" I ask.

"You are very talented, Violet, and I do truly believe your abilities can produce and sustain the results the

Duchess and I are working toward. But we are on a very tight schedule. This will help speed things up. Please remove your robe and lie facedown on the bed."

"What—what are you going to do?"

"Lie down, please," Dr. Blythe says again.

I can't swallow—it takes all my energy to make my legs move, to stand and turn around. I let my robe fall from my shoulders and lie down on the crisp white sheet that smells like lemon and ammonia. My skin shrinks away from the doctor's touch as he places a hand on my lower back. I realize he hasn't put an electrode there this time.

"I want you to take several deep breaths, Violet. Relax." He must be seriously deluded if he thinks I'll be able to relax right now. But I take the deep breaths anyway. "Good. It's better if you stay still—I'm afraid this will hurt."

The next second, the needle sinks into me and my lower back is on fire. I scream, and the doctor presses his hand down, trying to hold me still; instinctively, I wrench my body away and white-hot agony rips down my spine.

Then the pain is gone.

"There we are," he says. "All done."

Tears spill over my eyelids, making dark spots on the white sheet. My body is limp, my breath coming out in shallow pants.

Dr. Blythe spreads something cool across my lower back and says, "The potential in surrogates is unlimited. But sometimes you get in your own way—doubt, anger, and fear can affect your abilities, either positively or negatively. Thanks to modern medicine, we've found a way to stabilize that. So today, we are going to get our first glimpse of what you're really capable of." The excitement in his voice makes me nauseous. "Please stay just as you are."

I don't think I could move if I wanted to; it's like my limbs belong to someone else. I hear the sounds of a jar being unscrewed, the clinking of glass and metal.

"All right." The doctor comes into view. In one hand, he holds a strange silver object, almost like a gun, but in place of the barrel, there is a glowing white cylinder. "This is called a stimulant gun. It will stimulate the Auguries and help us unleash your full potential."

He presses something into my hand and I see that it's a seed, about the size of an acorn. "Can you feel it?" he asks. "The life inside?"

Of course I can. It's like a tiny heartbeat, as light and fast as a hummingbird's wings.

"Yes," I whisper.

Dr. Blythe's warm green eyes turn sad. "Excellent," he says softly.

He raises the gun and presses the glowing cylinder against my spine where the needle went in.

I think I scream. I can't be sure.

The pain is everywhere. It consumes me. A bouquet of needles explodes inside my brain. My veins are filled with razor blades that rake through my body with every beat of my heart. My eyeballs are on fire. My skin burns.

I can feel the seed react. It breaks open in my hand and begins to grow at a tremendous rate, but I can't see anything because my vision is blurred with tears. I hear a metallic crash and a sharp snapping sound. Something hot and wet pours out of my nose and drips into my mouth. I choke on the taste of my own blood.

Then, it stops. I gag and sputter, coughing up blood and saliva.

"There, there," Dr. Blythe says, wiping my nose and eyes with a soft, wet cloth. "There, there . . ."

He walks away, and I hear him tapping on the screen. "You may sit up whenever you are ready," he says.

It's a while before my breathing returns to normal. I come back to my body little by little, feeling the sheet under my skin and my hair tickling my neck and shoulders. Very slowly, I roll onto my side, then push myself up into a sitting position.

The entire medical bed is covered in thick green vines that outline the shape of my body. The tray of silver instruments has been knocked over, the more delicate tools snapped in pieces. Vines crawl up the pole that connects the screen to the ceiling. Part of the sheet is stained red with my blood. I can still sense the vine's life inside me. My body feels battered, bruised from the inside out, and my head throbs.

"You did very, very well," Dr. Blythe says, handing me the robe. I'm afraid that if I speak, I might throw up. "I just need to take a blood sample, and then we're all done for the day."

I barely feel the pinch of the needle in my arm.

I thought this man was sort of like a friend. How could I have been so stupid? He works for the Duchess. He doesn't care about me at all.

Dr. Blythe finishes drawing my blood, then stares around him at the vine-covered medical room.

"Never in all my twenty-nine years as a physician have I ever seen anything like this," he murmurs.

I want to wrap one of the vines around his throat and strangle him with it. But Lucien's voice whispers in my ear. *You will be a model surrogate.*

Even so, I can't stop myself.

"I hate you," I say quietly.

Dr. Blythe's eyes are sad again as he meets my gaze. "Yes," he says. "I imagine you do."

I SPEND THE REST OF THE DAY, AND THE FOLLOWING ONE, in bed.

The slightest movement hurts. My bones feel brittle, like they've been turned to glass. Annabelle brings me tea and soup, but I don't have much of an appetite.

I will be obedient, I keep telling myself. *I will not complain. And I will get out of here.*

A few days later, I'm recovered, though my lower back is still sore. Annabelle and I are sitting on my bed, playing a game of Halma before turning in for the night, when there is a knock on the door and the Duchess enters.

I can't remember the Duchess knocking on a door, ever. Least of all my door.

"Leave us," she says. Annabelle collects the game and hurries out, with one quick, worried glance in my direction.

The Duchess's dress glitters in the light of the dying fire as she moves to sit on the sofa. She looks exhausted. When she speaks, her voice is quiet, almost gentle.

"Please," she says, resting a hand on the empty space beside her. "Sit by me."

The sofa is so small that our knees are only a few inches apart when I sit down. The smell of her perfume makes my stomach turn.

The Duchess smooths out her skirts. "I have been trying to go about this the right way, and I am not sure . . . I am having difficulty . . ." She shakes her head and smiles. "It is not often that I find myself at a loss for words. You are very important to me. Sometimes, I have a problem with my temper. I apologize for that."

I can't think of anything to say. For some reason, this strange, soft-spoken Duchess unsettles me more than the cold, angry one.

"I envy you," she confesses. "Your . . . abilities." She must see the incredulity in my eyes, because she laughs. "Oh, you may not believe me, but it's true. We all envy the surrogates. Do you not think that, if I could do this myself, I would? I have wealth, yes, and a title and power. But you have a power I do not. *I* cannot create life."

I remember the lioness's words, at Dahlia's funeral. *We make their children. We have the power.*

"So we turn you into property," the Duchess continues. "We parade you around and dress you up and make you our pets. That is how the Jewel operates. Status is our sole occupation. Gossip is our currency." She gives me a piercing look. "You can do this, you know. I read the doctor's report, I saw the results of the stimulant gun. Your abilities are far beyond what I had even dared to dream. Do you have any idea what we will accomplish together? We will make history, you and I."

It is so hard to hold back the retort, not to snap at her

that she has absolutely no role in this process except to provide an embryo. We are not doing anything *together*.

The Duchess studies me, as if she can read my thoughts.
"I've angered you," she says.

I take a breath before answering. "I just don't understand, my lady," I say carefully. "This obsession. Being first.
Why not just have a regular baby in a regular time?"

Her eyes grow distant as she stares at the embers of the
fire. It's quiet for a while. "I was meant to be the Electress,
you know," she says softly.

My eyes widen.

"I was a month old when the arrangement was made,
sixteen when it was broken. The Exetor and I . . . we were
very close. It was a perfect match. A founding House and
the future Exetor. My life was meant for greatness." She
looks younger somehow, vulnerable, and I think I see something glisten in the corner of her eye. "My life was meant to
be happy," she whispers.

"What happened?" I ask tentatively.

The Duchess shrugs. "Men cannot be trusted. You are
lucky you will never have to discover that for yourself." She
sniffs and plays with a charm on her bracelet. "What was
your life like? Before Southgate, I mean. Was it happy?"

I don't want to share that with her. I don't want her
touching any part of who I was before I came here.

"Yes, my lady. It was very happy."

"Tell me about it."

I look past her into the fire and pretend I'm in the sitting room at Southgate, talking to Raven. "I have a younger
brother and sister. I used to take care of them when my

parents were working. My sister and I liked to play tricks on my brother." That should be enough.

"I had a sister, too," the Duchess muses. "Carnelian's mother. We did not get along."

I frown. "I thought the royalty could only have one boy and one girl."

"Yes. But occasionally, twins do happen. Usually it's the simple matter of terminating one, but my darling mother wasn't strong enough to make that decision and my father indulged her." Her mouth twists, like she's tasted something unpleasant. "You loved your mother, I imagine."

"I still do."

The Duchess smiles a broken, half smile. "Of course." She looks at me with an unfathomable expression. "All I want is for my daughter to be happy," she says. "I will do anything to give her a better life. Is that such a terrible thing?" She laughs, and there is no edge to it, no sharpness. "I sound awfully sentimental, don't I? My father must be turning in his grave."

Abruptly, she stands, and the softness falls away, replaced with the rigid mask I'm accustomed to. "I wish for you to feel at home here. As such, you will no longer require an escort while within the palace. Your new cello will arrive tomorrow. I hope you find it satisfactory." She sweeps to the door and pauses with her hand on the knob.

"Hope is a precious thing, isn't it," she says. "And yet, we don't really appreciate it until it's gone."

She closes the door behind her, and I sink back against the couch, wondering what exactly just happened.

Twenty

My cello arrives the next day, as promised.

Though I don't tell Annabelle about my conversation with the Duchess, she already knows that I don't require an escort around the palace anymore. When I tell her I'm going to play in the concert hall, she simply smiles and nods, and continues changing the sheets on my bed.

I play for twenty minutes or so, but my mind isn't focused on the vibration of the strings or the movement of the bow. That stimulant gun made the doctor and the Duchess very happy—too happy. I should ask Lucien about it next time we speak.

I wonder if that's what Raven meant when she asked me if I'd seen a doctor yet. Is the stimulant gun the cause of her hollowed eyes? Is she being tortured with it in the House of the Stone?

I have to check on my violet. I need to know it's still there for her.

I leave my cello on the stage and hurry downstairs and out the back door into the garden. I didn't bring a coat, and the wind whips my hair around my face and slices through the thin fabric of my dress. I make my way to the west wall and stare up at the violet, swaying in the breeze.

My breath catches in my throat. There's another flower wrapped around it. A lily, but instead of white, its petals are jet black.

Hope ignites in my chest. Raven saw my violet.

And now, I think as I send a second violet up to join the first, *she knows I'm close.*

I GET BACK TO THE CONCERT HALL AS QUICKLY AS I CAN.

Lucien probably wouldn't approve of me sending flower messages to my best friend, but I don't care. No one else could possibly know what it means, or that it even means anything at all. And now I know Raven is all right.

I breathe in the scent of velvet and floor polish. The cello fits snugly between my knees, and I play a few scales, just to make sure it's still in tune.

I start with a sarabande in D Minor, then a courante in the same key, then another sarabande in F Major. As long as I'm playing, my mind is still. I don't have to think about the pain Dr. Blythe caused me or the demands the Duchess has put on me. As long as I'm playing, I'm not a surrogate. I can simply be.

I remember what Ash said, the night of the Exetor's Ball. How the royalty acted like they owned my music. As if they could ever *own* this.

As I finish the sarabande, a soft clapping begins and I look around, startled.

Ash stands offstage, just behind the curtain, and for a second, I think he might be a figment of my imagination. He stops clapping and puts his hands in his pockets.

I should leave. I need to leave now. I *cannot* talk to him—not out in the open here where anyone can see.

But my cello makes a tiny thump when I set it down, and my satin slippers whisper across the stage as I join him. The choice isn't a conscious one—it comes from a place in me without logic or fear.

It's warm and dark behind the curtain. We are so close, it's like someone has spiked my veins with adrenaline. I feel lightheaded. My skin tingles.

"What are you doing here?" I ask. He wears a collared shirt with the sleeves rolled up. I have the strongest urge to run my fingers over his forearms.

"I wanted to see you play. I thought I was invited." He sounds nervous.

"Oh." My verbal skills seem to disappear when he's around. The foot of space between us feels charged with electricity. "Right. Did you like it?"

"Very much."

He takes a step toward me and I'm surprised I can't see tiny sparks of light exploding in the air around us. This is wrong, I know this is wrong, but at the moment, I can't seem to remember why.

"I . . . I . . ." He shakes his head and looks down. "I can't stop thinking about you," he confesses.

We are so close, the hem of my skirt brushes the tips of his shoes. "Really?" I ask.

He laughs. "And I thought I was being obvious."

"I—I don't have much experience with this."

"No," he says softly. "I don't imagine you do."

"None, actually," I admit.

"To be fair, I don't have much experience in this particular area, either."

I frown. "Isn't this what you do with Carnelian?"

As soon as I say her name, I wish I hadn't. A shadow passes across Ash's face.

"You don't know what you're talking about," he says.

"I just thought—"

"That I seduce every woman I see?" he asks wearily.

"No," I say. "It's just . . . I've seen you two together."

His eyes blaze the way they did at the Exetor's Ball, like gray-green fire. "Do you ever obey an order from the Duchess even though you don't want to?"

"All the time."

"And have you ever disobeyed her?"

I bite my lip, thinking of the ruined cello on my bedroom floor.

"I know. There are consequences." His fingertips dust across the back of my hand. "Do you want me to leave?"

Be a model surrogate, Lucien whispers.

"No," I reply.

A tiny smile lights up Ash's face. "May I ask you something?"

My heart is so swollen I think it might burst. I inhale his scent of soap and clean linen and something that must be boy. "Anything."

"What is your name?"

My heart explodes into a million glittering fragments that rain down like fireworks through my chest.

"Violet," I whisper.

He closes his eyes and breathes it in, like it's the answer to a riddle or a secret key. "Violet," he murmurs. Then his mouth is on mine.

I feel entirely new. Ash's lips are gentle, moving with mine in unfamiliar, exciting ways, and I discover a new Violet, a Violet I never imagined existed. How can my body contain all these feelings? It's like I didn't really know myself until this moment.

Ash pulls away, tenderly cradling my face in his hands, his forehead resting against mine. "This is dangerous."

"Yes."

"It's not safe here."

"No," I agree, though whether he's referring to the concert hall, or the palace, or the Jewel itself, I'm not sure.

"Can you meet me in the library in fifteen minutes?"

I feel like I could meet him on the moon if he asked me to. "Yes."

"Be at the last stack on the east side by the windows. Look for Cadmium Blake's *Essays on Cross-Pollination*."

I laugh at his bizarre instructions. "What?"

He grins. "Trust me." Then his face turns solemn. "Think about this carefully. It's your choice—I'll understand if you decide not to come."

I nod, and he disappears out the backstage door.

To meet him in the library would not only get me in trouble with Lucien, but if the Duchess found out . . . I don't even want to think about what would happen. Something very, *very* bad. I shouldn't do it. I told Lucien he could trust me. I promised him I would behave.

But all I do is follow orders. Whether they're the Duchess's orders or Lucien's or the doctor's, I'm never in control. And if I'm going to run away and hide for the rest of my life, well, first I'm going to do one thing for me. Call it selfish or disrespectful or stupid—I don't care. At least I can look back on this—on being with Ash—and say *I* made a choice.

I'm giddy as I take my cello back up to my chambers.

The sky has darkened, and the fires have been lit against the cold November winds—two footmen are lighting the lamps when I arrive at the library. They bow to me before continuing with their work. Ash said the east wall, all the way toward the windows—the easiest route is to cut through the central reading area. I'm so aware of myself as I walk out into the wide circle of armchairs, the way my arms move, the length of each step.

And then I stop short, jerked back to reality by a familiar, pungent scent that makes my nose wrinkle.

The Duke is sitting in one of the chairs by the crest table, puffing on a cigar, a ledger open in his lap, a glass of amber liquid on the table beside him. His eyes are red-rimmed and he makes a notation in the ledger, muttering something that sounds like "frivolous woman." I freeze. I've never seen the Duke in here before.

He looks up. "Oh. It's you."

I don't know what to say, so I make an awkward curtsy.

He takes a long pull on his cigar, blowing out a cloud of foul-smelling smoke. "Well?"

My eyes widen a fraction. *Well what?*

He laughs. "You aren't very smart, are you?" He taps the cigar against a crystal ashtray, then waves his hand in the air. "Aren't you here to get a book?" he asks a little too loud, like I'm a child who doesn't understand his language.

"Y-yes, my lord," I stammer.

"Get on with it, then." He downs the rest of his drink and turns his attention back to the ledger. I curtsy again and head directly into the stacks, heart racing, eager to get away from him. Of all the days he had to come here.

I'm shaking as I get to the east wall and follow the shelves all the way to the windows. This tiny corner of the library is deserted, and I can see why. All the books look incredibly dull, dissertations on plants and animal husbandry and methods of irrigation. I wonder why the Duchess even has books like these. I run my fingers over the titles until I find the one I'm looking for: Cadmium Blake's *Essays on Cross-Pollination.*

"You're late."

I jump. Ash is leaning against a shelf on the other side of the aisle. His arms are folded across his chest, a playful expression on his face.

"Hi," I breathe.

He grins and pushes off the shelf, taking a few steps toward me. "You didn't have any trouble finding the place, did you?"

"No, I just . . ." I make a face. "I ran into the Duke."

"Yes, I thought I smelled his vile cigars." Ash grimaces. "One of these days, I believe the Duchess will murder him in his bed."

I laugh, but he doesn't, so I stop. Is he serious?

"So, um . . . what are we doing here?" I ask. It's a secluded place, sure, but still . . . there's the Duke, and the footmen lighting the lamps, and anyone else who feels like borrowing a book to be worried about. The concert hall was actually more private.

His mouth pulls up into a sort of crooked, half smile. "Can you keep a secret?"

I have to laugh. "Yes," I say. "I can keep a secret."

He joins me at the bookshelf and, with exaggerated care, pulls at the top of Cadmium Blake's *Essays on Cross-Pollination* so that it tilts at an angle. The entire shelf swings open, revealing a dark space behind it.

Glowglobes hang from the ceiling, illuminating walls of plain, rough stone. A tunnel curves out of sight just ahead of us.

I can feel the blank shock on my face, and quickly snap my gaping mouth shut. "Where does it go?" I whisper.

Ash takes my hand, and I feel a jolt of excitement. "Come on," he says, pulling me forward and closing the bookshelf behind us.

He presses a finger to his lips and squeezes my hand, leading me down the tunnel, which winds and curves so that I lose all sense of direction—sometimes, other tunnels branch off the one we're on.

At some point, we begin to climb, then the light stops

ahead of us, and I see a smooth wooden door with a heavy iron handle.

Ash turns the handle and dull gray light leaks into the tunnel. He motions for me to go first.

I recognize the parlor immediately. It's the place where Ash and I first met. I remember the claw-footed sofa, the low coffee table, the armchair by the lone window. The window looks out onto the lake, but from a different angle than my room. Tiny rivulets of rain run down the panes of glass.

A quiet snap makes me turn. Ash has closed the secret door, which is hidden behind the oil painting of the man in the green hunting jacket with the dog at his side.

I glance at the two visible doors. One I remember sneaking in through. Does that mean the other one leads to his bedchamber? My ears feel hot.

There is an awkward silence. Ash runs a hand through his hair and clears his throat. "Would you like something to drink?" he asks politely.

"Um, yes, all right. Thank you." Everything felt secret and safe in the dimness of the concert hall and the darkness of the tunnel. In the cold, gray light of this parlor, I'm not entirely sure how to act. I take a seat on the sofa as Ash pours us tea from a pot on the side table.

"Well," he says, handing me a cup and sitting down beside me.

"Well," I say, for lack of a better idea.

The clock on the mantel ticks loudly. I take a sip of tea.

"Perhaps we should formally introduce ourselves," Ash

says. "I'm Ash Lockwood."

"Violet Lasting," I say, then I grin.

"Is something funny?"

"No, it's just . . . I can remember the exact moment when I thought Violet Lasting was gone forever."

What am I talking about? Why would I bring that memory up now?

"When?"

I blink. "What?"

"When was that moment?"

"Oh." I look down and speak to my tea. "At the ceremony on the train platform at Southgate. Before I came here." That moment is so clear in my mind: the fat man with the ruby ring, the faces of all the other surrogates, the caretakers . . .

"Before you went to the Auction?" Ash asks.

I nod. "That morning."

"You must have been very scared."

I shrug.

"What was it like?"

"What do you think it was like?" I can't keep the bite out of my voice. "They made me stand on a stage, alone. Women offered to pay money for me. They took away my name. They took away my home. They took . . . everything."

There is a long silence. I take another sip of tea. This isn't how I wanted our conversation to go, and I wish I could change the subject.

"I'm sorry," I say. "I'm—"

"They took my home away, too," Ash says. I look up. His face is utterly serious. A lock of brown hair has fallen over his forehead and I have the strongest urge to brush it back, to run my fingers through his hair.

"They did?" I ask.

"The difference is, I let them."

"Why?"

"My little sister was ill. I skipped school one day and took her to the free clinic. We waited all day to see the doctor. That was where Madame Curio found me." He smiles at the memory, but his smile is incredibly sad. "'I bet you drive all the girls crazy.' That's what she said to me. I had no idea what she was talking about."

"What happened to your sister?" I ask.

"She had black lung. Common in the Smoke. Treatable, if you can afford the medicines. We couldn't. When we got home, Madame Curio was waiting for me. She said I could help Cinder—that's my sister. She said she could give me a job, money enough not just to pay for Cinder's medicine but to take care of my family, to make sure they never wanted for anything. Just one little condition: I could never see them again." He swallows hard. "I left with her the next day."

He puts his cup down on the table, his voice becoming formal. "I am so sorry. This is not . . . appropriate conversation. I shouldn't . . . I'm not accustomed to talking about myself so much. It's not permitted. I apologize."

"We're breaking lots of rules today, aren't we?"

Ash grins and relaxes a little. "It would seem so."

"That was a very brave thing you did for your sister."

"It wasn't much of a choice."

"Still," I murmur. "If I had had a choice . . . well, I don't know what I would have done."

"I don't believe that," Ash says.

He's right. If it was Hazel being sent away on that train and I could save her by taking her place, I would do it in a heartbeat.

"How old were you?" he asks.

"Twelve." I can still remember waiting in line at the testing office, holding my mother's hand. The cold, probing fingers of the doctor. The sharp smell of the antiseptic. The sting of the needle. "Testing is mandatory for all girls after . . . you know, once you . . . become a woman." My cheeks burn and I can't look at him. "Anyway, that night they came for me."

I blink away the memory, hiding my face in another sip of tea. It's gone cold.

"Sometimes, I feel like I'm remembering someone else's life," Ash says. "Like that person doesn't exist anymore."

"He does," I whisper.

"It's hard to remember who you were when you're constantly pretending to be someone you're not."

"I'm sure there must be some moments when you can be yourself," I say.

Ash's whole face softens. "You haven't been here very long."

I bristle. "Maybe not, but I can understand what you mean. Besides, you have more freedom than I do. You can talk whenever you want, and dress how you want, and go wherever you want. They treat you with respect."

"Do you really think it's *respect*, when the Duchess eyes me at dinner, or Carnelian demands that I dance with her over and over? Do you think they care if I am tired or hungry, or if I actually hate dancing? They don't respect me, Violet. They own me."

We're quiet for a moment, lost in our own thoughts.

"No, they don't," I say suddenly, sitting up. Ash raises one eyebrow. "If they owned you, you wouldn't have come to the concert hall today. And if they truly owned me, I wouldn't be here."

"That is a very optimistic way to look at it," Ash says.

"You disagree?"

"I—" Ash sighs. "I've lived here too long. It's hard to be optimistic." He cups his hand around my neck, stroking his thumb down the length of my jaw. "But I will say this— when I woke up this morning, it was like I could breathe again. Like some weight had been lifted and I felt like myself for the first time in years."

"What happened this morning?"

He smiles. "I decided to find you."

Silence wraps around us, but it's not an uncomfortable one. Ash moves his hand from my neck and rests it on the back of the sofa.

"What do you miss most?" he asks. "From your life before."

"My family," I say. I put my cold tea down on the coffee table. "Especially my little sister, Hazel. She's so grown up now." I smile sadly. "She looks just like our father."

"Who do you look like?"

I laugh. "No one. My father used to joke that my mother must have had an affair with the milkman." Something warm and sad trickles into my chest.

Ash twines one of my curls around his finger. "Is he a good man, your father?"

"He's dead," I say quietly.

His hand freezes. "Violet, I—I'm so sorry."

"It's all right. It was a long time ago."

"How old were you?"

"Eleven."

He unwinds the curl. "May I ask what happened?"

I look out the window while I speak. "He was coming home after working the late shift in the Smoke. There was a fight outside a tavern by the train station—two men were beating another man badly. My father . . . he tried to stop them." I swallow. "One of the men stabbed him. By the time the Regimentals brought him to our house, he was dead." I close my eyes and the image appears—my father, blood and rain and mud soaking his clothes and skin, lying lifeless on our kitchen table. My mother wailing, making an awful, inhuman sound. I took Hazel and Ochre to our bedroom, but we could still hear her. The three of us huddled on the bed and cried all night. In the morning, Father was gone.

A tear drips down my cheek and I brush it away quickly, embarrassed. This is not the time to be crying. "I'm sorry," I say. "I haven't thought about that night in a long time."

"He was trying to help someone," Ash murmurs. "That was a very brave thing to do."

I shrug. "I guess."

"I'm so sorry."

"What about your family?" I ask.

"What about them?"

"I don't know. Tell me about them. Were you very close with your father?"

Ash chuckles once, a hard sound. "No. I was not close with my father. We did not . . . understand one another. I wasn't like my two older brothers. They're twins—Rip and Panel. They . . . I don't know, they like roughhousing and getting into fights and making a lot of noise, and they were much bigger than I was. I preferred the quiet. If we'd had any books in the house, I'm certain I would have been happy to sit by the stove and read."

"Is that why you were out in the gazebo?" I ask. "At the Exetor's Ball. It was so loud inside."

His hand curls around mine and all my focus pours into that place where our skin touches. "Yes, partly. And partly so I would stop staring at you."

"Oh, sure," I say, flushing.

"It's true." He slides closer to me. "Violet, if we don't stop this now, I'm afraid . . . I'm afraid I'll never want to stop."

Never. The word doesn't seem like an exaggeration. I don't think I will ever want this to stop, either. A sobering thought occurs to me—when I leave the Jewel, I leave Ash, too.

I push it away. That thought can wait for another time. He is here now, and I am here, and there is nothing stopping us from having this moment together.

I lean toward him. Ash's fingers graze my cheek, and my skin tingles with anticipation. "Are you going to kiss me again?" I ask hopefully.

He smiles. "Yes, Violet. I'm going to kiss you again."

His lips touch mine, softly at first, then urgently, and I wrap my arms around him as we sink back together on the couch.

~ Twenty-One ~

"ARE YOU READY, VIOLET? VIOLET?"

Dr. Blythe and I are in the garden, by the oak tree. Late-afternoon sunshine filters through its leaves.

Time has been acting strangely since my afternoon with Ash yesterday. Sometimes every minute feels like an hour, and other times it passes in huge dollops, so that I arrive in one place without really remembering how I got there.

"Sorry," I say. "Yes. I'm ready."

I take off my gloves and put them in the pockets of my coat. Dr. Blythe smiles.

"You seem a little distracted today," he says. "It's all right to be nervous. But I think you'll find that, after our appointment on Monday, you may surprise yourself."

I have absolutely no illusions that I'll be able to affect this tree at all. But I hitch a smile on my face and nod. I find a small knot in the bark and run my fingers over it, back and forth. It has a spiral feel, like a snail shell.

Once to see it as it is. Twice to see it in your mind. Thrice to bend it to your will.

An image appears, of the tree in winter, bare branches black against a pale gray sky. A light snow falls, swirling flakes of white that melt when they touch the ground. There is something sad and beautiful about it. It makes me homesick, though I can't explain why.

I sense the life of the tree, as powerful as it was the first time. I'm better prepared for the power now. I acknowledge it as it throbs against my palm, and I welcome it thrilling through my veins. I very badly want the image in my mind to be real.

The tree recognizes me—I can feel it acknowledge my presence, react to the familiar thrum of life inside me. I gasp and fall to my knees, but I keep my hand firmly placed on the knot. I've never felt such raw emotion. It's dizzying, like nothing I've ever experienced, because the oak tree cannot feel in the same way that I do. I'm bewildered by a grief so tender it makes me want to cry, and exhilarated by an agelessness, a feeling of being ancient and brand-new at the same time.

I focus, pulling at the thick cables of life inside the oak. To my surprise, one moves. I coax it closer to my hand, and just as I feel a tickling between my fingers, it snaps away, and my body snaps with it, one quick, rigid motion that sends a painful buzz down my spine, like the way my elbow feels when I hit my funny bone.

I fall backward, blood dripping from my nose into the dirt. The suddenness of no longer being attached to the tree is disorienting, and my fingers claw at the earth, searching for the connection.

Dr. Blythe begins to clap.

"Bravo, Violet," he says with quiet sincerity. "Bravo."

He hands me a handkerchief. I press it to my nose and look back at the tree. A tiny leaf flutters in the wind, protruding from the knot.

"You see," he says, crouching beside me and opening his medical bag, "the stimulant gun heightens your abilities, but it weakens you physically. If overused, it can have some very nasty side effects. I wanted to make sure your body had time to recover. But you, Violet, you have such a strong, *natural* power, that with one application, you've already exceeded my expectations. I've worked with many surrogates in my career, and not a single one of them could accomplish what you have just done." He rubs an ointment under my nose that stings and smells like eucalyptus, but it stops the bleeding. "The Duchess was wise to wait for you. I feel the task ahead of us will be positively easy."

He helps me to my feet and cleans my face with a piece of gauze and some rubbing alcohol. "There. Good as new."

My skin feels thin and fragile. My insides float like they're trying to rearrange themselves. The life of the tree swirls around my rib cage.

"I think we're done for the day," Dr. Blythe says, patting my shoulder. "I'll see you tomorrow."

He walks away down the tangled path. I stay with the tree for a moment and stare at the leaf I created. It's shaped like a little mitten, a delicate greenish-brown. I catch it between my fingers and rub my thumb across its veined surface.

"I'm sorry," I whisper to the tree.

I try to picture what it would be like, to have a child grow inside me at the rate that this leaf suddenly sprang out of the knot. I shudder at the image of my belly swelling up so quickly.

You don't have to worry about that anymore, I tell myself. *Lucien will get you out.*

I shiver—the air has cooled, the sun veiled by a thin layer of cloud. I make my way to the western wall and stare up at the flowers, twined around each other. My first violet is beginning to wilt.

I have to send another message. For as long as I'm here, Raven needs to know I haven't forgotten her. More flowers might be too conspicuous, with winter approaching. I search my coat pockets and find an old hair ribbon, frayed at the ends, a delicate pink. Raven would hate the color, so I quickly draw up a new image, and cracks of pale blue spread across the satiny surface. I create a new sprout of ivy and wrap the ribbon around it. Then I send it over the wall.

I put my gloves on and head back to the palace. As I'm passing the ballroom window, movement catches my eye. Cautiously, I approach and peer inside. My heart freezes and drops like a stone into the pit of my stomach.

Ash and Carnelian are dancing together. His arm curves around her waist, his hand resting on the small of her back, their faces close together. One of her arms is draped around his neck, the other clasping his free hand. His movements are smooth and graceful, but Carnelian follows his lead stiffly.

I should not be watching this. But I can't seem to look away.

And then, as if time slows down in a moment that lasts an eternity, he leans forward and his lips touch hers. Pain splinters inside me, and I clutch the window for support. My hand scrapes the glass, and I throw myself against the wall, hoping they didn't see me, my heart hammering so hard it sends tremors through my whole body.

Then I start to run.

I stumble blindly along the gravel paths until I reach the maze and dive into it, taking lefts and rights at random, losing myself among the hedges. All I can see is him kissing her.

I collapse at a dead end, gasping for breath. I feel unbelievably stupid. A foolish little girl who doesn't know anything about love. All this time he was *kissing* her.

I hate him. But I hate myself more, for being idiotic enough to believe that I could have that sort of happiness. Or any happiness. For thinking I made a choice that *meant* something. I disobeyed Lucien, I broke his trust, and for nothing.

I don't know how long I stay there, my head resting on my knees, tears seeping into my coat, the cool air playing with tendrils of my hair.

"Violet?" His voice makes me jump, but I don't answer or look up.

I hear him sit beside me, feel the warmth of him. "Violet, I'm so sorry. Let me explain." A pause. "Will you look at me, please?"

"No." If I look at him, I'll start crying again. I don't want to cry in front of him.

He sighs. "What you saw . . . that's my *job*, Violet. I have to do that. I have to . . . kiss her." I hear the hesitation before he says the word. "But it's not what I *want*. I thought . . . I thought you would understand that." I hear his weight shift. "Do you have any idea how much I hate my life? I have to lie, *all* the time. I lie to these girls, and tell them whatever they want to hear, and the worst part is, they don't seem to care. They don't care if what I say is true. They don't care about *me* at all. They don't see me, they don't know me. I am a piece of property to them, something to wear on their arm to a ball. I may not have experienced the Auction, but I am continually being bought and sold, all the same."

After a second, I lift my head and meet his eyes. Words lodge in my throat, unable to escape. Because I do understand. I know exactly how he feels. And I can't judge him, or blame him for it.

Ash smiles my favorite smile, the one that makes him look like he has a secret. "May I tell you something?"

I nod.

"The day we met, I heard you laughing. That's why I came into the parlor." I remember the hysterical laughter after my narrow escape with the two maids. "There you were, all flushed and smiling, and I thought you were the most beautiful girl I'd ever seen. And you looked at me with this stunned expression . . ." He laughs softly and tucks a lock of hair behind my ear.

"And I walked into the coffee table," I say with a grimace.

Ash laughs again, a little louder. "Yes. But you made me feel like . . . like a person again. You see *me*, Violet. Does that make sense?"

I don't understand why this is happening. Why *now*? I sit in this maze and stare at the one person who truly understands. And the *right* thing to do, the *smart* thing to do is reject him. To listen to Lucien and just obey.

It isn't fair. And I can't do it.

I'll have to leave him anyway, eventually. That should be punishment enough. I'll have to leave him, and I'll have to lie to him.

"Violet?" Ash looks nervous, and I wonder what my expression is.

There are only a few weeks left until the Longest Night. Surely that can't hurt anyone. Just a few short weeks to be with him. I think it's worth the risk.

I grab him by his coat and pull him to me, crushing my mouth against his. We are the same, he and I, both controlled by the royalty, neither of us free to make our own choices. But we can choose to be together. The royalty cannot own this moment. I sense his surprise, feel his shoulders tense and then relax, his fingers sinking into my hair, and we fall back together on the cool grass.

THE NEXT MORNING, I SIT IN MY FAVORITE ARMCHAIR BY the window in my tea parlor and watch the traffic coming in and out of the Duchess's palace.

There's much more than usual—footmen hurry back and forth carrying small tables and yards of fabric and armfuls of flowers.

"What's going on?" I ask Annabelle. Her face falls and her cheeks turn pink.

"What?" I ask. "Annabelle, what is it?"

She shrugs.

G is engaged

"Garnet?"

She nods.

"To who?"

House of Downs

"Oh."

Eng party tmrw

"How does Garnet feel about it?"

Annabelle smiles wryly and raises an eyebrow.

"Yeah." I laugh. "I bet he's hating it."

Suddenly, the door to my parlor opens and the Duchess sweeps in.

"Come with me," she says. I glance at Annabelle—her face has gone paler than usual, her expression alarmed.

"Where are we going, my lady?" I ask as she leads me down the hall of flowers. She doesn't respond, but when we reach the elevator, I know.

Dr. Blythe is standing with his back to us, and my stomach swoops with fear. Is he going to use that gun again?

"How are you feeling today?" the doctor asks.

I assume he's not talking to the Duchess. "Fine," I reply.

"The weather's gotten a bit colder—no sniffles, coughing, sore throat, anything of that sort?"

"I'm fine," I say again. Why is the Duchess still here?

"Are you ready, Doctor?" the Duchess asks impatiently. She takes a viselike grip on my arm, as if I might try to run away. As if there was anyplace to go.

"Just about, my lady," Dr. Blythe says.

"You said the timing had to be precise," the Duchess says.

"That won't be a problem, my lady." I detect a suppressed excitement in his voice; he turns and smiles at me, a warm smile that immediately sets me on edge. He walks toward me with careful steps. "Do not be alarmed," he says.

It's then that I notice the stirrups, gleaming silver, protruding from the end of the bed.

I don't see the needle in his hand until it's too late.

There is a sharp sting on the side of my neck, and the world goes black.

Twenty-Two

I CAN HEAR A FAINT HUMMING, ALMOST LIKE THE ARCANA.

I try to open my eyes, but they're so heavy. My tongue is swollen, and it takes an effort to swallow.

"She's waking up, Doctor."

The Duchess's voice pierces through the thick fog of darkness. I can feel something sticking in my arm—I try to scratch at it, but I can't seem to move.

"Not to worry, my lady. We're nearly finished."

Doctor Blythe. The medical room. The needle. The stirrups.

Consciousness comes back to me in a rush and I force my heavy eyelids open. At first I can't make sense of anything but a bright white glow. Then slowly, the world comes into focus.

I wish I'd stayed unconscious.

My arms are restrained with straps, and there is a strap across my shoulders as well. An IV pokes into my skin at the crook of my elbow. My legs are propped up and open, a sheet of stiff white fabric draped over my knees like a tent.

My lungs feel compressed—I can't seem to catch my breath.

The Duchess's face appears in my view. "Calm down," she says, dabbing at my forehead with a damp cloth. "You'll hyperventilate."

The air is too thin, like I can't get enough oxygen. My heart thrums in my chest, too fast, far too fast. "What's . . . happening?" I gasp.

"Deep breaths." Dr. Blythe's voice comes from behind the drape. "Relax. You're all right."

"I can't . . . I can't . . . feel my legs . . ." I'm suffocating—white lights pop in front of my eyes. My heart feels like it's about to explode.

"My lady, there is an oxygen mask just to your left. Would you mind placing it over her nose and mouth?"

I feel something hard and plastic on my face, then I inhale a wonderfully clean, fresh breath of air. My heartbeat slows.

"There now, see? You're fine." The Duchess pats my head again with the cloth. "You shouldn't have woken up so soon," she says, as though it's my fault.

"All done," Dr. Blythe says, emerging from behind the drape and removing a light blue procedure mask. I cringe at the snap of latex as he takes off his gloves. "Everything went just fine, my lady."

"Excellent," the Duchess says brusquely. "I have an engagement party to organize."

I hear the elevator doors open then close. Gently, the doctor removes my feet from the stirrups. My legs dangle limply off the end of the bed.

"I've given you a mild sedative," he says, pressing his fingers against the inside of my wrist to check my pulse. "It should be wearing off now." He takes a small penlight and flashes it in my eyes, then makes some notations on the screen. "I think we can remove these," he says, undoing the straps on my arms and across my shoulders. I try to sit up, but the room tilts and a wave of vertigo hits me.

"Lie back, Violet," Dr. Blythe says. I don't have a choice. I stare at the smooth white ceiling and wait for the dizziness to subside. There is a tiny sting in my arm as the doctor takes the IV out. "Do you still need the oxygen mask?"

I shake my head. I want to get out of here. Tears prick the corners of my eyes. Dr. Blythe removes the mask. I feel a tingling sensation, like pins and needles, in my toes. I want to know what happened, but the question sits like a lump in my throat. I don't want to hear the answer. Dr. Blythe just sits there, watching me, waiting.

The tingling sensation spreads up my calves and into my thighs. The vertigo fades. Very slowly, I slide myself back on the bed, into a more upright position. My body feels like dead weight, my movements clunky.

Dr. Blythe smiles. "Would you like some water?"

I nod. He holds up a cup with a straw and I take a small sip—my lips are dry and the cool water feels good.

"You may experience some mild cramping tonight," the doctor says brusquely, "but by tomorrow, you'll be feeling just like your old self, I promise. We should know the results in about a week."

"Results?" I croak.

"Yes, Violet. The results." Dr. Blythe squeezes my hand. "In one week, we are going to find out if you're pregnant."

PREGNANT.

The word sounds strange in my head, foreign, like the more I think about it, the less sense it makes. I lie in bed that night, staring at the frothy canopy above me, and try to notice some difference. I press my hands against my stomach, as if I might feel a tiny heartbeat or a small bump. Nothing. There's nothing.

"Please don't let it work," I whisper, as if by wishing it out loud, it might come true. "Please . . ."

I feel contaminated. They put something inside me, without my permission, against my will. Knowing that it would happen and experiencing it are two entirely different things.

At least I'm not crying anymore. I cried all afternoon, until I ran out of tears and it was just an awful, dry, aching sob that shuddered through my chest. I called Lucien's name over and over into the arcana, until I got so frustrated by the silence that I threw it against the wall. The arcana is back in its hiding place now.

I try very hard not to think about Ash. How stupid of me, to worry about the risks of being with him. Our time is over.

There is a tentative knock on the door, and Annabelle pokes her head in. She scribbles something on her slate, but

I don't look at it. I just keep staring at the ceiling.

The slate appears in my line of vision.

D is here

Without a word, I slide up into a sitting position, hugging my knees to my chest. Annabelle gives my wrist a squeeze and flits out the door. The Duchess enters slowly, almost like she's afraid she'll startle me.

"How are you feeling?" she asks.

"Fine, my lady," I say through clenched teeth.

She walks forward and sits on the edge of my bed.

"I know this must be difficult for you," she says.

"No," I say in a flat voice, unable to lie in this instance. "You don't."

"Don't sit there and sulk and pretend as though you didn't know this was going to happen," the Duchess says. "The doctor said the procedure went very well."

"Yes, my lady."

"If there is anything you need, you will let me or Annabelle know immediately."

I glare at her. "I'd like to be left alone."

"Why do you look at me like that?" she snaps. "As if *I* am the villain. Why are you not grateful for everything I am giving you? Fine clothes, the best food, a new cello, jewelry, balls . . . I am *trying* to take care of you. I am trying to make you happy."

"You stole my body and my *life* and you expect me to be grateful?" I need to calm down, but it's so hard. I'm too angry.

"What life?" she says. "Would you rather be living in poverty? Starving and filthy in a hovel in the Marsh?"

"Yes!" I cry. "A thousand times over if I could be with my family again. If I could have my own life, make my own choices. I would do anything for that sort of freedom."

"I have given you freedom!" she shrieks.

"Walking around the palace without an escort is *not* freedom!" I shout.

There is a tense silence as we glare at each other. The Duchess inhales deeply through her nose.

"*I* did not make these rules," she says. "*I* did not take you away from your family. I didn't create the Auction. There are many in the Jewel who would not have given you a fraction of what I have given."

I look away, refusing to respond. The Duchess sighs. "Did you know that the Electress wishes to abolish the Auction?"

I turn back to her, hope swelling inside my chest. "Really?"

The Duchess laughs at my expression. "Oh no, she doesn't wish to end surrogacy. Just the Auction. She despises the surrogates."

"Why?"

The Duchess gives me a pitying look. "Because she did not *need* one. She isn't royalty, remember? She was perfectly capable of bearing her own children. But in order to marry the Exetor, she was forced to give up that power. All royal women are sterilized upon marriage—a necessary precaution against pregnancy." Something flickers in her eyes, an emotion I can't quite place. "Do you remember when I told you about the two schools of thought concerning surrogates? I believe your personalities are necessary. There are many who disagree, and the Electress has sided with them.

She has a plan to . . . adjust the surrogates."

"Adjust us how?" I ask.

"Why bother training your surrogate? Why spend the money, risk an unfavorable result because your surrogate has a character flaw, or does not try hard enough, or resents you? All we really need are your bodies. The stimulant gun can induce the Auguries. The Electress subscribes to the view that your minds are of no use to us."

I gasp. "What, she wants to . . . lobotomize surrogates?"

"That is exactly what she wants."

I feel sick. "She can't do that."

"Yes, she can. She is the Electress. The Exetor has no interest in surrogacy—like all the other men in the Jewel, he considers it a 'lady's issue.'" The Duchess rolls her eyes. "If she has enough support from the right people, there is no reason why she couldn't create a new law."

"What's stopping her?"

"So far, the experiments haven't worked. But once they do . . ." The Duchess shrugs. "No more holding facilities. No more compensation for the families. Once a girl is ready to be impregnated, she will simply disappear." She looks me full in the face, her black eyes sparkling. "You do realize there are others who wish to secure the young Exetor's hand, to put a daughter in the Royal Palace who will continue the Electress's work. We cannot let that happen."

I don't like the way she's put us together, on the same side, even though it's exactly what Lucien has been hoping for. "Why do you hate her so much?" I ask. "Just because she married the Exetor and you didn't?"

All the color drains from the Duchess's face. "You have

absolutely no idea what you are talking about. That woman *cannot* be permitted to make new law. I will not allow her to come into my circle—*my* circle, the circle *my family* built—with her dirty blood and her coarse manners and expect to change the shape of history."

"But . . . even if you arrange a match, your daughter will be too young to do anything. She'll only be a baby."

The Duchess's mouth curves into a small, cruel smile. "Oh, you do not need to concern yourself with that. Your only job is to produce her as fast as you can."

My stomach tightens. "I know what my job is, my lady."

Her smile widens. "Good."

"Doesn't anyone *love* anyone here?" I ask. "Isn't there any part of you that just wants a child?"

The Duchess's face becomes very still. "I have loved more deeply than you can possibly imagine," she says. For an instant, she looks like an entirely different person. I am too stunned to speak.

The Duchess seems to realize she's revealed too much of herself. She rises, straightening her skirts. "That's that, then. As you may have heard, my son is engaged. The party is tomorrow evening. You will attend. I have arranged for you to play a small concert." She looks around my room as if searching for the right words to end this conversation, then gives up. "Good night," she says, without meeting my eyes.

As she leaves, I hear her say to Annabelle, "Make sure she looks stunning."

~ Twenty-Three ~

ANNABELLE DOESN'T DISAPPOINT.

At five to seven, I stand outside the doors to the ballroom dressed in a pale green gown that makes the footman's eyes pop before he can stop himself. The bodice leaves my shoulders bare, and the skirt falls to the floor in layers like the petals of a flower, their edges woven with glittering crystals. A choker of diamonds wraps around my neck and diamond earrings hang from my ears.

There is a hum of voices coming from behind the door, along with light strains of music. The footman bows to me before opening it.

"The surrogate of the House of the Lake," he announces. Only the people closest to him hear.

The ballroom is filled with men in tuxedos and women in colorful dresses—their laughter bounces off the painted ceiling. Garnet is standing woodenly beside a girl about my age; he looks miserable. The girl's blond curls and big blue eyes remind me of Lily. The Lady and Lord of the Glass are offering Garnet their congratulations. I wonder how their baby is. Their surrogate must be in one of the holding facilities now.

I find the Duchess, wearing a gown of pale gold with capped lace sleeves, and head toward her. She is in conversation with the Electress—I try to keep my expression neutral as I move to the Duchess's side.

"My goodness, isn't she just a vision," the Electress gushes. She wears a gown of rich crimson velvet with a large dragon embroidered on its skirts—it seems like too much material for her small frame—and her lips are painted bright red. Like at the Auction, I am strongly reminded of a child playing dress-up. It's hard to imagine her experimenting on young girls, cutting out pieces of their brains. Though she probably has someone else to do that for her. "When do you intend to start trying?"

"When the doctor thinks she is ready, Your Grace," the Duchess lies smoothly.

"You don't want to wait too long. The Lady of the Mirror's surrogate is pregnant already, and the Lady of the Star's as well. You don't want to get left behind."

The Duchess shrugs and takes a sip of champagne. "I'm not worried, Your Grace. But I thank you for your concern."

The Electress eyes me curiously. I grit my teeth and force the corners of my mouth up.

Lucien appears at her side, handing her a glass of champagne, and my heart jumps.

"Thank you, Lucien," the Electress says brightly, before turning to the Duchess. "I hope you don't mind—it's from my own cellar. I've become terribly choosy about what I drink, so I decided to bring my own."

I suppose I would, too, if my surrogate had been poisoned.

"Of course, Your Grace," the Duchess says with a fake smile. I hear someone else being announced at the door, but I can't make out who.

"Oh! Lapis!" The Electress waves over a woman with auburn hair in a golden dress similar to the Duchess's. "Congratulations. The House of the Downs must be thrilled with this engagement."

The Lady of the Downs sinks into a curtsy. "Yes, Your Grace. My daughter could not have hoped for a better match."

We all look over at the couple—Garnet chooses this moment to scratch himself in a very inappropriate place. I barely stifle my laugh. The Lady of the Downs's cheeks redden.

"Yes," the Electress says with a smirk. "He is quite a catch. Ah, Carnelian."

My heart plummets so fast it leaves my head spinning. Carnelian and Ash join us.

I can't bring myself to look up, for fear that I might just fling my arms around him. It's been so long since I've seen his face. Instead, I stare at the ruby pendant hanging around Carnelian's neck.

"It will be your turn next, my dear," the Electress is saying.

"Yes, Your Grace," Carnelian replies. "I'm looking forward to it."

A waltz begins to play and the Electress claps her hands together. "Oh, one of my favorites. I must dance. Excuse me, ladies, while I find my husband."

The party continues, with dancing and laughter and lots of champagne, though the Duchess makes sure to inform me straightaway that I'm not permitted to drink any this time. The Countess of the Stone doesn't appear to have been invited, so I don't get to see Raven again. I hope she's found my ribbon. I spend most of my time by a table piled with brightly colored macarons, trying not to watch Ash on the dance floor and hoping Lucien will find an excuse to get me alone.

After a few hours, the Duchess calls for silence. She stands at one end of the ballroom, the Duke by her side, Garnet and his fiancée close by.

"Thank you all for joining me in celebrating this very special occasion!" the Duchess exclaims. "Let us raise a glass to the happy couple—Garnet, of the House of the Lake, and Coral, of the House of the Downs."

Everyone raises their glasses and cheers.

"And now," the Duchess says, "my surrogate will perform a short program for you. Shall we all proceed to the concert hall?"

A footman leads me out and down a different hall from everyone else—I assume he's taking me to the backstage door—when he is intercepted.

"Her Ladyship requested that I escort the surrogate," Lucien says. "You may go back to your post."

The footman hesitates, then bows. "Of course."

Once he's gone, Lucien smiles at me. "Shall we?" he says, offering his arm.

I grin and take it.

"How are you?" he asks.

The words get tangled in my throat. Lucien stops walking. He lifts my chin and studies my face.

"Has it happened?" he asks. I nod. "When?"

"Yesterday," I whisper.

"So you don't know the results yet."

I shake my head.

Lucien brushes my cheek with his fingers. "It's all right. It's not ideal, but we'll get through this. The Longest Night is just around the corner, right?"

I bite my lip. "Lucien, do you know about the Electress's plan? About lobotomizing the surrogates?"

Lucien raises an eyebrow. "Who told you that?"

"The Duchess."

Lucien purses his lips. "Yes, I am aware of it. But we can't focus on that. And we have no idea if the operation will ever be performed successfully, so for the time being, let's concentrate on keeping you safe, shall we? Remember what our goal is."

"But the other girls, Lucien. I can't—"

"Listen to me." Lucien stops outside the backstage door and puts his hands on my shoulders. "This is not just about saving you. There is much more at stake here, Violet."

A shiver runs through me. "What do you mean?" I whisper.

Lucien smiles a secretive smile. "It only takes one small stone to start an avalanche. I am going to help the other girls, in more ways than you can guess. I am going to help everyone under the thumb of the royalty. But none of that will matter if I can't help *you*."

He opens the door before I can press him further. I can hear the chatter of my audience as they take their seats. My cello and music stand are already set up.

"Are you ready?" he asks.

My questions vanish as my stomach twists unpleasantly with nerves.

"Yes," I reply.

He kisses me lightly on the forehead. "Good luck."

I take a deep breath and walk out onstage, to thunderous applause.

This is so much better than at the Exetor's Ball. The excitement of the crowd is palpable, with none of the antagonism in the air. This audience is genuinely excited to hear me play, not eager to see me lose some ridiculous competition. I sit and prop my cello between my knees, then look out over the rows and rows of seats, all of them filled.

It's what I've always imagined, made into reality.

The Duchess has chosen my repertoire. I open the first page and find that she's selected the prelude in G Major to start—no doubt to remind everyone of my previous performance. I smile and begin to play.

Immediately, I know something is wrong. Instead of relaxing, the nerves in my stomach seem to get worse as the song progresses, like a dull cramp. I finish the prelude, and smile politely at the applause. It certainly wasn't my best performance, but they don't seem to notice.

I reach out and turn the page to the next piece—the movement sends a dull ache through my lower back, and I wince. The Duchess has chosen another prelude, this one in D Minor, similar to the nocturne the iced cake danced to. I lift the bow to the strings.

I only manage the first few bars before the pain becomes unbearable—my stomach is cramping severely, and my lower back is on fire. But it's not until I feel a wetness between my thighs that my bow falters, screeching across the A string and falling to the floor.

I look down at my lap and see a bright red stain, veins of color spreading across the pale green petals of my dress like the first Augury. But I'm not performing an Augury.

I don't realize I've dropped the cello until I hear the jarring crash of it hitting the floor. There is a flash of white from offstage in my peripheral vision. I press my hands against the stain, my fingers becoming sticky with blood, a dull pounding in my ears muting all the sounds of the room.

"Help," I whisper.

Then I fall.

I expect to hit the floor, but a pair of soft hands catches me.

Sound comes back in a rush.

"Get the doctor!" Lucien yells. There are shouts and cries, a confusing babble, and people are running up to the stage, but everything seems blurry. Another cramp wrenches in my gut.

I moan as Lucien lays me down gently on the stage and brushes a hand against my forehead.

Then the Duchess is standing over me. "The doctor is in the Bank," she says. Her face is pale, her eyes full of fear. I've never seen her look scared before.

"We'll send someone immediately," the Exetor's voice comes from somewhere to my right.

"There's no time, we have to stop the bleeding," Lucien says. "My lady, where is your medical room?" The Duchess can only stare at me. "My lady!"

She starts. "This way."

Lucien lifts me up in his arms—he is surprisingly strong—and carries me off the stage and through the concert hall. Concerned faces swirl around me in a golden haze, but one stands out clearly. Ash's gray-green eyes are wide with panic.

Pain rips through my abdomen, and I cry out.

"We're almost there, honey," Lucien whispers in my ear. "Hold on. We're almost there."

"It hurts," I whimper.

"I know."

I hear the grate of the elevator open, then darkness, then the bright lights of the medical room. Lucien lays me on the bed and I curl up in the fetal position, my hands soaked with blood.

"Is she all right?" The Duchess's voice is somewhere off to my left, strangled and frightened. "Is she going to be all right?"

Lucien's face fills my vision, and I feel his fingers probe my elbow, sinking a needle into my veins.

My eyelids grow heavy. Lucien's face blurs and becomes Ash's. I want to reach out and stroke his cheek, but I can't lift my arms. When he speaks, it's Ash's voice I hear, coming from the end of a long tunnel.

"That's right. Go to sleep."

Darkness engulfs me.

Twenty-Four

SOMETHING COOL AND WET BRUSHES AGAINST MY FORE-
head. It feels nice.

My eyelids flutter open.

I'm in my bedroom. The Duchess is leaning over me
with a damp cloth.

"Doctor," she calls. She sits beside me on the bed. "How
are you feeling?"

My mouth is dry, my lips sticking together. My tongue
feels swollen. The Duchess fills a glass with water from the
jug on the nightstand and holds it to my lips.

"There you are," she says gently. I take a few small sips.
Some water dribbles down my chin and the Duchess wipes
it away. The door opens and Dr. Blythe rushes in.

"Is she awake?" He hurries to the bed, the Duchess moving aside, and smiles at me as he presses two fingers against the inside of my wrist. "It's good to see your eyes open again."

"What . . . happened?" I croak.

"The first attempt often fails. However, your body's reaction was unusually violent. You very nearly died. We must proceed with absolute caution," Dr. Blythe says.

"We are already behind schedule," the Duchess protests.

"If we lose her," the doctor says sharply, "none of that will matter."

My head is spinning. "So I'm not . . . pregnant?"

The doctor opens his medical bag. "Not anymore."

He takes out a thermometer and pops it under my tongue.

"How do we proceed?" the Duchess asks.

"We wait at least another full cycle before the next attempt. Four or five weeks at the earliest. She must be allowed to heal."

"Very well," the Duchess says. "But you will stay here. I will arrange for a room to be set up for you this afternoon."

"As you wish, my lady."

The idea of the doctor living here is not particularly comforting. But I've been given time—four or five weeks. The Longest Night is five and a half weeks away. Lucien can get me the serum before they try again. The doctor removes the thermometer.

"Where's Lucien?" I ask. Dr. Blythe frowns and the Duchess looks confused. And I realize I'm probably not supposed to know Lucien.

"He's back at the Royal Palace, of course," the doctor says.

"He saved my life," I say, hoping that will be enough to justify my question.

"He did," the doctor replies. "You are very fortunate he was here." He puts the thermometer back in the bag. "The best thing you can do now is rest."

I nod, exhausted.

"I'll send someone to fetch your things," the Duchess says to the doctor. She dabs the cloth against my forehead one more time, a surprisingly tender gesture, then sets it on my nightstand and hurries out the door.

"Someone has been waiting most impatiently to see you," Dr. Blythe says with a smile. He opens the door and leaves the room as Annabelle rushes in.

"Annabelle," I cry weakly. She kneels beside the bed and takes my hand in hers, pressing it against her cheek. She doesn't need to use her slate to express herself—I know what she's thinking. "I'm all right," I say. "Just tired."

She nods, but tears fill her eyes.

"Oh, Annabelle. I'm okay. Really."

She kisses the back of my hand.

"I think I need to sleep now," I say. "Will you stay here?"

Annabelle climbs onto the bed beside me. I rest my head on her shoulder.

"Thanks," I whisper. Her lips press softly against my hair.

I SPEND THE NEXT FEW DAYS CONFINED TO MY BED.

The doctor comes in to check on me every morning, and the Duchess visits in the afternoons, but I spend most of my time reading and playing Halma with Annabelle.

Every day that passes is one day closer to freedom. I tick them off in my head, a countdown to the Longest Night. They won't have a chance to hurt me again—not the Duchess or the doctor or anyone.

I wonder what Lucien meant, when he said there's more at stake than just saving my life. Is he planning some sort of revolt against the royalty? By taking away the surrogates, he threatens the very basis of royal life—they can't make new royalty without us. But then he'd have to hide every girl in every holding facility, plus all the surrogates in the Jewel. And if he *is* trying to overthrow the royalty, I want in. And not just to be whisked away to some safe zone in the Farm. The Duchess deserves to know how it feels to be on the other end of a leash.

I say good-bye to Ash a thousand times in my head, as if the more I say it, the easier it will be to accept. Being impregnated almost killed me. Other surrogates are dying and I might have the ability to help them. If Lucien can get me out, he can get them out. I have to take this seriously—I have to do what Lucien says. No more secret meetings, or kisses in the garden maze. I will be a model surrogate. There is too much at stake.

I tell myself it's better this way. It was always going to end, so why not sooner rather than later? I pretend this is a good thing. I pretend I'm happy about it.

I hope Raven is all right. I wish I could have seen her at the engagement party. Although I'm glad she didn't have to watch me bleeding all over the stage.

Finally, Dr. Blythe pronounces me well enough to walk around the palace again.

"Can we go to the garden?" I ask Annabelle. "I want to be outside again."

She wraps me up in my warmest coat and scarf, and we head out the back door by the ballroom. I pretend to wander aimlessly, back and forth across the garden until Annabelle sits on a bench for a few minutes. I make my way to the western wall.

Our flowers are dead, both mine and Raven's. I press my hand against the wall and whisper, "I miss you." What would Raven do if she was here? She'd probably be berating Lucien for taking so long to get her out.

A glint of silver catches my eye. I brush aside a few dead leaves and find a new vine, its slender tendril wrapped around a little charm, a silver terrier. Raven and Crow had a terrier growing up—they named him Danger, because he was so small and they thought it would inspire him to be tough. Her mother sold him to a magistrate when they couldn't afford to feed him anymore.

I kiss the charm and put it in my pocket. At least I know Raven is okay, that she still remembers me. Then I yank a button off my coat, wrap Raven's vine around it, and send it over the wall to her.

I drift farther back into the heavier woods. It's nice to be outside. Breathing in the cold air is refreshing, cleansing me from the inside out. I wander down a path I've never taken before, not really paying attention to where I'm going. When I emerge at a tiny pond filled with brightly colored fish—golden and orange and soft white—I stop short and gasp.

Seated on a bench on the opposite side of the pond is Ash.

He jumps to his feet. He's wearing a simple brown coat and a gray scarf, and he fits into the woodsy backdrop perfectly. "Violet?"

"Hi," I say.

"Are you . . ." He blinks very fast and swallows. "Are you all right?"

"Oh yes," I say, feeling oddly formal. "I'm fine. Thank you."

The space between us seems to expand and contract at the same time.

"I was so worried," he says. "I heard . . . they were saying you almost died."

I shrug. "I'm better now," I mumble. I tell my feet to move, to turn around and walk away, but they're not listening. My eyes won't stop staring at him.

"Why are you looking at me like that?" he asks.

"Like what?"

Ash frowns. "Like *that*. Like you're scared of me."

"I don't . . ." I clear my throat and turn away. "I have to go."

"Go?" he says, shocked. "The last time I saw you, you were bleeding to death, and now you're leaving?"

I stumble away from him, from the promise of comfort, the warmth of his arms around me. I can't have it anymore. I have to let him go.

"Violet, stop."

My body obeys, even if my brain is screaming at me to run. I hear the crunch of leaves beneath his boots, feel the gentle touch of his hand on my shoulder. "What is going on?" he asks.

I slip out of his grasp and turn around. "We can't keep seeing each other," I say.

Lucien would be proud. But everything inside me hurts.

Ash looks stunned. For one moment, he is like a statue frozen in front of me. Then he comes to life and takes a step back. He looks around, at the pond, at the bench, the trees, as if something in this garden will tell him what to do, what to say. He closes his eyes and when he opens them, something cracks in his expression—for a fleeting instant, I see pain, jagged and raw. Then he smooths out his face as neatly as Annabelle smooths out my bed sheets.

"Very well," he says. He sounds pleasant, detached.

"I—I'm so sorry," I whisper. Now that it's happened, I wish I could take it back. I don't like this Ash, the polite mask, the clipped manners. It's the royalty's Ash, not mine.

"If you will excuse me, Carnelian must be done with her etiquette lesson."

He brushes past me and I instinctively grab his arm.

"Ash, wait—"

He yanks his arm out of my grasp.

"No," he says. I can feel his anger—it radiates off him in waves. "You do not get to tell me what to do. You have lost that privilege."

It's like I'm underwater. Everything is slow and muddy. My lungs aren't working right.

Then the impact of what I've done hits me hard, and the world sharpens, and I'm furious. It isn't fair that he's angry at me when all I'm trying to do is help other girls, and it's infuriating that I can't explain that to him. Both my palms smack into his chest, sending him stumbling backward.

"Do you think this is *easy* for me? Do you think this is what I *want*?"

I raise my hand to hit him again, but he catches my wrist.

"Do you think this is easy for *me*?" he hisses. "Do you have *any* idea . . ."

He pulls on my wrist, hard enough to bring our faces within inches of each other. I'm suddenly very aware of how strong he is.

"You do *not* know," he growls. "You talk as though I am accustomed to what we—what I thought we had. Sex, oh yes, I know about that, and lust and lies and betrayal. But this?" His grip tightens. "I risk my *life* every time I'm with you. Do you get that? If we're caught, they will execute me."

I feel myself go limp, all the fight bleeding out of me. "What?"

"Oh, come on, Violet. What did you think would happen? You've only been here a short while but you know how these people are."

"But . . . but *why* then? Why did you ever kiss me in the first place?"

"Because this is not something I was supposed to have!" Ash shouts. "I look at you and I feel human again. I look at you and I feel whole. You don't know me that well, Violet, but trust me when I say I was *broken* before I met you. I *can't* go back to that."

He seems to realize he's still holding my wrist. My fingers have gone numb. Ash releases me and shoves his hands into his pockets. Blood rushes back to my fingertips, which prickle with pins and needles.

"And even if we aren't caught," he continues in a more subdued tone, "I will never be able to introduce you to my family. I will never get to walk down the streets of the Smoke with you hand in hand, or take you to the Commissioner of the Peace and make you my wife. As soon as Carnelian is engaged, I'll be gone. I'll be sold to another family, and the cycle of my life will continue as though you had never touched it. But you have. I can't ever forget that." He blinks and looks at my wrist. "I did not mean to hurt you. I'm so sorry."

My frail resolve wavers. I think about what sort of person I want to be. I owe Lucien my life, and I will be loyal to him until the end. But Ash has nothing to do with that. Ash is separate, a part of my life that is just mine. There are things that are bigger than us, it's true. Saving the surrogates. Destroying the royalty. Is loving Ash worth the risk?

But when I look into his eyes, the eyes that saw me first, I see everything that Lucien is trying to save. Because what is a life without love? Ash and I were never meant to happen, but against impossible odds, we found each other—and more importantly, we chose to be together.

After I've left this place, when I look back on these last few weeks, amid all the memories and tangled-up emotions there will be a gaping hole of regret in my life, the empty echo of what could have been, if I'd only had the courage to stand up and say, "I want you for as much time as I can possibly have."

Ash deserves to be with someone as brave as he is.

"Ash, don't leave." I take a tentative step forward. "I was wrong. I'm sorry. Stay with me."

He doesn't move. "I don't know if I can, Violet. I don't

know if I can trust you anymore."

"What, because I was trying to be responsible? Because I made a mistake? Well, guess what—I'm human. I'm not perfect. I was *trying* to do the right thing, but you know what? I don't care anymore. I don't want to be right, I don't want to be good. I wasn't supposed to have you any more than you were supposed to have me. And if you can't forgive me for having a moment of weakness or a second of uncertainty, then maybe you're right, maybe I don't know you at all. But don't think that I don't want you, because I do and maybe I'm just not as good at saying it out loud. I want you forever, Ash, but that's not going to happen and I get that. But I'll take you for as much time as I can have, and I won't waste a single second of it."

There is a long silence. We stare each other down, my brain working furiously to think of something else to say.

A slow smile creeps across Ash's face. "For someone who's not good at saying it out loud, that was . . . pretty impressive."

I flush. "Well, you made me mad."

"Oh, really? *I* made *you* mad?"

"Okay, I might have started it, but—"

Ash reaches out and presses his finger against my lips.

"You're allowed to end this," he says quietly.

"I know," I say. "I don't want to. You make me feel whole, too. In this place that takes little bits and pieces of us, you remind me of who I am. Of who I was."

He wraps one arm around my waist and pulls me close. It's like I can finally breathe again. He smells like dry leaves and wool.

"Don't ever do this to me again."

"I won't," I promise. Guilt twinges in my stomach, but I ignore it.

"I'm serious, Violet. Because I can't—"

"Ash," I say. My skin is on fire, my nerves are singing, because he is so very close and yet not close enough. "Please. Shut up and kiss me."

He smiles and presses his lips softly against mine. But I don't want soft.

I throw my arms around his neck as if I could pull him even closer, as if I could fuse us together. He holds me tighter, and I feel the shift in both of us. Our kiss becomes rough and wild, unpracticed, and I know I will never forget what this feels like, not if I live to be a hundred years old.

This is what it feels like to belong with someone.

~ Twenty-Five ~

THE NEXT FOUR WEEKS ARE THE HAPPIEST OF MY LIFE IN the Jewel.

Happy, because the doctor has promised not to impregnate me again and the Duchess, busy arranging Garnet's wedding, keeps her distance and lets me be. Dr. Blythe and I visit the oak tree once a week, but I never make it grow again without the force of the stimulant gun.

I speak to Lucien every Sunday at midnight through the arcana. I tell him I'm being perfectly obedient, which is mostly true—as far as the Duchess is concerned, I am the model surrogate. He is relieved by the news of the delay of my next impregnation. He won't give me any more information about where it is I'm supposed to end up hiding for the rest of my life, or what his ultimate goal is, though I press him a lot on that point. I get the feeling that whatever it is, it's too dangerous to talk about in this circle, even over the arcana. But he does reassure me that plans are being finalized, and that he will shuttle more girls out of the Jewel after me. I just wish there was more I could do to *help*.

I see Ash nearly every day—he leaves me notes in *Essays on Cross-Pollination* with a date and time, and it's easy enough to find excuses to go to the library on my own and slip down the secret passage. It's only ever for an hour, maybe less, stolen moments when Carnelian is at a lesson and I'm not with the doctor. We talk about Before—about our homes, our families, our friends. I teach him how to play Halma. Sometimes, we read to each other. Other times we just lie on his couch, with no need for conversation. Just to be together.

Raven and I communicate as often as we can, using the ivy. We give each other trinkets that look meaningless to anyone else. A scrap of lace. A lock of hair. A marble from my Halma set. A watch spring.

But to us, they say, "I'm here. I'm okay."

ONE CLOUDY DECEMBER AFTERNOON, ASH AND I LIE ON his couch, my head on his chest, his fingers twined in my hair. My skirt spreads out like a fan over us, and I can feel his heart beating against my cheek.

There is only one more week until the Longest Night. Seven short days left before I leave the Jewel forever. I wish I could tell him. I hate lying. Every time he makes a reference to "next year," or muses about how long we might have together, or mentions how grateful he is that Carnelian is proving so difficult to marry off, guilt hits me like a punch in the gut. Once or twice, I've been tempted to just blurt it out and tell him I'm leaving, but Lucien's voice always whispers in my ear, holding me back.

"What's wrong?" Ash asks. He's gotten very good at sensing my moods. I tilt my head up to look at him.

"I don't want to be without you," I say. It's the most honest answer I can give.

Ash kisses my forehead. "If we look on the bright side, Carnelian received another rejection this afternoon, from the House of the Leaves. It looks like you might be stuck with me for a little while longer."

I always feel worse when he says things like that.

"What if the doctor succeeds and I get pregnant?" I say. "You won't want to be with me then."

Ash frowns—we don't usually talk about the logistics of my surrogacy. "Violet, if you had webbed feet and a third eye, I'd still want to be with you. And it's not as if I'm unaware of your . . . position in this house."

I roll my eyes. "Did they teach you how to be euphemistic in companion school, or is it a natural ability?"

Ash grins. "A little of both, I think."

I fiddle with one of the buttons on his shirt, so tempted to open it, to feel his bare skin. We've been so close over these past weeks, and yet there is another closeness, a different sort of intimacy, that we haven't experienced. And now that I only have a few days left, everything seems more immediate.

We could do it, Ash and I. Right now. It's the perfect time. We're alone together. On this couch. You're supposed to do it lying down, right? My breath catches in my throat. I wonder what it will feel like. I wonder if it will hurt.

"What are you thinking about?" Ash murmurs. Heat floods my cheeks. Carefully, I loop the button on his shirt out of its hole, letting my fingers trace his skin. It is smooth and I can feel the hard muscle underneath tense.

"Violet?" he asks warily.

"Um . . ." I can't bring myself to say it out loud, so my hand moves to the next button. I'm shaking, but isn't it natural to be nervous? My fingers fumble a little, but I get the second button undone.

Ash's fingers close around my hand. "What are you doing?" he asks gently.

"I . . . Don't you know?"

"I have a theory," he says, but he doesn't let go of my hand.

"And?" My heart is pumping in my chest.

"Violet, I don't think that's a good idea."

Rejection washes through me, hot and prickly. "Oh," I say.

In one swift movement, Ash sits up, keeping my legs draped over his lap, taking my chin gently between his fingers. I can't meet his eyes. "Hey," he says. "Look at me."

Reluctantly, I lift my gaze. "You've done it before."

"Yes," he says. "I have."

Carnelian's face flashes across my mind. "You just don't want to do it with me."

"No, Violet, that's not—you know I want to. You must know that."

I shrug. How would I? I don't know anything about boys. "This is all new to me," I mumble.

He smiles. "You may have forgotten, but it's new to me, too."

"Then why not? Is there something wrong with me?"

I don't know why I'm pushing the issue.

Ash laughs sadly. "No, there is nothing wrong with *you*." I stare at him, curious. He looks away, like he's regretting what he said. "Never mind."

I nearly topple off the couch as he stands up and moves to the window, buttoning up his shirt.

"Ash," I say. "Whatever it is, you can tell me."

"Trust me," he says bitterly. "You don't want to know."

I sit up straighter. "Trust me," I insist. "I do."

There is a long silence, but I have the sense not to break it.

His eyes are hard as he turns to face me. "It is forbidden for any companion to sleep with his client. But often the lady of the House takes a . . . special interest."

The Duchess's face looms in front of my eyes. "What?" I gasp.

"Not the Duchess," Ash says quickly, as if reading my thoughts. "No, her attentions are focused elsewhere."

Relief washes over me, heady and strong. "Not the Duchess," I repeat.

"No. But the other girls I've companioned for . . ." His jaw tightens.

"You slept with their mothers?" I ask timidly.

"Yes. I have to—I am theirs. They have . . . paid for me.

This is how I must support my family. This is how I keep my sister alive." He sinks into the armchair, his head between his hands. "I told you, that day in the garden. I'm not a good person." His voice is so quiet. "I understand if you are disgusted. I disgust myself."

I have no idea what to say. To be honest, the idea of Ash sleeping with the older royal women is horrifying. I think about the ones I know, the Countess of the Rose with her gray hair and wrinkles, the Countess of the Stone, her fleshy arms and cruel eyes . . . I shudder.

I don't realize Ash is watching me until he sighs. "I understand," he says.

"What? Ash, no." I hurry over and kneel beside him. "I'm not—just give me a minute, okay? This is . . . not what I was expecting."

His expression is strained, and he nods once. I take his hand in mine. It feels the same as it did a minute ago, before I knew. Is what he's been forced to endure any worse than what I've been through? They are awful in their own unique ways.

"Ash, do you honestly think that what they've *made* you do affects who you *are*? You are a good person, and don't ever let anyone make you feel differently." I press my hand against his cheek. "This, right here, is who we really are. I see you, remember? I know you. We have something they can't touch, something they can't take away. What they force us to do doesn't matter."

He pulls me up into his lap and I kiss his forehead. He runs his fingers over the beaded design on my skirt.

"Violet," he says, and when he looks in my eyes, my

stomach somersaults. "I think . . . I think I love you."

I feel myself dissolve into a thousand molecules, amazed at how three small words can completely alter my state of being.

"I think I love you, too," I whisper.

~ Twenty-Six ~

MY MIND IS A BLUR AS I MAKE MY WAY BACK DOWN THE tunnel.

I didn't want to leave, but Carnelian should be finished with her lessons by now and Annabelle might come looking for me. I let my hand trail along the rough stone wall, hearing his whispered words in my head.

I'm in love. Ash loves me.

I open the hidden door to the library, still lost in the bliss of the moment.

"What are *you* doing back here?" a reedy voice asks.

I whip around. Carnelian stands in the shadows, a small smile on her lips. She runs her finger down the spine of one of the books. "Looking for some bedtime reading, were you?"

My heart slams against my ribs. "I was just walking around," I say, trying to keep my voice casual.

"That's funny." She takes a step closer to me. "I've been here for half an hour and I haven't seen you."

"I thought you had etiquette lessons." The words slip out before I can stop them.

Carnelian's eyes narrow. "How do *you* know that?"

"Um, Annabelle mentioned it, I think." I try to will the blush to fade from my cheeks, but that only seems to make it worse. "Anyway, it's a big library. Maybe you just didn't see me."

Carnelian takes another step, so there's only a foot of space between us. A pimple is forming on the side of her chin. "I don't know what you're up to," she says. "But I'm going to find out."

I swallow. "I'm not 'up to' anything. I just . . . like books."

Carnelian snorts. "Right. We'll see."

"Is there a problem here, ladies?" We both jump as Garnet emerges from the stacks.

"What are you doing here?" Carnelian asks. "I thought you were supposed to be getting measured for your tuxedo."

Garnet feigns surprise. "Am I? Why, it completely slipped my mind." He looks me up and down. "Are you tormenting the surrogate, cousin? Better not let Mother catch you."

"I'm not afraid of her," Carnelian says, jutting out her chin.

"Yes, you are," Garnet replies. "Hey, where's that companion she bought you? I heard you never leave his side."

Red blotches appear on Carnelian's cheeks. For a second, I think she might cry. She gives me a scathing look, then turns on her heel and disappears.

"She always was a little sensitive," he says with a shrug. "Oh, I'm Garnet, by the way."

"I know," I say.

He laughs. "Of course you do." Then he gives me a flourishing bow. "Shall I escort you back to your rooms?"

"Oh, um, that's all right," I say. Garnet is amusing, but to be honest, he sort of frightens me. I remember what the Lady of the Flame called him—unpredictable.

"I insist." He takes my elbow. "Tell me," he says as we make our way out of the library. "Who do you hate more? My mother or my father?"

"Excuse me?" I can't believe he'd ask me that. As if I'd give him a truthful answer.

"I'd have to go with my mother," Garnet says, as if I hadn't spoken. A Regimental stops in the hall and stands at attention as we pass—I can feel his eyes on me, curious and scrutinizing. "My father is dull as a post, so at least he's easy to overlook. But there's just no ignoring my mother."

I decide to act mute. I won't participate in this conversation.

"She's gotten even worse since Carnelian came to live here. Poor kid. First her father dies, then her mother commits suicide. Very shocking. Scandalous for the House of the Lake."

"Carnelian's mother killed herself?" I gasp.

Garnet nods. "She was a strange woman, my aunt. Strange and sad. I never really got to know her well—my mother despised her. I think Carnelian hates her and misses her in equal measure. It makes her a very unpleasant person to be around."

"Why does she hate her?" I ask.

"Because her mother left her alone," Garnet says simply.

I see it now. Carnelian is all alone. The Duchess hates her, the royalty laughs at her, and Ash . . . no wonder she adores him. He's the only person in this place who's nice to her.

I feel a twinge of guilt. I don't want to feel sorry for Carnelian.

"Why did the Duchess despise your aunt?" I ask.

Garnet gives me a quizzical look, like he's not sure if I'm being serious. "Because she left. You do get the papers in the Marsh, don't you?" Before I can answer, though, he continues. "Aunt Opal was not House of the Lake material. Especially not after she turned her back on her royal lineage and ran off with some newspaper man from the Bank." He grins. "Really, my mother has had it quite hard. A crazy sister, a broken engagement—to the Exetor, of all people—and . . . me. Ah, here we are."

We've reached my chambers. Garnet knocks on the door and Annabelle opens it.

"Annabelle!" Garnet cries, wrapping an arm around her. Annabelle turns bright red. She tries to curtsy, but it's difficult with Garnet in the way.

"I've returned the surrogate, safe and sound," he says. Annabelle ducks her head in thanks. "It was lovely meeting you—officially. I'm sure I'll see you again soon. And stay out of Carnelian's way if you can help it," he adds with a wink, before heading back down the hall. "I think she's got it in for you."

THAT NIGHT, I CAN'T SLEEP.

The things Ash has revealed to me about the royalty, about his profession, about how he's treated within the walls of the Jewel . . . to anyone else I think it would be impossible to understand why he would do it, or how he could. But not to me. They took something inside him and they broke it, just like they took something inside me.

I know the pain of obeying an order that every part of you screams to resist. But Ash and I found each other. And we broke all their rules.

I can still hear his voice, whispering in my ear.

I love you.

It takes me only a few seconds to decide—I can't wait another minute. I'm running out of time. If I really want this, I have to do it now.

I throw back the covers and quietly slip out of my chambers.

The halls of the palace look different at night, all shadows and unfamiliar shapes, but I could walk this path blindfolded. The silence is eerie. I make it to the library, and flit past shelves that loom like sentinels in the darkness. The secret door creaks a little as I open it and hurry down the tunnel, into his parlor. There is no curtain on the window, and moonlight gives everything a silvery glow. I tiptoe across the rug and open the door to Ash's room.

I've never been in his bedchamber before.

The curtains are drawn, but I can see his outline under

a pale blue comforter, the faint movement of his body as he breathes in and out. I creep to his side—only his head is exposed. The rest of his body is hidden under a swath of blankets. I put a hand on his shoulder.

"Ash," I whisper, shaking him gently.

He makes a small, sighing sound.

"Ash," I say again, shaking him a little harder.

He opens his eyes and yelps, sitting up so fast that I jump back. His chest is bare, his hair rumpled with sleep, and I feel a surge of desire and a stab of fear.

"Violet?" he hisses. "You nearly gave me a heart attack! What are you *doing* here?"

"I . . . I . . ." I've suddenly lost the power of speech. All I can see is his skin glowing faintly in the light of the open door.

Ash throws off the covers, and I see that he is wearing a pair of loose cotton pajama pants.

"Violet," he says, getting up and putting his hands on my arms, as if to steady me. Am I shaking? I guess I am. His fingers are warm against my skin. "Are you all right? Did something happen?"

"I—I love you," I stammer.

For a second, he just looks stunned. Then he smiles and pulls me against him. "Is that why you're here?" A strange sound escapes my throat, somewhere between a sob and a squeak. His breath is hot against my ear as he murmurs, "I love you, too."

My heart is in a panic now, throwing itself against my ribs as I wrap my arms around him, feeling the indentations of his shoulder blades, tracing the curve of his spine. His scent is everywhere, and I press my cheek against his chest. One of his hands curls around my waist, the other strokes the length of my hair, out of its pins, falling freely down my back.

I turn my head so that our lips can meet.

At first it's just a regular kiss, comforting and familiar and warm. But then it deepens into something else, something more, and a yearning blossoms inside me. My hands move from his back to his stomach, tracing the lines of his chest and neck until my fingers are brushing his cheekbones. Desire twists in me so fiercely it hurts.

I don't realize I've been pushing him backward until we fall onto the bed. My hair hangs like a curtain around us, and he holds it back with his hands.

"Violet," he says, and there is a warning in his voice. But I can't stop. I can't stop kissing him. I feel him give in, sinking his hands into my hair, the muscles in his arms tense and tight. I press myself against him.

"Violet, stop," he gasps, rolling me over so that I'm lying on my back.

"I—I—I'm sorry." Hot tears fill my eyes. "I'm sorry."

Suddenly, he is stroking my face, kissing my hair. "Please don't say that," he murmurs. "You know I want to. You know I do."

"Then why not?" I can't hide the desperation in my voice.

"I could hurt you," he confesses quietly. "I've never . . . I mean . . ."

"It's all I want," I whisper. My voice sounds so fragile. I feel breakable. "You're all I want."

Ash hesitates. I run my hand across his chest and press my lips against his shoulder.

He leans in and kisses my neck, the soft spot just under my jaw, my collarbone . . . My head starts to spin as his fingers trace my arm until he reaches my waist, seizing a handful of my nightdress; I'm suddenly aware of how little separates us, just thin layers of silk and cotton.

His lips graze my throat. "Are you sure?"

I've never been so sure of anything in my entire life, but words fail me in this moment. My nerves are on fire, buzzing with a strange and fierce vitality, and I wrap my arm around his lower back and pull him closer to me. A low moan escapes his throat and then his mouth is on mine.

IT DOES HURT. BUT PAIN IS NOT NEW TO ME; I HAVE FELT pain before.

This is different. This pain is worth it. And this time, I am not alone.

~ Twenty-Seven ~

I AM A NEW PERSON.

I sit up in bed. My own bed. I didn't want to leave Ash
last night, but I had to. I press my fingers to my lips and
smile, letting the memories take me, the shape of his body,
the feel of him . . .

I am weightless. I climb out of bed and walk across my
room, marveling at the wonderful strangeness of my body.
It's like my joints have become unhinged. Like my feet are
barely touching the floor. My skin feels unnaturally warm,
as if I've become a tiny sun, radiating light and heat and I
love it.

I love him.

I open the door to my tea parlor and gasp as every flower

in every vase throughout the room suddenly blossoms, buds unfolding, petals growing bigger in brighter and more vibrant colors than they were before. This is me—it has to be. I don't know how, but there's no other explanation. An accidental Augury. I brace myself for the pain, but there's none. Just a pleasant buzzing sensation in my chest and stomach.

The door opens and Annabelle enters, carrying my breakfast tray. She stops short, her eyes wide as she takes in the explosion of color—some of the plants are still growing.

"Good morning," I say cheerfully.

Annabelle puts the tray down and pours me some coffee. I sit in my favorite armchair and take a sip. It's bitter.

"Annabelle, can I have some more sugar?" I ask. She usually makes it better than this.

She blushes and adds another spoonful, but I'm already far away, in a darkened bedroom, Ash's phantom fingertips against my skin, his hot breath in my ear . . .

The coffee is still too bitter. I put it down and a tingling numbness spreads through my fingers. "Annabelle, something's . . . something . . ." My mouth feels clumsy, and it's hard to form the words I want.

Annabelle appears in my vision—guilt is etched across her face. The room becomes blurry.

She drugged me.

Annabelle doesn't use her slate, she only mouths, "I'm sorry."

I fall forward into her arms and darkness takes me.

WHEN I WAKE UP, I HAVE NO IDEA WHERE I AM.

As my eyes adjust, I see that I'm in my bed, in my room.

Someone has dressed me in my nightgown.

The doctor is sleeping in a chair next to me, his chin resting on his chest. I switch on the light and he starts, blinking around, dazed.

"Good evening," he says, stifling a yawn. "Or perhaps, good morning is more appropriate."

"What are you doing here?" I ask.

"I wanted to be here when you woke up," he says. "Annabelle was a little heavy-handed with the sedative I gave her. Overcompensating for last time, I think—she didn't want you waking up during the process again."

The process. My stomach churns. I touch the inside of my elbow—there is a tiny bump where they put the IV in.

"You did it again," I whisper.

"Yes. I'm hoping there won't be any complications this time, but just in case, I am ordering you on complete bed rest for a while, until we can determine whether or not this attempt was successful. Someone will be with you at all times."

"What?" I gasp. "No."

Dr. Blythe pats my shoulder. "Not to worry. The Duchess will attend to your every need. I'm sure the time will fly by."

THE TIME DOES NOT FLY BY.

True to his word, the doctor doesn't allow me to be alone for even one minute. Either Annabelle, or Cora, or a handful of other maids are with me all the time. Even at night, someone is always sleeping on a cot in my bedroom.

I feel that, somehow, Lucien will find out what's

happened. Ash must have heard, too. But I won't be able to send anything to Raven.

I wish there was some way to get a message to Ash. He needs to know that I won't forget him, no matter what happens.

I love him. He loves me.

I hold on to that thought over the following days. He loves me. I remember the look in my mother's eyes when I gave her back my father's ring, and I think I understand her better now. How hard it must have been to give that small piece of him away. How hard it must be to live without him.

At least, once I'm gone, I'll have some consolation knowing that Ash is alive. He won't be as far away as my father.

Each day that passes is one day closer to the Longest Night. I begin to worry that the Duchess won't allow me to go to the Winter Ball. Dr. Blythe comes in to check on me twice a day, once in the morning, and once just before dinner, and every time I ask him if I'm allowed to leave my bed. He always says no.

Sometimes, Cora reads to me aloud, and sometimes Annabelle and I play Halma, and once the Duchess sent a string quartet. That was frustrating more than pleasurable, though. The cellist wasn't very good.

I am only allowed out of bed to shower and use the bathroom.

I am running out of time.

The day before the Winter Ball, I decide I've got to do something drastic.

"Get the Duchess up here," I say to Annabelle. "Tell her I want to see her. Now."

Annabelle's eyes are wide. She hesitates, unsure what to do.

"I don't care if this isn't following protocol," I say. "I need to see her."

The Duchess arrives twenty minutes later, her expression murderous. She slams the door of my bedroom behind her.

"Who do you think you are?" she demands. "You do *not* call for me, do you understand?"

"I'm very sorry, my lady, but"—I take a breath, not really believing I'm about to say this—"seeing as *I'm* the one carrying what might potentially be the future Electress of the Lone City, I thought maybe you could spare a few minutes."

She stares at me, her eyes narrowing. "What do you want?"

"I want to get out of this bed. I feel fine. I don't want to be guarded day and night. And I want to go to the Winter Ball tomorrow."

The Duchess raises an eyebrow. "And why should I grant any of these requests?"

"Because . . . because we are in a partnership, remember? You need me to be a willing participant. You want me to work as hard as I can to make this baby grow as quickly as possible, right? This is what I want in exchange for that."

The Duchess purses her lips and takes a minute before answering.

"Very well," she says. "I will talk to the doctor about lifting your bed rest. But you will report any pain, or abnormality, or anything immediately."

"Of course, my lady."

"Annabelle will see to it that you have a new dress for the ball."

"Thank you, my lady."

She pauses at the door, one hand on the knob, and smiles. "You're a smart girl," she says. "I was wise to have bought you."

I wouldn't be so sure about that, my lady, I think.

I TELL ANNABELLE I WANT TO GO OUTSIDE.

We walk through the garden arm in arm. I can sense that she's not about to leave me alone, even for a second, but I have to check on Raven. It's been a week since I sent her anything—the last time was the day I learned about Ash's true profession.

I decide it doesn't matter if Annabelle sees a token from Raven. She won't understand it, and I'll be gone soon anyway. I lead her to the west wall, where the ivy is heavier due to my and Raven's vines. There's a spot where pieces of ivy have been snapped off or twisted, and I can't remember if that's how the vines have always looked, or if maybe someone else has come to this place while I was confined. Could someone have taken Raven's token? Does someone in this palace know?

I find the place where Raven's gifts always wait for me. It's empty.

I search through the vines, ripping some of them off the

wall, as Annabelle watches me with a confused expression.

There's nothing.

Dread creeps up on me, slow and heavy.

Something is wrong. Something is *very* wrong.

~ Twenty-Eight ~

THE LONGEST NIGHT IS SO NAMED BECAUSE IT IS THE shortest day of the year, and therefore, the longest night.

It also symbolizes the darkest time in the city's history, just after the forming of the Lone City, when the ocean threatened to engulf the island and the royalty funded the building of the Great Wall. There was no electricity then, so it's tradition for all electric lights to be turned off and candles lit—this was never a problem in the Marsh, where electricity was so rare anyway. Gifts are exchanged at midnight. I remember the year my father gave me a brass-plated harmonica. I thought it was the most amazing present, even if I couldn't quite figure out how to play anything on it. He promised to teach me. That was the last year we celebrated the Longest Night with him; he was killed a few days later.

It's also tradition to wear white, after the five-petaled hellebore that blooms during the winter months. I study myself in the mirror now, as Annabelle curls my hair. My dress is strapless, layers of ivory chiffon floating to the floor. A necklace of diamonds and rubies sparkles at my throat. Annabelle piles my curls up on my head, securing them with pins that are adorned with jeweled flowers, tiny sprinkles of white and red. She smiles at me in the mirror.

I study my reflection. Something is different. I'm not the frightened young girl who sat here the night Cora and Annabelle got me ready for that first dinner. I have experienced so much in my short time in the Jewel. I have been changed, forged into someone wiser and stronger than I used to be. I have grown up.

Annabelle covers me in a white fur cloak and we make our way to the foyer.

I allow my eyes three full seconds to drink Ash in as I walk down the main staircase. He wears a white tuxedo jacket over a black vest and tie, but all I can see are the lines of his body in that darkened room.

Ash spares me the briefest glance, then turns away, the hint of a smile on his lips. Carnelian is watching me with her arms crossed, her white lace dress covering her up to her neck. Her stare reminds me to be cautious. The Duke is draping a long cloak over the Duchess's shoulders. Garnet leans against the newel post and whistles as I come down the stairs. My cheeks flush, and the Duchess cringes, touching her temples like she has a headache.

"Garnet, please," she says, threading her hand through the Duke's arm. "Let's get going."

It's cold outside, and tiny flakes of snow drift lazily from the night sky. In the motorcar, I'm reminded of my last ride to the Royal Palace. It's like my life is repeating itself, but in a stranger form.

"Have you been to the Royal Palace yet?" Garnet asks me.

I stare at him for a second, wondering if he's joking. "Yes," I say. "You . . . you bumped into me at the Exetor's Ball."

Carnelian snorts.

"Did I?" Garnet's eyebrows pinch together. "Huh. Well, you haven't seen anything until you've seen the Winter Ball decorations."

When we arrive at the Royal Palace, we are escorted to an extension made entirely out of glass. It is lit with thousands of candles, giving the room a beautiful golden glow. Women in white look like delicate snowflakes, milling about and drinking champagne from crystal flutes, hanging on the arms of men in white tuxedo jackets. Boughs of hellebore dangle from candle-filled chandeliers, interspersed with bright splashes of red and green holly. The floor is made out of blue glass, and enormous ice sculptures glitter in the flickering light.

I see what Garnet meant—the whole effect is magnificent.

There is a loud banging, and I see the Exetor and the Electress at the far end of the room, on a crystal dais, both standing with their glasses raised.

"Welcome," the Exetor says, "to the Winter Ball, and the celebration of the Longest Night."

THE WINTER BALL IS MORE EXUBERANT THAN THE Exetor's Ball.

Or maybe it just starts out the way the Exetor's Ball finished. I keep well away from the dance floor, ignoring the sight of Ash and Carnelian dancing together, and scan the room for Raven. I need to see her face, to know that she's all right.

Instead, I glimpse Lucien, on the crystal dais, speaking to the Electress. I wonder what excuse he'll use to get me alone and give me the serum. I stand quietly beside an ice sculpture of a winged horse, grateful that no one seems to notice me, and that the Duchess has left me on my own. It's like she's proving that she trusts me. It's exactly what Lucien wanted.

Dance after dance . . . I stay in the shadow of the winged horse, waiting for Lucien to find me, searching for Raven's face in the crowds. People mill around, chattering and laughing, but I don't pay attention to their conversation until I hear a familiar, childlike laugh.

"I told you she would be a handful, Ebony," the Electress says. She is on the opposite side of the sculpture—I can barely make out her figure, distorted by the ice. "But you insisted on picking the most headstrong lot in the Auction."

"Why start with anything less than the greatest challenge?" The Countess of the Stone's voice sends a chill through me. "If I succeed with her, the others will be easy."

They must be talking about Raven. I keep very still, straining to hear over the music and laughter.

"Don't push too hard. Remember what happened with the last one. It was wise of you to leave this one at home." The Electress sighs. "If only there was an easier way . . ."

"Greatness is never achieved easily, Your Grace," the Countess of the Stone replies. "If we prevail, you will become the most revered Electress since Diamante the Great, who started the first Auction. You will change the face of history."

The Electress giggles, and my stomach squirms. "Yes. I will prove to this arrogant circle that bloodline isn't everything. And the Duchess of the Lake will fall so far in the standings that she will have to beg for an invitation to a third-tier garden party. Did you know, she *lied* to me at her son's engagement party? She said she hadn't started trying for a child, and then her surrogate up and nearly bleeds to death onstage."

"Caution and care, Your Grace. Caution and care. Pearl has done nothing to threaten us. Yet."

"Oh yes, yes, I know. Come, enough of this somber talk. It is the Longest Night. I must dance. The Lady of the Veil has recently acquired a most agreeable companion . . . do you think he would favor me with his hand?"

She laughs again, and I hear them move away. I feel as frozen as the sculpture beside me, struggling to make sense of their conversation. If the Electress is seeking to lobotomize the surrogates, it sounds like they're testing it on *Raven*. That must be what Raven meant, when she told me the Countess was trying to take her memories away.

A new dance begins and the Duchess leaves the floor to join the Lady of the Glass, Carnelian, and Ash. She beckons me over and takes a glass of champagne from a passing waiter.

"Now, I don't want to speak too soon, Iolite," the Duchess is saying—she and the Lady of the Glass are both flushed and smiling. "But I may have some very exciting news in the next day or so."

She reaches out and pats my stomach with her hand. I'm still in a daze, picturing my best friend strapped to a table, being experimented on. They can't do that. Not to Raven. She's too strong, she's too brave. . . .

"Oh!" the Lady of the Glass practically shrieks. "Oh, Pearl, how marvelous."

"Calm down, calm down," the Duchess says, laughing. "Nothing is certain yet. But Dr. Blythe is quite confident this time. She's been on complete bed rest all week. No more mishaps."

A muscle in Ash's jaw twitches.

"Oh," the Duchess exclaims, pointing. "There's the Lady of the Light with her son. Come, Carnelian, let's see if we can't find someone willing to take you off my hands." Carnelian reaches out for Ash, but the Duchess smacks her hand away. "Don't be stupid, girl, you can't bring your companion with you." The Lady of the Glass snickers.

Carnelian allows herself to be dragged off, glancing back pitifully at Ash. He and I stand side by side, not daring to look at each other.

"I need to see you," Ash breathes. "Alone. Now."

The sound of his voice sends tiny shivers through me.

He turns without waiting for a response, knowing I'll come. I wait a moment, then follow, staying a few feet behind him, keeping my head down and slipping through the crowd and out the glass doors, into a quiet hallway lined with plush carpets. His back disappears around a corner and I hurry to keep up.

This hallway is smaller, more narrow. Halfway down, Ash opens a door and vanishes. I turn the knob quickly when I reach it—the room behind is dark. Ash's fingers close around my wrist, pulling me inside.

"Ash, I—"

But he doesn't allow me to finish my sentence. His lips are eager and my body reacts instinctively. His fingers caress the exposed skin on my back and I shudder with longing.

"This is a really bad idea," I gasp.

"I know," he says, his lips on my throat. "But I couldn't—"

I pull his mouth back to mine. My blood is singing as I run my hands over his chest, feeling the hard muscle beneath his tuxedo shirt.

I hear a gasp and a light switches on. Ash and I jump apart. Lucien is standing in the doorway, his eyes wide, his face blank with shock.

I can't move. I can't think.

Lucien recovers quickly, closing the door and wheeling around to face us, his expression livid.

"*What* is going on?" he hisses. His eyes dart from me to Ash and back again. I feel shame well up inside me, hot and stinging; suddenly I can't look anywhere except the floor.

The silence swells and billows around me.

"Violet." Lucien's voice is cold, and for once, I don't enjoy hearing the sound of my name. I force myself to meet his eyes, and I can see the anger and incredulity there, mixed with something much worse. Disappointment. "Have you lost your *mind*?"

Ash looks back and forth between us. "You . . . you two know each other?"

"Um . . ." I don't know who to answer first.

Lucien ignores Ash. "What is wrong with you?" he snaps. "This isn't a game. Are you completely unaware of the danger you've put yourself in? He's a companion, Violet. A *companion*."

"I know who he is," I snap back. "I haven't told him anything. He has nothing to do with this."

"Nothing to do with what?" Ash asks.

"Get out," Lucien orders.

I realize that if Ash leaves right now, I will never be alone with him again. I will never get to say good-bye.

"Ash—I'm leaving," I stammer.

"Violet!" Lucien cries. But it's too late. The words are out.

"He won't tell anyone," I insist.

"Can someone please explain what's going on?" Ash asks.

"Lucien is getting me out. Of the Jewel. I leave . . . I leave tomorrow." The relief at finally telling him the truth is quickly overshadowed by the expression on his face. I thought Lucien's look of betrayal was the worst thing I'd seen.

"I don't understand," Ash says slowly.

"I'm so sorry," I whisper.

Ash blinks. "How? How could you even . . ."

"Lucien's made a serum," I say. Lucien makes a sharp sound of protest and I hold up my hand. "No. I've been lying to him for over a month. Please, let me finish."

"Over a month!" Lucien cries.

I ignore him, speaking quickly. "The serum will make me seem dead. Lucien will get my body out of the Jewel and hide me . . . somewhere. That's all I know."

"This is exactly why I haven't told you where you're going," Lucien snaps.

Ash's whole body seems to crumple. "You would let me think you were *dead*?" he asks.

"I . . ." Tears fill my eyes. "I made a promise."

"And what about your promises to me?" Ash says. "Or did those not really matter? Can I believe anything you've said to me? Was I just satisfying some urge before you ran away to who knows where?"

"Of course not," I protest. "Don't say that. What else could I have done?"

"You could have trusted me," Ash says.

"I do."

"Enough." Lucien stands between us, glaring Ash down. "Get out."

Ash glares right back. "Why are you doing this? What's in it for you? And don't pretend like there isn't *something*, because you and I both know, no one does anything in this circle for free."

Lucien's lip curls into a sneer. "I will not have my motives questioned by some lowlife companion."

"Lucien, don't—" I start to protest but Ash cuts me off.

"I've heard the rumors about you. Your laboratory, your experiments. Is that what she is? A test case? A laboratory rat?"

"Ash, that's not—" This time, I cut myself off. What is Ash talking about? I knew Lucien was an inventor, but what experiments?

"You know *nothing* about me," Lucien snarls. "She needs to be protected. She needs to be saved."

"She's stronger than you think," Ash retorts.

"She is more important than you could possibly fathom, and she is *leaving you*. Nothing she does is your concern anymore. So do everyone a favor and get. Out."

Ash turns to me.

"Is this it, then? This is how we end?"

I open my mouth, but nothing comes out. I have to leave, I know I do, but I don't know how to say good-bye to him.

"There is more at stake here than some silly romance," Lucien says sharply. "If Violet doesn't leave this place soon, and I mean *immediately*, she will die."

Ash and I stare at him, frozen with shock.

"What?" My voice is barely a whisper.

Lucien's gaze is still fixed on Ash. "Do you want to know what really happens to surrogates after the royal babies are born?" A cold bead of fear slides into the pit of my stomach. "They die. They all die. Childbirth kills them."

The room takes on a strange, hazy quality. I feel like I am watching someone else's life, like Lucien's words don't apply to me.

"No," Ash says. His voice sounds hollow. All the anger has drained out of him.

"Please," Lucien scoffs. "You know enough about the royalty—more than she does. Do you honestly believe they would build a facility for surrogates who are no longer useful? She'll die if she doesn't get out of here. Is that what you want?"

Ash is quiet for a long moment. I wish I could know what he's thinking.

"I should go," he says.

"Yes," Lucien says. "Finally."

"No!" I cry, finding my voice again. "Ash, please . . ." But there are no words that can keep him with me.

Ash stops at the door. "It would be easier to forget you," he says to me, "and these past weeks we've had together. It would be easier if I could hate you. But the sad truth is, I will more than likely love you for the rest of my life."

Then he's gone.

I'm suddenly aware of the panic snaking its way up my spine. Tears stream down my cheeks, but I don't bother wiping them away now. I swallow and turn to face Lucien.

"Am I really going to die?"

Lucien puts his hands gently on my shoulders. "If you have her baby," he says. "Yes."

"Why?" I ask. "How?"

Lucien shrugs. "Maybe your bodies aren't compatible with the fetus. Maybe it's to do with the Auguries. They don't know. They don't care enough to find out."

"Why didn't you tell me? How could you *not* tell me this, Lucien?"

"I . . ." Lucien sighs. "I wanted to protect you. I didn't want you to have another thing to worry about."

I wish I could sit down, but there's no furniture in this room.

"I cannot believe you had an affair with a companion," Lucien says. "I cannot *believe* you broke my trust."

I shake my head slowly, back and forth. The fact that Ash is gone, that I will never hear his laugh in my ear, or feel his heart beating against my skin, hasn't entirely sunk in yet. "He won't tell," I say.

"Let's hope not. Because if he becomes a threat, there are ways of dealing with it. One companion can easily disappear."

"Don't you dare," I growl.

"You do not give me orders, young lady. Remember what you promised. You do what I tell you—no questions, no complaints."

"Why are you doing this for me? Really. Why do you want to save me?" I demand. "I don't understand. Why me, why now? Was Ash right? Is this even about me, or is there something in it for you?"

Lucien's jaw clenches.

"I had a sister. Azalea." He says the name softly, his voice tight with emotion. "She was a surrogate. I tried to help her, tried to save her life, and for a while, I succeeded. Until one day, I failed." He shakes his head and turns away from me. "There was a time, only a few short months ago, when all I cared about was keeping her safe. That was all that mattered to me. And so what if nameless, faceless surrogates were dying, as long as my Azalea was protected.

But she became restless, rebellious. She wanted an end to the Auction, an end to the suffering of innocent young girls. She believed that surrogates could take their power into their own hands, use it to overthrow the royalty. There was another voice whispering in her ear, and in the end, that voice won out over a brother's love."

I'm shocked into stillness. *Use the Auguries to overthrow the royalty?*

Lucien rubs a hand across his forehead. "She left me a message before she died. 'This is how it begins,' she said." The words stir something in my memory, but it's too elusive to recall. "Her death forced me to action. Because I cannot ignore all the injustice anymore. Once a small crack reveals itself, suddenly a hundred others appear. And then the walls that have been so carefully constructed begin to crumble.

"Then I was looking through the photographs for the Auction and I saw you." His eyes meet mine. "You look so much like her. And if I had to choose a surrogate to help, why not the one who would always remind me of why I'm doing this." He smiles. "Once I met you, you reminded me of her in other ways, too. She was stubborn, and determined, and compassionate. And she had a good heart."

"So you think, somehow, I can help change the system?" I ask incredulously.

Lucien sighs. "I think you can help *end* the system. But I am not the one who can explain how. For that, you will need this."

Lucien takes my hand and slips a ring on my finger, a large oval topaz surrounded by tiny diamonds. "The serum is inside. There's a secret compartment in the stone." He shows me a tiny clasp, hidden by the diamonds. "Take it tomorrow at midnight."

I run my fingers over the jeweled surface.

"Thank you, Lucien," I say numbly.

He kisses my forehead. "We can do this. Trust me. Now, let's get you back to the Duchess."

~ Twenty-Nine ~

I WAKE THE NEXT MORNING WITH A WEIGHT PRESSING against my chest.

Today is the day. I will take the serum tonight. I'll leave Ash and Raven behind, because if I stay here, I will die.

I stare at the ceiling and wait for Annabelle to come with the breakfast tray.

But when my bedroom door opens, it isn't Annabelle who enters. It's Dr. Blythe.

"Good morning, Violet," he says cheerfully, placing his black bag on my bedside table. "Did you have a nice time at the ball?"

A nice time. No, Doctor. I did not.

"Yes, thank you," I say automatically.

"It's a very exciting day for us," the doctor says, rubbing his hands together. I am barely aware of him as he takes out a needle and syringe, and a flat square of plastic with two felt circles on it. He sinks the needle into my arm and draws a small amount of blood. Suddenly, I become more alert—he hasn't taken a blood sample in a while.

"Yes, a very exciting day indeed," he says, holding the syringe over the plastic square and soaking one of the felt circles with my blood. "If the other circle turns green, it indicates a positive result. If it stays white, a negative."

My lungs contract and my heart fills my throat. The doctor and I stare at the small circle of felt.

The seconds tick by.

A thought occurs to me then, a thought so glaringly obvious I'm surprised I didn't think of it before.

If it turns out I'm pregnant . . . what if the baby isn't the Duchess's?

Ash's darkened bedroom flashes before my eyes.

What if the baby is mine?

Suddenly, I think I might throw up.

"Excuse me," I gasp. Dr. Blythe moves aside as I scramble out of bed and run to my powder room. I make it just in time to vomit in the sink.

I turn on the tap and rinse out my mouth, then wipe my face with a soft blue towel. I stare at my reflection in the mirror. My skin is even paler than usual, and clammy, strands of black hair sticking to my forehead and cheeks.

I look terrified. I *am* terrified.

The baby could be mine.

I've never wanted to be pregnant, and I've certainly *never* envisioned a scenario in which the pregnancy was my own. Having something of the Duchess's inside me was such a hateful idea, and always the only option.

I move my hand down and press it gently against my stomach.

I don't *want* to be pregnant. But if the baby is part me and part Ash . . . how could I hate that?

Everything is all mixed up. I feel nauseous again.

"Violet?"

I jump. Dr. Blythe stands in the doorway. "Are you all right?"

I manage a nod. He holds up the pregnancy test. "Negative," he says sadly.

All the air whooshes out of me, leaving me dizzy. For once, Dr. Blythe seems to understand exactly what I need.

"I'll leave you alone for a minute. Her Ladyship must be informed at once."

I sink down onto the plush blue bathmat.

Negative.

I start to laugh, a heady, breathless laugh. I lean against the sink and laugh and laugh until my stomach hurts.

"Annabelle," I call. I hear the door to my bedroom open.

"Good morning." The Duchess's voice makes me jump, as she appears in the doorway.

I scramble to my feet. She wears a gold dressing gown, and her hair is hanging loose down her back. It's a strange contrast to the harsh look on her face.

"I shouldn't have gotten my hopes up," she says. I can't think of a response to that. We stand in silence.

"When my sister and I were born," the Duchess says, "my father said he knew immediately that I would be the one to do great things. I was his favorite. He spent his whole life preparing me to take the throne—he was a hard man, but he taught me many things. Strength. Cunning. Ambition. Determination. All the qualities that he admired, I possess. And look at me now." She smiles sadly.

"You are royalty," I say, frowning. What a ridiculous thing for her to say. "You have everything. What more could you possibly want?"

The Duchess's eyes flash. Her hand whips out and pain explodes in my cheek and eye. "I am exactly the woman my father wanted me to be and it is still not enough. You must try harder. I have risked everything on you."

Slowly, I straighten up, square my shoulders, and glare at her. I barely feel the pain. It doesn't matter. I will take the Duchess hitting me a thousand times. Because she cannot truly hurt me anymore.

When she realizes I'm not going to respond, she says, "I'm hosting a luncheon this afternoon. Annabelle will get you ready. Be in the dining room at two."

ANNABELLE BUTTONS ME INTO A PALE PINK BEADED dress, her eyes fixed on her work, sensing that I don't feel like talking.

I twist the topaz ring around my finger—I've put a couple of other rings on, and a bracelet as well. Not that anybody would notice anyway. I have more jewelry than anyone could keep track of. And I'm not letting this ring out of my sight today. Only ten more hours until I take the serum.

I make my way to the dining room. A footman bows to me and opens the door.

"The surrogate of the House of the Lake," he announces.

It's the same crowd as the family dinner, except the Countess of the Rose is also in attendance, with the lioness. I move to stand beside the Duchess. The Duke is with her, looking like he'd rather be somewhere else. Garnet leans against a side table, a glass of amber liquid in one hand, a wry grin on his face—he toasts me with his drink. Carnelian stands beside him, her expression sullen.

And just behind her, is Ash.

I feel an odd, swooping sensation in my chest, like I've missed a step going down a flight of stairs. His eyes burn into mine for a half a second before they turn blank. He keeps up a pleasant smile, but from the tense set of his shoulders, I know that he is angry. My lips part slightly, but I can't speak to him here.

I can't speak to him ever again.

The Duchess and the Lady of the Glass descend on me.

"You must be so disappointed," the Lady says in a hushed voice. "But she looks healthy."

"Yes, the doctor agrees we won't have to wait so long before the next attempt," the Duchess says.

The Countess of the Rose stumps over, leaning heavily on her cane. "Patience is the key," she says. "Though mine is wearing thin, I must admit."

She glances toward the windows where the lioness stands, dressed in black, hands clasped behind her, head down.

"Dr. Plume is worried she may not be compatible at all.

It is so frustrating—I wish they could sort the defective ones out before the Auction."

The Lady of the Glass nods sympathetically. The lioness does not look up, though I'm sure she can hear these women talking about her. I remember the girl I first saw in the Waiting Room at the Auction House, with the gold-threaded braids, and the rainbow tassels, and the fierce expression. The girl who bragged about a surrogate's power at Dahlia's funeral, and stole a flute of champagne at the Exetor's Ball. Now her shoulders hunch, like she's trying to make herself smaller, invisible.

The door to the dining room opens.

"The Countess of the Stone. And surrogate," a footman announces. My heart leaps—Raven! Raven is here.

"What?" the Lady of the Glass hisses.

"I thought you rescinded her invitation," the Countess murmurs.

"I did," the Duchess replies.

The Countess of the Stone is so large, she blocks Raven from view. She wears an enormous fur cloak, which she sweeps off her shoulders and holds out for the footman to take.

"Pearl," she says. "How kind of you to invite me."

She bears down on the Duchess, kissing the air beside each of her cheeks.

"Oh, it was my pleasure," the Duchess says with an icy smile. Two footmen hurriedly add more settings to the dining table.

The Countess of the Stone greets the Countess of the Rose in a similar fashion, but barely glances at the Lady of the Glass. Her eyes move to me—or more specifically, my stomach. "Still no luck, I take it?"

"Dr. Blythe is optimistic that the next—"

"Doctors are idiots," the Countess of the Stone replies. "It's the surrogate that counts." She snaps her fingers.

Raven shuffles out from behind the Countess. Seeing her makes my throat swell. Like the lioness, she keeps her head down, and her hair is longer than it used to be, hiding her face. But I can see that she is even thinner than she was at the Exetor's Ball, and her dress is tight, as if to accentuate it. Which is why, at first, I can't make sense of the small bump protruding from between her hips.

Not until Raven runs one bony hand over it tenderly.

I don't know how I keep my gasp inside, but I manage to stay quiet.

Raven is pregnant.

It doesn't make sense. Even if she got pregnant right after the Auction, she shouldn't be showing yet, should she? It's only been two months.

"You must be very excited," the Lady of the Glass says.

The Countess of the Stone ignores her. "She took to it on the first try. The first try. Imagine!"

"Imagine," the Duchess repeats dryly. "Though you might want to consider feeding her now and again."

The Countess shrugs. "She's naturally thin."

I can't stop staring at Raven. In a matter of months, my best friend will be dead.

I wish I didn't know. I wish Lucien had never told me. I blink back the tears that threaten to well up and spill over, because I cannot cry here. A bell rings and the Duchess claps her hands.

"Shall we sit?" she says.

I take my usual seat beside the Duchess—the lioness and Raven sit beside their mistresses as well. I try to catch Raven's eyes, but she keeps her head down. A frail, wispy man sits on the Countess of the Rose's other side, and I assume he must be the Count. How pathetic these royal men seem, compared to their wives. The Duke and the Lord of the Glass are on their way to getting drunk, laughing loudly and slapping each other on the back. The Lady of the Glass's eyes dart between her husband and the Countess of the Stone, as if afraid he's making a bad impression.

Footmen circle the table, pouring out glasses of wine and water, and placing the first course in front of us. Ash has not looked at me since I came in. Garnet is teasing Carnelian about something, making her face turn from pink to scarlet. Raven's head is still down. She hasn't touched her food. She hasn't even picked up her fork.

Then she looks up and I can't stop the sharp intake of breath at the sight of my once-beautiful best friend.

Her cheekbones stick out, and the skin stretched tightly over them has a grayish tinge. She looks hollow, vacant. Our eyes meet but I see no flicker of recognition in hers, just a blank stare.

It's as if Raven is dead already.

No. She can't be gone.

Suddenly, I am aware of the silence in the room. Everyone is staring at me.

I turn to the Duchess. "The Countess asked how you are feeling," she says.

I'm not sure which Countess she's talking about, so I try to make my answer general. "I'm feeling fine, my lady," I say to the room at large.

At the sound of my voice, Raven blinks and looks around, confused, like she's waking up from a dream. There is life in her eyes again, and when she sees me, the ghost of a smile pulls at her pale lips.

I feel a rush of relief so strong it's almost painful. She's still there. Raven is still in there.

I have to find a way to save her. I can't leave her in this place.

The rest of the meal resembles the many others I've been forced to sit through, the mindless chatter and gossip, the snide comments hidden under the guise of politeness. I try to think of some way I can communicate with Raven, who spends the luncheon going back and forth between being in the present and being somewhere else—sometimes her eyes glaze over, or she stares at her plate for too long, her fork frozen in midair.

Maybe it's because I'm so aware of her, or maybe it's because I know her so well, but I almost sense the pain before it happens.

Raven gasps—one hand slides across her stomach and the other grips the tablecloth. Veins of color spread out from her clenched fist, a deep, inky blue that crawls across the table, turning the white linen dark. Carnelian screams, and the Lord of the Glass topples out of his chair.

Suddenly, I know what I need to do.

"Get the doctor!" someone yells. In the commotion, I jump up and knock over my chair, pretending to get tangled in its legs and fall to the floor. I bring up the image in my head, swift and sure, and cracks of brilliant green spread across the carpet. The royal women shriek, the men hopping around to dodge the color that races over the ground. I crawl toward Raven and shove her out of the chair.

I wrench Lucien's ring off my finger and jam it onto hers.

"Don't take this off. There's a clasp in the diamonds," I

say quickly. "Drink what's inside at midnight."

Raven blinks. "Violet?" she whispers. Then she vomits a river of blood.

A massive hand grabs the back of my neck. In one swift movement, I'm on my feet, looking into the cold eyes of the Countess of the Stone.

"Get away from her," the Countess says.

"She—she's sick," I stammer. Blood stains the front of Raven's dress and runs down her chin. Her nose has started bleeding, too.

The Countess tosses me aside like a rag doll.

"Ebony!" the Duchess shouts. "Don't you dare lay a finger on my surrogate."

The carpet is fully green now. For a moment, the room is still. The two women stare at each other, one small, one massive. It's hard to decide who is more menacing.

"Get. Out." The Duchess's voice is sharp and commanding.

The Countess of the Stone's mouth twists. "As you wish, Pearl." She grabs Raven by the arm and pulls her upright. Raven follows her docilely out the door, Lucien's ring secure on her finger.

"Well," the Duchess says. "I think this luncheon is over." The table is a mess, spilled wine and food on top of the now-blue tablecloth. All the guests are wearing various expressions of confusion and panic. She turns to the Duke. "Darling, why don't you take the gentlemen to the smoking room. Garnet, will you join them?"

Garnet tosses the napkin he's holding on the table. "Thanks, Mother, but I'd rather gouge my own eyes out."

The Duchess's eyes harden. "Then find something useful to do. Preferably something that doesn't involve a kitchen maid."

The Duke has already herded the other royal men out the door. Garnet bows.

"As you wish, Mother."

"Are you all right?" the Duchess asks me.

"Yes, my lady."

"Have Annabelle take you for a walk in the garden. The fresh air will do you good." I curtsy. "Come, ladies, let's move to the sitting room."

As the Duchess sweeps out of the room, the royal women trailing behind her, I hear the Countess of the Rose murmur, "Very well trained, Pearl."

The lioness is the last to leave. She looks back at me and for a moment, I see a hint of the old fierceness in her eyes. It reminds me of the way she looked at Dahlia in the Waiting Room—like she was jealous.

I wonder what her life is like, in the House of the Rose. I don't even know her name.

The room is empty, except for me, Garnet, Carnelian, and Ash. Carnelian is staring at the bloodstained carpet.

Garnet clears his throat and says, in his typically blithe manner, "Well, I'm off to find a kitchen maid. See you all at dinner."

Footmen come in and begin to clean up the mess. Carnelian tugs on Ash's sleeve.

"Can we go for a drive, Ash?" she asks. "I'd love to get out of this house."

His smile is so genuine, it might've fooled me if I didn't

know him better. "Of course. I'll have them bring the car around."

Carnelian threads her arm through his, throwing me a smug look, and they walk out the door, leaving me alone with the hope that Raven understood my instructions and an emptiness where Lucien's ring used to be.

I LIE AWAKE THAT NIGHT, LISTENING TO THE CLOCK TICK-ing on my mantel.

Raven should be taking the serum now. I don't know why, but I'm certain that she heard me, that she understood. I wonder what Lucien will think, when it's her body in the morgue instead of mine.

I can wait. Whatever this plan of his is, however he thinks I can help destroy the royalty, all of it can wait. Because I couldn't let Raven die. Not like that. Not in that palace, with horrible things being done to her brain and someone else's baby growing inside her.

Maybe, at the end of the day, I'm just like Lucien. Will-ing to save Raven's life at the expense of others. Like he did with Azalea. Maybe I'm too selfish to be a savior of surrogates.

It doesn't matter. I made a choice. Now I have to make amends.

I throw off my covers and slip out the door, down the darkened halls of the palace, toward the library.

I quickly reach the east windows and for a terrifying sec-ond, I think I see a shadow move in the stacks. I freeze, my heart hammering. The shadow moves again, and I see that it's just the wind blowing a tree branch outside the window.

I hurry down the secret tunnel and into Ash's parlor, tiptoeing to his bedroom door and opening it quietly. He's asleep, one arm thrown over his face, his breathing slow and even.

"Ash," I say. He mumbles something unintelligible. "Ash." I shake his arm.

"Wha—" His whole body lurches awake. His hair is a mess, and he blinks around the room with unfocused eyes. When he sees me, he freezes. "What are you doing here?"

I sit down on the edge of the bed. "I gave it to Raven," I say.

"What?"

"Lucien's serum. I gave it to Raven."

Comprehension dawns on Ash's face—I've told him about Raven before. "The Countess of the Stone's surrogate. *That's* Raven?"

I nod.

Ash lets out a huff of air, like I've punched him in the stomach. He presses the heels of his hands against his eyes. I wait for him to say something, but he doesn't.

"I'm not leaving," I say timidly.

"Yes, I've gathered that." He's still holding his head in his hands.

"I couldn't do it, Ash. I couldn't let her die here. Not if I could save her."

"So what, it's all right if *you* die here?" Ash's head snaps up and he glares at me.

"We don't know what's going to happen."

"Yes, we do. We *do* know, Violet. Lucien knows what he's talking about. He's lived in the Royal Palace a long time, so if he tells you you'll die in childbirth, you can bet your life that you will." He grabs me and shakes me hard. "You can't die, Violet, don't you get that?"

His fingers dig into my arm, his face a mixture of anger and panic. I press one hand gently against his face.

"I made a choice, Ash," I say. "Just like I made the choice to be with you, that day in the concert hall."

"This isn't the same thing," he snaps.

I stroke his cheek. His skin is still warm with sleep. I didn't think I'd ever get to touch him again. "It's my life. You can't decide how I live it. Neither can Lucien."

For a second, I think he's going to keep yelling. But then he relaxes his grip on my arms. "You really are infuriatingly stubborn, aren't you?"

I smile bleakly. "Can you forgive me for lying to you?"

Ash sighs. "I can forgive you for not telling me about the escape and Lucien's involvement. That would have been unthinkably dangerous. But how could you have let me think you were *dead*?"

My hand slips from his cheek to his chest. His heart beats under my palm. "I'm sorry," I whisper.

"I know. That doesn't make it okay."

"I know," I agree. We hold each other's gaze for a long moment. "Can I stay?" I ask finally. He has every right to kick me out and never speak to me again.

He definitely looks like he's considering that option. Then he smiles my favorite smile and shakes his head. "I swear, you'll be the death of me."

"That's not funny."

Ash puts a hand on mine, leaning back against the

pillows and pulling me with him. I nestle into the crook of his shoulder.

"How angry do you think Lucien will be?" he asks. "When he finds out you've given the serum to someone else?"

I smile into his collarbone. "He'll probably pop a blood vessel."

"Or two. Or ten." Ash kisses my hair. "What happened today in the dining room?"

"You mean the Auguries?"

"I don't know. Is that what it's called? I've never seen anything like that."

I tilt my head up. "You don't know about the Auguries?"

Ash rolls his eyes. "Violet, I don't know anything about the surrogates. At the companion house, we were instructed to treat you like furniture. We were told you had some peculiarities and if we saw anything strange we were to ignore it. Not that any of us wanted to risk even thinking about a surrogate." His jaw tightens.

I kiss him just under his ear. "You're pretty brave, aren't you?"

He grins at me. "Not as brave as some."

Suddenly, there is a tremendous *bang*, followed by the sound of heavy boots, and then the door to the bedroom is kicked open. I shriek as Regimentals flood into Ash's room, their guns drawn and pointed. Ash and I scramble back against the headboard, his body slightly in front of mine, protecting me. My brain buzzes, every muscle taut. I can't seem to make sense of what I'm seeing. I can't stop looking at their guns.

"Well, well, well." My blood turns to ice as the Duchess saunters into the room. "What have we here?"

There is a long, agonizing silence.

"It isn't her fault," Ash says. "It is mine. I am the one who—"

The Duchess's eyes flicker to the Regimentals. They move like a lightning strike, two of them ripping him from the bed as another whips the butt of his pistol across Ash's face. Blood sprays over the pale blue comforter.

"No!" I scream as another Regimental yanks me out of bed, twisting my arm behind my back. I know I should feel pain, but I can't feel anything. The bloodied pistol smashes again and again into Ash's skull, slicing open the skin above his eye and raising a welt on his cheekbone.

"Stop it!" Carnelian's voice pierces through me. She is standing behind the Duchess, staring at Ash with an expression that mirrors my own. "You said you wouldn't hurt him."

The ice in my veins melts as fire floods in its place. *She* did this.

"Shut up, you stupid girl," the Duchess snarls. "What did you think would happen? Really, Carnelian, even when being useful, you are such a disappointment." She speaks to the Regimentals holding Ash. "Take him to the dungeons."

They drag his limp body out of the room.

"Ash!" I scream after him. This can't be happening. This can't be real. "Ash!"

But he's gone.

I'm still struggling against the Regimental's hold. The

Duchess approaches me carefully. "You have disappointed me, *Violet*."

The shock of hearing my name from her mouth stuns me into stillness. I gape at her.

"What?" she asks softly. "You didn't think I knew your name?" For a moment, we just stare at each other. Then her hand slams into my face, sparks exploding in front of my eyes. "I trusted you!" she shrieks. "And this is how you repay me? You little *whore*." She hits me again and I taste blood.

"Ash," I mumble.

"The companion is a traitor. And you know what happens to traitors in the Jewel, don't you, Violet?" She leans in so that her face is inches from mine. Her eyes are black fire. "They are executed."

She looks up at the Regimental. "Take her to her chambers and keep her there. Guard all the exits. Get her out of my sight."

She whirls around and leaves the room. Carnelian lingers in the doorway, her eyes wide.

"I didn't know," she whispers. "I swear, I didn't know. She said she wouldn't hurt him."

Strength comes back to me, and with a strangled yell, I tear myself out of the Regimental's grasp, barely aware of the pain shooting through my shoulder. My only thoughts are of Ash's bloodied face and that it is all Carnelian's fault. She cries out and stumbles backward and I raise my hands to wring her scrawny little neck.

Another Regimental plows into my side, slamming me into the wall—all the air expels from my lungs in a giant *whoosh*. Sparks explode and swirl in front of my eyes. Two more Regimentals grab my arms and I can't fight them, I can't do anything except struggle to breathe, but it's like a pillow is being pressed down over my nose and mouth. The Regimentals pull me forward; my legs falter and give way, so they drag me out of the bedroom, past a white-faced Carnelian and into the halls of the east wing.

Suddenly, blissfully, my lungs expand—I gulp for air, coughing and choking in my desperation to breathe.

"Ash," I wheeze as the Regimentals drag me down the glass hallway, the one I crept through the day I first met him. Tears spill down my cheeks. My breath is coming easier now, and the reality of my situation starts to sink in.

"Ash," I croak. She is going to kill him. The Duchess is going to kill him.

The Regimentals' fingers dig into my arms, and I stumble, trying to keep up with them, but they're walking so fast.

"Ash!" I cry, hoping he can hear me, wherever he is.

Two sleepy-looking maids huddle together near the sculpture room, holding a flickering lamp, watching me with curious eyes. I don't care. I don't care if I wake up the whole palace.

"ASH!" I scream his name over and over, the shadowy halls blurring as the tears fall thick and fast, and just as we reach my chambers, I see a willowy figure in a white nightdress, long copper hair flowing past her shoulders, and for half a second our eyes meet—Annabelle's eyes are wide with shock, and her lips part like she wants to say something. But then the Regimentals pull me into my drawing room, away from her.

They drag me to my bedroom, tossing me in roughly and locking the door. I throw myself against the wood, scratching at it with my nails, pounding on it with my fists, yanking on the doorknob, screaming.

Nothing answers me but silence.

My chest aches, and I give up, slumping against the door and sliding down to collapse on the floor, pressing my cheek against the soft green rug.

This can't be happening. This can't be real.

I close my eyes.

Please don't let this be real.

But it is real. Dread fills my chest like liquid lead, pulling me down into a void where nothing waits but misery and anguish, and eventually death, because I will never leave the Jewel. I will die here.

I don't know how long I lie on the floor, drowning in the certainty that this is it, that all I am and all I have been is over. But at some point, a noise filters in through my consciousness. A faint buzzing sound, which seems to be coming from my vanity.

I sit up, listening hard.

The arcana.

I scramble to my feet, pulling open the drawer and grabbing the jewelry box with the hidden compartment—the whole thing is vibrating. I empty it out, spilling pearl bracelets, diamond earrings, brooches, rings, and ruby pendants across the vanity's surface, pop out the bottom, and grab the arcana—it buzzes between my fingers.

"Lucien?" I whisper. "Lucien, is that you?"

For a moment, there is nothing, no answer, no sound

except the hum of the tuning fork in my hands.

Then a voice that isn't Lucien's speaks, and I nearly drop the arcana in pure shock.

"Don't worry," Garnet says, his usually confident tone gone and a fierce urgency in its place. "We're going to get you out."

Then the arcana goes still and falls from my hand, landing with a tiny clink against the sparkling jewels scattered across my vanity.

Acknowledgments

FIRST AND FOREMOST, TO MY AMAZING AGENT, CHARLIE Olsen, thank you for your unwavering support and boundless enthusiasm, and for being as big a nerd as I am. We are truly a match made in the Grey Havens. And to Lyndsey Blessing for your hard work handling all things international.

I was so fortunate to be able to work with Barbara Lalicki, my incredible first editor, whose insight made this book richer and stronger than I ever thought possible. And a huge vat of thanks to Karen Chaplin for taking up the reins with ease—I can't wait to work on the rest of this story with you. Rosemary Brosnan and Alyssa Miele, you made me feel right at home. The entire staff at HarperTeen has made this crazy process such a pleasure—Susan Katz, Kate Jackson, Andrea Pappenheimer and the sales team, Sandee Roston and Olivia deLeon and the publicity team, Diane Naughton, Kimberly VandeWater, Lindsay Blechman and the marketing team. Massive thanks to Barbara Fitzsimmons and Cara Petrus, and the whole design team, for my absolutely breathtaking cover. Josh Weiss and all the production editors, Gwen Morton, Melinda Weigel, and Anne Heausler, thanks for your sharp eyes and for reining in my love of exclamation points.

To Jess Verdi, for whom this book is dedicated—what can I say? Thank you does not seem sufficient. I cannot imagine writing this book (or any book) without having you in my corner. You were the first to hear this tiny spark of an idea, the shoulder I cried on when things seemed too impossible to continue, and the cheering squad that kept me going every step of the way. There's no one I'd rather drink wine and watch *Vampire Diaries* with. I am so lucky I get to be your friend. 1864.

To my awesome thesis group, Riddhi Parekh, Caela Carter, and Mary Thompson, thank you for your endless wisdom and encouragement during my last, frantic semester at The New School.

Huge thanks to my fabulous beta-readers, Corey Haydu, Alyson Gerber, and Dhonielle Clayton, for your time and patience and for loving Ash as much as I do.

The rest of the New School Writing for Children class of 2012—Sona Charaipotra, Kevin Joinville, Amber Hyppolite, and Jane Moon—you guys read so many pages that will never see the light of day. A thousand thanks.

Jill Santopolo, thesis advisor extraordinaire, thank you for taking this story and turning it into something publishable. Without you, the Auguries never would have existed.

To my first readers, Maura Smith, Rory Sheridan, Jonathan Levy, and Melissa Kavonic, thank you for all your support and for urging me to continue down this uncertain path.

To my friends and family, who have watched me struggle and stumble through life trying to find my place, I am here because of you. Thanks for sticking by me. And special thanks to Ben, Leah, and Otto.

To my parents, Dan and Carol Ewing, you guys are, quite simply, the greatest. You fostered my creative side from day one, and even when things were looking bleak, you encouraged me to keep going. I am the luckiest daughter in the world. Thank you for never insisting that I get a "real" job.

And, finally, to Faetra Petillo. I wish you were here to celebrate with me. I miss you every day.

JOIN

THE COMMUNITY AT

Epic Reads
Your World. Your Books.

DISCUSS
what's on
your reading
wish list

FIND
the latest
books

CREATE
your own book
news and
activities to share
with friends

ACCESS
exclusive
contests and
videos

**Don't miss out on any upcoming
EPIC READS!**

**Visit the site and browse the
categories to find out more.**

www.epicreads.com

HARPER TEEN
An Imprint of HarperCollinsPublishers